Cousins

The Thirteenth Carlisle & Holbrooke Naval Adventure

Chris Durbin

Chris Durbin

To Amelia

The first of the next generation.

Cousins At Arms

Copyright © 2023 by Chris Durbin. All Rights Reserved.

Chris Durbin has asserted his rights under the Copyright, Design and Patents Act, 1988, to be identified as the author of this work.

No part of this book may be reproduced in any form or by any electronic or mechanical means including information storage and retrieval systems, without permission in writing from the author. The only exception is by a reviewer, who may quote short excerpts in a review.

Editor: Lucia Durbin

Cover Artwork: Bob Payne

Cover Design: Book Beaver

This book is a work of historical fiction. Characters, places, and incidents either are products of the author's imagination or are used fictitiously. For further information on actual historical events, see the bibliography at the end of the book.

First Edition: February 2023

CONTENTS

	Nautical Terms	vii
	Principal Characters	viii
	Charts	x
	Introduction	1
Prologue	A Family Affair	4
Chapter 1	A New Adventure	9
Chapter 2	Lady Chiara	19
Chapter 3	The Spanish Consul	27
Chapter 4	The White Island	34
Chapter 5	Windward Passage	43
Chapter 6	A Chase	54
Chapter 7	Rocks and Shoals	64
Chapter 8	Wind and Tide	73
Chapter 9	Breaking Strain	83
Chapter 10	Temptation	92
Chapter 11	Havana Bay	102
Chapter 12	Their Excellencies	115
Chapter 13	Don Alonso	126
Chapter 14	Logwood and Mahogany	136
Chapter 15	The Sergeant of Artillery	147
Chapter 16	A Weighty Matter	157

Chapter 17	An Innocent Lugger	168
Chapter 18	Trapped!	179
Chapter 19	Stay or Go?	189
Chapter 20	Carpe Diem	194
Chapter 21	The Lure	200
Chapter 22	A Lee Shore	210
Chapter 23	Dispatches	222
Chapter 24	St. George's Island	229
Chapter 25	Evidence	239
Chapter 26	A God's Eye View	250
Chapter 27	A Promising Action	262
Chapter 28	Reunion	272
Chapter 29	Family Decisions	283
Chapter 30	A Solution	294
	Historical Epilogue	296
	Fact Meets Fiction	299
	The Series	302
	Bibliography	304
	The Author	306
	Feedback	308

Chris Durbin

LIST OF CHARTS

The Caribbean	x
The Old Bahama Straits	xi
Mobile Bay	xii
The Gulf of Honduras	xiii

NAUTICAL TERMS

Throughout the centuries, sailors have created their own language to describe the highly technical equipment and processes that they use to live and work at sea. This still holds true in the twenty-first century.

While counting the number of nautical terms that I've used in this series of novels, it became evident that a printed book wasn't the best place for them. I've therefore created a glossary of nautical terms on my website:

https://chris-durbin.com/glossary/

My nautical glossary is limited to those terms that I've mentioned in this series of novels as they were used in the middle of the eighteenth century. It's intended as a work of reference to accompany the Carlisle & Holbrooke series of naval adventure novels.

Some of the usages of these terms have changed over the years, so this glossary should be used with caution when referring to periods before 1740 or after 1780.

The glossary isn't exhaustive; Falconer's Universal Dictionary of the Marine, first published in 1769, contains a more comprehensive list. I haven't counted the number of terms that Falconer has defined, but he fills 328 pages with English language terms, followed by an additional eighty-three pages of French translations. It's a monumental work.

There is an online version of the 1769 edition of The Universal Dictionary that includes all the excellent diagrams that are in the print version. You can view it at this website:

https://archive.org/details/universaldiction00will/

PRINCIPAL CHARACTERS

Fictional

Captain Edward Carlisle: Commanding Officer, *Dartmouth*

Matthew Gresham: First Lieutenant, *Dartmouth*

David Wishart: Second Lieutenant, *Dartmouth*

Enrico Angelini: Third Lieutenant, *Dartmouth*

Arthur Beazley: Sailing Master, *Dartmouth*

Alfred Pontneuf: Marine First Lieutenant, *Dartmouth*

Frederick Simmonds: Captain's Clerk, *Dartmouth*

Jack Souter: Captain's Coxswain, *Dartmouth*

Nathaniel Whittle: Able Seaman, *Dartmouth*

Lady Chiara Angelini: Captain Carlisle's wife

Francis Hookway: Magistrate and Logger on the Yucatan coast

***

Historical

William Pitt: Leader of the House of Commons until October 1761

George Grenville: Leader of the House of Commons from October 1761

Lord George Anson: First Lord of the Admiralty

Ricardo Wall y Devereux: First Minister of Spain

Étienne François, Duc de Choiseul: Foreign Minister of France

Sir Henry Moore: Lieutenant-Governor of Jamaica

Commodore Sir James Douglas: Commander-In-Chief Leeward Islands

Rear Admiral Charles Holmes: Commander-In-Chief Jamaica

Juan de Prado Mayera Portocarrero y Luna: Governor-General of Cuba

Don Alonso Fernández de Heredia: Governor-General of Guatemala

***

Chris Durbin

The Caribbean

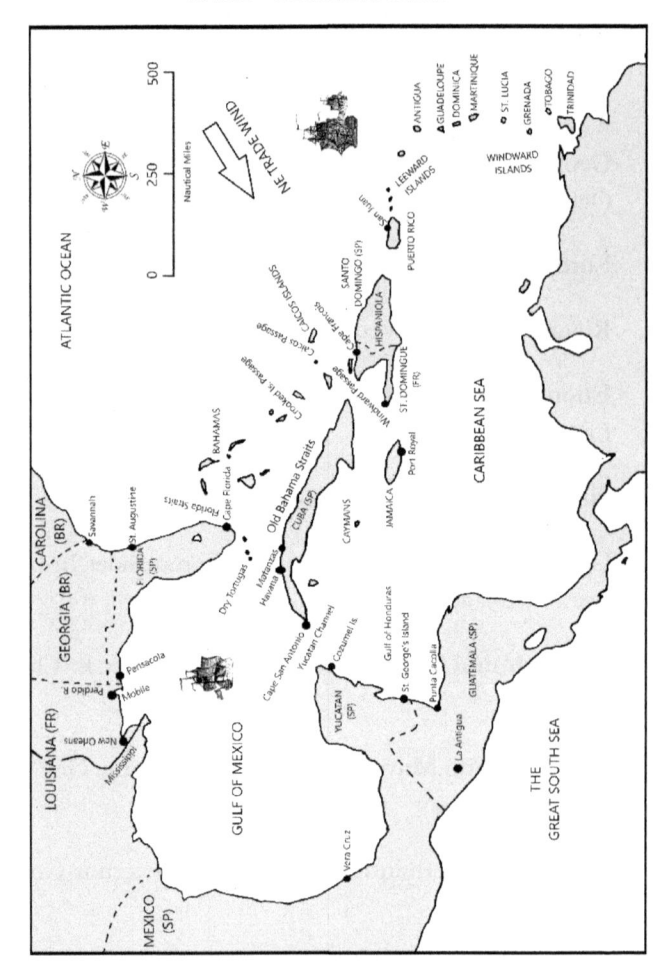

The Old Bahama Straits

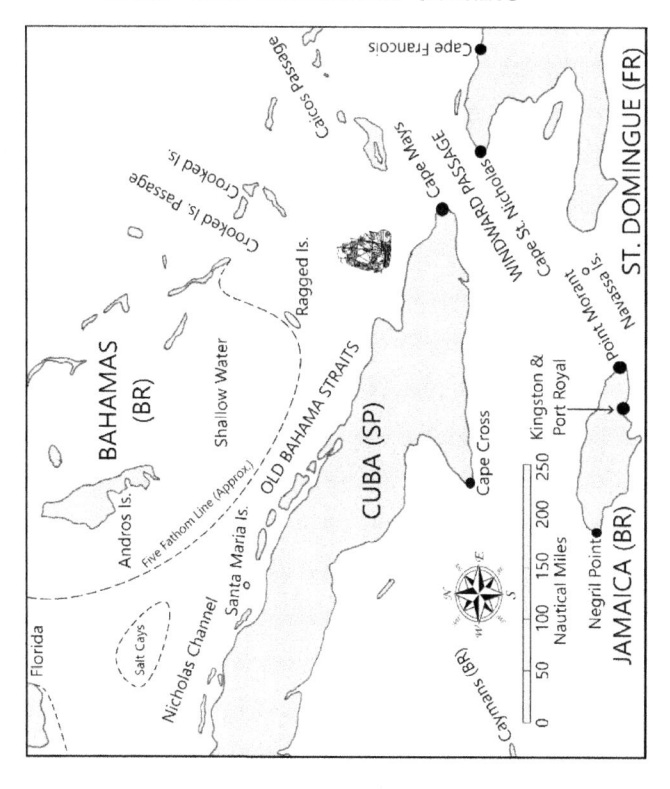

Mobile Bay

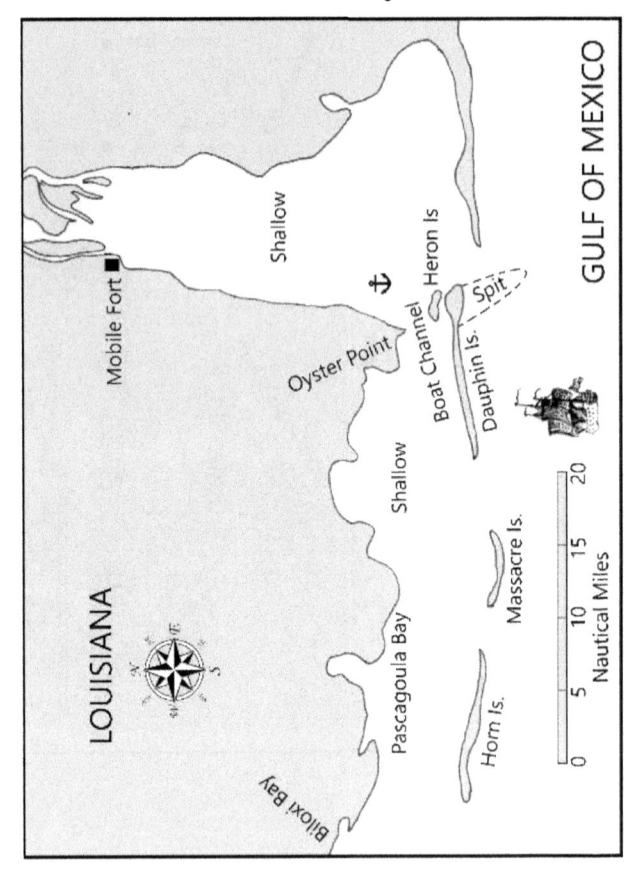

The Gulf of Honduras

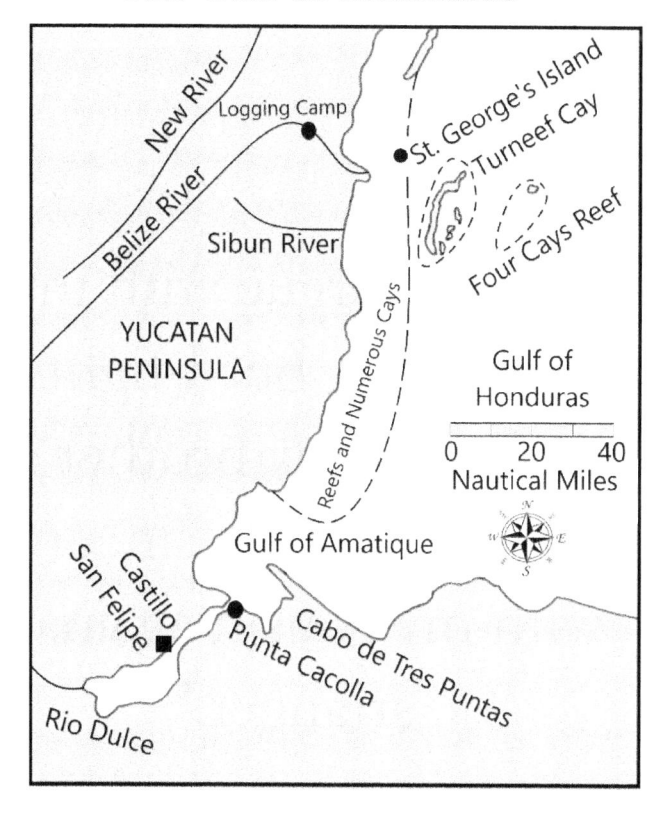

"I may argue with my brother, but I fight beside my brother against my cousin, and with my cousin against a stranger."

Old Arab adage

INTRODUCTION

The Seven Years War in Late 1761

By 1761 it was clear to even the most optimistic French minister that they were losing the war. Canada had fallen, and the French possessions in America were reduced to a toehold in the Gulf of Mexico and nominal ownership of the vast but unexploited hinterland that they called Louisiana. The Caribbean sugar islands that provided much of the state's wealth were being picked off one-by-one and all their plans for an invasion of England had come to nothing. The King's ships were either destroyed, blockaded or sailing under British colours and it would take years to rebuild the French fleet.

King Louis assumed that King George's German possession of Hanover would be his most valuable bargaining counter for peace talks with the British, and he drained his country's coffers in an attempt to take it. Despite the massing of huge French armies in Germany, Prince Ferdinand and his allied army obstinately defended Hanover, pushing back every fresh assault and raising new armies as each of his became exhausted.

In the east, Prince Frederick was under pressure from the combined armies of Austria and Russia and was forced into a defensive strategy to preserve the very existence of Prussia.

During the spring of 1761 the French approached the British government with an offer of peace. However, they had also approached Spain, hoping to form a third Bourbon family pact against their common enemy. A secret treaty with Spain was signed in August but, deliberately or unintentionally, news of the treaty inevitably leaked. When Britain heard of this secret treaty, her ministers were withdrawn from the negotiations.

France now staked everything on Spain's entry into the war and another hugely expensive push to take Hanover. However, Spain was slow to ready her navy for the coming conflict and her army was decaying and in no fit state to undertake her own project, the planned invasion of Britain's ally, Portugal. In Germany, Prince Ferdinand was training more soldiers for the coming campaign season.

Carlisle and Holbrooke

Edward Carlisle spent the early part of 1761 on the Leeward Islands Station where his fourth rate ship-of-the-line *Dartmouth* was used to blockade the French sugar islands. However, the New England merchants had seized the opportunity that the French defeat in Canada offered, and had started smuggling molasses from the French islands. Having arrested one such smuggler, Carlisle became embroiled in the tangled web of commercial interests in Rhode Island, and was lucky to escape being pursued through the courts in Newport. Back to the Caribbean and Carlisle intercepted a French squadron and captured a fifty-gun ship to add to his growing fortune from prize money. In June of 1761 he was delighted to find that his wife and son had followed him to Antigua. It looked as though he'd spend a pleasant hurricane season in the bosom of his family. This book starts as the hurricane season ends and the British ships start to deploy again.

In December 1760, Holbrooke's frigate *Argonaut* was sent to join Admiral Hawke's blockading squadron off the French Atlantic coast. He narrowly missed capturing a French frigate that had escaped from the Vilaine estuary in company with two ships-of-the-line. That was his first encounter with the Chevalier de Ternay, who would appear again in the story. Holbrooke was called to the Admiralty where he was given a new task, to insert and then extract agents from Brittany. He hazarded his ship and himself on moonlit beaches and estuaries, and didn't recognise the signs of his own mental fatigue. He had a respite when he joined the force to invade the French island of Belle-Isle, but then it was back to the blockade of the Vilaine, which ultimately took its toll. In the summer of 1761 he returned to his home in Wickham suffering from what we would now call post-traumatic stress disorder or PTSD. And there we leave George Holbrooke for the time being.

***

PROLOGUE

A Family Affair

Saturday, Fifteenth of August 1761.
The Escorial Palace, Spain.

The King studied the document that lay before him on the desk. He'd read it before of course, in its many drafts, but on every previous occasion his agreement had been hypothetical, another step on the long path of diplomacy between himself and his cousin, King Louis XV of France. Now he was being invited to sign the document, and suddenly its momentous nature was laid bare. He looked up at his chief minister who was seated opposite him across the austere desk.

'Well, General Wall, should I sign? Choiseul appears to be most eager for this treaty; perhaps that should make me suspicious.'

Ricardo Wall stifled an exasperated sigh. He'd inherited his Irish father's stoicism and he'd learned humility while following the interminable, hopeless Jacobite cause, but despite all that the King still tried his patience. Wall had been born in Spain, thought of himself as Spanish and yet he couldn't shake off the emotional baggage that came as an inescapable part of his Irish roots. He found it difficult to disguise his dismay at the tortuous process of decision making in the Spanish court. At least today he was alone with his King, free from the babble of voices that so confused his master. He knew what this treaty meant to King Carlos; he was already lauding it as the third Bourbon family compact and saw it as a building block of his legacy. A lasting treaty with the great and vigorous nation across the Pyrenees would free him from any fears for his land borders and allow him to concentrate on defending and reforming his vast overseas empire. Wall knew that the King would sign, and yet this was a good opportunity – probably his last chance – to remind him of why it was such a good idea.

'The Duc certainly wants this, your Majesty. France is near exhaustion and King Louis' navy can no longer prevent the British overrunning his remaining colonies. He must have peace with Britain or he must have your own navy to achieve some sort of balance, it's as simple as that. Choiseul will continue his negotiations with Britain, but they are not going well. King George wants more than France can concede with honour. King Louis may be moved by family loyalties but the Duc wants this treaty to be a threat in case the peace negotiations fail…'

'Excuse me, General,' King Carlos was unfailingly polite and rarely interrupted any of his ministers, 'but why, in that case, must this be a *secret* treaty. Surely that defeats its object.'

Wall smiled at that. Again, his master knew the answer very well, and he was merely settling all the factors in his mind.

'The important thing about a secret treaty, your Majesty, is that it can be revealed when either party deems it in their interests to do so. Choiseul will find a way to place a copy in William Pitt's hands – unattributably, of course – whenever it suits his purpose. He may have done so already, and naturally you always have that option yourself.'

The King pulled a wry face. He had an exalted opinion of his own morality and set himself lofty standards, but he also understood how diplomacy worked.

'Very well then, a secret treaty only so long as it serves my cousin's purpose, and our own. Now, how do you assess Choiseul's chances of making a peace before we are obliged to enter this war?'

Wall thought for a moment. The treaty committed Spain to declare war upon Britain in May of 1762, nine months in the future, unless by that time France had obtained a peace agreement. That gave a breathing space for the Spanish navy to be made ready for what would certainly be a stern test against the British fleet, and for the army to be prepared for its invasion of Portugal. Amazingly, Choiseul had agreed that France would make no peace without Spain's own grievances against Britain being addressed. In Wall's opinion that made it almost certain that there would be no peace in the near term, not unless the French reneged on the agreement. He shook his head emphatically.

'France has already lost America, India, West Africa, Belle Isle and, most importantly, half of its sugar islands in the West Indies. The only bargain they can make is to exchange Minorca for Belle Isle, and under the terms of the treaty France must cede Minorca to your sovereignty. King Louis has nothing that Britain wants. The threat to Hanover is losing its force, and this new King George has little enthusiasm for protecting what he sees as his father's German lands, not his own. One suspects that he would be glad to hear no more of Hanover. Britain is weary of the war and its crippling expense, for sure, but not weary enough to make sufficient concessions to allow France to make peace with its honour intact. Signing this treaty, your Majesty, commits Spain to war in nine months, you can be sure of that.'

King Carlos stood and walked to the window. He stared out at the neat, formal gardens for a few moments, then turned slowly.

'I know my cousin's mind in this. He won't be looking at the consequences of this war and how to end it on favourable terms, he'll be looking at a greater picture. He once told me that England is the natural enemy of both Spain and France, and always will be. In his view, if France makes war with England then so should Spain be at war, regardless of the short term costs, and *vice-versa*. Choiseul understands that too, he's of the same mind as his master, and in part I agree with them. And yet, I see the British navy sweeping all before it on the oceans, and I see King Louis' army checked at every turn by Prince Ferdinand. We can hardly help in Germany and in any case our whole strength will be needed to bring Portugal into our realm. Can our navy, combined with what's left of King Louis' ships, match the British? What say you, General?'

Wall had thought about little else for the past months. The Spanish fleet was considerable. On paper at least it could muster fifty ships-of-the-line as well forty-odd fourth rates and frigates; its deployment against the British should be decisive. Yet he was a man who always gave himself a way out and he was determined that his master should know all the risks that came with this treaty, and should take the responsibility for signing it.

'The British fleet is strong, your Majesty, but it's scattered across all the oceans of the world. When your ships and France's combine they'll outnumber the British fleet in the channel and allow King Louis to at least threaten an invasion of England. Lord Anson will be forced to bring his ships back from the Americas and the East Indies to protect the English Channel, and that will jeopardise all the work that he has done so far. With our dockyard at Havana available for the French ships and with reduced British squadrons at Jamaica and Antigua, the French will take back their lost territories and islands with ease. All that, of course, supposes that our ships are ready for sea next year, and that will require a certain amount of money to be diverted to the navy.'

Wall looked intently at his monarch, alert for any sign that he was going too far in outlining the dangers.

'However, there is the question of command, your Majesty. Navies are not like armies, and the combined power of allied squadrons can never equal the sum value of the separate parts; it's a question of concentration of force. We've seen the difficulty that the French navy has found in bringing its squadrons together. They've been defeated in detail before they could ever get in sight of each other, and that's made worse by the lack of communications at sea. Make no mistake, your Majesty, it will be a hard campaign, and we must balance the risks against the rewards.'

The two men lapsed into silence. Carlos was not an indecisive man, but he found that the decision placed before him was perhaps the most important of his reign. Would the British ravage his own extended and vulnerable empire in the way that they had his cousin's? It was certainly a risk, but then he could see that if they weren't stopped, the money-hungry British merchants would soon demand the right to trade freely in his territories, and the world knew where that led.

He looked again at the stately gardens, at the timeless regularity of it all, the fruits of his predecessors taking a long view of kingship and not counting the immediate costs. Yes, his cousin of France was right. Britain *was* the eternal enemy of his kingdom and the sworn enemy of his religion. Regardless of the risks, he knew that it was his duty to stand with his family; they would be cousins at arms.

'Very well, General Wall. Would you kindly make the arrangements for me to sign the document?'

***

Cousins At Arms

CHAPTER ONE

A New Adventure

Monday, Thirtieth of November 1761.
Dartmouth, at Anchor, Freeman's Bay, Antigua.

'Any moment now, sir.'

Arthur Beazley, sailing master of His Britannic Majesty's fourth rate ship-of-the-line *Dartmouth*, had waited like this in harbours from the frozen northern seas to the sweltering tropics, seemingly for half of his life. He had long ago learned that any show of nervousness on his part would be picked up by the other officers on the quarterdeck and swiftly transmitted to the crew, and now was not the time for skittishness on deck. For Beazley was about to execute a most difficult manoeuvre. He would bring *Dartmouth* out of the anchorage and away to sea without the help of boats and without endangering any of the dozen or so men-o'-war that clustered around them. It was a Leeward Islands Squadron affair, an unnecessary conceit that would either reinforce the ship's reputation or end in an embarrassing and costly disaster.

'Did you feel that?'

The officer of the watch held a wetted finger aloft in an attempt to detect the first stirrings of the land breeze. David Wishart was much younger than the sailing master – almost too young for his lofty position as second lieutenant in a ship-of-the-line – and he hadn't quite shaken off his natural excitability. Beazley didn't favour him with the slightest glance, yet he had also noticed that faintest of movement in the air. It was that breathless transition period in the early evening when the harbour waited in a hushed silence. The sea breeze had faltered and died over half an hour ago and the two-decker was already feeling the effect of the flooding tide, and was starting to swing on its anchor to face the open sea. All that was needed now was enough wind to waft them clear of the harbour, but not so much that it counteracted the tide and turned their bows back towards the land before they had won their anchor. With the squadron mostly in harbour, there was no space for turning once they were underway and it was imperative that *Dartmouth's* bows were facing the ocean before they loosed their grip on the harbour bed.

Beazley waited a few moments to make it clear that he wasn't reacting to Wishart's question, then he glanced aloft. Yes, there was a definite movement of the commissioning pennant. It was made of heavy flax bunting and it would take more than this infant breeze to make it fly free, but its belly was at least lifting away from the t'gallant mast in the direction of the sea. Fifteen more minutes, he estimated.

'My compliments to Captain Carlisle, Mister Young, and please to report that I would like to weigh anchor now.'

Midshipman Horace Young was even younger than Wishart and had yet to learn the stoicism that was proper on the quarterdeck. However, he'd been anticipating this command and now he positively skipped the few steps that led to the captain's cabin. These fifty-gun fourth rates had been built to take a commodore on foreign stations, but in wartime they were generally used as heavy cruisers, and their captains could luxuriate in a suite of cabins on the same deck as the quarterdeck. The marine sentry wordlessly opened the door to the dining cabin and the captain's clerk waved him straight through into the great cabin that stretched across the stern of the ship.

'He's in the stern gallery, Mister Young, with Lady Chiara.'

Frederick Simmonds messed with Horace Young in the gunroom – they were good friends and held roughly the same status within the ship – but a formal report to the captain demanded that he speak to Horace as though they hardly knew each other, and only the faintest wink betrayed him.

Cousins At Arms

The door to the stern gallery was open and Young could see through the windows to where Carlisle and Lady Chiara were standing on the starboard side of the narrow platform. From there they could look between Fort Berkeley and the careening wharf to see the King's Yard with the already night-grey hills rising behind. The sun was moving rapidly towards the high land to the left of the yard and the cranes and warehouses cast long, stark shadows that created a fine contrast with the yard's crushed white shells that served as both roadways and working surfaces. That colourless precision of shape and line was rarely ever seen outside the tropics and it was enhanced by the sun glancing off the little ruffles where the wind was just starting to stir the waters of Freeman's Bay and English Harbour. It was clear that the captain and his wife were enjoying this last view of the land before they set sail, and a more sensitive man might have paused before delivering his message. However, all this beauty was lost on Horace Young, who had but one thought in his mind, to deliver his report without the hesitation and errors that always brought a frown to his captain's brow.

Young stepped into the gallery, turned smartly to the left and removed his hat. It should have been an elegant movement, a dramatic sweep of his arm that would bring his hat from his head to his chest, but it was not to be. Horace had forgotten that the great stern lanterns partly overhung the gallery and the iron bracket for the larboard lantern neatly plucked his hat from his hand and sent it spinning towards the sea below. Young's hand twitched in the direction of his lost hat but he recovered himself before he'd made the probably fatal error of putting his personal property before his duty. It was a serious loss – that was his best hat, his number one deckhead scraper, and would cost a week's pay to replace – but it was nothing compared with the sheer horror of not reporting correctly to his captain.

'M-mister Beazley's compliments, sir,' he stammered, all his carefully prepared *sang froid* gone overboard with the hat, 'and he would like to w-weigh anchor… soon…'

Young new that there was something wrong in his report but his wits had gone under Carlisle's stern gaze. His discomfort was evident to both the captain and his wife but his salvation came from an unexpected source. A disembodied voice floated up from the water below, from the longboat that was standing by to give *Dartmouth* a nudge in the right direction if the wind should fail.

'I've got your hat, Mister Young, safe and sound and hardly wet at all. I'll send it up immediately.'

Jack Souter could read his captain's mood by a single glance, and he had a soft spot for the midshipman whom he'd known for the past two years. Young had already been serving in *Dartmouth* when Captain Carlisle took command at Quebec, in the shadow of the still-smoking, half-ruined fortress and city, and he had stayed to become a follower of this new captain. Souter, however, was a long-standing follower of Carlisle and had served in his previous ship. As the captain's coxswain he had a certain freedom to express himself that wasn't afforded to any other petty officers, or to midshipmen.

Carlisle looked severe.

'You'll need your hat as Mister Beazley is ready to weigh anchor *immediately*, I fancy.'

That was all the hint that Young needed and he recovered in an instant.

'I beg your pardon, sir, Mister Beazley would like to weigh anchor *now*, sir.'

Horace waited in awful dread, because he was certain that he was in for a right roasting. Captain Carlisle was very particular about the reports that his officers made to him, having suffered in his early years in command from midshipmen improving upon the exact words that they were supposed to say. He was about to deliver the expected rebuke when he felt a slight pressure from Chiara's hand on his arm. He was being manipulated, he knew, by both his coxswain and his wife. But secretly he was pleased to see an old and experienced seaman supporting his young officer and it would take a greater matter than this to go against his wife's wishes, even if they were delivered by nothing more than the light pressure of her fingers. He leaned over the stern gallery's rail.

'Souter, just hoist that hat up on the boathook, will you? Now, Mister Young,' he said as he replaced the hat unceremoniously on the midshipman's head, and his wife reached over to square it off, 'you may return to the quarterdeck properly dressed. My compliments to Mister Beazley and he may weigh anchor. I'll be on deck in a few moments.'

Horace Young bowed to his captain. It was an awkward movement because he didn't think it was quite right to remove his hat after the captain himself had placed it on his head, and yet bowing with his hat still in place risked it slipping over his forehead. He compromised with an inelegant half-bow, ignoring the trickle of seawater that ran down his forehead. Then he marched with as much dignity as he could muster back to the quarterdeck, followed by Lady Chiara's soft laughter.

***

Matthew Gresham leaned over the fo'c'sle rail to see the anchor cable stretching vertically down into the clear, blue water. It was evidently under considerable strain, but that was to be expected with the best bower weighing nearly two tons suspended by a cable of seventeen-and-a-half inches in circumference.

'Anchor's up-and-down, sir.'

'Very well.'

Carlisle didn't need to make any further comment. His first lieutenant wasn't waiting for an order, he was merely reporting that the ship was directly above the anchor which was still on the seabed but would imminently break free.

Gresham waited a moment before looking again over the side. He had heard the clicking of the capstan pawls so he knew that the anchor was coming home, but it seemed to be rather slower than he'd expected. He should see the cable swinging in a slow arc as soon as the anchor was clear of the ground, but it was still rigid and stretched vertically downwards into the water. He walked back to the fo'c'sle rail and looked down onto the upper deck.

'Mister Hewlett, is there a problem? The men seem to be straining.'

The bosun kicked the messenger with the sole of his boot, it was bar-taut, and now the pawls were clicking slower and slower.

'We may have fouled something, sir. It's coming home right enough but very slow.'

Gresham swore under his breath. This was all he needed, with the captain's wife on board and the sun setting in half an hour. It would be a sorry start to the voyage if they had to wait for the morning and be towed out against the sea breeze. He hurried forward to where he could see that the longboat had moved up to the ship's bows. Trust the captain's coxswain to be in the right place at the right time.

'Souter, can you see the anchor?'

Normally he would have ordered the boat to keep clear while the anchor was being heaved in, to prevent accidents, but now he needed that view from sea-level.

Souter gave a few orders for the oarsmen to bring the boat close to the anchor cable. He leaned far over the gunwale so that the back of his head was hiding the glare of the low sun.

'Looks like we've picked up another anchor, sir.'

Gresham swore again, but softly. He looked quickly around to conform what he already knew. Although there were ships all around him, they had been lying to their anchors with their heads seeking the sou'west breeze, and there was no chance that any of them had fouled *Dartmouth's* hawse. The anchor was still coming home, but at a miserable pace, as he'd expect with perhaps as much as four tons of cast iron weighing it down. He looked quickly over the fo'c'sle rail again. The bosun was urging on the men at the capstan bars, seventy-two of them between the two great machines, and a further twenty-four to pull on the swifters. With all the messenger-men, the nippers, the fo'c'sle hands standing by the cathead and those with the worst job of all, in the cable tiers, there was a total of some two hundred and forty seamen engaged in weighing anchor, and not a man was idle.

'Heave,' shouted the bosun, 'heave her home, men.'

Hewlett found it hard to express himself with the captain's wife on the quarterdeck where she could hear every word that he uttered. He could see the amusement in the faces at the capstan for the bosun was known to use a choice phrase or two when things weren't going well.

'It's another anchor, sure enough, sir,' called Souter from over the side, 'a frigate's bower anchor by the look of it.'

Gresham composed himself to make a full report, which must necessarily be done by shouting across the waist to the quarterdeck; he couldn't leave the fo'c'sle now.

'Captain, sir. Anchor's aweigh and coming home slowly but we've picked up a stray frigate's anchor. We can bring them both up but it will be slow.'

Carlisle's face showed no expression. He heard his first lieutenant's reports and he knew that he spoke the truth as he saw it, but it always looked worse from his necessarily narrow perspective. Gresham saw only the problems with the anchor and the long process of clearing away the tangle; he couldn't see the bigger picture. But Carlisle could feel the rising land breeze that was now lifting the whole of the commissioning pennant some twenty degrees from the vertical. His ship's head was cast towards the harbour entrance and there was no shallower water between him and the open sea. The fouled anchor was a problem but not a tragedy.

'Very well, Mister Gresham, heave away and we'll sort it out later, make sure the longboat is clear.'

He looked over the side. As he thought, the making tide was setting them back up the harbour, but so slowly that it was almost imperceptible.

'Mister Beazley, let fall the tops'l's and let's get underway. Take us slowly out of the harbour.'

The twenty seamen not engaged in anchoring were already in the fore and main tops, waiting for the order to set the tops'l's. At Beazley's command they rushed out along the horses to release the gaskets that held the furled sails to the yards. The tops'l's started to fill immediately and in a minute *Dartmouth* had enough way to counteract the flooding tide. They were motionless over the spot where their anchor and the errant frigate's anchor had been plucked from the bottom.

'I thought the master attendant had dragged the whole bay in the past six months, Mister Beazley.'

'That he did, sir, I saw much of it with my own eyes. It's mostly a fine white sandy bottom but there are a few coral heads here and there that can snag an anchor and the sweep won't get to them. There must be hundreds of tons of old iron down there still.'

Gresham hurried back to the quarterdeck.

'Anchor's breaking the surface now, sir. But good God, it's an old one, the stock's almost all eaten away. It must have lain here since King Charles' time, or earlier. Our fluke's caught in the ring. Do you want to jettison it or keep it, sir?'

'Oh, I think we can keep it, Mister Gresham. The King's yard at Jamaica can give it a new stock and hammer out its bends. It'll be good for another ship yet.'

Gresham tried not to grimace. It would be easy to bring the anchor inboard once their own anchor had been catted. But it would be a damned nuisance on the voyage, taking up space on the fo'c'sle and threatening to snag the tacks and sheets at every move. It would be far easier to pass a line around its fluke now and a few sharp heaves would break it free to fall back to the bottom of the bay and be someone else's problem in the future. But that wasn't Captain Carlisle's way, he knew. He looked around for the first time since the drama had started to unfold. *Dartmouth* was running at perhaps two knots and already Fort Berkeley and the Half Moon battery were abaft the beam. There were still a few merchantmen between them and the open sea, but the ship had steerage way, and with a gentle breeze and a modest tide, there was little chance of anything going wrong. His captain had been right to continue to weigh and in all likelihood he was right to salvage the anchor.

'I'll go back to the fo'c'sle then sir.'

'Very well, Mister Gresham, and now that we're clear, the longboat can tow astern.'

***

'Is it always that dramatic in a fourth rate, dear? I remember it being a rather smoother operation in *Medina*.'

Carlisle had to force himself to pay attention to his wife. She had been to sea with him before, in his previous command, the sixth rate frigate *Medina*, but that was four years ago. Now he thought about it, except for their brush with the Dutch pirates, it had been an uneventful trip to take the Spanish governor-general of Florida to St. Augustine. Certainly the seamanship aspects of that cruise had caused no trouble.

'Oh, we were just unfortunate but it could have been worse. If it was a larger anchor, a second rate's best bower for example, we'd have had to apply to the admiral for a diver to help sort ourselves out. That, or something akin to it, happens on nearly every cruise. I'm lucky to have such good officers who know their business and I was pleased to see how they handled a difficult situation. Of course everything is to a purpose, and the officers and the crew have had good practice in dealing with heavy anchors. You never know when you'll be working anchors on a lee shore with time running against you.'

He tapped the wood of the quarterdeck rail, just in case, and saw his wife's amused look at his superstition.

'Yes, I noticed that there was no anxiety among the men, and commendably little shouting.'

Carlisle said nothing. Few things happened at sea without shouting but there was a general view that it should all be toned down when Lady Chiara was on board. The fact was that the crew adored her, would do anything to elicit a smile, and a word of thanks made each of them her lifelong servant. No, there would be little shouting and no cursing at all on this voyage, at least not in Chiara's hearing. But then, in principle it should be a peaceful mission, to bring this cargo of the Spanish governor-general's furniture to Havana and to send the admiral's compliments by the mouth of a post-captain. It was a strange chance that had caused the Spanish merchantman to founder upon the rocks on the eastern side of Barbuda, and it was purely by good fortune that the cargo for the governor-general had been stored in the after part of the ship that had been driven hard up the rocks and had not been flooded. Sir James had just received a letter from the Admiralty exhorting him to be as amiable to the Spanish as he could. It had taken little persuading to decide that he could spare a fourth rate for a few months in the hope of favourably influencing his colonial neighbours. And it was a valuable cargo of furniture, as Carlisle had seen with his own eyes. It could have graced the Escorial Palace itself, and would appear hugely impressive in a colonial governor-general's palace, even in Havana, which by some measures was the most important city in the Spanish new world.

If he were lucky it would take a week to reach Jamaica. Then, unless he was detained by Admiral Holmes, who counted Havana within the sphere of his interest, it would be another week or so to their final destination. With the French navy almost swept from the seas, it should be a pleasant cruise and perhaps an interesting few days in Havana, if *Dartmouth* was allowed into the harbour. Then at least a month to return home again against the prevailing winds. Yes, a fine yachting expedition, if all went well.

***

CHAPTER TWO

Lady Chiara

Wednesday, Ninth of December 1761.
Kingston, Jamaica.

Lady Chiara angled the pages of the broadsheet to catch the low evening light that slanted through the window. She reached for her purse and looked quickly around the parlour of the rented house. It was a habitual gesture. She knew very well that she was alone and only her maid would enter at that time of day without knocking, but she was sensitive about the spectacles and hadn't yet come to terms with their necessity. The broadsheet article that so consumed her was a superficially well-informed speculation on the possibility of Spain joining the war on the side of France. She'd read it before, of course, because all news that reached Jamaica had to came via Antigua, but still, it was an interesting article and highly topical. She knew that few of the other officers' wives had read it, and those that did could hardly be expected to understand the nuances of diplomacy and family ties that could lead the King of Spain to embark on such a hazardous path. But Chiara had been brought up in the Sardinian court, and from an early age she had been expected to make intelligent conversation on the great events of the times. The torturous politics of Europe were an open book to her and Spain's agonising and self-mutilating efforts to maintain its pre-eminence in the New World were just a part of that greater story.

Chiara frowned as she studied the article, just as she had at its first reading. The London correspondent appeared to believe that there was still a chance of Spain sitting on the side-lines in this great war. He dismissed in a few pithy sentences the family ties that bound the two offshoots of the house of Bourbon, insisting that greater matters were at play than mere blood relations. Chiara shook her head in despair. How little he knew of the forces that motivated the old monarchies. Nobody who had grown up under the Georgian kings of England could understand the motivations of rulers such as Louis of France and Carlos – the writer called him Charles, in the English fashion – of Spain. They were absolute monarchs, unconstrained by a constitution that in Britain made the King a servant of Parliament. The wellbeing and survival of the royal families directed every action of the state. Spain would fight, she was sure, despite the entirely predictable national disaster that would follow.

A noise outside startled her and she whipped off her spectacles and looked towards the window. Those were her husband's footsteps on the cobblestones that led to the small house set back from the wharfs of Kingston – the same house that they'd rented when she was last in Jamaica – she'd recognise his purposeful stride anywhere. Five minutes before she'd noticed the little boy who worked about the place running back from the direction of the waterside to warn her maid that the master was on his way, but she'd been so engrossed that his actual arrival had taken her by surprise. She heard the front door open and caught the high-pitched, belligerent tones of her maid's welcome. Like the unsatisfactory house, she was all that could be found at short notice. Chiara assumed a pose of one who was absorbed in the broadsheet, despite the difficulty in reading the unfocussed words.

'Chiara, my dear. Still reading? That light can't be good for your eyes; I'll have a candle and reflector brought immediately. But how lovely you look in the last of the sunshine.'

Carlisle caught the maid's momentary curtsey and saw her move away towards the scullery.

'Is that the article about Spain? The flag captain mentioned it when I called on him this afternoon. He wanted to discuss it but I haven't had a chance to read it yet. In any case, he has enough to concern him at present, what with the admiral passing away so suddenly. The expectation here is that Rodney will take the station when he arrives and perhaps he'll take the Leeward Islands too, although where that will leave Sir James I can't tell. But none of that will affect us, as I hope we'll be long gone to Havana. All I could gather from the flag captain was that he believes that the article lays to rest the risk of Spain joining the war, and that our mission to Havana is still useful. But what do you think of the chances of King Charles joining the fray, dear?'

It had been as long and painful journey, but after four years of marriage Carlisle had at last learned to respect his wife's judgement where diplomacy was concerned. She had an uncanny ability to see into the minds of the great people of the time, and divine their every motive.

'If the great and good of Jamaica believe that Spain won't join this war then I believe they'll be sadly disappointed. This article is useful in a way, in that it lays out most of the known facts, but the analysis is faulty. The author has spent too long in London where trade is everything. He doesn't understand the way that Spain and France work. Do you know what your continental neighbours call the English, between themselves?'

Carlisle didn't reply but cocked his head to one side, waiting. He could have taken issue with being lumped in with all the other English people but then, in his native Virginia that is what they called themselves, and that's what they understood themselves to be, Englishmen.

'Shopkeepers. They believe you have placed trade and wealth above national glory.'

Carlisle gave a wry smile. There was too much truth in Chiara's blunt assertion for laughter. Britain and its colonies had become rich by Parliament's mercantilist policies, and it was that prosperity that fed the growth of the navy and it was the navy that protected the nation's trade and destroyed its enemy's commerce. A virtuous circle if ever there was one, or an evil ring-around if you were French or Spanish.

'Oh there'll be war, probably when the winter weather is over in Europe and the campaigning season begins. Your Duke of Newcastle and Mister Grenville have five or six months grace, I expect.'

'Then we'll all have to sharpen up. Spain has a respectable navy you know, and we'll be hard pressed here in the colonies, particularly if Anson brings his battle squadrons back to home waters as he surely must in the face of a combined French and Spanish fleet. But that's a problem for their Lordships and for a later day. For now, I have news.'

Chiara didn't meet Edward's eye; she had a horrible feeling that the news would be bad and would deprive her of this voyage to Havana. She bit her lower lip, always a bad sign, and prepared to have a disagreement with her husband. She knew that there was little that he could do about it, but even that little might help to change this unknown flag captain's mind and she was determined to send him back again to fight her corner. If that failed, she would demand to see the flag captain herself, and be damned to the protocol.

'*Dartmouth* is to sail in two days, but – and this is between you and I – we're to take the Windward Passage and the Old Bahama Straits.'

Carlisle glanced sidelong at Chiara to confirm that she understood what he was talking about. She did, of course, her long hours studying Beazley's charts were not for nothing. But he also noted her dogged expression and knew what it meant.

'It appears that one of Admiral Holmes' last instructions was that the straits were to be surveyed – in a cursory, passing-through sort of way – after that hurricane came through last month. His secretary recorded it, so the flag captain feels that he must take action, particularly as *Dartmouth* has fallen into his lap, so to speak. He can fulfil Sir James' mission to Havana and the admiral's last wish with one ship. He sucked his teeth a little when I told him that Sir James had asked that you join me on this voyage – apparently he has strong views on officers' wives at sea – but again he didn't feel that he was on firm enough ground to defy a commodore and commander-in-chief.'

Chiara's face relaxed and she favoured her husband with a dazzling smile.

Carlisle could guess for the most part what his wife was thinking, or at least he thought he could. She had waged a subtle and ultimately successful campaign to be allowed to come on this expedition, mostly through Lady Helen Douglas, the commodore's wife. The logic was impeccable; she spoke perfect Spanish and was well known to be able to hold her own in any social or diplomatic gathering. The only officer in *Dartmouth* who spoke any kind of Spanish was her cousin, and she shuddered to think of how his dreadful consonants would be received by the governor-general of Cuba. Furthermore, there was no Spanish speaker of rank in Antigua who was both available and willing to leave the island for a month or two, nor, as it seemed, in the whole of Jamaica. The decision had balanced on a knife edge for days, principally because Sir James had publicly expressed his determination that his captains' wives should not sail with them. It was a perennial problem for the navy in general, but a particular problem for the Leeward Islands Squadron and the Jamaica Squadron where of necessity those wives who had followed their husbands this far were living in temporary quarters. The commander-in-chief had to endure their complaints at every social event, and the cry was always the same: they hadn't followed their husbands across the wide Atlantic just to be left in some rented house on a fever-ridden island when their husband's ship was sent away. He had to have a firm policy – Chiara understood that – but he was undermined at every turn by Lady Helen, who colluded shamelessly with her fellow wives. Be that as it may, Chiara had been allowed – nay, she had, in the end, been requested – to sail to Havana in *Dartmouth*, and now that the post of Commander-in-Chief Jamaica was temporarily vacant and the flag captain had acquiesced, there was no authority that could prevent her.

No authority but her motherly feelings for her infant son. Young Joshua was three years old and Chiara felt a pang of guilt at leaving him in Antigua in the care of a nurse. It was only the reassuring presence of her man-servant, Rodrigo, that persuaded her that she could safely sail away with her husband for a few months. It was strange to give the man a name. She had known him all her life and in Nice he had always been named the Head of Household. Then, after Edward's old frigate *Fury* had visited Nice, his officers had dubbed him Black Rod, for his imposing demeanour, which would indeed have been fitting in the sergeant-at-arms of the British House of Lords. It was only when he'd had to declare a name to be taken on *Dartmouth's* books, when he was fleeing Nice, that he had stated his name was Rodrigo Black. Chiara didn't believe it for one moment – it sounded like he was mimicking his own nickname – but at least it suited him.

***

The muster book, the purser's accounts and the bosun's barely believable account of his expenditure of cordage had all been studied and signed. Simmonds had departed to be rowed back to the ship, weighed down by the mountain of paperwork, and Carlisle at last had a few moments alone to consider this next phase in his life. He'd never sailed the Old Bahama Straits before; few King's officers had ever had cause to pass that way. Those whose duties took them to the west of Jamaica and into the Gulf of Mexico took the obvious, well-trodden route through the Yucatan Channel. It would be stimulating to deal with the navigational difficulties to the north of Cuba, and if Spain did join the war that information would be valuable. It was hard to imagine a British squadron and army descending on Havana, not when the Spanish fleet was so large, and not when most line-of-battle ships would need to concentrate in home waters against a renewed threat of invasion. Yet, at sea, no information as to rocks and shoals, wind and tide was ever wasted, and he looked forward to the challenge.

He'd noticed a new attitude in himself, a sea-change perhaps. A year ago, even as little as six months ago, he was eagerly anticipating the end of the war so that he could come ashore and leave behind the ponderous responsibilities of command of a ship-of-the-line. He had even contemplated throwing it all up before the war ended and it was only the thought of the whispers behind his back that prevented him from doing so. He had been disgusted with everything to do with England and its navy and its haughty ambition. He longed to retire to his new home on the green in Williamsburg, to be in peace with his little family and to live the life of a colonial gentleman. He wanted to know his father better – his last link with the family that he remembered as a child – before the old man went to his long rest. Yes, he longed for all that, but in the past year he'd been both pushed and pulled in the opposite direction. Pushed. Aye, that was a fair use of the word.

He'd been appalled by the money-hungry merchants of New England and their willingness to trade anywhere that could show a penny of profit, even with the French in the middle of a bitter war. His eyes had been opened and he could see the same attitude in his home town in Virginia, although the merchants of Williamsburg were just a tone or two less avaricious, and just a fraction more aware of their own reputations and the greater good. He'd come close to being prosecuted in Newport, through political interests, and he didn't at all relish being involved in that grubby way of behaving. At the same time he had found new interests in the navy that were pulling him back in. He'd feared that command of a fourth rate would condemn him to hanging on the coat-tails of the battle squadron, with no freedom of action and no hope of distinguishing himself, but events had shown how wrong he was. He'd been living the life of a frigate captain, but doing so in a ship with enough force to really influence events. He knew it couldn't last. At some point their Lordships, or the commander-in-chief on the station, would move him into a third rate and then he'd really be condemned to the line-of-battle. But for now he was content. No, he was more than content, he was actually enjoying the life of a post-captain on a foreign station.

Of course, any decisions on the future would be taken out of his hands when the war ended. He'd be fortunate indeed if *Dartmouth* wasn't taken out of commission and placed in ordinary, to lie between head-and-stern anchors at Portsmouth, Plymouth or the London River. Yet this dreadful uncertainty pervaded his thoughts and dragged at his heels, and it was exacerbated by not knowing his wife's thoughts on the matter. It seemed that she could read him like a book but after four years of marriage he had no clearer idea of why she had chosen him, why she was content to leave her home in Nice to join him and most of all he had no real idea what she wanted for the future.

And then there was the question of their three-year-old son, Joshua. Chiara had brought him to Antigua, along with her manservant Rodrigo and a nurse, leaving their home to be inhabited by his father and its care to a Williamsburg lawyer. He still couldn't tell what had moved Chiara to make the snap decision to leave their comfortable Virginia home and embark on the itinerate life of a sea officer's wife in a time of war. He hadn't been consulted and the first he knew of it was when he saw her on the deck of a packet in English Harbour. Yet if that was difficult to understand, the second decision to leave Joshua, the nurse and Rodrigo in St. John's and set out on a cruise of uncertain length in her husband's ship was completely unfathomable. Well, it was a puzzle for another day and he just hoped that his wife didn't come to bitterly regret her decisions.

***

CHAPTER THREE

The Spanish Consul

Wednesday, Ninth of December 1761.
Kingston, Jamaica.

They'd invited Chiara's cousin for supper. Enrico was, strictly speaking, a lieutenant in the Sardinian Navy and he was only on secondment to *Dartmouth* to gain experience for when King Charles Emmanuel changed his navy from one principally compose of oared galleys to a modern square-rigged man-of-war navy. Yet Enrico had been with Carlisle so long that he'd become a fixture in his ship. In fact, it was hard to imagine how he could go back to Sardinia after he had been a party to the same disagreement with his powerful aunt – who had the ear of the King – that had seen Chiara's manservant banished. One day, when the balance of power in Milan favoured the French camp, as it did from time-to-time, he'd be recalled, or his commission would be terminated. Then, being a Catholic and unable to take a British commission, he'd have no business in a King's ship. However, for the time being he was a valued member of *Dartmouth's* wardroom.

'What's the news, Mister Angelini?'

'Mister Gresham sends his compliments, sir. All is well and the stores are coming onboard steadily. The gammoning has been freshened where it was wearing on the knightheads and we'll be complete and ready for sea by tomorrow afternoon. Oh, and Mister Simmonds asked me to bring this letter to you. He said that it's from the Spanish consul and there was nothing else of any consequence.'

The letter had been opened, of course. All his letters were read by his clerk and only those that required the captain's attention were passed to Carlisle. In that way, he only saw a small proportion of all the correspondence that entered the ship. The interminable letters from the navy board could usually be handled by his officers, and there was no reason why he should be bothered by matters that concerned only the bosun, the carpenter, the gunner, the purser or the surgeon.

'This is in Spanish, what the devil does he think I can make of it?'

Carlisle theatrically turned the letter on its side then upside down, as though to gain a sudden insight when the words were viewed from a different angle. No wonder Simmonds had sent it on with Enrico; there was no officer in *Dartmouth* that could read it, although Enrico should have been able to make some sort of a guess at its general contents. But then, Simmonds wouldn't have shown a letter from a foreign consul to any of the ship's officers before the captain had seen it, and Simmonds knew that Chiara would be on hand when it was delivered. He glanced at Enrico; no, his lieutenant hadn't read the letter.

'Allow me, Edward.'

Chiara wouldn't have used her husband's Christian name in front of any other of the officers, and not even in front of Enrico – who was, after all, family – on board the ship. However, here ashore she didn't have to pretend that Enrico wasn't her cousin and she could behave more normally.

Carlisle passed the letter to his wife and turned his head to confirm that the maid was pouring a glass of wine for Enrico.

Chiara studied the letter, holding it against the candle. It had been written in a tiny, cramped hand, as though the author was trying to save paper, and indeed his signature looked as though it had been shortened to keep to a single page. She realised to her embarrassment that her eyesight was not good enough to read such tiny script in the meagre candlelight, even with the reflector. She hesitated for a moment then reached in her purse and, with deliberate, be-damned-if-I-care movements, fitted her eye-glasses across her nose and behind her ears. She saw the quickly concealed surprise pass over Enrico's face and the exchange of glances with her husband. Enrico had never seen his elder cousin wearing spectacles, but he knew better than to make any comment. Even a *how well they look on you, Lady Chiara*, would have been a grave mistake. There was a deathly, nervous silence while Chiara read the now-visible words.

'I'll spare you the usual salutations, and the wishes that your Excellency is in good health,' she looked at her husband over the rim of her glasses making her appear like a child's governess of the most severe type. 'It seems that this consul wishes to view your cargo before you depart so that he can send with you a certificate attesting to its nature and condition. He proposes to do himself the honour of calling at the ship tomorrow in the forenoon.'

A quick frown passed across Carlisle's face. This sounded very much like an inspection, and a damned presumptuous one at that. The navy, with himself as its agent, was doing the governor-general a favour and it appeared that his good deed was being viewed with suspicion. His first thought was to refuse to allow this Spaniard aboard his ship.

'I wonder... I wonder what's behind this,' Chiara mused before Carlisle could speak. 'The first question of course is how the consul heard about your cargo.'

'Oh, it's been general knowledge since we arrived. Most likely the flag captain or even Sir Henry himself decided to tell the consul. Lieutenant-governors are a law unto themselves, you know.'

'I assume this cargo wouldn't have originally been intended to travel through Jamaica, Edward, is that the case?'

'That's certainly true, it was consigned directly to Havana with no intermediate ports. Of course, the ship's captain could touch at any convenient place if his ship were in danger, but he'd have avoided British ports if he could. It was only the tail-end of that hurricane blowing him onto Barbuda that interrupted his passage. Otherwise, if needed, he'd perhaps have called at San Juan, but nowhere else. But in any case he was bound north-about past Hispaniola and through the Old Bahama Straits, direct to Havana.'

'Then this consul has no business inquiring about the cargo, it must be a ruse to get on board. What could he want, Edward?'

'Well, if he wants a passage to Havana he can whistle at the wind for all the good it will do him. I'll have no Spaniards looking over my shoulder when I pass through the straits, watching where I take bearings and soundings. That could lead to a very sticky meeting in Havana. The Dons consider that to be their own back yard. It's the shortest route to Havana, you know.'

'Edward, could I see a map please, or a chart as I should say? I have an idea of this consul's motives. They're over there, Enrico, in the sideboard.'

Chiara had grown used to flinging out commands to her cousin and he had perforce fallen into a habit of obedience. It hadn't always been like this. When he had first joined Carlisle at sea he had considered himself naturally superior to Chiara, but the awful aura that surrounded a post-captain naturally envelopes his wife too, and Enrico had unwittingly, step-by-stumbling step, wandered into Chiara's web. He smoothed out the chart on the table in the centre of the room and brought the candle over.

Carlisle was intrigued and despite his natural desire to keep control of the conversation he waited as his wife, with her spectacles on the end of her nose – he only now noticed that they gave her an air of mystery – studied the chart. This was his own chart, not Beazley's, and it was an updated copy of one made in the year seventeen fifteen by Herman Moll, of whom he knew nothing except that he had described himself as a geographer and had sold charts and globes in London, right behind St. Paul's. Despite its age it was an excellent chart and Carlisle possessed none better. It displayed the whole of the Gulf of Mexico and the Caribbean Sea as far east as Barbados and it stretched from

Georgia in the north to New Granada in the south. It was no good for detailed navigation, it covered far too much ground and rendered the lesser ports as mere dots, but it was ideal for planning a passage. One of its chief glories was the detailed inset charts of a few of the principal Spanish ports: Havana, Porto Bello, St. Augustine, Vera Cruz, Cartagena. It was a salutary reminder that for all the pretensions of the newer colonial powers – Britain, France, the Netherlands and Denmark – it was Spain that had set down firm roots in the region, with no intention of leaving.

'Now, I don't understand your assertion that passing to the north of Cuba is the quickest way to Havana, Edward, it seems to me that we would have a clear run with the trade wind to Cape San Antonio.'

She pointed to the western tip of the island of Cuba, that formed one side of the Yucatan Channel, one of only two entrances to the Gulf of Mexico.

'From there it's but a short distance to Havana. Perhaps I'm missing something.'

Carlisle could see that Enrico was itching to display his knowledge. He inclined his head towards his lieutenant.

'Well, cousin,' he couldn't bring himself to use Chiara's Christian name in front of his captain, 'you are correct when we speak of distance to run, but you know, everything depends upon the trade winds and in this case their particular pattern in the Gulf of Mexico. You see, once we have rounded Cape San Antonio the wind blows dead foul for Havana twenty-nine days out of thirty, right on the nose.'

Carlisle smiled to hear Enrico so fluently using English idioms. It hadn't always been so.

'That means that we can either make short tacks along the coast or we can make a bold slant up towards Louisiana and catch the Loop Current that runs down towards Cape Florida. In either case a week would be an optimistic estimate to make port, and it would be more likely two or three weeks. Ships have had to beat up and down off that coast trying to reach Havana until their sails have worn thin.'

He looked up to see that his cousin was paying rapt attention, and suddenly realised how much, with her lower lip between her teeth, she looked like the very young lady that he knew as a child. It was the same expression of concentration that he remembered trying to copy when she was a great child and he nothing but a toddler. The spectacles, he noticed, rather enhanced the likeness although she had worn none in her younger years.

'But Enrico, doesn't the same hold true for this channel between Hispaniola and Cuba, the Windward Passage, I believe; even its name sounds discouraging. I can see those trade wind arrows slanting straight against us if we go that way.'

'You're right of course, in a way, and ships have spent days and weeks trying to beat to the north through there, but it's unusual. Generally there's a bit of easterly to the trade wind and we can make it in a single tack, or perhaps two. Then once we're past Cape Mays, here at the eastern end of Cuba, we have the trade wind and the current behind us and can make a fast passage through the Old Bahama Straits and reach Havana with ease…'

Carlisle interrupted his lieutenant.

'And there's one further factor, Chiara. If we spend a week tacking to and fro to the west of Havana, the Dons will have plenty of notice of our arrival, and I have no desire to give them that courtesy. The primary mission is to deliver the governor-general's furniture, but if you're correct, and we have to fight the Dons next year, then whatever information I can gather about Havana and its approaches will be useful. I really can't waste this opportunity to test the waters of the straits and to see the defences of Havana before they can be hidden from me. And in any case, that's the way I'm bidden.'

Chiara stared at the chart, committing it to memory.

'Is it common knowledge that you're taking this route?'

'No, that's a secret that I haven't even shared with my other officers yet.'

Carlisle gave Enrico a meaningful stare and the lieutenant nodded in reply.

'In fact nobody will expect it as it's generally understood that the Old Bahama Straits are too dangerous for a ship-o'-the-line, unless it's willing to anchor through each night and work the lead constantly each day. It's only possible because *Dartmouth* is the very smallest of that breed; that and our excellent sailing master of course.'

'Then, dear husband, this consul's mission is clear. He wishes to know when you will leave so that he can warn the governor-general. He'll assume that you are taking the Yucatan Channel, unless he sees you heading for the Windward Passage. I expect he has a fast vessel ready to take the news to Havana by whichever route you take.'

Carlisle stared abstractedly at the darkness outside the window. It was suddenly evident to him that anyone looking in from the street could see what they were studying and could discern by their hand movements which part of the Caribbean they were discussing. He walked over and drew the curtains firmly closed then returned to the chart.

***

CHAPTER FOUR

The White Island

Wednesday, Sixteenth of December 1761.
Dartmouth, off Point Morant, Jamaica.

'Beg your pardon, sir. Mister Gresham's compliments and the poop deck's swabbed and dried now.'

Midshipman Horace Young stood a yard back from the cabin door and spoke in hushed tones that sounded odd in a man-of-war. Normally he would have entered the cabin before delivering his message, but these were not normal times, not with Lady Chiara on board. It was well known that ladies in general and the captain's wife in particular considered the morning to start at eight o'clock, not four hours earlier as was generally understood in the navy, and he hoped that he might not disturb her.

'Very well, Mister Young. Is the sailing master on deck?'

'He's just stepped below to consult his instrument, sir.'

'Then my compliments to Mister Beazley and I would be pleased if he could join me on the poop deck when he's completed his records.'

Carlisle strode from the cabin, closing the door carefully behind him, and made his way onto the poop deck. From there he had an uninterrupted view to starboard, towards the east where the first glow of the rising sun was tinting the horizon. He watched in a state not far from ecstasy as the light spread rapidly to the left and to the right until a full four points of the compass were aglow and the high mare's tails clouds showed pink and gold against the blue-black sky. He waited a few more breathless seconds and as the ship's stern rose to a following wave, a speck of gold showed in the very centre of the gleaming arc. The stern fell and the speck disappeared. He felt the next swell lifting the stern and the golden speck reappeared, but larger than before. He gripped the taffrail and watched as at each successive upwards heave more and more of the sun became visible, until it hurt his eyes to look directly towards it. It wasn't yet a disc, nor even a part of a disc, for the curious effect of refraction widened its base where it was cut by the horizon, making it look like an apprentice glass blower's practice-piece melting into the sea. Then, abruptly, the sun broke its bond with the horizon and became a great glowing sphere, free of all constraint and ready to start its daily journey across the vault of the heavens. Carlisle reflected that nobody who spent their lives in the higher latitudes could ever know the glory of a tropical sunrise or sunset. In his native Virginia, even in midsummer the sun took a slanting passage across the horizon, and the transition from darkness to daylight and back again was only gradual; in far northern England it was even more so. But in the tropics the sun rose almost vertically and the slightest interruption – a report of the ships log speed, or attending to an ill-set sail – could mean that he missed the magical moment. He furtively leaned over the taffrail to confirm his suspicion, that Chiara was also watching the sunrise from the stern gallery, dressed in a damask robe against the morning damps.

A polite cough behind him alerted him to the presence of his sailing master.

'Ah, Mister Beazley, good morning to you. What do you make of those mare's tails, and this swell?'

Beazley was not a man to be rushed and he gazed for a moment at the long streamers of clouds with their curly, hooked edges. The sky above was surrendering its darkness and turning bluer by the second and the clouds were losing their outrageous colours, transforming into their daytime whiteness.

'It's almost too late for a hurricane, sir, perhaps a bit of a blow from the east but no more than that, I fancy.'

Carlisle nodded slowly. He'd lived through a hurricane before, some eighty leagues east of here, to the south of the great island of Hispaniola, and he had no wish to see another. And yet he caught the note almost of regret in

Beazley's voice, and he knew its cause. He turned away to hide his smile and feigned a study of the far horizon.

'What does your weather-glass tell us?'

Beazley gave his captain a sharp glance. For months he'd suffered the ribaldry and the scepticism of his fellow officers, and it was all because of his belief in his weather-glass. To be fair to Captain Carlisle, he was the only one of his fellow officers who saw that it could be of value in foretelling the weather, but even he reserved his full approbation. The problem lay in his lack of data derived from real observations. Most of the time the weather-glass confirmed what experienced sea officers knew from their own observations of the clouds, the feel of the wind and even the colour of the sea, and they tended to dismiss it as an irrelevance. Yet just occasionally it had shown that it could do better than the sea officers, and Beazley was sure that it could foretell a hurricane, if only they could find one. No sensible sailing master would ever wish for a full-blown hurricane – and Beazley was nothing if not sensible – but without one he couldn't positively assert that his instrument could forecast their approach. No, he didn't wish for a hurricane, and yet…

'The mercury is falling, sir, and we know that, in general, that foretells wind and rain.'

The sailing master paused and scanned the horizon astern.

'However, in this case, with the season almost over, I think more of a regular blow, sir, a trade wind blow perhaps, but nothing serious.'

'Then we'll keep our upper masts. I've no wish to further delay this passage.'

For delayed they were. The thought that his movements were being watched by the Spanish consul had prayed upon Carlisle's mind, to such an extent that he'd sought a way to disguise the ship's route. He'd sailed from Port Royal in the afternoon, leaving just enough time for any watchers to see him heading west, presumably intending to reach Havana through the Yucatan Channel. Then, as soon as darkness had fallen and he was certain that he couldn't be seen from the shore or by any of the little schooners that left with him, he'd ordered *Dartmouth* put onto the wind to beat back to the east. That had taken a full day, but now, at last, they had weathered Point Morant and were standing boldly into the Windward Passage with larboard tacks aboard.

'Aye sir, this bit of easterly in the wind can't be wasted. We might even weather Cape Mays on this tack.'

'Let me know if the mercury falls any lower, Mister Beazley.'

'Aye-aye sir, that I will.'

The sailing master tipped his hat and turned away to consult his weather-glass again. Hurricane or no, every recorded measurement was useful and he was daily becoming more confident in his predictions. One day he would stand in front of the elders of Trinity House and explain his findings with a such a mass of data that his conclusions would be irrefutable. And then, who knew where next? Perhaps even the Royal Society. He stroked the binnacle in passing, his own particular superstition to ward off the dreaded hex.

***

Carlisle lingered on the poop deck. If he went down to the quarterdeck he'd immediately be assailed by all the cares of command. In Matthew Gresham he had an excellent first lieutenant who intercepted most of the questions before they ever reached the captain, but all of his officers, whether they held a King's commissioned or a navy board warrant, had the right to bring their problems to the ultimate source of authority, and in a man-of-war that meant the captain. He could walk brusquely past his waiting officers and retreat to his cabin, but he knew that Chiara was up and about and he would only be in the way. Chiara had very set ideas about her appearance and even at sea she had to dress accordingly. That was no trivial task, evidently, and it took her maid's complete concentration. No, he was better out of the way.

In the few extra minutes he spent gazing astern the sun had climbed a hand's breadth above the horizon and its warmth was becoming pleasant. In an hour it would feel too warm, even with this strong trade wind, but for now it was almost perfect. A flying fish broke through the swell on the starboard quarter, then another and soon a huge shoal of them were skimming across the surface for perhaps fifty yards before plunging back into their natural habitat. Now he could see dark shapes twisting and lunging among the shoal, dolphins probably, the fish type, not the ones that sailors knew as porpoises or sea-hogs. They were fine eating, if they could be caught. So were the flying fish and he saw a good half dozen land in the longboat towing astern. He could rely upon his servant to claim a pair of those for the cabin breakfast. The thought of breakfast made his stomach complain. If he didn't have his wife at sea he could call his servant and the fish would be cooked and on his plate in twenty minutes, but he knew that Chiara wouldn't be ready for at least an hour. He turned away and started towards the ladder that led down to the quarterdeck where he could see his officers clustered. Casks of beef to be condemned, perhaps a punishment to be approved, a stays'l to be replaced; he secretly relished it all, but it was starting to wear a little.

'Land ho! High land three points on the starboard bow!'

Ah, a blessed relief, and just in time. Carlisle looked aloft to see the unmistakable form of his townsman from Virginia, Able Seaman Whittle, striking a heroic pose at the end of the t'gallant yard, with one hand on the standing part of the lift and the other shielding his eyes from the glare. Years ago Carlisle had seen another lookout in just that pose. On that occasion a landsman, confused by the bellowing of orders that he didn't understand, let loose the lift from the bitts on the main deck and the seaman had plunged to his death. The lookout had made the fatal mistake of holding onto the *fall* of the lift, of course, not the standing part. If anyone on deck should make the same mistake with the lifts today then Whittle would feel the standing part starting to go slack in time to swing down onto the horse and make his way safely back to the crosstree. Still, he valued Whittle and it was difficult to watch. He was showing off, of course, but that was just Whittle's way. He was after all, and not only by his own reckoning, the best lookout in the ship.

The first lieutenant snatched up the deck telescope before anyone else could reach it and he searched in vain for a sight of the land, but it was still below the horizon from the quarterdeck.

'I can't see it yet, sir, but that'll be Navassa Island. Not a penn'orth of good to man nor beast unless there's a value in bird's ah... excrement. The place is covered in the stuff, fathoms deep in places, and the stink would turn your stomach. I landed there once looking for wood and water. Firewood we found, cast upon the shore, but the water was so fouled we couldn't touch it. It's little wonder that no country has claimed it. However, it's a good marker for the passage and once we're past there we'll have French Hispaniola to windward.'

There was not an ounce of vanity in Matthew Gresham's body or soul and he gave the information as a matter of fact rather than a means of demonstrating his knowledge or his wide experience of these waters. He'd studied the sailing master's chart and was expecting the island to show during the morning watch, and there it was. The supplementary information was merely to remind his captain that they were close to the border between Santo Domingo and San Domingue, between Spanish Hispaniola and the French part of the island. By noon, the land on their starboard side would be French and any trading vessels they sighted were liable to be searched. If they were found to be enemy flagged, or a neutral carrying contraband to a French port, they would be seized as prizes. Or they could be but for the galling fact that both Sir James and the harried flag captain in Port Royal had expressly forbidden *Dartmouth* to engage in any actions that might slow its passage to Havana or put the governor-general's furniture in danger. And then, of course, sometime tomorrow they would be just forty leagues or so to leeward of the main port for the French navy in these waters, Cape François, and that brought a whole new set of issues. The French may have been defeated at sea, and they may have lost half of their islands in the Lesser Antilles, but they still occasionally gathered up enough ships and men to send small squadrons out from Brest and Rochefort and even Toulon to bring home the sugar convoys from Martinique and San Domingue. Those small squadrons ranged across the northern coast of Hispaniola and westwards as far as Cuba, and *Dartmouth* was approaching that danger zone with every league she made into the Windward Passage.

Beazley had come on deck at the cry of land and he was studying the sketched elevations in the margins of the chart, ready to compare them with the heights of the island should they become visible.

'Navassa Island, I'm sure, sir, and even if we see it from the deck we'll lose sight of it in another hour. Yet it gives us a good departure for the passage. The next land I expect to see after this will be Cape Mays, about this time tomorrow.'

'And you're certain we can't be seen from Point Morant, Mister Beazley.'

Carlisle looked involuntarily to leeward where the pure line of the horizon was smudged by the clouds that hung over the eastern tip of Jamaica. The sea was clear without so much as a local fishing boat in sight. It was those high mare's tails that were keeping small craft in port; they had an unhealthy look to them and fishermen would be staying close to home today.

'Nay, sir. We're a good twenty leagues clear and as you can see there's not a single vessel inbound to Port Royal this morning.'

Beazley didn't know for certain why Carlisle was so keen to keep their route to Havana a secret, but he had a good idea. He looked sidelong at his captain.

'No doubt we'll see some traffic heading into the passage but by the time any report of us reaches Port Royal we'll be half way to Havana, sir.'

Carlisle nodded, his face set in a non-committal mask. He could leave his sailing master to confirm the sighting of the island and to establish a good departure fix, but the smell of the flying fish in the pan was wafting from the galley to the poop deck and he could feel the saliva rising in his mouth.

'I'll be having breakfast, Mister Gresham. Call me if the island can be seen from the deck. I expect Lady Chiara will be interested.'

And with that he left for his cabin and his breakfast of flying fish in the company of his wife.

***

'I heard your officers laughing on deck, Edward. Pray, what was the joke?'

Carlisle was caught in the act of addressing a tasty morsel of flying fish. It was delicate white meat, not too oily, but full of tiny bones that caught in a man's throat if not eaten carefully. He was chewing it tentatively, alert for the first prick of a bone in his mouth, and it took him a moment to respond.

'Oh that'll be the land that Whittle sighted from the masthead, Navassa Island; you'll have heard the hail, no doubt. It's a rendezvous for gulls and suchlike, and it's covered in bird droppings so deep that it must have taken centuries to accumulate. It looks white from the sea, pure white from its pinnacle to nearly the shoreline, and in the sun it's so bright that it hurts the eyes to look at it. They know that I won't have coarse language on deck and not just because you are here; I won't have it under any circumstances. That's puzzled Whittle as to how he should report what he sees, how he should describe the bird droppings, and he's been tying himself in knots trying to find acceptable words to use.'

Carlisle crossed his fingers under the table. It was broadly true that he discouraged cursing, profanity, blasphemy and all kinds of coarse language, as the articles of war and general instructions insisted that he should. But even he'd been known to slip occasionally, when under stress.

'Well, that's admirable, Edward, and I'm pleased to hear that you keep such an orderly ship. Had I not known better I'd have said they were a crew of choirboys, so angelic is their turn of phrase.'

Chiara smiled sweetly at her husband. She'd been on board ship often enough to have heard most of the choice expressions used by seamen, and she knew very well that the prohibitions were more honoured in the breach than in the observance. Carlisle let it ride; he knew he couldn't win when his wife chose to be facetious, and he wasn't prepared to spoil his excellent breakfast by trying.

'Would you pass that napkin?' Carlisle asked in a strangled croak, 'and perhaps you wish to look away, I have a bone in my throat.'

***

CHAPTER FIVE

Windward Passage

Thursday, Seventeenth of December 1761.
Dartmouth, off Cape Mays, Windward Passage.

The wind started to rise late in the afternoon. It increased in force until Carlisle ordered the t'gallants to be sent down and the tops'ls reefed, then it backed a point. It looked as though *Dartmouth* would have to tack north through the passage after all. Nevertheless, the ship made good progress close-hauled on the starboard tack, flying to the north at a great rate, with her bows flinging the deep green waves aside in a shower of sparkling diamonds. Then with the sunset the wind increased further and all hands were called to double reef the tops'ls.

'What do you think now, Mister Beazley, a hurricane? If so then we must put the ship about and seek sea-room to the south.'

Carlisle was shouting into the sailing master's ear to make himself heard above the roar of the wind and the beating of the waves against the hull. Beazley took a moment to consider, as was his infuriating manner.

'I think not, sir. The season's nearly over – although hurricanes can still come upon us this late in the year, oh yes – but my weather-glass has started to rise again. I'm sure it's just that trade wind blow that I spoke of and it'll be over tomorrow.'

Carlisle looked up at the masts and walked over to test the weather main shrouds. They were bar-taut but he didn't have the feeling that they were being unduly strained. He certainly didn't want to turn back into the Caribbean Sea if he could avoid it. That could easily add a week to the voyage, and if this was just a normal blow he would look foolish or timid. He remembered the last hurricane he'd lived through, and he'd had sea-room then, hundreds of leagues of it to the south of Hispaniola. This Windward passage, squeezed between Cuba and Hispaniola didn't seem like a good place to ride out a full-blown Caribbean hurricane.

'The wind's veered a couple of points, sir. We should weather Cape Mays if it holds.'

Beazley was trying to persuade him to hold his course. How much of that was a desire to prove the efficacy of his weather-glass? Usually a sailing master urged caution while captains, in general, pushed their ships to the limit. No doubt, when Beazley presented his finding to Trinity House, it would sound well if he could claim to have predicted this blow while dismissing the chance of a hurricane. For men-of-war that kind of foreknowledge could mean the difference between success and failure in their mission, for merchantmen it could mean a profitable voyage rather than a loss-making one. As always, the choice was his. He could see it in Beazley's face; the sailing master had given his advice and now his captain had the responsibility, alone.

'What's your reckoning for our offing at Cape Mays?'

'Three leagues, sir, if the wind doesn't back again.'

Carlisle was becoming irritated by the master's temporising; he felt that he was being given problems without solutions. This damned weather-glass just added another layer of complexity, a layer whose value was not yet proven.

'And will it back, Mister Beazley? Can your weather-glass tell me at least that?'

Beazley stiffened. He recognised that his captain was challenging him and caught the slight hint of sarcasm in his voice. His answer was formal to the point of rudeness.

'The weather-glass can't tell us everything, sir, and our understanding is in its infancy. I can give you a *probable* wind strength, but I have nothing to say for wind direction. My experience – not related to the weather-glass, mark you – tells me that it will not veer any further to the south and in all probability it will hold in the east until we weather Cape Mays, sir. In all *probability*, it will blow no harder.'

Beazley affected to study the compass on the binnacle then turned to his chart. Carlisle stood in silence for a few more minutes, looking up at the commissioning pennant. He leaned over the gunwale to see the wake stretching away a point or so on the windward quarter, its passage marked by the moon's reflections. That showed how much leeway the ship was making, which was an important item of information when they were trying to weather a headland.

'Very well, we'll stand on. Mister Wishart, call me if the wind heads us or if it increases. Mister Beazley, I would be pleased to see the weather-glass records for the past day.'

***

Dartmouth plunged on through the gale. The flying clouds occasionally revealed the moon that looked down on them in apparent wonderment that any ship would not have sought shelter by now. For although by the calendar the hurricane season had ended, it was well known that late hurricanes – rare though they were – carried the most danger. Yet the wind held resolutely high and steady and from the east, never varying by more than half a point. Dawn found the two-decker still under double-reefed tops'ls with the low promontory of Cape Mays below the horizon on the leeward bow at six leagues, by the master's reckoning. Not another vessel was in sight in this howling wilderness.

'We'll pass four leagues clear, sir, as best as I can tell.'

Carlisle picked up the traverse board and studied the courses and log speeds that had been recorded overnight. Yes, that agreed with his calculation. It was galling, but it did appear that Beazley's weather predictions had again been proved correct. How much of that was due to his own very extensive experience and how much was owed to the weather-glass, was impossible to tell, but he deserved recognition in any case.

'Then it appears that I was almost guilty of timidly yesterday, Mister Beazley. I should know better than to doubt you, and of course your instrument.'

Beazley made no response, and Carlisle had expected none. His sailing master was excellent in all ways except for his sinful pride.

Carlisle removed himself to the poop deck where he could pace in privacy and where he could think without interruption. Soon his ship would be at the northern end of the Windward passage and he could bear away for the Old Bahama Straits. If this wind didn't moderate he'd reduce sail so that he didn't enter that dangerous stretch of shoal water at a racing gallop. The flag captain had insisted that he take the Old Bahama Straits, but he couldn't say why it was important. Admiral Holmes had spoken of it as he was ailing, apparently, but he hadn't been specific, and now he was beyond any human inquiry. Was it just a general precaution, to check that the straits were still navigable after the summer storms and the last hurricane, or was there some particular need that warranted a two-decker risking the passage? He was to survey the straits on his way through, to update the poor charts that showed little more than a long, narrow passage a hundred miles long, that in places was only thirteen miles wide and bordered by coral reefs and sandbars; a voyage that had claimed so many ships that most masters refused to sail that way at all.

If Chiara was to be believed, war with Spain was becoming inevitable, and in that case Havana would be an attractive target for an expedition. Yet it would be a bold move when many wise heads predicted a radical change in the naval balance of power when King Charles' fleet joined up with what remained of the French navy. Caution would suggest that the Channel Fleet should be reinforced against a renewed threat of invasion of England, and that would mean sending the bulk of the ships-of-the-line home. What then would be left to menace Spain's principal naval base in the New World?

He stopped and methodically quartered the horizon. If the master's reckoning was true, he wouldn't see Cape Mays from the deck, but he was surprised that there were no sails in sight, in this, the principal passage from the Caribbean to the American coast.

One more turn at the quarterdeck rail and he would have the officer of the watch hail the lookout at the masthead and demand a report. Surely he could do that without imperilling his dignity, couldn't he? But he knew well the answer to his own question. If the lookout had seen anything he would have reported it. By quizzing him he would betray his own anxious state of mind. But what was troubling him? With nothing to see and a clear ocean they could expect to pass unmolested. But there it was, an empty ocean, and that was the cause of his unease. Where was a ship-of-the line, or at least a frigate from the Jamaica Squadron? They must surely have been able to spare a single ship to watch this, the most important place in the whole command. With almost all the Windward and Leeward Islands in Britain's possession, France's only secure toehold in the whole, wide Caribbean was this half of the island of Hispaniola. And in all of San Domingue there was only one place capable of supporting major units of the French navy, and that was the natural harbour of Cape François just thirty leagues to windward. The British blockade was mounted from Monte Christi, even further to windward than Cape François, but it was normal for a frigate or a fourth rate to watch to leeward, here at the northern end of the Windward Passage. At least with so little seaborne traffic there was no chance of their presence being reported in time for the French admiral to do anything about it.

***

'Sail ho! Sail right on the ship's head.'

Carlisle stopped his pacing and leaned over the rail to look down at the quarterdeck.

'Mister Wishart. Send someone responsible to the masthead with the telescope. I want to know how that vessel lies, and is she a man-o'-war or a merchantman or a fisherman.'

Torrance, the mate of the watch, was running for the windward shrouds before Carlisle had finished speaking. Most likely it was a merchantman from Jamaica under reduced sail, just clearing Cape Mays and heading for the Crooked Island Passage, the fastest route to the American colonies. In fact, even if a merchantman was bound across the Atlantic she'd take the Crooked Island Passage in this easterly wind. It would be foolhardy indeed to beat to windward past Cape François, that known haunt of French frigates and privateers. Aye, a British merchantman most likely but there were a score of other enticing possibilities.

'Deck there, it's a merchant brig, I think, sailing large, and I can just make out another sail to the westward. I think the brig may have lost her main topmast, sir.'

Ah, now that changed things. A brig steering for the Old Bahama Straits must have come past Cape François, and was therefore most likely French, and she'd be slow without her upper mast. The sighting of that second sail suggested a convoy, perhaps, and any convoy in these waters would certainly have a naval escort. Carlisle was forbidden to cruise after prizes, but a French man-of-war was another matter entirely.

'Mister Torrance, stay up there and report as soon as you see anything new.'

'Aye-aye sir, and I can see Cape Mays six points on the larboard bow.'

The master stepped into his sea-cabin where he kept his precious charts. In this weather he could expect that Cape Mays would be seen at five leagues from the masthead, perhaps a little less. It was six points off the bow, according to Torrance. He made a tiny pencil mark where he had fixed the ship's position.

Carlisle on the poop deck was making the same calculation. With this fixed point now visible he could afford to make directly for the straits.

'Mister Wishart, bear away three points, if you please.'

Cape Mays was a low-lying point of land backed by hills that rose into the eastern Cuban highlands. If it wasn't so well known by generations of seafarers, Carlisle would have given it a wide berth, assuming that the waters off the Cape would be shallow. However, he knew that wasn't the case and the deep channel persisted right up to five cables from the Cape. That was all very well, but with this strong wind he had no wish to pass so close to a lee shore, an offing of five miles would be better.

'Ah Mister Gresham, this may add a little interest to the day, don't you think?'

'Frenchmen for a guinea, sir, steering for Louisiana I expect. Surely they must have an escort, but where is it?'

The reports from the masthead came thick and fast now as more and more sails broke the horizon. Four merchantmen, three ships and a brig and what looked like a heavy frigate leading. Probably a thirty-six with twelve pounders on her gun deck and sixes on the quarterdeck, a genuine fifth rate ship. There were few credible destinations for them through the Old Bahama Straits, with all of the American coast north of Florida in British hands. If they were indeed French, then Louisiana – New Orleans or Mobile Bay – seemed the most likely, as the French still clung on to that important coast and there were presumably French garrisons to be resupplied. Carlisle felt a little guilty that he knew so little of the situation in that, the gateway to the last French territory in North America. They could of course be Spanish, on passage for Havana, from San Juan or any of the smaller places on the north coast of Santo Domingo. He would know soon in any case.

'Mister Beazley, Mister Gresham. Do you see the situation? Good. Now I want to intercept those ships before they get too deep into the straits.'

Beazley scratched his head and stared hard at the naked horizon where the sails would soon be visible.

'Well, sir. If this wind holds we should be up with Ragged Island in the morning watch tomorrow, that's where the straits start to narrow. Ordinarily, I would say that our timing is good and we can be through the shoal water in the daytime, but unless they are remarkably slow, or remarkably fast, we'll catch them after sunset today. I take it you would prefer to meet them in daylight, sir.'

Carlisle had already considered this possibility. The Old Bahama Straits only became dangerous in the two-hundred-mile stretch after Ragged Island, and most mariners declined to make that passage in the dark. If they found their timing was out, they'd anchor overnight to the west of the island and get underway as soon as there was enough light to see the coral reefs, the shifting sandbanks and the isolated coral heads that bedevilled that area between Cuba and the Bahamas. It was no place for an engagement even in the daylight, and doubly so at night. Even if he could overtake the convoy before the sudden tropical sunset, it would be a risk to engage them in the gathering gloom, with the west-bound current dragging them inexorably onwards. But was he seeing too many dangers? He'd never been through the straits, and all he knew of them was from possibly exaggerated tales of hazards on every side.

'Well, gentlemen, I find you have the advantage of me as I believe you have both sailed through there.'

He waved his arm vaguely to the nor'west.

'What's your opinion? Must we tamely suffer them to pass through the straits in peace, and hang onto their coat tails until the morning? I'll say now that if they're French, I'd rather not engage close to Havana for fear of Spanish interference; the eastern end of the straits would be preferable.'

Beazley's habit of pausing before replying lost him the opportunity to speak first, for Gresham had no such affectation.

'I came this way in the last war, sir, and we passed without any problems. Mind, though, I was in *Squirrel*, a little twenty-gun sixth rate, barely more than a sloop. She had half our draught, and I was just rated midshipman. I spent most of the passage lashed to the main t'gallant pole, as I was so light in those days, looking out for shoal water. It was easy enough in daylight, sir, but at night… I would want a good chart and a local pilot.'

Beazley nodded his agreement.

'It's a dangerous passage all right, but not if you take it slow and easy in good weather and in good light. Mostly it's deep water and there's perhaps twelve or thirteen miles at the narrowest point. The problem is that the shoals and the coral stretch so far out from the dry land that there's nothing to see to fix your position. The main channel may be deep and wide but there's no way of knowing when you're in it, and the coral heads come up so suddenly that you can be upon them from one cast of the lead the next. Full light with the sun upon the water and good weather is what's needed, sir.'

Carlisle looked thoughtful. That frigate would certainly stay between the convoy and *Dartmouth*, and he'd have to fight it before he did anything else. Most likely the merchantmen would escape while he engaged the frigate if its captain knew his business. Two hours, that was what he wanted, two hours to deal with the frigate before sunset then he could catch the convoy when they came out of the narrows at Santa Maria Island the next morning. That would give him another twenty leagues before he reached the Nicholas Channel, where the straits narrowed again and where he could expect to see a Spanish cruiser.

'Then I find it all rests on our speed today. Mister Beazley, you'll oblige me by supervising the sail trimming. Mister Gresham, it's been a long time since we cleared for action in earnest, it may be as well to beat to quarters now; we can send away the watch below when you've checked that all is in order. I hope, I very much hope, that our guns will speak before this day ends.'

***

'You know, tomorrow we'll be in the waters where the great Columbus made his first discoveries, we'll be running along the same track that he took, for at least part of the voyage.'

Carlisle had left the deck for a bite of dinner and Chiara had persuaded him that he should sit and eat like a civilised man. The sight of the dining cabin laid out for the two of them, with a variety of hot dishes, had seduced him away from his obsessive pacing of the quarterdeck, much to the relief of his officers. It was hard enough to get every fraction of a knot of speed out of the ship without the captain looking suspiciously at every sheet that was touched, and every movement of the wheel.

'Really dear, I understood that he discovered America, is that not so? Have I been deceived all these years?'

Carlisle glanced suspiciously at Chiara. He'd been fooled before, but it really did appear that she was ignorant of the great discoveries. He continued, emboldened by her meek, inquiring expression.

'I regret that may be the case. In his first two voyages he found only the islands, Cuba being the largest, and in his third and fourth he came to the coast of what we would now call the Spanish Main, or South America. He didn't reach even as far as Florida, more less Carolina or Virginia or the northern colonies. He discovered the New World, certainly, but he had no notion of its extent and left this earth with only a vague idea that there may be a great and profitable country to the north. He first touched land in the Bahamas, and found his way south through the cays until he came to this Old Bahama Straits that we are about to enter. He initially turned west. Then – and the Good Lord alone knows how he achieved it – he turned east *against* the wind and the current, and found his way to the north coast of Hispaniola and thence home to Spain. A remarkable man, and a most persistent one. It's a pity he had to be Spanish.'

Chiara raised an eyebrow and smiled archly.

'Spanish? Nothing of the sort! Columbus was Genoese. He grew up in Savona, a good Ligurian town, and the viscountess always maintained that his family was related to ours, although of a lesser branch, of course. He merely hired his services to the King of Spain, but his blood was Genoese. Spanish! Ha! I'm surprised you believe such stuff, Edward. The problem with you English is that you have no real sense of history. For you this is quite literally the New World, and yet Europeans have been here for nearly three hundred years. It's a national weakness and it proliferates with each new generation.'

Carlisle muttered an apology. In a flash of inspiration he guessed that his wife knew all about the discoveries and feigned ignorance merely to lead him into this trap. If so, it was well laid and expertly sprung. Yes, it was well done, and it took his mind off this chase even though only for a brief half hour as they discussed the world as it was before the English came west.

***

CHAPTER SIX

A Chase

Thursday, Seventeenth of December 1761.
Dartmouth, Crooked Island northeast 20 leagues.

'Sunset in thirty minutes, sir, and with this cloud we'll lose sight of them in an hour.'

Beazley stared impassively at the towering ranks of canvas that stretched far above the deck into the darkening sky. *Dartmouth* had the wind a few points on her starboard quarter, her best point of sailing, and she was spreading every stitch of canvas that could find a place on a yard or stay. From her t'gallants and stuns'ls to her sprits'l tops'l, every sail was drawing, but oh so weakly. The gale that had blown them through the Windward Passage had faltered during the forenoon and for a brief hour it looked as though the nor'easterly trade wind would blow with its accustomed vigour. However, it wasn't to be, and by the change of the watch it was apparent that they'd be in for a day of light winds.

Carlisle desperately wanted to come up with that frigate today, but it was looking less likely by the minute. The whole ship was hoping for a miracle; he could see it in the faces of the gun crews who looked at him expectantly.

'It may pick up when the sun's below the horizon,' he said, half to himself.

Gresham had been watching the range carefully, squinting into the setting sun that had dropped below the covering of cloud and yet still glared through the spaces between the frigate's masts and sails like some malevolent hobgoblin. He was measuring the gap between the two ships by vertical angles. He'd guessed at the height of the frigate's main masthead and was using his octant to measure the arc subtended between it and the waterline, and thus, by applying the figure to a simple table, he came to the distance that separated *Dartmouth* and the chase. Probably someone in the frigate was doing the same because there was no doubt at all that the French ship could outsail the two-decker in these light winds. All through the dog watches, as the pursuer drew closer, the Frenchman had been filling and spilling to stay between the convoy and the enemy, while keeping out of range of *Dartmouth's* guns. Fifteen minutes ago they'd sheeted home their tops'ls when it looked as though the range was closing dangerously and the tiny, knurled wheel on Gresham's octant had to be turned back again to keep the image of the masthead on the horizon.

Dartmouth's twenty-four pounders could be expected to throw a round shot just under three thousand yards – one and a half nautical miles – at ten degrees elevation. That was the maximum that the gun carriages allowed when the quoins were knocked right out to allow the breach to rest directly on the carriage bed. It was the crudest possible gunnery and a hit at that range would be by pure good fortune. However, with ten of the heavy guns in each broadside there was at least a chance.

'What do you think, Mister Gresham. If we yaw now and give him a broadside, will the shot carry?'

Gresham lowered his octant and shook his head; he didn't need to read from the table. He'd been drawing the arm of his octant closer to his body these last fifteen minutes, and that meant only one thing.

'Somewhat more than three thousand five hundred yards, sir, and that's taking an optimistic guess at her masthead height. If she's taller then it'll be even further.'

'Well, I won't waste powder and shot on her.'

He looked again to see that the setting sun was almost touching the frigate's deck.

'Now, Mister Beazley, the chart, if you please.'

***

The sailing master stared doggedly at the chart. His dividers were poised over the pencil mark that indicated *Dartmouth's* position by dead reckoning, some twenty leagues to the southwest of Crooked Island, right in the centre of the passage.

'Here's my best reckoning, sir, taking into account our headings and log readings, and adjusting for leeway and what we know of the current. Now the problem is that we're off the normal track of British shipping, we left it as soon as Crooked Island was abeam, and the strength of the westbound current here is a matter for conjecture. Some have reported no current at all and some have given it as five knots. We haven't had a sight of land since Cape Mays from the masthead at the end of the morning watch, so I must warn you that in reality we could be anywhere inside here.'

He drew a lozenge shape centred on their reckoned position, stretched parallel to Cuba's north coast on an east-southeast to west-northwest axis, some eight leagues in length and five leagues in breadth.

'Then we could be ashore on the coast of Cuba at this moment, Mister Beazley, by your reckoning.'

Carlisle's voice was heavy with sarcasm. He knew that Beazley was stacking up the objections, making a case to anchor before it became fully dark. He didn't want to sail into these unfamiliar straits on what looked like being a bible-black night.

'Evidently not, sir, as we appear to be still underway.' Beazley could answer sarcasm with sarcasm, he was an old hand at this game. 'But as we move further west the coral reefs and little cays to the north and south will start to close in and we could be aground without ever sighting dry land. That's all very well in the daylight when we can see the colour of the water ahead, and get some warning of the rocks and shoals, but at night we have nothing to guide us, and with this cloud overhead I didn't even manage a noon sight. We should anchor, sir, while we can still see our way.'

Carlisle stared at the chart as though looking for inspiration. No doubt the sailing master was right and it would be foolhardy to follow the French convoy into the darkening straits, but the thought of a frigate and four merchantmen slipping through his fingers was almost more than he could bear.

Gresham glanced out of the stern windows. The sea astern, to the east, was already a dark bluish grey that faded into the thick layer of cloud overhead. In twenty minutes they'd have to grope with the lead lines to find a safe overnight anchorage. He voiced what they were all wondering.

'Will the French anchor? I'd dearly love to know the answer to that! They're showing no sign of it; there have been no signals flying, no guns. Perhaps they know this passage better than we do.'

That was the critical piece of information that they needed. Would the French anchor? If they didn't find a snug berth soon then like *Dartmouth* they'd have to feel their way into a safe anchorage. Surely that wouldn't be an attractive proposition. However, if they were seen to anchor, then they'd be easy prey for an overnight cutting-out expedition. No, if they anchored at all they'd do it when they couldn't be observed. When the sun slipped below the horizon, they'd turn aside from the straits and find some patch of sand in five fathoms or so, sheltered from the east wind, and ride out the night. Or they could press on through the night. Was it likely that they knew the straits better than Beazley did? Yes, probably, but did that mean they were confident enough to risk a night passage?

'Just reach into that cabinet would you, Mister Gresham? You'll find my Caribbean chart there. Mister Beazley, step onto the deck if you please and ask Mister Wishart, with my compliments, to call all hands and stand by to reduce to tops'ls and mizzen and start soundings with the twenty-fathom lead. Have both bower anchors ready for letting go.'

Carlisle's Caribbean chart was more-or-less centred on the Old Bahama Straits. What he wanted to know – and he felt a pang of guilt that he hadn't already armed himself with this information – was whether the French were likely to have often used this route. Certainly they had business beyond Cuba; the whole of the north coast of the Gulf was theirs, from the Perdido River that formed the boundary with Spanish Florida all the way west to Mexico. France had been at war with Britain for much of the last century, and for all of that time Britain had maintained a strong naval presence at Jamaica, effectively dominating the central Caribbean. That must have forced the French traffic for Louisiana to sail north of Cuba, through these very same waters that *Dartmouth* was now sailing. Surely, surely they must have a good knowledge of the navigation of the straits, certainly it would be better than their British adversaries who had only an occasional need to pass this way.

Carlisle heard the pipes and the bellows, and the rush of feet as all hands poured up on deck to shorten sail. Beazley quietly opened the door and took his place again.

'Ready to shorten sail when you give the word, sir, and the bosun's compliments, the anchors have been ready to let go these two hours, sir.'

'Could you still see the chase, Mister Beazley?'

'Aye sir, they'll be in sight for a few minutes yet.'

He looked hard at the sailing master who he could see was deliberately being economical with his information.

'Is there any sign that they're anchoring?'

'No sir, and they haven't shortened sail either.'

Carlisle was becoming less than enchanted with the sailing master's obstinacy. He grimaced and turned for the door and strode out onto the quarterdeck. Wishart heard the scuffing sounds as the marine sentry was forced back on his heels. He winked at the mate of the watch and then assumed a wooden expression. Carlisle afforded him barely a glance.

'I'll be on the fo'c'sle, Mister Wishart.'

The deck was crowded with men but they parted like the waters of the Red Sea as their captain barged his way forward. He stopped at the fife rail and trained his telescope at the fast-disappearing shapes ahead. It was a Dolland instrument with lenses specially ground to capture any available illumination and it was excellent for use in these sort of twilight conditions. Through the lenses the shapes took on a more distinct form. No signal flags, no lights, and evidently no guns. The straits held no terrors for these captains, of that he was sure. They looked as though they would pass through under full sail, darkness or no.

'My compliments to Mister Wishart,' he said to nobody in particular, 'and what was our speed at the last cast?' He heard his question being relayed back to the quarterdeck and the answer was brought at the run by a worried-looking midshipman.

'Mister Wishart's respects, sir and the log speed was two knots and a fathom just half a glass ago. He'll cast the log again this instant.'

Carlisle made no reply but continued his study of the chase. This was an old trick of his, to keep the telescope to his eye so that his officers would be shy of interrupting. It gave him a few valuable seconds to think things through.

They weren't going to anchor before dark, of that he was sure. Possibly they had a favourite anchorage in mind some way into the straits, but he thought that unlikely. No, those ships had a purposeful look about them and he was sure they'd carry all the sail their spars would bear, right through the night. But should he follow? If he didn't they were lost, that was a certainty. He couldn't possibly make up that distance before they passed Havana, and he couldn't stretch his orders to follow them into the Gulf of Mexico, not before he'd delivered the damned governor-general's twice-damned furniture. He straightened, snapped his telescope closed, and strode back to the quarterdeck.

'It appears that our chase has no plans to anchor for the night, and therefore nor do I. Mister Gresham, you are to take the watch and the hands are to remain on deck throughout the night. The lead is to be worked and both anchors are to be ready to be slipped at a moment's notice.'

He was issuing his orders in a rapid staccato, leaving no breaks long enough to sound like indecision.

'Mister Wishart or Mister Angelini are to be on the bowsprit looking out for signs of shoaling, and they are to relieve each other every hour. Mister Beazley, you'll be on deck unless you need to consult your charts. I'm to be informed of our speed and the sounding every fifteen minutes unless either should change significantly, when I'm to be called immediately. Now, I aim to have these gentlemen in sight when the sun rises, and perhaps we can have a resolution to this chase tomorrow.'

***

Dartmouth maintained a stately pace through the tropical night. The trade wind was barely a whisper of its usual self and the sky was covered by a vast blanket of high cloud, blocking out the moon and the stars. It was a peaceful night, with the gentle breeze barely causing a stir among the masts, the yards and the rigging, and yet the deck was unquiet. Over a hundred men crowded the fo'c'sle and the waist through the night, and a further two hundred dozed at their stations on the lower gundeck, finding whatever nooks and crannies they could to make themselves comfortable. Few slept soundly and the constant murmur of conversation hung like a physical thing over the benighted ship. The only faint light came from the shaded lantern in the binnacle, by which pale glow the steersman kept an eye on the compass and adjusted the wheel to keep his course, west-nor'west a half west, into the treacherous straits. Even the bell was muffled by the marine sentry clasping its rim as he swung the clapper to mark the half hours.

'No bottom, no bottom on this line!'

That had been the leadsman's strangled cry all through the first watch and yet it gave no comfort to Carlisle. He'd seen the master's chart and he knew how abruptly the depths diminished to the north and south of the straits. The lead line was twenty fathoms long and it would perhaps be too late when the leadsman first found a bottom. He could have called for the deep-sea lead, a hundred fathoms long, but to cast that the ship had to heave to and reduce its speed to as near nothing as possible, and that he wouldn't do.

At midnight he was called into his cabin for supper and he left the deck to Gresham. Walker had fitted the wooden deadlights over all the windows, and the single candle gave the table a feeling of intimacy as the rest of the dining cabin was lost in the shadows. The cloth was spread with cold beef and mutton ham and potted char, and Port Royal bread that had only just lost its softness and merely needed to be toasted to be agreeable. Chiara had called for a bottle of Madeira, knowing that her husband might need it.

'And will you catch your Frenchmen, Edward?'

Chiara was spreading potted char onto toast by the candlelight. The char had been shipped all the way from the northwest of England, from an area of lakes and hills and tiny streams in some counties with the interesting names of Westmorland and Cumberland. It sounded a delightful place and Chiara hoped that she could one day visit, perhaps in the summer. The potted fish had survived the journey well. Its intense savoury flavour, unadulterated by the fiery spices that were ubiquitous in the West Indies, made a pleasant change to the normal fare.

'I wish I could tell, but you know, they might very easily have hauled their wind and let us pass them in the dark and we wouldn't know until the morning. And then again they could have passed further ahead, being better acquainted with these straits than we are.'

Chiara paused for a moment as her husband stared at his supper. She could tell that he was troubled.

'And is catching these French ships more important than carrying out your orders, dear? I don't mean delivering the governor-general's furniture, that's trivial, but as I understand it you have been charged with surveying these straits and unless there is something that I don't understand, that can hardly be accomplished at night under full sail.'

Carlisle looked affectionately at his wife. She hadn't read his orders – that would be a breach of security that not even he would countenance – and yet she'd picked up the essentials from scraps of conversation.

'Oh, we all have a general duty to annoy the enemy as much as is in our power, but as for surveying the straits, that's just a dream. It would be a task of months to do that with any accuracy and in any case it's already been done, to at least some degree. What that part of my orders really means is that I'm to look out for any changes to the straits that may hinder passage. Perhaps a new sandbank has been thrown up by that last hurricane, or the Spaniards may have fortified one of the cays. A new wreck perhaps, that should be noted. That's about all that can be achieved on passage, and that's all that is needed. In this case, my dear, I'm confident that I'm obeying my instructions. In fact I believe my conduct to be exemplary.'

He grinned at his wife, almost believing it himself.

'I'm trying my very best to take, sink or burn these ships before they are close enough to Havana to create an incident.'

'Yes, I do believe it would make Spain's path to war all the shorter. It's all very well fighting the French in the islands or off San Domingue, but I imagine the governor-general considers the waters off Havana to be his very own.'

Carlisle nodded in agreement while he spread a spoonful of mustard over a slice of toasted bread before covering it with a generous slab of mutton ham.

'Well, he wouldn't have the law on his side, such as it is recognised this far west. Three miles is becoming the accepted distance that a nation commands the seas from its shores. But I agree with you, once we are out of the straits, we enter a region where Spain has long assumed sovereignty.'

He paused to chew at his mutton ham on toast.

'Three miles? Then why don't the Frenchmen merely anchor perhaps two miles off the Cuban coast and defy you to do your worst?'

Carlisle swallowed, wiped his mouth with a napkin and smiled at his wife.

'Well, for a start the shoals to the south start well before any sight of land, and they'd be hard pressed to find a suitable berth within three miles of the shore without running hard aground. And I doubt whether they trust my observance of that rule in any case. There are few Spanish naval or military posts along this shore, and I would be very tempted to fall back on an older rule that a nation's writ only holds good for the waters that are actually commanded by guns on the shore. No, they won't put their faith in my adherence of what is only an *emergent* law. If there's a lawless place in this whole sea, it's these Old Bahama Straits, or perhaps the Yucatan Peninsula on the Spanish Main. It's dog-eat-dog here and the devil take the hindmost!'

***

CHAPTER SEVEN

Rocks and Shoals

Friday, Eighteenth of December 1761.
Dartmouth, Andros Island north-northeast 22 leagues.

The middle watch came and went like a dream. The night offered no substantial points of reference with the stars hidden by the thick, broad cloud that stretched overhead. So light was the wind that it barely raised a ripple overside and only the half-hourly bells lent any real impression of the passing time, and they were muted, like the church bells that tolled for the passing of a Christian soul. There was no change of the watch as all hands were at their quarters ready to fight or to anchor, at a moment's notice. As far as Carlisle could tell *Dartmouth* might have been drifting alone in the universe, sundered from the normal constraints of space and time.

Eight bells sounded from the fo'c'sle and Carlisle had to think hard before deciding which watch had just ended. Gresham came to report, removing his hat and holding it before his chest in the modern fashion.

'The watch is changing, or would be if the hands weren't all on deck or at their guns, sir.'

He stumbled in his delivery as he realised that his captain could take that as a complaint against his disruption of the ship's routine by this pressing on through the night. He made a belated effort to make amends.

'I beg your pardon, sir, that was clumsily put, may I rephrase it?'

The first lieutenant took a breath and looked cautiously at his captain's face, or at least he gazed at the pale orb that was all that he could see on this dark, dark night.

'Eight bells in the middle watch, sir. The wind's blowing light and steady from the east-nor'east, the ship's making two knots and there was no bottom at twenty fathoms on the last cast of the lead. Mister Beazley reckons our position twenty-two leagues to the sou'-sou'west of Andros Island, inside the straits still. The moon rose twenty minutes ago but we've had no sight of it, and sunrise is at half past six.'

'No bottom, sir, no sounding on this line, nothing to report!'

If the darkness wasn't hiding his captain's face, Gresham would have been truly shocked at the savage expression that passed across it. Carlisle turned quickly to the bosun, shouting so that his words were heard from forward to aft in this unnatural stillness.

'Mister Hewlett, remind the leadsman that he is to make his reports in the correct form and is not to attempt to improve upon them. If I hear anything like that again I'll see him next at the grating, he or anyone else who presumes to ignore my standing orders. Make that clear to him, if you please.'

Carlisle stalked up to the poop deck to walk off his bad humour in solitude, leaving a shaken and nervous quarterdeck behind him. Gresham and Beazley knew very well what was worrying him, and his other officers could make shrewd guesses. He had started to calculate how far out the master's reckoning could be now, after nearly twenty-four hours since the last sight of land and eight hours of drifting along with an unknown force of current carrying them through a dangerous passage at God-knows-what speed. The truth was that they could be aground in a moment on either the north or south side of the channel, and a twenty-fathom lead line would afford them scant notice of the impending disaster.

His nerves were wearing thin, he knew. Perhaps it was the result of over five years in command in wartime, but there was a very particular and immediate cause. He knew deep inside him that he had been foolish in following the French convoy into these unknown waters on a dark, moonless night. Foolish, yes, but there was little that he could do now to remedy the situation. He couldn't anchor in this depth of water, and any attempt to lie-to or haul his wind would put him entirely at the mercy of this mysterious current. At least this two knots on the log gave him steerage way to react to any dangers; if he abandoned that his ship would be little better than a leaf spinning in a mill-pool. And in any case, he told himself, in less than two hours he would have enough light to see any obstructions. He'd also be able to see the convoy, if it hadn't found an overnight anchorage or made better progress than his old, lumbering *Dartmouth*.

An hour of walking restored his humour, somewhat, and was that the first hint of dawn? Out on the starboard quarter the horizon was just starting to glow with the faintest of orange light. There wasn't enough yet to help with navigation, but second-by-second it spread until he could almost believe that he could see the dividing line between sea and sky. And now he thought about it, the breeze was increasing. It wasn't anything like the true trade wind, but it was perhaps a harbinger.

'No bottom, no bottom on this line!'

That was the same leadsman that he had admonished, and the man clearly hadn't forgotten it. He could detect the sulky tone to his voice, which wasn't what he wanted to hear from a man who'd been entrusted with such an important function. He heard Hewlett's gruff tones as he berated the man, reminding him of his duty. Hewlett should replace him; he wanted no disaffected seaman swinging the lead in the Old Bahama Straits, and that would mean the man must be punished. Probably it would be a half dozen strokes of the cat for such a crime. Carlisle stepped down to the quarterdeck to call the bosun over, but he was intercepted by Gresham. He realised with a start that he could clearly see his first lieutenant's face; would he ever become accustomed to the speed of the tropical sunrise?

'Four bells in a few minutes, sir, and sunrise in thirty. We'll be able to see where we're going presently, and the wind's starting to get up, from nor'east-by-east, I fancy. Maybe we'll see that convoy in a few minutes.'

Carlisle couldn't help responding to the first lieutenant's optimism. That fit of the blue devils had almost dissipated now and he was inclined to look upon the world in a more kindly light.

And now he could see Hewlett hauling away the leadsman by his shirt collar, and another man taking his place. That was good, but he already regretted the inevitable punishment he would have to order. He avoided it wherever possible, but sulkiness in reporting a sounding was not something that could be excused.

'Sail ho! Sail on the larboard beam, sir. Four, no five of 'em. It looks like that convoy, and there's the brig, still missing her main topmast.'

The visibility was improving at an extraordinary speed but the convoy wasn't yet visible from the quarterdeck. They must be six miles away, at least. Six miles, good God!

'Mister Beazley, take the deck. Bear away and make a course to intercept the convoy.'

Six miles on the beam, perhaps more. Then if the French were in the centre of the channel, *Dartmouth* must be right at the northern edge.

'Mister Beazley, belay that. Wear ship and make your course south. Mister Hewlett, get that leadsman moving!'

There was still confusion at the starboard main chains and the new leadsman was coiling his line and had not yet passed his safety strop around the lanyards. It looked like the man who'd been relieved had thrown down the lead line in protest. A punishment for certain. But meanwhile there had been no report for at least five minutes.

'Quarterdeck! I see shallows ahead. Ahead and to larboard!'

Enrico's voice had an edge to it. That most imperturbable man was clearly shaken by what he was reporting.

'South, Mister Beazley, take us south!'

Carlisle ran forward and looked ahead and then across to the larboard bow. He saw the danger immediately and now he could see the speed of the current that was sweeping them down onto the shoals; three knots at least.

Behind him the ship was turning urgently to larboard. The sail handlers were hauling on sheets and tacks as the stern came through the wind. The water was clear ahead now, a deep and enticing blue, but the current held sway still and even though their head was to the south they were being swept sideways to the west at a fast walk.

'Sand with coral heads, sir, I can see it quite clearly now.'

At least Enrico was keeping his nerve.

Carlisle looked at where Enrico was pointing. They couldn't possibly avoid being swept onto the shoal, but there was at least a chance of avoiding destruction.

'Mister Beazley, Mister Beazley, get the sails off her, furl everything and bring her head into the wind. Mister Gresham, Mister Hewlett, let go the larboard anchor.'

There were only seconds to make the decision and Carlisle knew it needed longer than that to weigh up the options. If he tried to claw his way to the south he'd strike the shallows beam-on, almost certainly, and quite probably one of those coral heads would bilge the ship, and it would be a total loss. If he put his ship's head to the west he could run up on the sand between the coral heads – they were plain enough to see now that the sun had popped over the horizon and the clouds were hurrying away to the westward – but he'd probably be dismasted by the impact. He had a chance – just a chance – of anchoring before he struck. But if the anchor didn't immediately hold he'd be driven stern-first onto the sand and coral, and he'd lose his rudder as well as his masts. It was worth the hazard, and he knew in a flash that it was the right decision.

The decks were all aglow in the light of this new day as if in mockery of these tiny mortals who were now wrestling with the fluid elements and with the solid earth for their very existence. Carlisle was almost bowled over by Hewlett and his party of men who ran for the larboard cathead.

Dartmouth's sails were coming in fast and those that were still drawing were starting to luff as her bows sought the wind.

'Clear below!'

That was the mate of the watch, below the fo'c'sle where the cable was handled. He was confirming that the cable was free to run out of the hawse.

'Slip!'

Gresham put all the urgency that he knew into that bellow. The cable ran hot through the hawse but it only took a few seconds for the anchor to find the bottom, so shallow was the water. *Dartmouth's* bows swung swiftly and firmly into the wind and the fast current. Carlisle ran aft along the gangway and vaulted the poop deck ladder in his haste to see over taffrail. God, they were close.

'Belay the cable, hold at that, Mister Gresham.'

He felt his ship snub as the cable was nipped and then the solid and satisfying groan as the weight was taken on the bitts.

'Sails are furled, sir.'

Gresham's call told Carlisle that there was no unwanted pressure from the wind. Only the current and the windage of the masts and spars and rigging were pushing *Dartmouth's* stern towards the reef. They were safe, for now, and Carlisle took another look over the side. They'd brought-to above a providential patch of sand; he could see it plainly over the side with its garden of long weeds streaming away on the fast-flowing current. To starboard – to the south – he could see a massive coral head not a ship's length away, and to larboard a small one a little further off.

'By the mark, five.'

Five fathoms! The sand was just eleven feet below *Dartmouth's* keel, and that was the sounding forward. The merest glance over the side showed that the bank beneath them sloped up towards the west. So the rudder would have less clearance, perhaps three or four fathoms. He'd have to kedge off, but this was no time for rash judgement.

'Mister Beazley, what's the state of the tide?'

'Hard to say, sir, but my guess is it's flooding to the westward, about half tide I'd say. Perhaps a fathom yet to rise, but I could be wrong at that, I only have uncertain notes from previous ships to go by.'

'Then take a sounding yourself, Mister Beazley, and another in half an hour and see where we stand. What do you make of the current?'

'Three knots, sir,' Beazley was on more certain ground here and he'd already ordered the log to be streamed to get an accurate measurement, 'and I expect half of that's the tidal stream and half the current. At slack water we may have only a knot or so.'

'Very well. Now, gentlemen,' he looked at Gresham and Beazley and Hewlett, 'I intend to kedge her off at slack water at the top of the tide; that will give us a few hours of moderate current to get off and away. If the tide's ebbing, then we'll try as soon as the kedge is laid out. The one thing I can be certain of is that we're at neap tides now,' he pointed to the quarter moon high overhead, whose pallid rays hadn't yet been extinguished by the rising sun, 'so no day will be better than today. Will the kedge anchor suffice, do you think?'

The three men looked thoughtful. The kedge was carried specifically for occasions such as this; it was the lightest anchor and could easily be borne by the longboat, but being the lightest it had the least holding power. It wasn't really intended to hold the ship against both wind and current. It would do no good to make all the preparations and find that the kedge wouldn't hold. It would likely mean the loss of a day and nobody knew what the wind would do in that time. In fact the wind was the greatest unknown quantity. If the master was wrong about the tide and it was ebbing, well, they could deal with that, but if another gale should come screaming in from the east they'd be hard pressed to avoid dragging onto the shoal and losing the ship. In that case all thoughts of kedging off would have to wait. And every day, as the moon waned, the tidal stream would increase.

Beazley and Hewlett both looked at Gresham.

'I think, sir, that it must be the starboard bower, we should be able to lay it out it in three hours.'

He almost added that it would be the devil of a job, but that would have been superfluous. The Longboat would be almost swamped by its weight and it would take the most delicate manoeuvres to sling it under the boat's keel.

The sailing master and the bosun looked relieved. They'd wanted to say that themselves, but deferred to their superior.

Carlisle walked again to the side. Was it possible that the current was already slacking? If so then Beazley was correct and in three hours from now they'd have the best opportunity to get the ship away from the shoal. If they missed it, they'd have to suffer a low tide with only a few feet under the vulnerable rudder. He shuddered involuntarily at the thought.

'The wind, Mister Beazley?'

Now Beazley looked even more concerned. He tilted his head up to see the regular trade wind clouds high above and he could feel the keen wind right on the ship's bow.

'As you see it, sir. My guess is we have at least a day of this.'

'It won't moderate then?'

'No, sir, and the weather-glass is steady. It's the right trade wind and it's here to stay.'

Carlisle had never heard the weather-glass being spoken of in such a positive way. It was a pity, all the same, because what they really needed was last night's light airs. Now they'd have to haul the great two-decker into the teeth of the wind and the current, with no real chance of a calm to ease the strain.

'Then the starboard bower it is. You'll need to carry it a full cable-length to windward, Mister Gresham, and I hope

– I trust – that we'll be able to take advantage of the ebbing tide to bring her off. My compliments to Mister Angelini and he's to take the cutter and survey the ground to the south of us. I want to know whether there are any further obstructions between us and the main passage of the strait.'

How lightly he had decided to save that anchor in Freeman's Bay! Yet that practice at dealing with the unwieldy weight of a bower anchor would stand them in good stead today.

***

CHAPTER EIGHT

Wind and Tide

Friday, Eighteenth of December 1761.
Dartmouth, at Anchor, Andros Island north-northeast 19 leagues.

The second bower anchor weighed thirty-nine hundredweight – two-and-a-quarter tons – and with the two cable-lengths of seventeen-and-a-half inch three-strand hemp rope bent together end-on-end, it made a ponderous great weight to be carried by a thirty-foot longboat. Carlisle remembered with a gulp that the longboat itself weighed only two tons, or thereabouts, and it was built with carrying the small kedge anchor in mind, and that weighed only five-and-a-quarter hundredweight. Indeed, it would have been impossible to ship the bower anchor inboard on the longboat: the only way that it could be brought to its intended resting place was by slinging it *underneath* the boat.

'Aye, she'll take it, sir,' the carpenter stated in answer to Carlisle's question, 'when my boys have rigged a canvas upstand for the gunwales. They'll have to tack it all around with hot pitch between the cloths and the wood and it'll make a right mess to be cleaned up before your Honour needs it in Havana, but that can't be helped. There'll be no holes for the oars of course, but that don't matter because the yawl will tow her into position.'

Carlisle hadn't come that far in his thinking. Of course, he knew that the anchor would have to be slung underneath the longboat, but he hadn't reckoned how much freeboard that would leave. He looked again at the sea. The trade wind had raised a respectable chop, and it would only take a few waves coming over the gunwales for the whole lot, boat and anchor and cable, to be dragged abruptly to the bottom. That would be the ruination of his plans. With the longboat gone, none of the other boats were remotely big enough to take a bower anchor, even under-slung.

Gresham knew Chips for a garrulous man, and he hustled the carpenter away; there was no time to lose, and he needed the captain's attention.

'It'll be a hard pull for the yawl, sir, but they've only two cables to go, they'll manage that. The most dangerous part will be slipping the anchor, in case one side of the suspending cables releases before the other. That would tip the longboat over quicker than you could think. But Mister Hewlett has a scheme for the way the cables will be arranged. Of course the weight will have to be distributed from forward to aft and from starboard to larboard, otherwise the poor old boat could be snapped in half when it takes the strain. As chips said, there's no need for any openings in the canvas upstand, the longboat will be just a dumb lighter today. The sailmaker is ready to start work as soon as Chips has the upstands ready. Aye, it'll work, sir, just you see.'

***

Gresham was everywhere, cajoling and pushing and issuing orders at a rate that made the mind spin. Carlisle stood back, leaving him to this, for he knew that he could do no better than the first lieutenant and probably his efforts would be a great deal worse. For Carlisle had been promoted to commander quite early and had spent too little time as a midshipman and lieutenant to really understand the sailor's arts. Gresham had infinitely more experience at this kind of work. It was doubtful whether he'd ever before had to lay out a fourth rate's bower anchor from a longboat, but he knew the limitations – aye, and the strengths – of the people and material he had to work with, and probably his dreams included just such outrageous acts of seamanship. Carlisle's interference would do no good.

'Beg your pardon, sir.'

Beazley had been supervising a cast of the lead from the taffrail.

'The tide's flooding, as I thought, but I reckon it's just an hour now to slack water, and in this long strait it should have a stand of an hour or so.'

'Two hours then, Mister Beazley. Two hours to have that anchor laid out. After that we're losing advantage with every extra hour that slips by.'

'Aye, sir…' Beazley paused as though embarrassed to speak, '…and I hardly like to mention it, but the weather-glass has started to fall. It could be another blow, sir.'

Carlisle set his face, staring to windward as though trying to divine what was coming towards them over the far horizon.

'Well, your instrument hasn't played us foul yet, Master, although I believe we have a very long way to go before we fully understand its mysteries. So, as I understand it, in seven hours our rudder will start touching the bottom, the tide will start running to the west, and a trade wind blow may be upon us. The gods surely are toying with us.'

Beazley nodded miserably. This mounting disaster was none of his doing – he'd specifically warned his captain against attempting the straits in the dark – but it was his ship that was in danger.

'As soon as the carpenter has finished with the longboat we must talk about how we can unship the rudder, if that becomes necessary. And then, of course how to ship it again when the weather moderates.'

Beazley nodded glumly. They'd done it before in Villa Franca harbour in the far Mediterranean, and they'd achieved it while the captain was ashore, but this was different. Villa Franca was a perfectly sheltered haven, while here they were exposed to a constant swell overlaid by the choppy waves that were being thrown up by the current as it was forced up onto the bank. In but a few hours they'd have a rising gale and wind against tide. It beggared belief how that massive rudder could be lifted clear of its pintles here on this treacherous lee shore.

'I hope that won't be necessary, sir.'

'I trust it won't, Mister Beazley, but we must be prepared for the worst. Now, assuming we can lay out that anchor in the next two hours or so, and assuming it holds well enough for us to haul the ship bodily off this reef, how will you cast the ship's head to the south to get away from here?'

'Well, sir…'

Beazley was on firm ground now. The balancing of backed tops'ls against staysails and the mizzen, to bring the ship's head off the wind before the anchor was weighed was child's play to him and he'd outlined his plan to Carlisle in just a few minutes.

***

Carlisle called for his telescope and fixed the French convoy with a malevolent stare. They were running to the west under this new, prosperous wind, and must have clearly seen their pursuer's difficulty. Had they planned this? Had he run into a trap? It was unlikely, for the captain of that French frigate couldn't have known what course *Dartmouth* would take through the night. But surely there must have been wise heads on that quarterdeck who foresaw just this turn of events. It must have seemed like madness to them for a two-decker to blunder through the straits under full sail on a moonless night. All that was conjecture, but Carlisle was certain that there would be no sympathy for him from those Frenchmen. He heard soft footfalls behind him and became aware of his wife's presence. He'd almost forgotten her existence in these past few hours and now he felt the cold fingers of guilt at the way he'd ignored her.

'Are we in great danger, Edward? I see so many worried faces that I can't help being concerned myself.'

The easy lie formed on Carlisle's lips; he was tempted to tell her there was nothing to be concerned about, but in a flash of empathy he saw that it wouldn't do to treat his wife as a child. She deserved to know the truth, and he told her now in short, brutal sentences, how they'd come to this pass and what the consequences could be if they couldn't get away before the tide fell and the wind rose. Once *Dartmouth's* keel started slamming on that hard sand bank it would be all over in a matter of hours, and they would have to take to the boats. The nearest land was Andros Island some thirty miles to the north. It was nominally British, administered by Nassau a few leagues further to the nor'west, although King George had little to say in the management of that lawless place. With luck they should be able to ferry everybody to safety. However, if they struck one of those coral heads and if the wind blew up again, like the gale in the Windward Passage, it could become very tricky.

'Then I'll prepare myself in case I should need to spend some time in a boat. But Edward, I have more faith in your powers than you seem to have.'

Chiara leaned forward and kissed her husband on the cheek, then she was gone into the cabin calling for her maid as she went.

Carlisle stood still, savouring that tender moment, until Chiara had disappeared down the ladder to the quarterdeck, then he strode purposefully towards the rail and looked down into the waist and aft towards the stern of the ship. The longboat had been brought to the starboard quarter and as luck would have it there was a tiny lee there, where the current was pushing the ship's bows across the wind. It looked strangely forlorn, without its bowsprit and with its mast and yards removed and sent into the ship. Everything that could be unshipped had been, so that the once proud longboat was indeed nothing more than a dumb lighter. For it was the total weight of the longboat and the anchor, and all the cables and anything else that was necessary, that determined how high the false gunwale had to be built.

The yawl and the cutter had been hoisted over the side and they were both swarming with men; it was a scene of urgent activity. The carpenter had already nailed battens to the longboat's gunwales and the sailmaker was busy with lengths of number four canvas, extending the freeboard by the eighteen inches that the carpenter thought was sufficient, which happily was the standard breadth of a cloth of naval canvas. He had only two seams to sew, at the bows and at the transom because a single cloth that was provided for a main tops'l could easily spread the length of a thirty-foot boat. A pair of carpenter's mates were busy with the pitch-pot, leaning across from the yawl to seal the bottom edge of the cloths to the longboat's wooden gunwale, and a second pair were following in the cutter with a bag of tacks, fastening the canvas to the wood of the longboat's gunwale capping and forcing the hot pitch into the weave, to make it as watertight as possible. Carlisle nodded in approval. That would give the boat enough reserve of buoyancy to carry the bower anchor, and he could have guessed how the carpenter and the sailmaker would go about that business. However, it was the work inboard the longboat that was more intriguing. He called down to the carpenter who was directing the final two of his six-man crew in a most interesting task.

'Chips, how's it going?'

The carpenter raised his head for just a moment then bent to his task, favouring his captain with only a few words, and those spat through a mouthful of ten penny nails. Carlisle had never known him so short with his words.

'We'll be finished in half an hour, sir...' was all that Carlisle heard. The muttered final few words, '...if I can be left to myself,' were thankfully lost in the general hubbub of sound.

The carpenter was creating a frame that would sit high above the extended gunwales and upon which would rest the cables that would hold the bower anchor under the longboat's keel. *Dartmouth's* spare main tops'l yard was some sixty feet in length and twelve inches in diameter at its greatest, in the middle, where it would normally be slung from the crosstree. It had been sawn in half and the two thirty-foot lengths were lying ready on the thwarts. The spare fore tops'l yard had been sacrificed to make six uprights that would hold the two great beams above the gunwales, on either side. A cable had been wound right around the boat and hauled taut with a Spanish windlass, to stop the frame forcing the gunwales apart when it took the weight of the anchor. Carlisle could see the carpenter's mates pouring extra pitch around the cable where it crossed over the gunwales; that pitch would fill the gap that would otherwise have been made between the cable, the gunwales and the canvas upstand.

'You see, sir,' said Hewlett who had left the anchor work to explain the plan to his captain, 'that old anchor will be slung from a strop over the anchor stock so that it lies up-and-down under the boat. I won't use the ring; it would make the anchor hang two feet lower. Now, normally we'd sling it horizontally, but there's enough water here, as we're not slinging through the ring, and we must have a smooth slip or it'll have the boat over. I'll be using the ten-inch cable that's properly for the kedge to go through the strop and right up over the gunwales and over that frame.'

Carlisle could see how it would be done and he was working through the hazards in his mind.

'Now, sir, you're perhaps wondering how I'll slip it. Well, the cable will be seized in the middle of the frame and I'll just cut the seizing when the time is right.'

'Won't there be a sideways pull as the cable snakes through the strop, Mister Hewlett? That could haul the gunwales under, even with the extra height.'

'Oh no, sir. Once the seizing has been passed, I'll cut the cable so that there's only a foot or two spare on either side of the seizing. It's a sad waste of a good cable, but I expect you'll sign off anything that goes overboard today, sir.'

Hewlett turned his head away and winked at one of his mates who was passing by with a bight of the ten-inch cable over his shoulder. Every expenditure of his stores had to be tallied, and it was certain that a whole storeroom of things that he couldn't otherwise account for would be presented to Carlisle for signature. Some of those stores would really have been lost in this difficult operation, but some, by the time-hallowed customs of the sea, would be spirited ashore to be sold to the merchantmen. That was how a bosun made his pay stretch from one month to the next.

Carlisle nodded. If all went well it would be a clean slip and the anchor would fall away without anything snagging.

'But the really trick part, sir, and that's what Mister Gresham has in hand, is slinging the anchor under the longboat. Now, the main yard extends fourteen feet past the ship's side. Two lengths of the kedge cable will be rigged from the stuns'l iron at the yardarm and passed through the anchor's new strop and then to a block on another strop on the main yard, that my mate's making up now. It's to be twenty feet outboard of the slings, right over the ship's gunwale. When Mister Gresham has that all ready, and when Chips has finished pinning and lashing the frame together, we'll pull the longboat through the bights of cable so that it's right above the anchor. Then we'll take one of those lengths of cable and seize it around the frame, then lower away on the other until the weight is taken by the strop and the longboat. Easy as you like, sir.'

Carlisle could see that the anchor had been slipped from the cathead and was dangling with its flukes in the water and its eye still showing above the surface. Two seamen were sitting astride the stock, and he could see that they were splicing the strop that would be held in place by the huge oak beams that made up the stock.

Hewlett could guess what Carlisle was thinking: time was passing.

'They'll have that splice done in a jiffy, sir, and then we can pass the cables.'

Probably Hewlett had already in his long career considered how he'd use a bower anchor as a kedge, so he would have been prepared with this elegant solution to the problem, but even so, he was doing well to bring all the parts of the puzzle together so quickly. It was a side of his bosun that he hadn't seen before.

Carlisle raised his voice to shout to the first lieutenant.

'Mister Gresham. Let me know when you're ready to bring the longboat under the main yard.'

'Aye-aye sir! It should be half an hour, maybe a little less.'

Half an hour! And that was just to position the longboat to take the anchor. They still had to transfer the weight of the anchor to the boat – a most delicate operation – and after that they still had to tow the longboat some four hundred yards into the wind and the constant current. Then, and only then, the larboard bower had to be weighed – he didn't want to slip it and lose it forever – and then they would embark upon the backbreaking business of drawing the great two decker against wind and current until it was clear of the reef and could be sailed away into deep water to the south. They were cutting it fine, but just a glance confirmed that every man was working as fast as he could. This was indeed an epic battle between a ship and her men and the inexorable march of wind and tide, and it wasn't yet clear who would win. Carlisle walked back to where the sailing master was supervising another cast of the lead.

'Tide's still rising, sir and the flood's slacking a little, the log's showing two knots now.'

'Very well, Mister Beazley. Now, can you give the longboat more of a lee when they're ready to pull her under the main yard?

Beazley felt the wind and looked over the side at the current rushing past.

'If I give her a bit of the fore topmast stays'l, that should suffice, sir.'

Carlisle nodded in agreement. The leverage forward would push the bows across the wind and create a better lee. Anything would help.

***

Carlisle made his way slowly to the mizzen top, with his telescope slung over his shoulder by a lanyard. It wouldn't do for him to display any anxiety, not with the safety of the ship hanging in the balance. A panicked captain transmitted his unease to the ship's company as quick as lightning. It was that sense of despair, that feeling that their captain was no longer in control of events, that spooked the men and became its own devastating self-fulfilling prophecy. Men who were anxious and could see that their officers were also uneasy, were much, much more likely to make mistakes, and then, in the extreme, an unsettled crew was prone to abandon its duty, leaving the ship to the mercy of wind and wave, tide and current, and the violence of the enemy.

He settled himself in the top and swept the horizon all round. There was nothing to see, nothing to suggest that *Dartmouth* was navigating in a dangerous strait, surrounded by shoal water and wicked coral heads. A casual observer would have concluded that he was safely anchored in a calm sea with a steady trade wind blowing, and no dangers for many leagues. Nothing to see all around the horizon, except over towards the west; no, a little to the north of west, where a tiny group of barely recognisable objects broke the purity of the line. Then the French convoy and its escort had not been enticed to interfere with their pursuer's attempts to save his ship. It was easy to forget, when this extraordinary act of seamanship took up every man's full concentration, that *Dartmouth* was still at war. Moreover, the ship was immobilised with the nearest naval bases belonging to their sworn enemy, the French, and to their lukewarm friends the Spanish. At this moment, Carlisle was probably the only man in the ship giving a thought to its wider role in this great war, and that was why it was so essential to have good officers who could allow him to break away from the immediate, pressing concerns.

***

CHAPTER NINE

Breaking Strain

Friday, Eighteenth of December 1761.
Dartmouth, at Anchor, Andros Island north-northeast 19 leagues.

Lieutenant Gresham looked eager and confident, as though he was to be given a birthday treat rather than take responsibility for an operation of such complexity, and with such a high chance of failure, that it would make most men quail at the very thought.

'I'm ready sir. If you can give me that lee now, we can get the longboat in place and start transferring the load.'

Carlisle wasn't going to be rushed. There was too much at stake and a single error could be fatal. He walked forward and gazed critically at the first lieutenant's arrangements. The great bower anchor had been lowered so that it hung far enough below the surface for the longboat to be brought over it. The bower anchor's own cable led from the anchor ring to the hawse, while one of the kedge cables passed from the main yardarm, through the strop that was slung around the anchor stock, and up to another strop that had been worked over the main yard vertically above the ship's gunwale. The second kedge cable also passed through the strop and was loosely suspended from the main yard; this would be the cable that would carry the anchor below the longboat. The longboat itself looked strange indeed with its added eighteen inches of freeboard, the tight turns of cable around its hull, and the massive framework looming over it all. The yawl was ahead of its bows and the cutter astern, each secured to the longboat by a painter, and at each painter a seaman was stationed with an axe, to cut the smaller boats free if the weight of the anchor should take the longboat straight to the bottom. Losing the longboat would be bad, but losing the yawl and cutter would leave Carlisle without the means to save his ship's company if the worst happened.

Hewlett and his two mates were alone in the longboat, ready with a long roll of seizing twine and a sharp knife. Hewlett would stay in the boat while his mates would leave before it took the anchor's weight. If it all went wrong, the bosun would be the only one carried to the bottom, for he'd have little chance of escaping through that mass of spars and ropes that he was crouching under. He winked up at Carlisle.

'The starboard cable's on the bitts, Mister Gresham?'

'Aye sir, and Mister Angelini's below ready to veer away as needed, and ready to heave in the larboard anchor.'

Almost half of *Dartmouth's* crew would be at the capstan bars, and even with that amount of muscle, they'd find the next hour or so a severe trial. His officers were becoming restless, he could see.

'Very well. Mister Beazley, hoist the fore topmast stays'l.'

The transformation was immediate. The wind hauled forward onto the larboard bow and the longboat found its lee and steadied under the starboard quarter. The flip side of the coin was that *Dartmouth* started to roll a little with the wind further off the bow. That was why Carlisle had left it until the last moment before ordering the stays'l hoisted. Until now, it was the ship that needed to be steady, but for the next hour the longboat must be sheltered at whatever cost to the ship.

Carlisle looked over the side again.

'You may proceed, Mister Gresham.'

Gresham drew a breath.

'Heave away on the yawl, heave away.'

A long rope led from the bows of the yawl through the bight of the kedge cables and all the way forward to a block at the starboard boomkin. From there it passed back to the fo'c'sle where a party of waisters under a petty officer were ready to heave the yawl, the longboat and the cutter, in one long procession forward, until the longboat rested under the main yard. A second rope led from the stern of the cutter to the snatch block on the poop deck, where a smaller group waited.

'Steady now,' shouted Gresham. He ran to the side and looked over. 'Six feet forward… one more… hold her aft.'

The last was delivered in a full-throated bellow to the poop-deck party who had to arrest the forward movement of the three boats at just the right point so that the longboat was properly positioned.

'Now, just take down the slack forward and we'll be there.'

The fo'c'sle party leaned back on the rope and belayed it on the bitts beside the foremast. Now the three boats were fixed firmly in position with the longboat directly under the main yard.

'Very good, very good.'

Gresham rubbed his hands. That was the easy part. He looked over to see the bosun's face grinning back at him from beneath his cat's cradle of ropes and spars. He glanced at the captain who made no sign whatever, then he looked to windward, choosing his moment as the serried ranks of the trade wind swell marched towards the ship.

'Mister Wishart, check away handsomely.'

Wishart had the critical task of ensuring that the slack kedge cable was veered so that the bosun could get at the ends. He saw one of Hewlett's mates stretch out and catch the inboard fall while another used a boathook to snag the outboard fall. They heaved them in together, no easy task with a ten-inch cable, until Hewlett could reach them to take a temporary seizing. Now, as Wishart gave them more slack, they were able to cross the two bights over the framework above the longboat. Hewlett held up his hand.

'Belay there, Mister Wishart. Thus and no further.'

Hewlett looked over the side to gauge how much slack rope was hanging below the boat. He motioned to his mates, both strong men, to heave in until the cable was as taut as it could be without yet taking the weight of the anchor. It would do no good to have the anchor dangling so far below the boat that it would snag on a shallow patch. He took a few more turns of seizing then reached for the knife that the armourer had honed specially for him. Still, it took an agonising few minutes to cleave through the ten-inch hemp rope. At last it was done and the two ends could be laid alongside each other end-for-end, ready for the seizings. Hewlett took the long length of cordage, knotted it to the two bights of rope and then, using a massive serving mallet that was normally reserved for the shroud lanyards, passed two dozen tight turns around the cables, drawing them close together so that the join was as strong as each individual cable. He knotted the end and cut off the waste. Then he spent a moment inspecting the seizing, tapping it to make sure there was no slack. Finally, he looked up and gave a raised thumb to the first lieutenant. His mates jumped from the longboat through a gunport, leaving this most dangerous part to the bosun alone.

'Mister Wishart, the second kedge cable, veer away, now.'

This was the first really dangerous moment and every man on deck knew it. The second kedge cable was bearing the entire weight of the huge bower anchor. Slowly, slowly Wishart's party walked the cable forward, letting the friction on the bitts take the strain. Gresham watched the longboat carefully. He could see Hewlett smashing at the first cables with his serving mallet, encouraging them into their exact places on the paired halves of the main topmast yards. Slowly the slack came off the first cable, and the second cable started to lose its rigidity. Now the serving mallet was useless, no power on earth would shift the cable once it felt the full weight of the anchor. The framework groaned; it visibly subsided into the boat, and the boat settled deeper in the water until the lower ends of the canvas were wetted each time an errant wave reached it. But it held. The framework was steady, and the boat hadn't been dragged straight down to the depth, nor had the framework been forced through the boat's planking or split it apart like a shelled peapod.

Gresham exhaled, the first sign of nerves that he'd shown.

'Mister Wishart, run in the second cable and jump down into the yawl.'

The first part was over. The anchor was slung beneath the longboat by a massive strop made from the kedge cable, while its true seventeen inch cable snaked away towards the ship's hawse. The bowman pushed the yawl away from the ship's side and Wishart gave the orders to start the slow pull into the teeth of the wind and current.

***

The yawl's crew may have had the most physically demanding task, but it was Gresham on the fo'c'sle who directed the whole operation and who could bring about its ruin in a moment of inattention. The yawl could fairly easily have towed the longboat and the bower anchor four hundred yards into the wind and current, but that was the smallest part of the weight that the oarsmen had to fight against. The anchor's cable had a weight of its own and that weight was increasing with every yard that Wishart's men gained towards the point where Hewlett could slip the anchor. But not only was the cable's weight increasing, it was also dragging at the longboat as it was paid out through *Dartmouth's* hawse. For the cable couldn't be merely let go, that would so far increase the weight that pulled downwards on the longboat that it would certainly sink it. Gresham had the task of paying out the anchor cable only at the rate that the longboat was moving away from the ship. But he had one more trick up his sleeve.

'Souter, away with the cutter.'

The captain's coxswain gave the orders that propelled the cutter towards *Dartmouth's* starboard bow. His was another dangerous task and he had reduced the cutter's crew to just four oarsmen, and each of them had a tightly bunged empty water breaker that they held by a lanyard to help them swim, if it became necessary. Souter steered the boat under the hawse so that the anchor cable scraped against the gunwale. The two oarsmen on the starboard side boated their oars and lashed the massive cable to the thwarts, so that the cutter now took the weight of a portion of the cable transversally across the centre of the boat. The cutter was, in effect, buoying the bight of the bower anchor's cable at a point some fifty yards from the longboat, taking some of the strain that was threatening to drag the longboat under despite its raised gunwales.

Gresham had wanted to use the pinnace as a second buoy, to supplement the cutter, but Carlisle had refused. He could see the potential for this operation going so badly awry that all the boats involved could be lost or irreparably damaged; dragged under or smashed by the weight of the bower anchor, if the longboat should be swamped. He had no intention of being cast upon this reef with no means to leave his doomed ship. At thirty-two feet the pinnace was longer than the longboat but it was much lighter built and was in no way capable of carrying the bower anchor, but it could take twenty or so people to Andros Island to summon help.

Slowly, slowly the strange procession of boats inched its way to windward. Through his telescope Carlisle could see the straining oarsmen in the yawl, with Wishart encouraging them, his body swaying forward and aft as he gave the time for the strokes. The longboat was doing well and he could see Hewitt now sitting atop the framework with his own stopped cask under his arm and his knife flashing in the sunshine. He saw the choppy waves splashing against the boat's bows, but nothing but a few capfuls of spray were coming inboard, as far as he could tell. He looked further left and it was evident that the cutter wasn't faring so well. Souter was in the stern with two of his oarsmen and the other two were in the bows, but the weight of the cable was pulling the gunwales closer and closer to the waiting sea. He could see that all five men were baling, using the canvas buckets that they had taken against just this emergency.

What would happen if the cutter sank? Would the extra weight on the longboat pull it under?

The join between the two cables had passed through the hawse some ten minutes ago, so the longboat was over half way towards the point where the anchor could be slipped. Beazley was using a hand compass to direct the yawl, flashing up a green flag for Wishart to pull more to starboard and a red flag for him to angle the boat to larboard.

'Just a hundred yards to go, sir, I reckon.'

The master had another flag ready for use, lying at his feet, a yellow square that would indicate to Hewitt when he could slip the anchor.

Carlisle could hardly breathe. At any moment the cutter could be pulled under and then the yawl would surely be able to pull no further. Souter's crew were bailing faster now, almost frantically, and he could see the waves lapping at the gunwales. Should he order the anchor slipped now? He felt his wife's presence behind him. She had no business on the quarterdeck at a time like this and he thought for a moment of ordering her below. He lowered his telescope and started to turn, but Beazley's urgent call stopped him.

'The cutter's turning turtle, sir.'

Carlisle could see as much without the telescope. The weight of the anchor cable between the ship and the cutter was pulling down on the boat's larboard side. A larger wave must have been its undoing and he could see that it had been pulled right over. Heads were bobbing in the water.

'Slip the anchor Mister Beazley, make the signal.'

Beazley had picked up the yellow flag as soon as the cutter had started to roll and he waved it urgently, holding out the fly so that Hewitt could see the whole of the flag. There was an agonising moment as the bosun's knife sawed at the seizings and then, so suddenly that it took them all by surprise, the longboat bobbed up a clear three feet, looking suddenly huge in the disturbed water.

'Belay the cable,' Gresham shouted.

A half dozen agile men and boys passed the stoppers that would hold the cable fast against the messenger, preventing any more escaping through the hawse.

Carlisle watched in fascination as the cutter disappeared, pulled down by the weight of the anchor. He counted the heads in the water; four, then a fifth bobbed into sight. Then a massive shape rose among the swimmers, with water cascading from it. It rose clear of the water then fell back to slip forever below the waves. It was the cutter's stern. The boat must have been snapped in two by the weight of the anchor plummeting towards the bottom. Perhaps the bow section was still attached to the anchor cable. It could foul the whole arrangement, making it difficult or impossible to heave the anchor all the way home, but there was no help for it.

'Away pinnace crew! Away pinnace crew. Pick up those men, fast as you can.'

Gresham was issuing orders rapidly now, rescuing the survivors from the cutter, bringing the yawl and the longboat back alongside, completely focussed on the immediate tasks.

'Mister Gresham,' Carlisle called, 'the boats can look after themselves. Heave in the larboard bower.'

Gresham looked stunned. He'd momentarily lost sight of the bigger picture. Time was still the critical factor and they had to weigh one anchor and heave the ship up to the new anchor that now lay some three-hundred-and-fifty yards to the southeast. That was a mighty piece of labour in itself and in a few hours they'd be in danger of grounding.

'The wind's picked up a little, sir,' Beazley was gauging the strength of the wind from the dog-vanes on the mizzen shrouds, 'and there's a deal of cloud gathering to windward.'

Carlisle looked where the master was pointing. He could see the high trade wind clouds but beyond them, above and below, a bank of grey was coming up fast. Should he chop the larboard anchor cable? That might be the prudent thing to do and it would save them at least half an hour over the time it would take to heave it in until it was clear of the water. He looked again to the east. Two hours, he reckoned, at least he had a time that he must work to. The threatening gale was giving them just enough time to save the larboard anchor and still get underway to the south before it hit them.

He felt something bump against the ship's bow, then a scraping as it passed astern. Beazley craned over the gunwale and called back to Carlisle.

'That's the cutter's forward half, sir, brought down on the current. Then it's not still attached to the cable. Thank the Lord for small mercies!'

***

The next two hours passed in a frenzy of urgent activity. The remaining three boats and Souter and his four oarsmen were recovered quickly and the boats were secured astern, on stout cables against the expected blow. And it was just as well that all those men were recovered because the work still to be done would require all hands that were fit to push on a capstan bar or haul on a swifter. The larboard bower was brought up until its ring just showed clear of the water. It could be catted and fished later. Then the backbreaking work of hauling in the starboard cable could commence. A sold hour it took, and it was fortunate that the tide was slack, because heaving against the rising wind and the regular current was hard enough. But eventually it was done and, as the starboard bower broke free from the sand *Dartmouth's* head cast to starboard, and she filled her sails on the larboard tack, standing away to the south, seeking the centre of the strait, to deep water and a safe passage to the west.

***

CHAPTER TEN

Temptation

Saturday, Nineteenth of December 1761.
Dartmouth, at Sea, Old Bahama Straits.

Gresham strode onto the quarterdeck and leaned out to peer over the quarter. He had a look of intense satisfaction; not only had he just completed a masterstroke of seamanship in getting his ship clear of a dangerous mess of sandbanks and reefs, but he'd done it with the loss of only one boat, and he'd brought all his men back aboard. But most of all, they'd got the ship clear before the coming gale had struck. And now that he thought of it, he hadn't left behind a single anchor, which was a signal achievement in itself.

'Any moment now, I think,' he said to the quarterdeck at large, 'and what a blessed, timely blow it will be if it gets us through this damned passage before we lose the light.'

He rubbed his hands at the thought of the open spaces beyond the straits where the ship could spread its wings day or night without the fear of foundering on some hidden reef.

'We'll have a fast run down to Havana if this wind holds true. What do you think Mister Beazley?'

'I think we don't have the right and proper trade wind yet, Mister Gresham, and that'll be a nasty blow when it comes, although I do believe it'll stay abaft the beam. The weather-glass is falling and as we all know…'

What they all were supposed to know wasn't revealed for at that moment the captain's head appeared at the poop deck rail and Gresham remembered why he'd come from the gundeck to the quarterdeck.

'The boats are all snugged down safe, sir. Doubled bridles through the aftermost gunports on the gun deck, and bow-graces in case they're thrown upon our stern. They're as safe as if we had hoisted them in.'

Carlisle nodded. Normally they towed the longboat to save space and brought all the other boats inboard and stowed them on the extra spars in the waist. However, they would have to heave to if they wanted to bring the pinnace and yawl inboard, and there was not time for that, not with those grey clouds blotting out the eastern horizon. He was about to turn away when he realised that his normal mute acknowledgement was insufficient for the moment.

'My congratulations and my thanks, Mister Gresham. That was a piece of seamanship that I don't expect I'll see again in my lifetime. I think the men are due an extra issue of grog with their supper. Perhaps you would let the purser know.'

This he said in a loud enough voice for the quartermaster and the steersmen, and the marine sentry to hear. He'd always felt self-conscious making these sort of prepared speeches, but he recognised the need. The men had indeed done well; the slightest hesitation or a botched lashing could have been the ruin of them all, and yet they acted in the steadiest manner possible. But there was always something to spoil the mood, and today it was the leadsman who was in a certain degree responsible for the ship being in that dangerous position. He'd have to pronounce the man's punishment in the next hour or so, and get it over with before dinner, so that it didn't hang over them while they were in Havana.

The bell struck five times, startling Carlisle. He hadn't realised that the forenoon was so far progressed. He'd be hard pressed to finish the business before eight bells, and he felt strongly that a flogging after such a superhuman effort was hardly the right way to show his appreciation. And was that the master-at-arms lurking there? He'd know that the man must be dealt with immediately, only a crime that warranted a court martial was left unpunished more than a day or so. Carlisle felt a pressure in his chest, the same discomfort that he always experienced when he was being forced into making a decision that he'd rather defer or not make at all. Damn them! He turned deliberately for his cabin, ignoring the master-at-arms, his good mood spoiled.

***

'Well, Edward, the ship has a real holiday feel about it. I don't believe I've ever known such high spirits.'

'They did well today,' Carlisle replied looking fondly at his wife, some of his ill humour evaporating at the sight of her. 'I don't believe another ship in the whole squadron could have brought us out of that dangerous corner. Do you know, the men we fished out of the water after the cutter sank were laughing and joking as though they'd been on a run ashore.'

'It was Matthew Gresham's doing, in a large part, I understand.'

'Just so, just so. The man's a paragon of seamanship. And you're right about the high spirits, but I regret that I'm going to put a damper on it all after I've had this coffee.'

He told his wife about the seaman whose sullen attitude had nearly caused the loss of the ship, and the need to have him punished within the hour, before the men had their dinner and their grog. It was always dangerous to flog a man after grog had been issued and his messmates' animal spirits were roused. He'd known ships in his youth, before this war, where an ill-timed flogging in the afternoon had led to half a dozen more, all of which could have been avoided by rigging the grating before dinner. Chiara looked thoughtful, stirring the coffee in her cup; she understood her husband's dilemma better than he could guess.

'I do wonder, Edward, what would have become of me, a meek and helpless woman, if the ship couldn't have been brought out of the shallows before the wind rose.'

Carlisle raised an eyebrow at Chiara's description of herself as *meek*, it wasn't a word he'd have associate with his wife, and *helpless*! He almost laughed aloud.

'Oh, we'd have brought you to safety, somehow…'

'Yes, yes, I'm sure. But think of the inconvenience, and as you are constantly telling me, danger lurks around every corner at sea and more so without the reassurance of solid, thick planking underfoot. I wonder, would it be appropriate for me to show my appreciation in some public way. I heard that you've ordered a second issue of rum this evening, so it can't be that…'

Carlisle knew very well that he was being manoeuvred. He wasn't a great flogger, and he'd so far avoided letting the cat out of its bag with his wife on board. The offence was indeed heinous and normally it would be bad for the discipline of the ship if the criminal were to get away scot-free, but if it were known that his wife had pleaded his case, then perhaps it would work out well. The leadsman wasn't a bad seaman, far from it, and he wouldn't have been sent to cast the lead if he wasn't competent. Perhaps it was his birthday, or for some other reason his messmates had plied him with hoarded spirits. Carlisle would never know the truth; it would be locked behind a wall of silence, but perhaps a close brush with corporal punishment, and a providential escape, would do more good than a flogging.

'Will you join me on the quarterdeck, my dear? You won't need to say anything.'

***

The master-at-arms was waiting on the gangway with the errant leadsman behind him, his head hanging in shame. Whatever defiance had overcome his normal character had clearly fled, which reinforced Carlisle's view that it was drink-related. Gresham stepped forward, then hesitated, surprised to see Lady Chiara close behind the captain.

'I beg your pardon, sir, my business can wait…'

'Thank you, Mister Gresham, but if it's concerned with yesterday's incident at the main chains, then let's see Foster immediately.'

Gresham hid his surprise. Naval crime and punishment were hardly suitable subjects for a lady, but he waved for the master-at-arms to come forward with his prisoner. There was a hush on the quarterdeck and men stopped their work all over the deck to hear Foster's sentence. The only sounds were the rising wind in the rigging and the creak of the steering gear as the steersmen hauled the wheel this way or that to counteract the swell that tended to throw the ship off course. Carlisle had a moment to notice how well Chiara balanced against the unpredictable heave and fall of the ship as the waves passed under her keel.

The master-at-arms was an officious man, proud of his position and inured to the ship's company's hatred that was an inevitable consequence of his duties. He started speaking in a formal tone.

'Well, sir, Able Seaman Foster, here…'

'Thank you, master-at-arms. I'm very well aware of the facts. Now, Foster, do you have anything to say?'

Foster barely raised his head and started to mumble until a savage thrust in the ribs from the master-at-arms' truncheon brought his head up. He looked Carlisle in the eye and cleared his throat.

'I beg your pardon, your Honour, for failing in my duty. I don't rightly know what came over me but I'm… I'm resolved to never let it happen again.'

Foster's head stayed up but his eyes swivelled left and right as though they had a separate life to the body that contained them. They finally alighted on Lady Chiara. He hadn't noticed her before and at the sight of her his shame almost overcame him and he hung his head again.

'Well Foster, you certainly deserve punishment,' Carlisle stared at the seaman for what seemed like an eternity, 'and you can be grateful to your shipmates for their skill in getting the ship away from the reef that your actions brought us to.'

Foster nerved himself to hear his punishment. Probably he'd never been flogged before, but he must have seen it often enough. He'd be aware that in principle a captain couldn't order more than a dozen strokes of the cat, but he'd have heard the stories of captains who ignored that rule, and he must know that his was a serious offence. A dozen then, or perhaps two dozen if the captain was feeling vindictive. It wasn't the pain that worried him, and the cat rarely drew much blood until after the first dozen, but he feared the humiliation of being seized up to a grating and having his shirt pulled from his back before all his messmates. And then there was the captain's lady, would she witness his disgrace?

Carlisle continued to study the man in front of him. He knew enough about the common seamen to have a good idea of what was going through his mind.

'Yes, you can thank the men who brought us off that reef, and saved the ship and the lives of a good many of us, I don't doubt. But as for your punishment; Lady Chiara wishes to mark her appreciation for her deliverance from the perils of the sea, and she has interceded on your behalf.'

He turned to the master-at-arms.

'A week's stoppage of grog for Foster, and I trust that this will be a salutary lesson to him.'

***

Carlisle reflected on the past hour. It had been a master-stroke to spare Foster his flogging. He could tell that it was a popular decision by the men's high spirits and it would do Foster no harm to go without his rum for a week. Yet Carlisle understood his men better than they could have guessed. The fact was that Foster would be treated with consideration by his messmates, and he'd be given as much of their issue of rum as he would have had of his own, perhaps more. No doubt the master-at-arms would be watching that mess, but it would take more than one man to prevent seamen offering a friend a taste of their grog. In any case the punishment had dubious legality; the articles of war allowed him to flog a man but not to refuse him his rations, and if pushed too far some messdeck lawyer might even complain formally.

That was so often the way with punishments in the navy, they become more symbolic than real. He had lost count of the number of times that after some misdemeanour ashore he'd withdrawn a man's privilege of leave in the knowledge that the ship would sail in a few hours and there'd be no leave for anyone for at least a month. It was the same with extra cleaning duties and he'd seen a whole mess turn to with brushes and mops to help out their mate. The only punishment that the men really feared was a flogging, and even then it was only for the humiliation, not the pain, which was less than they felt in their daily duties in laying out on a tops'l yard in a gale. Yes, flogging was the only real deterrent at sea, and for that reason a wise captain used it sparingly.

He looked sideways at his wife who was reading by the scant illumination that came through the stern windows. The angles of her face were shown in stark relief by the steel-grey light, and she looked severe and – although he'd never dare to tell her – she looked older than her years. Yes, that was no longer a youthful face, but then she hadn't looked particularly young when he'd first seen her on the deck of a tartane in the Straits of Bonifacio some six years ago. Six years! And in that time, and with only a few months at sea in men-of-war, his wife had somehow acquired more wisdom in how to handle the people than he or any of his officers. He understood that an observer could always see more objectively than one who was immersed in the problems of managing a company of three-hundred-and-fifty men on a daily basis, but even so, Chiara had shown remarkably good judgement in pleading for Foster.

'Do you know today's date, Edward?'

'It's the nineteenth of December, dear, why do you ask?'

'Well, you've been so busy since we sailed from Port Royal that I haven't found a good time to mention it, and with this gale chasing us down the strait, this may also be a bad time, but four days ago was the sixth anniversary of the day that we met. Do you remember? I do, I recall how you looked so young and handsome, and you haven't changed at all in those years.'

Carlisle was dumbstruck. Had she been reading his mind? It wouldn't have surprised him; he'd become fatalistic at the steady stream of her unlikely talents. They were offered for his admiration at regular intervals, as though they should be paraded sparingly, to avoid them becoming tarnished by over-use. He garbled a reply, to the effect that his wife was as beautiful as the day they met and her charms grew upon him with every year that passed. He knew he'd made a hash of it, but Chiara smiled nevertheless as she pushed her spectacles back onto the bridge of her nose and returned to her reading.

***

The gale overtook *Dartmouth* just as the men finished their dinner and their grog. The tops'ls had been double-reefed in anticipation and the t'gallants had been lowered in the last hour of the forenoon watch. Now that they were nearly through the dangerous Nicholas Channel the great two-decker could run down the longitude in safety and even in some degree of comfort. Carlisle had left the cabin to his wife and now he was standing on the quarterdeck beside the binnacle, studying the set of the sails and feeling the rhythm of the ship as it rose and fell under the influence of the mounting waves and the screaming wind. He knew that he couldn't improve upon the master's sail plan, nor could he better the way that Gresham had made all secure in anticipation of the weather, yet it was still his responsibility. It constantly fascinated him when he considered all the expert officers who collaborated to make the ship float, sail and fight. Within their specialisations, they reigned supreme and he, their captain, could add little of value. However –

and he knew he must never forgot this – it was his guiding hand that brought their combined knowledge and experience together and made *Dartmouth* into such a formidable fighting machine. Only he directed when they should fight and when they should flee and only he could balance the competing demands of a carpenter whose only concern was to prevent the ship sinking, against the first lieutenant who in the heat of an action thought only of keeping his guns firing.

His reverie was interrupted by Wishart, who had the first dog watch.

'I beg your pardon, sir, but there are five sails in sight, a point on the starboard bow at about five miles. It looks like the French convoy, sir.'

'I heard no hail, Mister Wishart.'

'No, sir. The weather's thick down to leeward and the masthead can see no further than we can from the deck. The relief lookout reported them as soon as he got aloft.'

'Very well, Mister Wishart. It appears that the lookout may have been warming the bell.'

Carlisle could easily imagine what had happened. It would be uncomfortable at the main topmast crosstrees and the man who had been there for thirty minutes would have been more concerned with ensuring that he had a timely relief than in scanning the grey wall of cloud that cut out everything beyond a few miles. He picked up his telescope from the hook on the binnacle and walked up the poop deck ladder for a clearer view ahead.

It took only seconds to find the sails and through the telescope he could see them quite clearly. The French convoy: four merchantmen running for all they were worth and the frigate trailing astern, keeping between them and the deadly danger of a British two decker in pursuit. They were being held back by the wounded brig, otherwise they would be far to the west by now, and it must have come as a shock to see *Dartmouth* only six miles behind him. They had every right to believe that the British ship would have found a permanent resting place on that shoal, what with the thick weather and a brewing storm to windward. It brought home to Carlisle just how fortunate he had been to get his ship clear before the gale struck.

He could see now that the convoy had hauled its wind a point or two as soon as it had cleared the Nicholas Channel. Then they weren't heading for Havana and the only other possible destinations were deep in the Gulf of Mexico in French Louisiana. He caught himself actually licking his lips. This gale would blow through in the night and then, when the sun rose, it would be an easy task to find the French ships. They were all at the mercy of the trade wind and the current through the Old Bahama Straits, and it was ten-to-one that the convoy was steering to round the Dry Tortugas and shape its course for Mobile Bay or New Orleans. A brief scrap with the frigate – her captain should withdraw after a few guns for the honour of the flag – and then the merchantmen would be prizes. If he ordered *Dartmouth* to bear up a point now, it would be merely a matter of following in their path. Tempting indeed, but he knew it would never do. If he could have overhauled them before they had entered the Nicholas Channel, he would have gone for them, but he had his orders and, strange to say, it was more important at this point in the war to deliver the governor-general of Havana's furniture and to avoid making prizes of his King's cousin's ships on his own doorstep, than it was to deprive the French of four fat merchantmen. No, he must turn his face from prizes, even such tempting ones as these. Carlisle took one last look at the convoy, then called down to the quarterdeck.

'Are you ready to bear away for Havana, Mister Beazley? We must be clear of the channel now.'

The sailing master scratched his head and stared abstractedly at the veiled horizon to larboard.

'I'd prefer to stand on for another few hours, sir. I haven't had a good fix since we left the Windward Passage.'

***

CHAPTER ELEVEN

Havana Bay

Sunday, Twentieth of December 1761.
Dartmouth, at Sea, off Havana, Cuba.

The gale was nasty enough while it lasted, and it kicked up a violent sea in the Nicholas Channel where the current and the wind-blown waves were channelled between the Salt Cays at the far sou'west of the Bahamas bank and the confused archipelago that lay off the northern part of Cuba. *Dartmouth* had stood on further than needed for a passage to Havana, which must have given the French convoy an uneasy couple of hours as they saw the two-decker apparently following them into the Gulf of Mexico. With no good fix from the land, and with Beazley visibly nervous at the possibility of repeating the previous day's navigational errors, Carlisle bowed to the moral pressure and agreed that it was wisest to steer west-by-north through the night and hope that in the morning they would find enough of the nor'easterly trade wind to waft them sou'west to Havana Bay. But it was not to be and sunrise found them in a failing wind, too far off the land to benefit from any sea breeze. *Dartmouth* barely had enough way to stem the current that threatened to send them north through the Florida Straits and out into the broad Atlantic.

'I reckon we passed Matanzas in the night, sir, and the high land that you can see to larboard is to the east of Havana. The entrance to Havana Bay is still some ten leagues further to the west.'

Carlisle looked sharply at the sailing master. It was unlike him to be so vague about the ship's position, but then, in this meeting place of three ocean currents and without a certain fix, any navigator could be excused for being puzzled. Here the current that had hurried *Dartmouth* through the straits met the famous Loop Current that had hastened *Medina* on its way to St. Augustine back in 'fifty-seven. Here also was the start of the infant Atlantic Drift that fed off the other two currents and passed up the east coast of Florida and thence into the wide ocean, to deliver its warm waters to the shores of Britain. All were of unknown and unknowable speeds, and no navigator could be certain of his position until he had a sight of land that could be recognised.

Beazley referred again to the elevations in the corner of his chart and squinted at the far distant mountain range. Yes, it certainly looked like the mountains between Matanzas and Havana, but he was wary; it was all too easy to apply wishful thinking when comparing a sketched elevation and hazy, distant mountains.

'The log shows four knots and two fathoms, sir. The Loop Current runs at about three knots here, dead against us by all accounts, and we do appear to be making a knot or so over the ground.'

'Yes, when I last came this way we found four knots a few leagues further north, but of course it was in our favour as we were bound through the Florida Straits.'

'Did you not sight the land at all, sir?'

Carlisle laughed as he remembered that odd mission to deliver the Spanish governor-general of Florida to his seat at St. Augustine. Don Alonso Fernández de Heredia – he even remembered his full name – hadn't wanted to be seen off Havana. He was in some sort of a dispute with the governor-general of Cuba, over precedence and rank. He was concerned that once he was seen by a Spanish man-of-war he would inevitably have to land in Havana, and he felt that he would not easily get away again. And of course, Don Alonzo had been wounded in a fight with Dutch pirates and very much wished for the comfort of his own palace.

'No, Mister Beazley. *Medina* passed fifteen leagues north of Havana, hugging the north side of the channel near the Dry Tortugas. We saw nothing at all of Cuba after we had passed Cape San Antonio a few days before. But you know, it's easy to see why the Dons chose Havana as their principal city in these parts. It has a wonderful harbour, of course, but just look at how the winds and currents make approaching the place so difficult. We know now how dangerous it is to make a passage along the north coast of Cuba.'

'Aye, sir. I'd happily do it again in a single ship in daylight, with no chase in sight, but not pursuing a convoy and not with an invasion fleet and not at night, oh dear me no.'

Carlisle privately agreed with the master, but he had a strong suspicion that the Old Bahama Straits were seen by Anson as a way to outflank the enemy's defences. He'd been sent that way for a set purpose, although only poor Admiral Holmes knew what that was.

'Yes, Mister Beazley. The Florida Straits of course has that strong current that will make any approach from the north long and tedious, and if a fleet rounds Cape San Antonio then they have to tack against the trade wind or take the Loop Current far into the Gulf of Mexico. Every route except the Old Bahama Straits will give Havana days or weeks of notice that they are being attacked. Aye, Havana will be a hard nut to crack, if it should ever come to that.'

'Well, be that as it may, sir, but I think our luck is about to change.'

He nodded towards the east where fluffy white clouds were forming in the middle regions of the air, with their familiar elongated shape. Trade wind clouds. The steady, predictable breezes that bore the great explorers to all corners of the world in their search for new lands and their riches. Now they were the engines of transatlantic commerce and dictated the tracks of invasion fleets as the colonial powers battled each other for dominance in the new worlds beyond Europe. It was a pleasure to see them after their absence over the last few days.

***

Dartmouth came-to off the Morro Castle, beyond the range of its guns, and fired a single shot to seaward, then they waited as the sun passed overhead and started dipping towards the west. There was no answering gun from the fort, no official acknowledgement of their arrival. Save for the flag on the tower of the Morro Castle, there was no sign that this was the principal seat of power for the Spanish empire of the Indies.

Carlisle climbed into the mizzen top and studied the harbour entrance. It was busy enough, and trading vessels of the smaller sort came and went and the ubiquitous fishing boats cast their nets along the shore, but he couldn't see into the harbour.

'Mister Beazley, take the ship half a mile further west.'

Dartmouth filled her tops'ls and in ten minutes she lay nor'west of the fort in the beautiful bay with Point Bravo to leeward and no appreciable current to move her from this vantage position. Now Carlisle could see right into the entrance channel that led to the anchorage and wharves in Havana Bay. It looked to be between one and two cables wide and probably a mile long. There were Spanish men-of-war at anchor in the bay; he could clearly see at least half a dozen ships-of-the-line and the same number of frigates and sloops. Beyond them the masts of further ships poked above the spit of land that hid their hulls. He had a glimpse of the city with its stoutest walls facing the flat land to the west, the obvious approach for a besieging army. On the eastern bank of the channel, beyond the Morro Castle, the land rose in a wooded ridge, *La Cabaña* it was called, that followed the course of the narrow passage. He thought he could see batteries on that higher land, with flagpoles and low enclosing walls. To the west a smaller fort matched its larger parent across the channel. It was all well and good, but that little fort was untenable if an enemy should gain possession of the Morro Castle. With just four hundred yards of water separating them, its guns would be silenced in half an hour.

The sun was high and he wiped the tears from his eye and a bead of sweat from his brow, then looked again through the telescope. There were two obvious ways of attacking the city, then. The first required a regular siege of the western walls, and as far as he could see the ground beyond the walls was mostly flat, and quite suitable for a besieging army to cut its parallel trenches. But a siege was a slow process and in the tropics it was always a race between the progress of the siege and the progress of disease in the besieging army. Aye, and not only on the land. Fleets and squadrons had been decimated by disease in these waters. Any action must be swift and decisive in the Caribbean; those that weren't were doomed, and the poor sailors and soldiers paid for it in their unquiet graves, as Admiral Hosier's Ghost could attest. He recalled a few lines of a poem, or was it a song? Probably both, he decide.

O'er these waves forever mourning,
Shall we roam depriv'd of rest.

Carlisle lowered his telescope and considered the whole panorama again. There was a better, more imaginative option. Ignore the city walls entirely and storm the Morro Castle by land and sea, which would quickly make the high ground to the east of the channel untenable for the defenders. A few heavy guns on that ridge would soon bring the city to its senses without the need for a protracted siege. He looked down onto the poop deck where a group of his officers were busy making sketches. Beazley would choose the best to be sent to the navy offices at Seething Lane, to be copied and distributed as necessary to guide future navigators. However, Carlisle's main interest was in the defences, and he was reassured to see his third lieutenant there with his paper and pencils. Enrico was by far the best topographical artist he had ever known and his sketches would be worth more than their weight in gold – far more – in any future campaign.

Cousins At Arms

In half an hour a sleek, gaily painted lug-rigged boat shot out of the harbour's mouth and set a course hard on the wind to fetch this unexpected British ship. The sketchers packed up their papers and pencils; it wouldn't do for their visitor to see them thus recording his city's defences.

A Spanish navy captain climbed the side and was duly piped on board, but there was another man waiting in the boat, a pilot by the look of him. The captain spoke no English, of course, but he was enchanted to find that his interpreter was a noble lady, and they spoke rapidly together for some minutes before Chiara was ready to relay the information that she had gained to her husband.

'Well husband, it appears that Captain Spinola and I are cousins, of a sort, although rather distant. He was born Genoese, or Ligurian at least – I have heard the family name often – and he's rather proud of it because of the connection with Columbus. He is the port commissioner, which is why he has come, and I am sure that his lack of spoken English is real. I see no signs that he understands the conversations around him. He sends greetings from the governor-general who would be obliged to know on what errand a British ship-of-the-line arrives so unexpectedly at Havana. I explained about the furniture – you will have seen him almost laugh before he remembered that anything belonging to the governor-general is no laughing matter – and he has requested to see it before he makes a decision as to whether you can enter the port today, or must wait for the governor-general's decision tomorrow.'

'Would you show him this?'

Carlisle held out the certificate that the Spanish consul in Jamaica had given him, after his own inspection of the cargo.

Spinola read the certificate, shrugged and said something in rapid Spanish to Chiara.

'He says that the certificate is all well and good, and he regrets the imposition, but he finds that he must view the furniture for himself.'

Carlisle wouldn't for anything let his irritation show on his face. He reminded himself that it was natural that the Spanish should be suspicious. After all, most people believed that war was imminent and in fact with the extended lines of communication with Europe, it could already have begun. The governor-general of Havana must live uneasily with the knowledge that at any moment a British fleet could appear and lay siege to his city.

'Very well. Mister Gresham, be so good as to take the deck while I escort the captain below, and would you pass the word for the cooper? He will need a few of his tools. Mister Young, a lantern, if you please, and Mister Pontneuf, I'll be obliged if you'll post marines along the route with Sergeant Wilson to see good order. I'll entertain Captain Spinola in my cabin for a few minutes.'

Carlisle was surprised to find that his ear was becoming attuned to the Spanish conversation, and as long as they didn't speak too quickly, he could understand most of what passed between his wife and the port commissioner. Nevertheless, he could understand the language better than he could speak it and he was pleased that Chiara was relieving him of the need to make a stilted, awkward conversation. There was indeed a pilot in the boat but Spinola was making it quite clear that if he wasn't satisfied he'd have to return to the city and leave *Dartmouth* to spend the night at sea off the harbour entrance.

A knock at the door brought Pontneuf, stiff and formal in his scarlet regimentals.

'Sentries are posted, sir, and the purser is at the storeroom with the keys.'

There were three sets of ladders to the orlop deck where the commodore's store room was situated, and they made a curious procession with Midshipman Young leading the way, followed by Chiara and then Captain Spinola and Carlisle, with Pontneuf bringing up the rear. Spinola negotiated the ladders easily, as would be expected of a sea officer, and he showed no surprise at the dark and dank lower regions where the governor-general's goods were stored. It must have been a similar arrangement in Spanish ships.

The furniture was all crated and packed tight with wood shavings and paper. Spinola pointed to a few of the boxes and the cooper levered each one open with a small crowbar. What he was searching for wasn't clear, perhaps it was a recognisable trade mark of a Spanish workshop, but whether he found it or not, after some ten minutes he straightened and addressed Chiara again.

'He is satisfied, Edward,' Chiara said after a rapid-fire dialogue, 'and he says that it is indeed the kind of furniture that the governor-general might have ordered from Spain. He even went as far as to declare that the governor-general was expecting it a month ago, and had nearly given up hope. He has made a decision on his own responsibility to bring the ship into the harbour, before the light fades. If you will permit, the pilot is waiting in the boat.'

'With all my heart, tell him the pilot may board immediately. Let us make our way back to the quarterdeck. I didn't relish the thought of backing and filling off the harbour mouth through the night.'

***

Back on the quarterdeck he found Gresham studying something through his telescope.

'Do you see that awkward looking schooner tacking in towards the harbour, sir? I can hardly credit it, but it looks so like one that was lying off number six wharf at Kingston that it can only believe they are one and the same. There can't be two such cranky looking bottoms in all of the Caribbean.'

Gresham studied the little vessel tapping the telescope tube with his forefinger as he struck off the points of recognition.

'Foremast the same length as the main. Fore-topmast but a yard or so shorter. See the size of that jib, it looks fit for a schooner twice its size, and that counter stern looks ready to fall off…'

Carlisle followed the first lieutenant's pointing telescope. He hadn't noticed the schooner at Kingston, but he knew that Gresham was a keen observer of all kinds of waterborne craft. He could hold forth on the rigging of a French first rate as easily as he could for a Hooghly River trash-scow.

'And now I come to think of it, that fellow put to sea just before we did and seemed to hesitate off the cays. In the end I saw him bear away and hug the coast heading west, I imagined he was bound for some port in Jamaica, and we lost sight of him at sunset, before we hauled our wind. Now here he is, large as life and ugly as sin. He did well to tack up from Cape San Antonio in such a short time, or perhaps he was fortunate with the wind.'

Carlisle had no doubt about Gresham's story, and he could have added to it, if he had felt so inclined. He would bet that this schooner was carrying a message from that impertinent consul, if not carrying the consul himself. With its schooner rig its master would reasonably have expected to be a day quicker than the lumbering two-decker, probably more. It was evident from Spinola's reception that *Dartmouth* had not been expected at Havana, and now he knew why. Well, there was nothing the consul's letter or even the consul himself could say that Captain Spinola hadn't already discovered.

Chiara came over to see what was so interesting, and Carlisle left it to Gresham to tell her. His officers seemed to live for the moment when they could have her undivided attention. He saw her look through his telescope as Gresham pointed out the interesting features of the schooner, and he was rewarded with a discreet, knowing smile when she handed the telescope back. He remembered that it was Chiara who first suggested that the consul would send a message ahead, and she'd been right. Without that warning *Dartmouth* would have headed directly for the Windward Passage after leaving Port Royal, and the schooner would have overhauled them and been days ahead at Havana. How would that have changed the reception from the Spanish? It was impossible to know, but he was privately delighted that his plan – Chiara's plan, really – had succeeded so well.

***

It was that moment of truce that all ports in the track of the trade winds experienced almost every day. The sea breeze had faded a few hours ago and the land breeze wouldn't start until the sun had nearly touched the horizon. For now, the trade wind dominated this interregnum even in this close harbour entrance. With the longboat rowing ahead and the pinnace astern, in case the wind shifted, *Dartmouth* made her stately way, sailing a point free on the larboard tack under tops'ls and jib, past the guns of the Morro Castle and into the narrow channel. Carlisle had tried to ascertain when a British ship-of-the-line had last sailed into this harbour, but nobody in Jamaica knew. Certainly it must have been many years ago, before the last war. He'd half expected to be denied entry and he was prepared to land the governor-general's furniture by boat, and sail away without ever penetrating into the heart of this potential enemy's capital. There was an outside chance that he was sailing into a trap, but he didn't think so. News of war could hardly have reached this far west without it being known in Kingston before he left, and Spinola's friendliness was so evident that it could hardly be feigned. He could see him now, chatting to Chiara seemingly without a care in the world, and Enrico had joined them. He saw Chiara introduce his lieutenant to Spinola, presumably laying emphasis on his position in Sardinian nobility, rather than his naval rank. Carlisle noticed that Spinola bowed at the end of every sentence; Chiara – *Lady* Chiara – had that effect on Mediterranean people.

He reassured himself with the knowledge that if it was a trap then there was little that he could do about it. Should the worst happen, he wouldn't even attempt to fight his way out. The best he could do was to set fire to his ship, but even that would probably be impossible, if the Spanish sprung the trap efficiently. He looked up at the castle's guns leering down upon him, then at the batteries that dotted the heights of La Cabaña to larboard, then across to the smaller emplacements in the city walls to starboard and finally to the Spanish men-o'-war anchored in the harbour. There was an air of neglect about them all: forts, guns and ships, as though they had been ignored since Spain's last war with Britain. Nevertheless, in good repair or bad, there was enough shot and shell to hold the passage against half the world's fleets. No, there was nothing to be done now but behave as though he was on a mission from a friendly power, which – he reminded himself – he was, at least in principle.

'The governor-general's palace is on the right there, Edward. I'm assured that your salute will be returned gun-for-gun.'

Yes, he could see it now. Perhaps it was described as a palace, as befit a colonial governor-general of this magnitude, but its walls were stout and at each embrasure he could see a cannon's mouth, ready to contest the passage in thunder, flame and smoke.

'And Captain Spinola is sure there's no need to salute that admiral's flag?'

Chiara turned to the captain and said a few words, pointing to the tall seventy-four gun ship that lay closest to the palace.

'No, it is not their custom when the governor-general is in residence.'

'Very well.'

Carlisle was irritated with himself. He had slipped into treating his wife as he would one of his officers, and now he was even using quarterdeck language to reply to her. And he could see that she had noticed it; he knew that self-satisfied smile of old.

***

Dartmouth came to anchor just a few minutes before sunset, only a cable distant from the Spanish flagship.

'Captain Spinola says that it is as well that you are safe in the harbour, Edward, there will be a northerly wind tonight and it would be uncomfortable at sea and so close to the land.'

'Really?'

Carlisle looked up at the clouds that showed no sign of a change of weather.

'Mister Beazley, a northerly blow, the locals say. What do you think?'

Beazley looked past the Morro Castle to the far horizon.

'You see that haze with the low clouds beyond, sir? I'm no expert in these parts but that does look like a blow to me, and it could well be northerly.'

'Then I trust that Frenchman has spread his sails or he'll be a long time making Mobile Bay, or wherever he's bound.'

'That's true, sir,' Beazley had clearly cast the French convoy from his mind, 'and that brig's main topmast didn't look too cheerful to me either.'

Barely had they secured the anchor than a boat arrived from the admiral inviting Carlisle to supper. Carlisle showed it to Spinola who immediately had himself rowed over to the flagship. He returned in an hour, with a revised invitation that included Chiara and Enrico. Then Chiara had managed to get her cousin invited to dinner. She understood very well the hierarchy in a British man-of-war, but no power on earth would persuade her that it took precedence over family ties and ancient blood-lines.

By the time Spinola returned the land breeze had started to cool the ships, and the fo'c'sle and waist were crowded with sailors staring longingly at the shore. And it was true that the lights of the town and the forts and the batteries made a romantic spectacle, but there would be no shore leave here, not in the present uncertain state of affairs. Chiara had guessed Spinola's errand, and already she was taking the air on the poop deck, dressed in a carefully

selected outfit, as though a Spanish colonial capital, astride the tropic line, was her natural habitat.
***

CHAPTER TWELVE

Their Excellencies

Monday, Twenty-First of December 1761.
Dartmouth, at Anchor, Havana, Cuba.

His Excellency Juan de Prado Mayera Portocarrero y Luna considered this British captain with interest. The governor-general was no fool; he'd been in this post for nearly a year and throughout that time he'd heard from afar the drums of war that beat insistently and loudly in Madrid. He knew that he'd be at war with Britain, probably before another year of his governorship had run, and it was inconceivable that the British navy had sent a ship-of-the-line all the way from the Leeward Islands merely to deliver his furniture. And yet, what did they hope to gain? Havana carried on a brisk seaborne trade with both Britain and its American and West Indian colonies, and there must be a hundred merchant masters that could describe the navigation of the harbour and its defences in detail. There had to be something more, or were the heretics just toying with him? And this business of using his wife as an interpreter? He wouldn't have believed it if he wasn't witnessing it with his own eyes and ears. Still, he should be polite. After all, the furniture that he had feared lost on the passage from Cadiz was at this moment being unpacked and polished, ready to add to the lustre and grace of his palace. It was a little gesture in the grand affairs of nations, but it may mean something. He hoped it was significant, for his Excellency didn't want to go to war, and certainly not with this lusty seafaring nation that had already humbled Spain's cousins in France. And he'd seen war at first hand, had been a soldier himself, and he didn't wish that upon this beautiful island. Perhaps there was hope. It was just possible that this was a tentative olive branch, an earnest of good will to test the waters.

'Is there anything else I can do for you Captain? Do you require any provisions?'

Carlisle could understand that much Spanish, and he recognised that the governor-general was politely inquiring about *Dartmouth's* intended length of stay. His ear was becoming accustomed to the language and he was starting to remember words and phrases that he thought he had forgotten. Nevertheless, he waited for the translation, and made his reply through Chiara.

'I would be grateful if I might be permitted to send my purser ashore to the market for fresh vegetables and a few other items, your Excellency. Otherwise I have enough provisions and water. Now that I have discharged my mission and delivered your property, I only intend to stay one day more. I plan to sail from here on Wednesday.'

'Of course. There is a fine market in the town tomorrow; I will order an escort for your officer, and a man who can speak some English and knows what prices should be paid. Now, as I will have the pleasure of your company for at least one more day, I have the greatest happiness in inviting you and Lady Chiara to dine with me today. Shall we say at three o'clock? The new governor-general of Guatemala has been staying with me for a week, on his way to take up his position. I don't expect you have met him before, but he speaks English to some extent.'

***

Dartmouth's pinnace rowed Carlisle and Chiara back across the harbour to the ship. Midshipman Young had the tiller, looking primped and pompous with the enormous responsibility of acting as the captain's coxswain. Chiara waited until they were well away from the wharf, then turned to her husband so that her words wouldn't carry.

'I heard the name of the new governor-general of Guatemala, whom we are to meet this afternoon, it was being spoken of openly in the palace.'

'Now, how on earth do you hear these things? It's all I can do to avoid tripping over my own tongue without attending to other's conversations.'

'You should listen more, Edward, you'd be amazed at what you might learn. Now, would you like to know the name?'

Carlisle looked at his wife quizzically. Why was she speaking so confidentially? The name of this unknown *Excellency* could hardly be a matter that must be spoken of in whispers. Then it struck him. He knew only one other Spaniard of that rank. Could it be…?

'Don Alonso Fernández de Heredia, dear Edward, you remember the name now, perhaps, and you might even remember his wife the Countess San Clemente?'

Carlisle was stunned. He had taken Don Alonso to St. Augustine when the ship that was carrying him and his family was first attacked by Dutch pirates then came close to foundering in a hurricane to the south of Hispaniola. That was how he knew about the winds in the Gulf of Mexico and the Florida Straits, and the almost mythical Loop Current that had allowed them to make for St. Augustine while avoiding the complications of Havana. Yes, he remembered Don Alonso. They had been friends of a sort, at least they had grown to respect each other. Then another thought occurred to Carlisle.

'The countess, will she be at the dinner…?'

Chiara laughed and the oarsmen all smiled at the sound, but fortunately they couldn't hear what she said to her husband.

'No, she won't be there, and nor will that scheming, forward strumpet of a daughter of theirs – I know why you look so worried Edward – but they are still in Old Spain, waiting until Don Alonso calls for them to join him in Guatemala. I won't have to protect you, and Señorita Maria will be saved any further embarrassment. In any case, I would lay a substantial bet that she's married by now, probably to one of those decorative young subalterns who lounged around Don Alonso's palace. Although I don't hold out much hope of her behaviour being greatly affected by such a small matter as a husband.'

Carlisle breathed a sigh of relief. He would never have thought it could be so wearing on the spirit to be pursued remorselessly and shamelessly by an attractive young lady, until it happened to him. And so much passion from Chiara! He had no idea that she resented the episode that happened so long ago, she had never once mentioned it since they left St. Augustine.

'Well, I expect he will hardly recognise us, Chiara, and we'll only see him for a few hours, but how extraordinary that our paths should cross again. It's rather like ships at sea. There's a whole wide ocean to inhabit but the currents and winds and the headlands and channels and havens dictate that at any moment nine out of ten craft – no, more than that, perhaps ninety-nine in a hundred – occupy a tiny fraction of the sea's surface. Events that should never happen, such as meetings at sea and collisions, become regular occurrences, as we know from experience. It must be like that in diplomatic circles.'

Chiara patted her husband's knee, as one would a child's.

'It is dear, it is just like that.'

'Attend to your stroke there, Davies,' Midshipman Young growled in his best imitation of the first lieutenant.

***

Evidently Don Alonso had been advised – of course he had – of the name of the British captain with whom he was going to dine, and he greeted Carlisle and Lady Chiara warmly, striding across the floor of the governor-general's reception hall as though he and not Juan de Prado were the governor and captain-general of Cuba. Carlisle caught the flash of irritation on his host's face; it appeared that nobody had warned *him*. Now, was there something between these two men? They were of nominally equal rank, although the governorship of Guatemala couldn't be compared to that of Cuba, and perhaps there was some jealousy.

'My dear Captain Carlisle, and Lady Chiara, how charming to meet you again,' he declared loudly, speaking the excellent but accented English that Carlisle remembered, and bending low to kiss Chiara's hand, 'but you have a new ship! I have such fond memories of your frigate, *Medina*, wasn't it?'

Carlisle was about to reply, but Juan de Prado interjected, apparently in an attempt to re-impose his authority over the gathering. Yes, Carlisle was certain, there was a tension between the two governors-general. Perhaps it was always like that with men in their positions. It certainly was with admirals; it was hard to find two who could bear to be in the same room as each other. And Don Alonso's English greeting must have been calculated to put Juan de Prado at a disadvantage. Of course, there had been a tension between Don Alonso and the previous governor-general of Cuba. Even when he was dangerously wounded, Don Alonso had been insistent that they should not touch at Havana, and as he remembered it was for the fear of being – most politely – detained by the senior governor-general.

'I gather you are already acquainted. Well, it's for the best that you are not seated together, or the remainder of this company would have nothing to talk about.'

The governor-general set about introducing the other guests, although he was clearly rattled, and Don Alonso's beaming smile and his exaggerated pleasure at meeting an old friend was doing nothing to help. The governor-general's lady was present, presumably for Chiara's benefit, but otherwise it was a naval and military affair and the governor-general had dressed for the occasion in his elaborate uniform as the colony's captain-general. The captain of the Morro Castle, an anonymous brigadier-general, the flag captain to the admiral whom Carlisle had met at supper the previous evening, and two or three junior officers made up the numbers. Carlisle was expected to understand that it was a carefully selected gathering, enough men of quality to do honour to a visiting foreign officer, but not too many or of too great consequence to flatter a mere post-captain. Probably Don Alonso had invited himself as soon as he heard Carlisle's name, even before Juan de Prado had decided upon the dinner; it didn't seem at all unlikely.

Carlisle was seated between the governor-general and the brigadier, and he had to rely upon Chiara's help in maintaining a conversation. The brigadier shamelessly quizzed Carlisle about the route he took to reach Havana, and it seemed futile to deny that he had come through the Old Bahama Straits. In a moment of inspiration he described how *Dartmouth* had come close to being wrecked, without mentioning the pursuit of the French convoy. He could follow most of Chiara's translation and could only listen in admiration as she elaborated to give the impression that a ship-of-the-line would have to think twice before taking the north-about route to Havana. She did it more adroitly than Carlisle could ever have imagined, and he was convinced that she left a strong impression that the British navy felt the Old Bahama Straits was too dangerous for a battle squadron or a fleet of transport.

The governor-general had little to say once the food had been laid before them. Quite possibly he was regretting inviting Carlisle to dinner. Most certainly he regretted agreeing to Don Alonso's presence. When he looked up from his plate his eyes went directly to his fellow governor-general who appeared to be enjoying his host's discomfort. Despite sitting far away from Carlisle, he flung comments across the table freely, expounding on Carlisle's navigation skills and at one point launching into a description of the fight with the Dutch pirates where he was wounded. It was inconceivable, he knew, but Carlisle could almost believe that Don Alonso would strip his waistcoat and shirt and show the scar across his chest where a Dutch musket ball had bounced from rib to rib in a futile attempt to gain entry to his vitals.

***

Carlisle and Chiara were escorted the few yards from the palace to the wharf by the governor-general himself, and it was difficult to shake off the belief that he had done them this honour merely to prevent Don Alonso doing so. This seemed a perfectly normal end to a dinner but for one final incident. Just before the boat pushed off a young officer – a subaltern perhaps, although the Spanish rank insignia were a mystery to Carlisle – approached the boat at almost a run. He saluted smartly and handed a sealed letter to Carlisle who thrust it in his pocket to read later. He could guess who had sent it.

As the boat pulled towards *Dartmouth*, Carlisle looked back at the wharf to see the governor-general quizzing the subaltern, presumably about the author of the letter and whatever the subaltern knew of the contents. He saw the governor-general turn away and stalk back to his palace. Even over the hundred yards that now separated them, Carlisle could see that he was furious. Not for the world would Carlisle have the governor-general see him so impatient as to open that letter in the boat, and it remained firmly hidden until he reached *Dartmouth's* great cabin.

***

'Well, are you going to open it Edward? I think we can guess who sent it, and I must admit to a certain curiosity.'

Carlisle had never seen his wife so absorbed in an intrigue, for that was clearly what it was. Don Alonso must have a good reason to want to communicate with Carlisle, good enough to risk offending his host, who he must have known would see the letter being delivered. Chiara linked her arm in his so that she might read the contents at the same time as her husband. It was most uncharacteristic, but Carlisle could hardly push her away.

My dear Captain Carlisle…

The letter was evidently written in haste and it omitted the usual lengthy salutations that the Spanish found so essential.

I regret that we were separated at dinner as I did want to talk with you, to reminisce about that eventful voyage we took together. I flatter myself that you would also value the opportunity to speak of old times, and I propose to do myself the inestimable honour of visiting you in your ship at seven o'clock this evening. If this is not convenient then hoist a blue flag on a yardarm where I can easily see it from the governor-general's palace. If I see no flag I will take it that my proposed visit meets with my approval.

Perhaps you could send a boat to the wharf at the palace?

Don Alonso Fernández de Heredia, Governor and Captain-General of Guatemala.

Carlisle and Chiara looked at each other, then back at the letter.

'Well,' said Chiara, 'taken at face value it's an entirely innocent letter between old travelling companions, but I wonder what the other governor-general would have made of it, if he had seen it. I expect Don Alonso gave that officer a story to tell the governor-general, and there must have been a danger of this letter being intercepted before it reached us. Yet innocent it is not.'

Carlisle turned the paper over and held it up to the evening light that was flooding through the stern windows, as though he expected some secret script, only to be revealed by the direct rays of the sun, perhaps. There was nothing, of course. He looked troubled for a moment.

'I fear we may be stepping into a dispute that has nothing to do with us. Remember that we'll probably be at war with Spain sometime next year. I don't want to give the governor-general of Cuba any excuse to detain *Dartmouth*, not even for a few days, and I certainly don't want to do anything that hastens Spain's path to war. I suppose we must see Don Alonso. If I send the pinnace with a lieutenant – Enrico perhaps – to the wharf under the palace walls, it can hardly be construed as a secret mission. I'll have him fly an ensign, just so that there is no doubt.'

'Yes, that's probably the best thing to do. Now, he'll be here at the hour for supper. I'll speak to Walker about what we could offer.'

***

The sun had set when Don Alonso came on board, so the ceremony for greeting a foreign dignitary could safely be reduced to nothing more than a guard of marines and the ship's lieutenants and sailing master. He'd already been re-acquainted with Enrico in the boat, and he was gracious enough to remember Wishart, who was the only other officer who had followed Carlisle from *Medina* into *Dartmouth*. After introductions to Gresham and Beazley, he was escorted aft to the great cabin which had been scrubbed and polished to within an inch of its life. Even the marine sentry at the cabin door was shining. That he was standing upright went without saying, but he was unnaturally rigid, even for a marine, because his coat had been brought new from the store but an hour before and it was so stiff that it permitted only a limited range of movement.

There were just the three of them for supper. Carlisle had now become reliant upon his wife where anything beyond the normal realms of naval business was concerned, and particularly where her command of the southern languages could be used.

Walker had laid out a supper of cold meats and fruit, and a bottle of Madeira, mysteriously chilled, was waiting in a silver ice bucket.

'Ah, Madeira!' exclaimed Don Alonso. 'How well I remember that from *Medina*. We don't drink it in Spain you know, we have our wines from the region of Jerez – Sherry you call it – and they seems to fill the need for an afternoon wine or when a meal isn't in prospect.'

He took a sip from the glass that Walker offered.

'How well it tastes at the right temperature.'

They did speak about their voyage together and Chiara asked after the countess and Maria. Don Alonso answered frankly, as might have been the case among very intimate friends, but he was skilled enough in conversation to give no hint of his real mission.

After a few minutes they addressed the supper that Walker had laid out in the dining cabin. The rather too-warm cold meats were less appetising than the Madeira but the fruits were fresh from the Havana market and all-in-all they made a good companionable meal and then retired to comfortable chairs in the great cabin.

'It is good to hear about your family, Captain,' said Don Alonso after he had taken another sip of Madeira, his third or fourth glass by Carlisle's count, 'and I congratulate you on your new home in Williamsburg. A wise investment, I believe. If you can keep the French contained in the south of the continent, then land values will surely rise when the war is over. However, I didn't invite myself for the pleasure of re-acquainting us, pleasant though that has been.'

Carlisle inclined his head in a sort of low diagonal bow. It was his best non-committal gesture and he found it most useful when he wasn't sure what to say. He saw the amused look that Chiara gave him; she knew that gesture only too well.

'You will remember that the last time we met I was reluctant to be landed at Havana. Well, I was unable to avoid it this time, as the only ship that could bring me to Guatemala in the time period that my master King Carlos dictated was bound first to Havana. I had expected to be given a ship to take me on the last leg of my journey, but I've been here a week now and no King's ship has been made available. His Excellency of course has a good reason because it won't come as any surprise to you that with the uncertain state of affairs he feels the need to keep a substantial squadron here in Havana. In short, there are no ships to spare to carry a royal governor-general to his colony and I must bide here until one should become available. The alternative is to take passage in a merchantman, but that is hardly appropriate and you will remember that I have enemies at sea, even though I have heard no news of them for some years.'

'I might put your mind at ease, your Excellency. Those two ships followed us from St. Augustine but we utterly destroyed them in the Caicos Passage. The man who bore such enmity towards you is dead and will trouble you no more. His wife also perished in Jamaica.'

Don Alonso thought for a moment.

'I hadn't heard that, Captain, and I am most grateful, for myself and for my family. That sort of feud can only be resolved by the destruction of one of the parties, and I am relieved that it wasn't me. Nevertheless, I am still in want of a passage to Guatemala, and as our countries remain on friendly terms, I am hoping that I can beg a passage on your ship. If I'm not mistaken you must pass Cape San Antonio on your way home, and the shortest route to my capital at La Antigua is through the Gulf of Honduras. It will add perhaps a week to your voyage, Captain.'

Carlisle sat in stunned amazement. It was barely credible that the governor and captain-general of a Spanish colony should be begging a passage on a British man-of-war. At least he was realistic about the time it would take. It was easy enough to enter the Gulf of Honduras, but oftentimes the trade wind penetrated even that deep inlet and it could take days to beat out again. And he was sailing tomorrow, but presumably Don Alonso already knew that. What was the wording in his orders? To accede to any reasonable request of the governor-general of Cuba until he should have firm knowledge that war was imminent. Don Alonso wasn't the governor-general of Cuba, but surely his position came within the spirit of the orders. He glanced briefly at Chiara who, even though her face was composed in a friendly smile, managed to nudge him towards his decision.

'I find, your Excellency, that my own master, King George, would wish me to agree to your request.'

***

CHAPTER THIRTEEN

Don Alonso

Friday, Twenty-Fifth of December 1761.
Dartmouth, at Sea, Gulf of Honduras.

'I wish you the joy of the season, sir.'

Carlisle hadn't heard Gresham come up the ladder from the quarterdeck and just for a moment he was irritated at the intrusion. Then he caught hold of himself. He was too easily annoyed by trivial matters, and it was certainly right for the first lieutenant to greet his captain on this new day, even though the sun had not yet sprung with its customary exuberance from the eastern horizon. He turned to see Gresham's massive frame at the poop deck rail, his hat held formally over his chest, and his face showing a genuine pleasure at meeting his captain so early in the morning.

'Thank you, Mister Gresham, and my compliments to you also. I hope you're looking forward to today's feast, although I fear you'll find it somewhat cramped in the wardroom.'

'Oh, we'll manage, sir, it's only three more than our usual number, just Don Alonso's senior staff officers, except for the colonel. Mister Beazley has volunteered to stand the watch and Mister Angelini is with you. We always reckon for one of our number to be on deck, so it's only two more, in fact.'

'Ah. Then what are his other followers doing to mark the day?'

'They're feasting with the young gentlemen, and I don't doubt they'll be well entertained. I saw two creatures that bore a passing resemblance to geese being brought aboard by the purser's steward and handed over to Mister Young.'

Carlisle laughed; he'd seen them also and a generous soul could possibly call them Christmas geese, but they didn't look as though they had spent much time on the water. They were more like the wild turkeys that could be found in the forests of Virginia than anything that was raised in an English farmyard.

'Yes, and my apologies again for not being able to join you, but I feel I must entertain our guest and Colonel Arana; he ranks with a post-captain after all. The chaplain seems to go wherever Don Alonso goes, and I really do need Mister Angelini to help with the conversation. Don Alonso's English is passable while the colonel and the chaplain speak nothing but Spanish and French. It will be a dull diner without another Spanish speaker on my side. What do you think of this wind.'

'Dying, dying, sir. Mister Beazley warned us that we'd lose the trade wind once we passed Cozumel Island, and so we have. We may get a little sea breeze when the sun's up and that should suffice to take us up to the head of the Gulf.'

Carlisle looked thoughtful. Yes, the head of the Gulf, but he really had no good idea what he would find when he arrived there. There was a town and a port of sorts in a shallow bay – the Gulf of Amatique – but Beazley's only chart was unpromising, showing an anchorage with nine or ten fathoms some five miles from the port, and no real detail. That was deep enough for *Dartmouth*, but there was no indication of when it was surveyed or by whom. It could be just second-hand information from a man who'd spoken to someone who might have visited there in a jolly boat.

Carlisle waved his arm over to starboard, where the blackness was just starting to be relieved by the first loom of the rising sun.

'There are British settlements over to the west, once we get deeper into the Gulf. They're logwood cutters and suchlike; I wonder whether we'll see anything of them.'

'Aye, sir. We rescued a boat load of them in the last war. They were fleeing a Spanish attack and were trying to make Jamaica in a leaky, overloaded canoe type of affair.'

He continued in a lowered voice, conscious that Don Alonso was in the great cabin below their feet.

'The Dons fairly well cleared them all out, but as I understand it they've never bothered to settle the area themselves, and the loggers all went back after the peace.'

Carlisle nodded. It was just part of the diplomatic puzzle that he was attempting to understand. There had been temporary British settlements on that coast for a hundred years, pirates to start with, who preyed upon the Spanish trade to Vera Cruz, and the Spanish logwood cutters. The infamous Blackbeard started his career in that business, before he moved to richer pastures in the Carolinas. After the pirates had been suppressed, the remaining British settlers turned to cutting their own logwood and later on, when the fashion for brown furniture swept Britain and her colonies, they turned to the huge mahogany trees. Now there was a more-or-less permanent settlement on St. George's Cay, and it traded happily with Jamaica and had even set up its own magistracy and followed British common law. Britain laid no claim to the territory, but did insist upon the settlers' right to the logwood and the mahogany.

'We'll see what we'll see, Mister Gresham, but meanwhile you may have to get the stuns'ls in with this wind veering so.'

Carlisle leaned on the hammock cranes, gazing out to the west. Had he overstepped the mark in agreeing to take Don Alonso into this awkward corner of the Caribbean? He remembered what the flag captain in Jamaica had said, apparently repeating Admiral Holmes' advice before he died. Until war was declared with Spain it was best to be as obliging as possible, in case there was a chance of keeping them out of the war. Sir Henry at Jamaica had said something similar although it was naturally not phrased as an order. And the flag captain had told Carlisle to use his best judgement, and to accede to any reasonable requests of the governor-general at Havana. Well, Juan de Prado hadn't exactly asked Carlisle to carry Don Alonso and his suite, in fact he had looked askance at the idea, but he hadn't forbidden it. The tension between the two Spanish governors-general coloured all their dealings with each other, and it was difficult for an outsider to steer a path between the warring factions. Perhaps that was only natural, but he wasn't aware of such a constraint within the British colonies. He'd agreed, but he'd limited Don Alonso's party to his immediate staff officers and servants and the chaplain. He wouldn't have any of the rank-and-file soldiers that had come from Spain with Don Alonso, and the Spaniard had agreed with a smile of understanding. Both men knew that their countries could be at war with each other at any moment, and Carlisle didn't want a score of well-armed Spaniards on his deck if they should hear of it before they reached their destination.

***

The Christmas feast was enjoyed in the scorching heat of an almost-windless afternoon just nineteen degrees north of the line. The purser had done better than just fresh fruit and vegetables in the Havana market. He'd bought a young hog that had been roasted on the galley range for the captain and the wardroom, and an assortment of smaller fowl that had been variously roasted and baked. Together with the turtle soup and the vegetables, it made a fine spread and Don Alonso, Colonel Arana and the chaplain clearly enjoyed the meal. Chiara excused herself after the fruit had been served, and the chaplain followed close on her heels, leaving Carlisle, Enrico, Don Alonso and the colonel.

'May I ask, your Excellency, how you will make your way to La Antigua?'

'Well may you ask, Captain,' Don Alonso replied with a laugh. 'Now, I have never been to this coast nor to my capital, although Colonel Arana and two of my staff officers have, so things may not turn out in the way that I expect. In fact, Colonel Arana is almost a native of Guatemala and this visit to Spain was only his second, is that not so?'

Arana had said little throughout the meal but now, when talk had turned to a subject with which he was confident, he became positively eloquent and Carlisle had difficulty in keeping up with the rapid flow of words in a strangely accented Spanish.

'I was born at La Antigua, Señor, and I love the country. It could be the jewel in the Spanish crown if only we could secure its borders and exploit its resources without interference…'

Now, was that a warning glance from Don Alonso? Carlisle thought it might have been but what it meant was difficult to say. Chiara had noticed that the colonel had been drinking heavily and Carlisle suspected that she'd withdrawn before it became embarrassing. Probably Don Alonso was just attempting to prevent the colonel becoming too loquacious, but could it be something else?

Colonel Arana looked from Don Alonso to Carlisle and lapsed into a sullen silence. Don Alonso stepped in as though nothing had happened.

'The great thing, as I understand it, is to travel as far as possible by water before taking to the road. Do you have that chart that you showed me yesterday?'

At a nod from Carlisle, Enrico bowed and walked forward to the master's cabin where he knew that Beazley would have left the chart.

'Ah, thank you, Mister Angelini. You see this small dot, that's a little port where the Rio Dulce meets Amatique Bay, Punta Cacolla it's called. Its sole purpose is to be a stage on the route from La Antigua to the ocean. There is a shallow bar where the river meets the bay, so there is no question of *Dartmouth* proceeding any further, and I regret that we will have to part company at last. A few boats are kept there for just such a need as this, and they can carry me the seven leagues to the Castillo San Felipe. From there I can take a reasonably sized vessel across the lake and then there is a good road to La Antigua.'

Carlisle studied the chart as Don Alonso was speaking. Evidently this was the most frequented route from the colony's capital to the sea, and it was to be expected that there would be facilities for transporting a new governor-general.

'Do your officers have any better information on the depths of water in the bay, your Excellency?'

Don Alonso grimaced the laughed. He glanced again at the colonel who showed no signs of helping his governor-general. It occurred to Carlisle that the colonel was playing a dangerous game. Don Alonso was the King's direct representative in Guatemala and he could no doubt break a mere colonel with the stroke of a pen. But perhaps it was just the wine and the brandy. He'd noticed that Walker had filled up Arana's glass at the rate of twice or three times for every glass that Don Alonso took.

'You are asking too much of plain soldiers, Captain, but I assume you know how to deal with such matters.'

Carlisle did indeed. It would cost them a day, but he wouldn't cross the twenty-fathom line without sending the longboat ahead with Beazley to take soundings, and he'd have all his boats in the water to manoeuvre the great two-decker out of trouble if the wind should fail or if they should find themselves on a lee shore. He was grateful at that moment that they hadn't been forced to leave an anchor behind in the Old Bahama Straits.

'I'll need to send a boat ahead to find an anchorage, but I hope that I'll be able to carry you to within a few miles of that port.'

'Splendid. Now, the sight of your fine ship might alarm some of my people, so I think it would be advisable to send a boat into Punta Cacolla before you enter the bay. Is that possible?'

Carlisle thought for a moment. He was short of a boat but the pinnace was of little use as a work boat; it was too light and its timbers were too frail. He could afford to send it away – he stretched his fingers across the chart, twelve miles – and still have enough boats for his needs. But was that entirely wise? It was just possible that war had been declared by either Britain or Spain, and – stretching the probability as far as it would go – the word could have already reached Guatemala. In that case could he be sailing into a trap? He glanced at his guests; Colonel Arana stared doggedly at the table, evidently still smarting from his master's implied rebuke. Don Alonso, however, looked directly at his host with a hint of a smile playing across his face. Carlisle had the uncomfortable feeling that his thoughts were being read, that Don Alonso understood his motives and that he was thinking one step ahead. Oh, to hell with it! He'd come this far and might as well carry his convictions all the way to the coast of Guatemala. If Don Alonso thought to play him false, it was hard to see what force could be arrayed against a two-decked man-of-war in this out-of-the-way corner of the Spanish Empire. And he was as certain as he could be that no hint of war had come to Havana when he left two days ago, so it was hardly likely to have come to Punta Cacolla. If there should be word of war, then it was Don Alonso who was in danger, not Captain Carlisle or His Britannic Majesty's Ship *Dartmouth*!

Don Alonso was studying the chart as though he was seeing it afresh.

'Captain Carlisle, do you know this coast at all? I mean the part of the Yucatan Peninsula that we are passing now.'

Carlisle looked again at the chart and shook his head. Don Alonso's finger was hovering over a tiny island – a *cay* in the language of these parts – that was boldly labelled *St. George's Cay (British)*. It was conspicuous as the only English place name on the whole coast, all the rest were a mixture of Spanish and the obscure language of the native Indians. It was the only chart of the coast that Beazley could produce and the Cheapside printer must have copied it from a Spanish chart, merely adding the sole British place name that he knew of. Don Alonso was looking thoughtful as though he was planning his next move. Could this little island, the refuge for the English-speaking loggers on this coast, have been discussed in Madrid? All that Carlisle knew was that the coast wasn't formally claimed by any country.

Spain had decided that there was no value in owning it and Britain, while encouraging the settlers, had also rejected the idea of claiming it for the Crown. He was vaguely aware that Spain had tried to evict the settlers in the earlier wars of the century, but he wasn't aware of any settled British policy or any commitment to defend it. Arana looked interested, and he leaned across to study the chart, his eyes greedily taking in the details.

Once again, it seemed that Don Alonso was reading Carlisle's mind, and finding no answer, he elaborated on the original question.

'It's a strange anomaly, don't you think. Captain?'

Now here was the great chasm that separated a governor and captain-general of a Spanish province and a post-captain in command of a man-of-war. Don Alonso could speak easily about territorial anomalies. He was secure in the patent that had been issued by his King, giving him wide powers over how he governed, powers that were deliberately vague about the actual extent of the territory. His performance would be judged on greater matters than the fate of a little-known and economically insignificant stretch of coast, fenced in by dangerous reefs and an inhospitable hinterland. Carlisle was all too aware that he had nothing like that freedom of action. An incautious word regarding King George's interest or otherwise in this area could find him without a ship and doomed to half pay for the rest of his life. A little devil on his shoulder chuckled and just for a moment that prospect didn't sound so bad. Nevertheless, he must take care not to imply any British interest in the Yucatan, nor to imply that Britain had *no* interest.

'I regret that I know nothing of this coast, your Excellency, beyond the bare fact that there is an English-speaking settlement on that island.'

Don Alonso smiled in his enigmatic way.

'You'll make a diplomat yet, Captain Carlisle. I'm told that there are a few hundred of your countrymen – I beg your pardon, I know you call Virginia your home – a few hundred *Englishmen* who cut logwood and butcher cattle on that coast. That, I regret to say, is all I know. No doubt I'll be told my policy when I reach La Antigua. Do you know the English expression *a monkey on one's back*? Well, you have your monkeys in the form of admirals and senior captains, and I also have a King and his ministers to make my life difficult. However, I also have much subtler monkeys, and they claw at my back every day, not just when letters arrive from Madrid or Havana. My political advisors, chamberlains, generals, regional governors, city mayors all believe they know better than I, and they presume to instruct me and cajole me without mercy. You can be sure that one of these feels that the Yucatan coast is of utmost importance and I will have to waste an hour listening to him and then another half an hour telling him – in the politest possible way – that he is misguided and that he should return to whatever occupies him during the working day. Like you, I have no policy on this coast and will have none until one is forced upon me. Your occupation and mine are not so dissimilar Captain.'

Carlisle returned Don Alonso's gaze then turned his eyes to Colonel Arana who was still studying the chart as though to commit to memory what the British thought was important on the Yucatan coast. Carlisle could see that Arana didn't share the governor-general's view of this coast; he didn't think it insignificant at all.

***

Carlisle was glad to be clear of Amatique Bay. Oh, it had all turned out well, he had to admit, and there was no trap and no difficulty with Don Alonso's travel arrangements. The Spanish had been using this route for over two hundred years, and governors-general had come and gone, using the very same road that Don Alonso had to take. Perhaps that accounted for Colonel Arana's attitude. He called Guatemala home and he probably resented the long succession of Madrid appointees, each of whom brought his own ideas, stayed a few years without achieving anything noteworthy, then left with a good proportion of the country's wealth in the hold of his ship.

In fact, from the moment that the pinnace shot away from *Dartmouth*, spreading its sail to the quartering breeze with Colonel Arana on board, the whole affair had run remarkably smoothly, and Carlisle thought he could congratulate himself on a fine piece of diplomacy. If only he could get out of his mind that look on Colonel Arana's face as he studied the chart of Yucatan, and if only he hadn't seen the way he stabbed his finger at the dot that represented St. George's Cay, as though he would scrub it out of existence.

By the time that the two-decker rounded Cabo Tres Puntas – The Cape of Three Headlands – the pinnace was rowing back towards them having deposited the colonel at Punta Cacolla where he was presumably making arrangements for his master's reception.

Beazley had found a fine anchorage in six fathoms just a league off the little port, and Don Alonso had been rowed ashore with *Dartmouth's* gun salute raising flocks of seabirds from the shallows. And that was the end of that short interlude. Beazley was keen to take advantage of the evening's land breeze, and Carlisle felt that it wasn't right to linger in this enclosed bay, not with the winds of war blowing this way from Europe, so *Dartmouth* weighed anchor after a bare few hours and reached out into the Gulf of Honduras.

***

CHAPTER FOURTEEN

Logwood and Mahogany

Monday, Twenty-Eighth of December 1761.
Dartmouth, at Sea, Gulf of Honduras.

Carlisle was enjoying breakfast with his wife when he heard a hail from the masthead. He ignored it; he didn't want to interrupt his meal so he waited for the midshipman to make his report.

'Beg your pardon, sir, your Ladyship,' the midshipman said, bowing low to Chiara, 'Mister Wishart sends his respects and there's a sail in sight four points on the larboard bow, making towards us. It looks like a little sloop, sir.'

'Very well. My compliments to Mister Wishart and I'll be on deck presently, but he's to call me when the vessel is within hailing distance.'

It was amazing how only a few days of having a guest in the cabin spoiled the harmonious routine of life. Don Alonso had been the perfect company, polite, cultured and willing to be friendly, and they had come to an understanding, to a friendship even, and if it were ever possible that the two should meet again, they would do so in perfect amity. But for all that he'd been an intruder, and Carlisle had been unable to relax in his presence, and now he was unwilling to have his breakfast disturbed even for the unusual sight of a sail apparently heading towards them. In these waters, in peace or conflict, wise vessels stayed well clear of men-of-war, at least until they were sure of the nationality.

'You appear remarkably sanguine about this vessel, Edward, there is none of your usual mad desire to know who, what, where bound?'

Chiara was making her best imitation of a quarterdeck British accent. She had long thought the ship's officers too excitable and for herself she would be quite content to await the turn of events.

'Ah, well, we passed the Four Cays reef in the night and now we have leagues and leagues of deep water to leeward. The vessel can hardly be French, not here and not boldly approaching a two-decked man-o'-war, even if they mistake our nationality. Spanish? I think not, for much the same reason. However, St. George's Cay is some fifteen leagues to the west and it's odds-on that they're British. If they wish to speak, then they have only to hold their course. Wishart will tell me if we start to head-reach upon them.'

Chiara buttered a piece of bread which while it was not exactly soft, neither was it hard like ship's biscuit. Oh, how she longed for the bakeries and patisseries of her childhood, for the fresh, hard-shelled baguettes and the dainty, sugary, gaily-coloured confections. She searched through her memory for the meaning of *head-reach* and decided that it must refer to one vessel overtaking another. Perhaps it was more specific than that but the essence of the phrase seemed about right.

'Do you know, you sea officers amaze me. You have deduced so much from a simple report. I can hardly make out which side of the ship this vessel is approaching from and you have already determined its nationality and intentions. No doubt you have determined why it is so intent on speaking with us.'

'Ah, now that I don't know, but I will, soon enough.'

***

Carlisle and Chiara walked onto the quarterdeck in time to see the vessel round-to on *Dartmouth's* larboard quarter. It was a trading sloop, a single-masted cutter-rigged craft of the sort that hauled the produce of this coast to the markets in Jamaica. Logwood was the main produce, used as a basis for dyes in the English woollen industry, but mahogany was approaching parity in value. However, this sloop was in ballast and her gunwales rode high above the sluggish waves.

Wishart stood on the hammock cranes, grasping the

main shrouds, and raised the speaking trumpet.

'What ship, where bound?'

The man who replied was dressed in an open shirt and breeches without stockings, and though he wore a good tricorn hat his feet were bare. A blue-and-red striped sash was wrapped around his waist and from it protruded the worn, brown butts of a pair of pistols. Carlisle was disappointed to see that there was no great curved cutlass twinkling in the morning sun. He spoke English, but of a quality that hadn't been heard in Britain for a hundred years. All-in-all he looked like the penny prints of wild buccaneers that could be bought in any English town, and his voice sounded like a call from a different age.

'Sloop *Daisy*. From St. George's Island and come to sea begging a word with your captain.'

Carlisle and Chiara exchanged amused glances; she was evidently enjoying this exotic encounter. Just yesterday evening Chiara had opened a box of watercolours that she'd bought in Kingston – it had been her first opportunity clear of gales, reefs and guests, since they had left Jamaica – and Carlisle could tell that she was sizing up this strange person as a subject for her first essay into painting.

'Tell him he may send a boat, Mister Wishart, then heave-to on the larboard tack, if you please.'

Wishart had barely started his message when the sloop's captain cut him short.

'Never you mind a boat, sir, I'll just put the sloop alongside and jump aboard.'

Carlisle held up his hand to Wishart.

'Belay heaving-to. Let's see how he does this.'

Dartmouth was making perhaps three knots with the wind a point ahead of the beam. This sloop-master clearly knew his business and he dropped astern to get a clean wind in his sails. Then, with two-or-three knots advantage over the two-decker, he shot up onto *Dartmouth's* beam. His sails slatted in the great ship's shadow and he put the sloop alongside the main chains as neatly as could be. Two of his crew were ready to fend off but it wasn't necessary, and the master jumped easily onto *Dartmouth's* side ladder and ran up it as agile as a monkey, leaving his sloop to sheer away and drop back handily into *Dartmouth's* lee quarter.

Beazley looked disgusted.

'There's been more good men lost at sea from those greasy side ladders than, than…'

'…than useful predictions from the weather-glass?' Wishart added helpfully.

The sailing master ignored the comment and turned to study the compass. The midshipman winked, and the boy who stood ready for messages laughed incontinently, earning himself a cuff from the quartermaster.

'Francis Hookway,' the piratical apparition announced to the world at large as he alighted on the gangway above the waist, 'master of the *Daisy* and elected magistrate of St. George's Island.'

And with that and forgoing any invitation, he strode aft to the quarterdeck before anyone could prevent him. He was clearly familiar with men-of-war and Carlisle briefly wondered whether he'd seen service in the King's navy.

'At your service, your Honour.'

Hookway extended a leg, bowed low on one knee and removed his hat with a flourish, looking sideways at Chiara and evidently unsure how to address her.

Carlisle returned his bow in a more conventional manner and suppressed a smile at the strangely archaic address. He was aware of two hundred pairs of eyes watching this odd encounter, many openly grinning. It didn't accord with the dignity of a King's ship, but then in this odd corner of the oceans, who knew what passed for dignity?

'Captain Edward Carlisle of His Britannic Majesty's Ship *Dartmouth*, and this is Lady Chiara Carlisle. Would you step into the cabin, Mister Hookway?'

***

Francis Hookway would certainly take a glass of Madeira, even at this early hour, and he evidently didn't think that Chiara's presence should inhibit him. He tossed it off in one go and looked around expectantly for the second glass.

'Well, Mister Hookway, what do you have to tell me?'

'It's the Dons, your Honour, they're on the move, just like they were in the last war. They grasp every opportunity to take away our land and our livelihood, but it's gotten worse these last few months. We lost two good men last week, and we don't know whether they were killed or taken, but it makes little difference once they are in Spanish hands. I was hoping you could tell me, are we at war again? I heard rumours of it when I was in Kingston last month, but nothing definite. Fact is, sir, if they're coming again we'll have to pull our loggers off the mainland and back to the Island, like we did in the last war. We call it St. George's *Island*, sir, not *Cay*, Island being the English word. In any case, I'd rather bring the men back before we lose any more.'

Carlisle studied the man before him. He had seen his mode of dress before he came aboard, but now he had a chance to study the man himself. He was of middling height and powerfully built, as you would expect of one who earned his bread by felling trees deep in the forest then hauling them to the shore. His skin was burned dark by the sun, as dark as any of the *Dartmouths,* and his hair was light brown and tied roughly in a queue with a piece of black ribbon. In all, he was an unremarkable specimen for one who clung to the precarious trade of a Honduras logger. Yes, quite ordinary, except for his eye, for he had only one and that was of the brightest blue that Carlisle had ever seen. The left eye was covered by a leather patch and below the patch an ugly scar, long healed, ran slantwise to the hinge of his jaw, just below the ear.

Hookway was evidently used to being studied because he gave no indication that he either welcomed or resented the inspection. He stood impassively, awaiting Carlisle's reply.

'That may be a long answer, Mister Hookway, but before we get to that, I'm intrigued. How did you know that my ship would be passing this way today? We're too far off for you to have seen us, and I find it hard to believe that this is a chance meeting.'

Hookway smiled for the first time since he came on board, and with the smile his left ear rotated forward as it was pulled by his scar. It would be a fine party trick to amuse the children and it didn't seem to worry Hookway at all.

'Aye, you're right there, sir, and I know a lot more about you than you may imagine. My people have been on this coast for over a hundred years, generation after generation, and we've made our peace with the local Indians. We live in harmony, most of the time, and we have a common cause against the Dons, so we work together more than you might imagine. We've learned to watch the movement of those Spaniards up at Amatique Bay as a sort of bellwether, an indication of trouble ahead. We keep a lookout up that way, normally with a fast pirogue with one of our men and an Indian or two, and I hear what goes on almost before it's happened. I know that you carried the new Spanish governor-general and a few of his people from Havana and I know that he is making for his capital at La Antigua; the Indians found that from their kin in the town. And I know that devil Arana was with the governor-general. We were lucky and there were two pirogues there, changing the watch you might say, so one of them brought the news as soon as you arrived, and the second brought the details as soon as you had weighed. I heard all this yesterday evening and also that you were making your way back down the Gulf. Now, don't take this wrong, but any of our pirogues can make double the speed that this ship can make, and even more in these light airs, and they can take a passage inside the reefs.

I thought that you might be able to tell us what's afoot, so I jumped into the sloop hoping to meet you, and here I am.'

Carlisle smiled outright at that explanation. They'd seen a number of native craft in the bay, some fishing and others going about whatever business was to be done in such a backward part of the world. One or two of them could indeed have belonged to the loggers and Carlisle had to admit that they could certainly move faster than *Dartmouth* in these difficult waters, and by taking a route inside the reefs that fringed the shore they could steal a march on the cumbersome two-decker. Hookway's account was certainly plausible and his question was an obvious one, but there was another question that he wasn't asking, perhaps through politeness. What was a British man-of-war doing delivering a Spanish governor-general to his new domain? Carlisle turned away to look through the stern windows for a moment, marshalling his thoughts. Wishart had sensibly reduced sail while the logger was aboard and *Dartmouth's* great bulk barely disturbed the brilliant blue of the sea. For once, there was no noise of waves smashing against the hull and almost nothing from the wind. It was a peaceful vista and the longboat towing astern and the sloop keeping pace on the lee quarter added focal points to the composition.

'War with Spain? I wish I could tell you, Mister Hookway. The last that I heard we were at peace and the King and Parliament were hoping to keep it that way, but the Spanish King could have thrown his lot in with the French two months ago and we wouldn't have heard. That's why I've been so obliging to the new governor-general – Don Alonso is his name, by the way – and agreed to carry him from Havana. But you mentioned Colonel Arana; you know him?'

Hookway touched his scar. It was an unconscious action that was so closely linked to the mention of Colonel Arana that it must be connected.

'I was wondering at that. It's been many years since a King's ship came this way, and to see you apparently in league with the Dons has rattled some of the people over there…'

He jerked his head to leeward, towards the Honduras coast.

'…but Arana! Yes, I know him. Everyone on this coast knows the name although few have as good a cause as me. He was a captain in the last war and he led the raid into our territory. He burned our camps and marched our people – those that he hadn't killed – down to Punta Cacolla and shipped us like cattle off to Jamaica. Then he burned St. George's. I understand that these things happen in a war but the damned Dons didn't even settle the coast themselves. After they cleared us out they just marched back from where they came. I was nothin' but a youngster but I got this – he touched his scar again – when I wouldn't stand aside to let them burn our hut. We thought our troubles were over when Arana was sent back to Old Spain; it's a shock to see him here again.'

Carlisle studied Hookway afresh. He was a phlegmatic man but talk of Colonel Arana had animated him. Whatever Arana had done twenty years before, he was a senior officer now and an aide to the governor-general. Presumably he was above raiding logging camps and settler towns. Yet, Carlisle had seen the way Arana had unconsciously tried to erase St. George's Cay from the chart, spurred on by strong drink. He was disturbed, but it was none of his business and he had to remember that Britain and Spain were still at peace, and unlikely though it sounded, could be at peace for a good number of years yet.

'I understand, and you may wish to tell them that it's necessary sometimes to do things that you wouldn't expect to do, to hold off the evils of war by a few months.'

The logger had been listening keenly and he caught that reference to a few months.

'Do you, then, believe that war is inevitable, sir?'

Carlisle again gazed out of the window. Was war inevitable? It was hard to be certain and how much should he tell this man of whom he knew nothing beyond the bare facts that he'd volunteered. Yet, there was something essentially honest about him and, after all, the loggers of the coast were mainly British, even if the Yucatan peninsula wasn't claimed as a colony.

'The French are having a bad time of it at sea and their colonies are suffering. They need more men-o'-war and even the French shipyards can't keep pace with the rate that they are being taken or destroyed. They have one untapped source, and that's the Spanish navy. Now, King Charles and King Louis are cousins and there is a history of family pacts in time of war. It's certain that Louis is putting pressure on Charles to join this war, but how much is he being heeded? I don't know the answer to that. It's a rather long-winded way of saying that your guess is as good as mine. The only man in this parts who may know more is Don Alonso. He was in Madrid only a few months ago, and would have heard rumours even if he wasn't explicitly briefed on the matter; but if he knew, he was saying nothing to me.'

Hookway looked thoughtful, as though he were coming to a decision.

'Well, if the Don's come we can expect no help from King George on this coast, and there's nothing new in that. I guess you're bound for Jamaica then, sir.'

'Jamaica, yes, Mister Hookway, to await events, just as you are doing.'

'Then you may want to know that another of our sloops saw a Frenchman making for the Yucatan Channel, or so it seemed. A merchant brig or snow, but her main topmasts had gone at the maintop and her foremast was jury-rigged. It looked like she'd been in a bit of a blow. In any case they were making hard work of it and I don't expect they're very far along their way by now. It's a crying shame that your admiralty court in Jamaica won't issue letters of marque to our sloops; that would have been a nice prize to take back to Kingston. Although, it seems like a strange place for a French merchantman, don't you think, sir?'

Carlisle did think it strange. To be in that position a French merchantman must have run the gauntlet of all the Windward and Leeward Islands – many of them held by Britain now – and Jamaica. Very strange indeed, unless…

'Where exactly was she seen, Mister Hookway?'

'Just to the east of that old shoal maybe thirty leagues west-sou'west of Grand Cayman, and struggling to stay to windward of it. There's no danger of grounding on the shoal, the least depth we've found is six fathom, but it does kick up a nasty sea and we avoid it. Perhaps you wouldn't even notice it in this grand ship.'

Hookway smiled again and his ear performed its rotation.

'And steering nor'west, you say?'

'Aye, sir. Nor'west for the Yucatan Channel but she weren't making more than three knots even with the wind on her quarter. And the funny thing was that when she was first sighted she was on the larboard tack, as hard on the wind as she could be with no topmasts, as though she was trying to beat up to the coast of Cuba, or maybe making for the Windward Passage. When she saw the sloop she bore away.'

'How did the master of the sloop know that she was French?'

Few ships flew their national ensigns at sea, they were just too expensive to expose to that unrelenting wear and tear.

'They spoke. The French master wouldn't give away anything useful and he probably feared that our sloop was a privateer. But it was obvious that he was French, from his dress and his speech. When last seen she was still sailing large.'

Carlisle realised that he was staring at Hookway. How he would love to have spoken to that anonymous sloop captain! There were all sorts of indications that may have given away the brig's intentions: was she in ballast? Was her bottom fouled? What was the state of her paintwork? But that opportunity had passed. Perhaps he was drawing too many conclusions on scant information but the presence of a French merchant brig in these waters was remarkable enough to stir the imagination. The French were so short of merchantmen that none could be spared for trading with the Spanish colonies. The only place that Carlisle could imagine as this ship's destination was Louisiana at the top of the Gulf of Mexico. Yet it beggared belief that any French ship – man-of-war or merchantman – would have sailed the breadth of the Caribbean Sea alone. The British navy would have dealt with the former and there were swarms of privateers in every port in the British islands that would have fallen upon a lone merchantman. Yet there was a reason for this strange sighting; the missing main topmast was just too much of a coincidence and the foremast could have been lost in the later blow, after that French convoy had passed through the Old Bahama Straits.

***

CHAPTER FIFTEEN

The Sergeant of Artillery

Wednesday, Thirtieth of December 1761.
Dartmouth, at Sea, the Yucatan Channel.

'What do you think, Arthur, will we find our lame brig?'

Gresham and Beazley were walking together on the poop deck, taking advantage of the last few minutes before the captain came on deck. The sun was just lightening the sky and the decks were already being swabbed around them.

Beazley pulled a long face and stepped around a pool of water that hadn't yet been flogged dry.

'It doesn't seem to add up. It would have taken rank incompetence for that Frenchman to have been blown all the way past Cape San Antonio. I can see that he might have tried to beat for the windward passage, having found himself where he was, but to think that he could pass Jamaica without being noticed, now that's a real stretch. No, Matthew, in my opinion this is a different brig altogether, and I suspect that sloop surprised her when she was trying to sort out her rig, and mistook it for an attempt to beat to windward. Probably the brig took fright at the sight of the sloop and bore away without staying to finish her repairs.'

'Then a fool's errand, you believe?'

'Oh, no, not at all. Unless the captain was deceived by that man Hookway, there's a French merchantman making very slow progress back into the Gulf. Whether he's making for Louisiana or taking the Florida straits for home, we stand a good chance of catching him.'

They walked on for a few steps. Even before the sun hit the decks they were shrouded in vapour as the last of the water was carried away by the growing warmth, leaving the planking looking fresh and clean.

'I agree with you, Arthur. That can hardly be our brig from the Old Bahama Straits. Here's my hypothesis…'

Beazley gave a short bark of a laugh. Hypothesis? Such a long word. He wasn't aware that the first lieutenant knew its meaning. Gresham ignored him. Over this long commission he'd become used to the sailing master's assumption of intellectual superiority.

'What the sloop saw was a French brig that had attempted the Florida Straits alone, but was beaten back by that gale. Probably that was when she lost her topmasts and she'd scudded with the wind until it dropped, when she found herself almost as far east as the Caymans. It makes sense that she'd only have enough spares for one new topmast. She's running back to the Gulf either to return to Louisiana to refit or to find a calm patch to make a better job of jury rigging her masts. Then she'll make for the straits and home. In either case and with luck – he touched the smooth wood of the poop deck rail – we'll have her!'

Beazley scratched his head and looked to windward.

'The North Atlantic in January with jury-rigged foremast and no main topmast, now that's a bold proposition. But be that as it may, it looks like the trade wind has remembered its duty even though it has chosen to veer a couple of points to the easterly, and my weather-glass is steady, neither rising nor falling. If she's still at sea I reckon you're right, and we'll have a prize today.'

He looked up at the t'gallants, the tops'ls and the courses all pulling away lustily with the wind nigh on a point abaft the beam.

'Now, will she take stuns'ls, do you think?'

***

Dartmouth bowled on with stuns'ls aloft and alow and sighted the brig at four bells in the afternoon watch. By the end of the first dog they had forced the chase to heave to by their sheer physical presence, not a gun had been needed, and with plenty of daylight left to transfer the French crew. They looked dejected and barely acknowledged the four of their fellows – the men of indeterminate nationality that were to be found in every ship, even in wartime – who chose to take the bounty and become sailors of King George. On the whole, it was a good choice; better than being incarcerated in *Dartmouth's* hold on short rations and perhaps ending up in a prison hulk, waiting for the war to end or for their name to come up on a prisoner exchange.

'The brig *Petite Marie*, sir. She's not the one we saw in the Old Bahama Straits; this one sailed from Mobile Bay three days ago and was bound direct for her home in Lorient. Half a cargo of furs belonging to a syndicate and the master has made up the space with timber on his own account. Fifteen crew, four have volunteered, and the master is waiting in the waist, sir…'

Carlisle was watching the sad procession as Wishart spoke. Each man carried his possessions in a bag – no sea chests were allowed – and the captain could easily be distinguished as he constantly edged away to distance himself from the crew. A ship's corporal had already taken charge of the volunteers and was leading them away. But there was one man who looked different to the rest, and as Carlisle looked closer he could see what looked like the ragged remnants of a blue uniform coat, although it was so patched and grubby and faded that its colour hardly showed at all.

'…and there's a British soldier sir, a prisoner they were taking to France. He says he's a sergeant of artillery and he certainly speaks English well enough. I've told Mister Pontneuf; perhaps he can find a use for him.'

Carlisle watched for a few more moments. They all had that resigned look of men who expected little else in life, and truth to tell, once they found themselves the wrong side of Cape San Antonio it was more likely that they would be captured than that they'd find their way back to the Brittany coast. The four volunteers looked no different to the others and their apprehension was written on their faces. Only the sergeant looked hopeful, casting eager glances around at the unfamiliar sights, and grinning feebly at the jests that were flung at him by *Dartmouth's* crew.

'My compliments to Mister Pontneuf and he's to see to the sergeant's comforts. I'll want to interview him as soon as I've spoken to the brig's master, say in thirty minutes. Send the master to my dining cabin, if you please, and pass the word for Mister Simmonds; ah here he is.'

***

The brig's master looked nervous but still he showed a touch of spirit. Probably he'd been captured before; he certainly looked old enough to have been at sea in the last war. For that matter, he could have been captured and exchanged a number of times in this war, such was the speed of the trade in captured merchant seaman. Neither Britain nor France wanted to feed useless mouths and it was in everyone's interest to exchange prisoners as promptly as possible. He bowed as he entered the dining cabin.

'Captain Duboeuf, sir, master of the brig *Petite Marie*, or I was until an hour ago.'

Carlisle studied Duboeuf while the Frenchman stood awkwardly with his cap in his hands. The accent sounded right and the man could certainly come from Brittany or thereabouts. And he looked as though he was familiar with a ship-of-the line. Living so close to Brest it was likely that he had at least some experience in King Louis' navy, probably he'd been a bosun or one of the lesser warrant officers. And he must be a determined man. Not only was he planning to sail boldly past the British colonies in America, but he was ready to brave the North Atlantic in winter and to take his chance slipping past the blockading squadrons that were now based at Belle Isle, just ten leagues from Lorient. He must have known that it was a desperate gamble, and he must surely have reckoned his chances of bringing his cargo back to France at no better than even.

'Captain Carlisle of His Britannic Majesty's Ship *Dartmouth*. Please take a seat Monsieur Duboeuf, and would you care for a cup of coffee?'

He was an easy man to talk to and he certainly understood the relationship between captor and captured, as it pertained to prizes in time of war. Carlisle had it in his power to make the man's time in *Dartmouth* and in his longer-term incarceration either easy or difficult. He could spend this period of enforced leisure in a screened-off area near the bosun's cabin and mess with the warrant officers or he could join his crew in the hold on two-thirds rations. He could have all his personal possessions brought over or they could stay in the prize to be condemned with the hull, the sails and the cargo. His decision: and he chose his comfort over any sense of patriotism.

'There's a good cargo of furs, sir. They come down the Ohio and the Mississippi now that they can't be shipped out through Quebec, and the timber will fetch something, if only for firewood.'

'Why only a half cargo of furs?'

Carlisle wanted the man to get used to talking before he asked him anything important.

Duboeuf shrugged.

'It's all that was available, sir, and another convoy was due to arrive in Mobile from France at any day, and then there would be no chance of filling my hold. Half a cargo now is better than half a cargo next month.'

Carlisle nodded sympathetically. That inbound convoy that he had expected must have been the same one that *Dartmouth* chased in the Old Bahama Straits.

'Why, may I ask, did you not wait for a homebound convoy? Surely you didn't expect to reach the coast of France without a chase.'

Duboeuf made a deep sound in his chest which could have been a laugh.

'A convoy for France, sir? I haven't seen such a thing this past two years and my owners won't have me waiting for months for a frigate that may never arrive. There won't be a King's ship leaving the Gulf for half a year; they're all bound for Mobile Bay and show no signs of leaving. There'll be no escorts and consequently no convoys from Mobile, sir, and the insurance rates are pegged accordingly. If I could have made a fast passage home I could have brought a company of soldiers back next time, with a regular navy convoy and the King to cover the insurance.'

Now this was interesting. A concentration of soldiers on the Gulf Coast could mean one of two things: either the French were determined to hold the only convenient means of access to the vast territories of Louisiana, or they were planning an expedition up the waterways into the interior to block any further British conquests across the Ohio and into the Mississippi basin. Carlisle knew that there were still large numbers of Frenchmen west of the Ohio and the British colonies were poised to move into these new territories. If the French could hold their ground until the war's end and the peace negotiations, they could yet retain territory in North America. It was unlikely that the French were planning anything offensive against Montreal, which had been in British hands for six months now, but it was reasonable to assume that they wanted to solidify their position to the west. Certainly, there was no hope for French Louisiana if they lost the Gulf ports, principally New Orleans and Mobile. A concentration of force there made every sense.

Carlisle questioned Duboeuf until it was clear that he had heard everything useful. The man knew nothing about which regiments were in Mobile, nothing about any planned movements inland, and cared only to reach home, as quickly as possible. He sent the Frenchman back under escort, to be delivered to the bosun to have his own tiny space on the orlop. The man was no threat now. He would have been a greater concern if he had been with his crew in the hold, where he could be a focus for any attempted uprising, not that such a thing was likely when they were surrounded by some three-hundred-and-fifty British sailors and marines.

'Just let me see your notes, Mister Simmonds, before the sergeant comes in.'

***

Cousins At Arms

Sergeant Turner appeared to be exactly who he said he was. He'd been taken earlier in the year when the French had attempted to re-capture Quebec after its British defenders had endured a hard winter in the shattered city. He'd moved, stage-by-stage, through Montreal – just one step ahead of its capitulation – and down the Ohio and the Mississippi until he reached New Orleans. From there he'd been shipped in a coasting yawl to Mobile Bay where he was held at the French fort to await a passage to France. It was but a short step from France to a cartel ship to England. He'd been reasonably well treated, on the whole, and he'd fed no worse in French captivity than he had through the long Canadian winter in Quebec. Carlisle soon discovered that he was an intelligent man – as could be expected of a sergeant of artillery – and he wasn't convinced that his fortunes had improved when *Petite Marie* was taken by this great two-decker. All he wanted now was to find a way home, but first he had a story to tell and a secret to reveal.

'I was on a foraging party, sir, when I was taken by a French patrol. It was stupid, really. There were only a handful of horses left in the city, just those belonging to the brigadier general and his staff. All the others had been eaten, even the artillery draught horses. So it was none of my duty to be foraging. The rest of my men were killed and scalped by the savages – the French always have a few at hand, you know – but I was taken back to the main force and questioned about Quebec's defences. Little comfort did I give them; I could see that they didn't have enough men for a siege and they had only a few field guns. Anyway, I didn't see the battle because I was marched back to Montreal before it started, but I did hear the guns. They told me afterwards that our men were chased back behind the walls They called it a great victory, but they couldn't make a breach in the wall, not without siege artillery, and they had to withdraw in the end.'

Carlisle listened in silence to the account of his journey south, which was mercifully short, and it was only when the sergeant's account reached New Orleans that he interrupted.

'What were the French doing at New Orleans, Sergeant? Were they moving up the river or retreating down it, would you say?'

'Oh, neither sir, they weren't moving at all, but they did appear to be *preparing* to move upriver. I didn't speak much French when I was caught, but I've learned a lot this past year. But still I couldn't really tell what was happening, although I did hear that there were at least two regiments in the town and another down towards the mouth of the river, I think. From the few words that I picked up it sounded like they were going to embark in river boats soon and move up the Mississippi to the Ohio.'

'Foot soldiers, I suppose. Was there any cavalry or artillery?'

'Cavalry, sir? I should think not in that country, but they had a few field guns, six pounders mostly with some three pounders and coehorns, but no siege artillery, or not any that I saw.'

Carlisle suppressed a sigh. There was nothing more to be gained from this sergeant.

'You'll mess with the marines, Sergeant Turner, no doubt Sergeant Wilson will see you properly dressed…'

'Excuse me, sir, but I didn't really get onto my time at Mobile Bay. You see, sir, I was two weeks billeted in a cell at the fort right at the head of the bay where the river comes out, and they put me to work in the gardens by the commandant's house. I heard a few things that might be useful.'

Carlisle was growing weary of these interviews and he could see Simmonds roll his eyes at the Sergeant's offer.

'Very well, sergeant, tell me what you know.'

'Well, sir, I was digging a little garden to be planted with corn and it was right under an air vent that came out of the commandant's office. I suppose they thought that not being near a window I wouldn't be able to hear anything, and in any case they probably supposed I was just another of the French soldiers on fatigue duty, what with the uniforms being so similar and me not wearing my ragged old coat for the heat. Whatever the reason, sir, I could hear every word that was said in the office, as plain as if I was standing there.'

The sergeant paused and drew a breath. He was evidently pleased to have a willing audience and was enjoying speaking English after so long struggling with French.

'I heard the commandant talking to someone important, someone who had recently come over from France, and they were talking about a treaty between France and Spain. It's King Carlos in Spain, isn't it, sir? Only we call him Charles, I think.'

That caught Carlisle's interest. Charles or Carlos, it was the same thing, and perhaps this sergeant had something of use after all, buried within his circumlocutions and his rambling account of his wanderings through America.

'The man from France – I could tell he was important by the way he was talking – was telling the commandant that the Spanish would be at war by the first day of May. You see, *May* sounds the same in French as in English and I know they were talking about months because they mentioned *Janvier* and *Avril*, and I know those words.'

Carlisle leaned forward.

'Now Sergeant, this is very important. Can you remember anything about the man who was telling the commandant this?'

'Well, I saw him close enough when he walked in the garden a few hours later. He was well dressed and as I said before, he seemed important-like. He'd just come in on a ship from Brest, this was two weeks ago. I'm certain of what he said. He described it as a secret treaty that only a few people knew about, and the reason he was telling the commandant was so that he would be prepared to help the Spanish if they should arrive at Mobile. He seemed to think that with Pensacola being so close to Mobile, they would be the first to encounter the Spanish. He spoke of this treaty as the turning point in the war and how Mobile and the Mississippi must be held until at least May when the Spanish would be committed. It sounded as though he was telling nobody else, only this commandant, because it was so secret.'

'And what was it about the first of May, Sergeant, was that the date that the Spanish would declare war?'

'Not exactly, sir. That was the date that they would declare against us if there was no peace with France by then. He hoped that they'd declare earlier than that, but it all depended on how far along their fleet was.'

***

CHAPTER SIXTEEN

A Weighty Matter

Thursday, Thirty-First of December 1761.
Dartmouth, at Sea, Cape San Antonio southeast 40 leagues.

Dartmouth and the brig *Petite Marie* lay hove-to, rising and falling to the long, low swell that the trade winds had generated on their thousand mile fetch across the broad Caribbean. The brig was a hive of activity and already a new main topmast was in place and the shrouds were being rattled down. Neither the carpenter nor the bosun liked the look of her jury fore topmast and a new one was lying in the waist, ready to be swayed up to its own particular position. They were massive affairs, far too big for the little brig, but they would keep her at sea long enough to be condemned at a prize court. But all that was being supervised by *Dartmouth's* carpenter and bosun; the commissioned officers and the sailing master who would normally have been involved in this most interesting evolution were notable by their absence.

Carlisle's lieutenants and the sailing master couldn't have been in the brig, for they were all gathered in *Dartmouth's* great cabin. They'd been offered wine and coffee and now they were eager to hear what their captain had to say, hoping he would keep it short so that they could get back to the brig's topmasts. They'd heard rumours of what the master of the brig had said, and a more definite account of the sergeant's tale, although he'd been warned against repeating everything that he'd told Carlisle. The secret treaty was to remain just that, secret.

'Well, gentlemen, I find that we must split our forces for a while…'

The door to the sleeping cabin opened and Chiara walked in, taking a seat without any invitation after all the officers had risen to their feet and Gresham had given up the best chair for her.

'...do join us, my dear.'

Carlisle was just a half second late in offering the invitation, making it sound dangerously like sarcasm, but not a hint of resentment showed on Chiara's face. She adjusted her dress and smiled broadly, favouring each man with a particular notice before finally nodding agreeably to her husband. Carlisle felt as though he had just lost an argument, which was no way to start a meeting with his officers. He tried to keep his emotions from his face but only succeeded in an unnatural grimace.

'Now, as I was saying, we must split our forces. The information that the brig's master gave me suggests that the French are reinforcing their places on the Gulf Coast and may even be considering an expedition into the interior. However, his testimony, even backed up by Sergeant Turner, isn't firm enough. I find that I must go at least to Mobile and possibly to New Orleans to gather some hard intelligence to take back to Jamaica.'

Carlisle looked at the faces in the cabin. So far he hadn't said anything that they couldn't have guessed but each was looking keen, knowing that there was more to come.

'Now, my orders are vague after our errand to Havana and I feel that we won't be missed for a while yet, so a cruise towards Mobile is perfectly within the scope of my instructions from Commodore Douglas and *post mortem* from Admiral Holmes.'

Beazley glanced sideways at Gresham who knew very well that the sailing master was trying to decide whether the first lieutenant knew what *post mortem* meant. Gresham had watched in amusement as Beazley had become increasingly obsessed with the notion that *Dartmouth's* second-in-command was lacking in education.

Carlisle continued, having missed the off-stage theatricals.

'But there is one other duty that I must attend to. Sergeant Turner gave me other information that is of an exceptionally sensitive nature – I regret that I cannot talk about it here – and that must go to Jamaica as soon as possible. The brig looks a handy vessel and it can lie almost as close to the wind as *Dartmouth*. It will need to if the trade wind doesn't return to its duty and shift a few points to the north. As you know, Chips and the bosun are rigging new topmasts from our own spares and they believe she'll be as good as new, if a little awkward-looking, by tomorrow forenoon. I plan to send my despatches to Jamaica in the brig as soon as she can be made ready.'

Wishart and Enrico exchanged glances. This wasn't a job for the *first* lieutenant, but it was a lieutenant's or at a stretch a master's mate's command, but neither of the mates had been invited to the cabin. It would take at least a week to beat eastwards against the trade wind if it didn't back into the nor'east, and in that week any kind of adventure was possible. There could be prizes! Their eagerness to be chosen was written plainly on their faces, but deep down they knew that there was only one outcome. Enrico's commission was from King Charles Emmanuel of Sardinia, not from King George, and that ruled him out of most independent missions. There would be too many awkward questions if he was taken by a French frigate or a privateer with no British sea officer to legitimise his presence.

Carlisle could see Enrico's immobile face and the start of a smile on Wishart's. How long could Enrico's anomalous position last? Well, that was a question for another day.

'Mister Wishart, do you fancy a cruise?'

***

David Wishart watched impatiently as the new foretopmast jerked its way upwards. It would have been futile to interfere when the bosun was supervising, and it would only end in tears. And, he had to admit, Hewlett had the task well in hand. The old, missing, topmast had been rigged in some French merchantman-style that the bosun had never seen before, but the new one was a proper fidded arrangement, navy-fashion, and it was being hauled up through the lower cap by a half-dozen hands at the windlass. A seaman was perched precariously at the foretop, with his knife ready to cut any of the spun-yarn stoppers that didn't snap as they passed the top-block, and the top-maul and the fid were within his easy reach, and secured to the trestle-trees with lanyards. Too many lives had been lost by those heavy objects falling onto the men below.

'Way-oh!'

The topmast-man held up his hand and the pawls on the windlass ceased clicking. He slapped the cap into place and gave it a few hefty blows with the top-maul to fix it securely.

'Haul away,' he shouted when he was well clear of the moving parts.

The topmast was vertical now and sliding upwards through the hole in the foremast cap. This was the tricky part. If the foremast was raised too far before it was secured, then the leverage that it exerted as the brig rolled could easily damage the foremast cap. In the extreme, the heavy block of elm could be snapped along the grain and the topmast could fall to the deck.

Inch-by-inch now, and the square hole in the heel started to show above the trestle-trees.

'Way oh!'

There was an edge of tension in the seaman's voice. If the topmast was hoisted too high, its heel could pass right through the trestle-trees and the cap and sweep him off the maintop.

'One more pawl.'

Click!

'One more.'

Click!

On deck they heard the satisfying thuds of the fid being hammered into place by the top-maul. Now, short of a gale, the topmast was safe until they could rig the stays and shrouds. There was a palpable air of relief on the deck.

Wishart found that he'd been gripping the binnacle tightly and there was a ring of red around one of his cuticles where the fingernail had been pressed backwards. He thrust that hand into his pocket so that nobody should see that he'd been anxious.

He'd seen this done dozens of times before. Not only was it a routine when bad weather was feared and when the ship was to lie in a yard for any time, but the first lieutenant drilled the crew frequently in sending down the topmasts and then swaying them up again. But this was different; it was the first time that it had been done in a vessel that he commanded. For Carlisle, anticipating a lengthy parting, had promised him a letter appointing him to command the prize *Petite Marie*. It wasn't a King's commission to command a man-of-war, it wasn't even close, but nobody short of the commander-in-chief could relieve him of his command until Carlisle was consulted. He reckoned it could take a week to reach Port Royal, then the brig would have to be handed over to the prize agent until its fate was decided by the vice-admiralty court. A week: it wasn't very long, but who knew what could happen? A brief fantasy crossed his mind, where whoever was acting as commander-in-chief at Jamaica commissioned him as an acting commander and sent him away in the brig, to find *Dartmouth* or to search for French privateers. But it was a very brief fantasy. With the navy at about its peak, promotions were hard to come by and would only get worse. There were favourite lieutenants in the flagship just waiting for a prize brig to be commissioned, and even if Carlisle were handed the ultimate accolade of a promotion from among his lieutenants, Gresham was far, far senior to him. No, he'd been too young to take advantage of the opportunities that came at the start of the war and now he'd probably have to wait for the next, with a spell on half-pay between. Nevertheless, it was still exciting to take this brig all the way to Jamaica.

***

Wishart watched until the fore topmast was secured. He didn't need to see all the stays and shrouds rattled down, nor the ratlines rigged, and in any case he'd just seen a boat coming over from *Dartmouth* with a person that looked very much like the captain sat in the stern sheets.

'Boat ahoy!'

That was Barker, the bosun's mate who had been given to him as acting bosun. He at least was keeping his eyes open even with such intense activity on the brig's deck.

'*Dartmouth*!'

The formal reply to Barker's hail told everyone in earshot that *Dartmouth's* captain was coming over to the brig. If *Petite Marie* had been in commission, there would be a bustle of bosun's mates with their pipes, sideboys and all of the ship's officers gathering at the gangway. However, for a mere prize, Carlisle would have to be satisfied with Barker and an able seaman to help him aboard, and Wishart to greet him, with his head bared in the awful presence of a post-captain.

The yawl nosed alongside and Carlisle pulled himself up the six feet from the boat to the brig's waist. He looked like a man with no time for niceties and beckoned Wishart below to where he assumed the master's cabin would be. There were no refreshments; Wishart's servant was in the yawl waiting for Carlisle to be greeted before he boarded the brig, and he of course had not yet found his way around the scullery that served as the captain's galley.

'Mister Beazley reckons that we're drifting to the west at three knots, what with the wind and that Loop Current. The sooner you can get underway the better. What's the present estimate?'

Wishart thought quickly. His last orders were to part company in the morning watch or the forenoon watch, as soon as the brig was fit for a long beat to windward. But he'd seen how quickly the work was progressing and he'd be happy with just the standing rigging complete, the yards crossed and the sails bent on, with enough of the running rigging to set the sails. The rest could wait and they should have plenty of time to have it all shipshape before they reached Port Royal.

'I could be underway at eight o'clock, sir. There'll be a crescent moon until ten o'clock and this easterly isn't bringing much in the way of cloud. There should be enough light to finish off and send the bosun and his men back to you.'

'You have your stores, your octant and tables, water?'

'Stored and watered and wooded for a month, sir, nigh on six months if we get desperate and break into the prize stores. I've everything I need, sir, and Mister Hewitt is happy with the new topmasts. We won't win any races but we can lie seven or eight points off the wind, I expect.'

'Well, that's more than can be said for many of the Jamaica Squadron, Mister Wishart, and we have no right to expect more. I'll expect you to get underway by the end of the last dog watch, and you're to send me word if you'll be any later than that. Now, here are my dispatches.'

Carlisle handed over a thick canvas-wrapped bundle. All the seams were sewn and sealed with pitch and there was no indication of the contents or to whom they should be delivered. The package felt heavy to Wishart, and there was a wide bulge at one end. He realised that it must be weighted to make it sink quickly, grapeshot probably. There was another letter, an ordinary sheet of paper sealed with a plain wafer.

'Take a seat, Mister Wishart, this may take a few minutes.'

They were interrupted by Wishart's servant who poked his nose around the cabin door, looking just like a comedy mouse in a theatre.

'Beg your pardon, sir, but I found the cabin spirit locker. There are a couple of bottles of brandy…'

'Yes, yes,' Carlisle answered curtly. 'We'll have a glass of brandy. Oh. I beg your pardon Mister Wishart – Captain Wishart as I should say – it's your cabin, not mine.'

But the servant had gone. He wasn't used to waiting upon Captain Carlisle and his brusque manner had terrified him.

'Yes, it's your cabin and you're to style yourself captain until you've handed her over to the prize agent at Port Royal. You know him well enough, I imagine.'

'Oh yes, sir, he's an old friend.'

'Well, old friend or not, he will need to be watched. Make sure you have an inventory of the brig's fittings and stores before he takes it, otherwise he'll be doing a brisk trade in everything from belaying pins to hogsheads of brandy before the prize court knows anything, and we won't see a penny of it. However, that's not why I'm here, I've every confidence that you can take a prize across the Caribbean without any instruction…'

Wishart tried not to smile, to take the compliment as though it was no more than his due, but these words of confidence from his captain filled him with joy, and he grinned foolishly.

'…Now, here's your letter appointing you to command the prize. It's not usually necessary but as there's an *interregnum* in Port Royal and as I have no real idea when I'll get back there, you should have this as a legal authority. It may be that your men will be put to work in the yard, but you must resist them being sent to other ships. I know how that goes and we may never see them again. Test the water, but it may be best to volunteer them to the master attendant before anyone else knows you're there. Remember, you have some of my best seamen and I want to see them all again.'

They paused to hear the bosun's cries for the shrouds to be sent up to the tops. Carlisle nodded, eight o'clock seemed feasible.

'This however,' he said picking up the canvas package and dropping it to the table, where it fell with enough force to create a tremor in the cabin deck, 'this is of much more weight, in every sense. I chose not to tell you all of what I heard from the sergeant – who, by the way, I'm sending over to you before you part company – but in case of accidents, you should know what's in the package. It should be understood that this is for your ears only. The only circumstance where I expect you to report what I've told you is if you meet a British ship with a post-captain in command or if you have been forced to drop the package over the side. And that you must do at the slightest hint of danger, long before you are boarded or even fired upon. This must not fall into French or Spanish hands; or anyone else for that matter. It's to be handed to the commander-in-chief's secretary or to any post-captain that you should meet at sea, and then he can deal with it. Nobody else, is that clear?'

Wishart nodded stupidly. He'd never been responsible for anything like this and he wasn't at all sure that he liked it. Still, it gave him a thrill to know that he was being entrusted with... with what, exactly?

'Send you servant forward, if you please, Mister Wishart, where he can't overhear us.'

There wasn't a cabin in anything less than a third rate where conversations couldn't be heard from the scullery, where the domestics usually lurked.

After the door had closed on the retreating servant, Carlisle leaned closer and told Wishart all he knew about the secret treaty that would bring Spain into the war. He explained why the sergeant had convinced him of the truth of his story, and why it was unlikely that the commandant at the Mobile fort guessed that the secret had escaped.

'It may be that you have to give similar words of encouragement to the admiral, if there is one, or his secretary or even to Sir Henry, so it's important that you understand how this information came into my hands. Sergeant Turner can be brought forward if necessary to verify the facts, and that's why he'll be coming to you before you get underway. Now, if you were the commander of the Spanish fleet lying at Havana and you were told to make war on Britain and her colonies, where would your eye fall first?'

Wishart was startled at being asked such a question and he racked his brain for an answer, not wanting to disappoint his captain. He called to mind a map of the Caribbean. All the British possessions were to windward of Havana and none could be reached easily. The American colonies were certainly the easiest to reach – Georgia, the Carolinas and Virginia – but sending a fleet that far north would leave all of New Spain exposed. The Bahamas, but they were of little consequence and not worth the effort. Jamaica then? The jewel in the crown of the British colonies, the island that alone generated the majority of the profits for British merchants and the perpetual thorn in the side of New Spain.

'Jamaica, sir, it must be.'

Carlisle eyed his lieutenant speculatively. He knew him as a competent sea officer, but perhaps there was more to him. Perhaps he was seeing the early stages of the gestation of a future admiral, deploying squadrons and determining the fate of colonies not yet imagined.

'Jamaica indeed, and that's why you mustn't fail to take this information to Port Royal. Jamaica is wide open to invasion from the west and every indication of Spain's intent is worth its weight in gold to the lieutenant-governor. There, now you know why this is so important. Oh, and there's another letter in there explaining why I'm taking *Dartmouth* to Mobile bay. You know the background to that. I hope to be back in Port Royal in two weeks or so, and I'll see you there.'

***

Wishart saw his captain over the side then called to the bosun to give him the new time for parting company. Hewitt just shrugged and pointed to the where the shrouds were being let down from the tops, where experienced hands were seizing them to deadeyes and then rigging the lanyards to the lower deadeyes at the chains. Wishart brought out his watch just as the bell struck eight times for the end of the afternoon watch. Four hours until he had to be underway; it would be tight.

***

CHAPTER SEVENTEEN

An Innocent Lugger

Saturday, Second of January 1762.
The Longboat, at Sea, off Massacre Island, the Gulf of Mexico.

Gresham looked up at the unfamiliar shape of the lugsail, towering above him into the starlit sky. It had been easy enough to turn the gaff-rigged longboat into a lugger. The carpenter and bosun between them had effected the transformation in the day that *Dartmouth* had taken to cross the Gulf of Mexico from the Yucatan Channel to her present position, just below the horizon off Massacre Island. And this was what he delighted in, it could be said that he lived for times such as this: a ship's boat on a dark night sailing into the enemy's bosom with nobody to tell him which way to steer or when to fight or flee. He was lucky, he knew, because this was usually a mission for the second or third lieutenant, but it had fallen into his lap. Wishart was away to Port Royal with the prize and Angelini couldn't possibly undertake this kind of risky operation, not with only a Sardinian commission between him and the gallows, and Sardinia still neutral in this war.

'Harden in a touch Souter, let's give her a little more offing.'

Jack Souter put the helm down and the longboat responded by coming a point into the wind. Two of the seamen hauled in the mainsheet until its luff stopped lifting while another did the same for the jib. Then it settled down on its new course, shouldering aside the untidy waves that rippled the face of the long, low swell. The wind was nearly southerly now, and when the sun was up they could expect it to back dramatically so that they could bear away into Mobile Bay on the morning sea breeze.

'How far to the bay's entrance, sir?'

Souter was the captain's coxswain and held a privileged position that allowed him to ask questions of the first lieutenant. Few others would dare to do so, even in the relaxed atmosphere of an open boat detached from its mother.

'Fifteen miles, I reckon. That's the western tip of Dauphin Island over there to larboard, or at least I hope it is.'

Carlisle had set them off from a position just below the horizon off the ominously-named Massacre Island, the next in the chain that ran westward from Dauphin Island. The plan was to steer for the shore until the chain of islands were two miles off, then bear up for Mobile Bay as though they had left New Orleans, or Biloxi or even Pascagoula. Neither Carlisle nor Gresham had any real idea of the patterns of traffic on the French Gulf Coast and they had to rely upon what they heard from the French brig master. It sounded a weak source of information, but in fact the Frenchman was being so well entertained by the bosun's mess that he was inclined to talk freely to anyone who would listen, even when they could hardly understand a word that he said. As Hewlett said wearily, the problem was not in persuading him to talk but in getting him to stop. He told of a steady stream of merchant traffic travelling northeast towards Mobile Bay from New Orleans and the Mississippi. They all took the passage outside the islands because of the shifting shallows inside, and only used the lagoons to shelter from storms. Other traffic from Biloxi and Pascagoula and a dozen smaller places inside the islands came out of the lagoon through the nearest break in the chain and joined the regular flow of traffic. They were predominantly small craft and the thirty-foot longboat wouldn't look out of place, particularly with a lug rig. The deception was completed with a dozen or so burlap-covered bales that bulked out the midships of the longboat; they could be taken for furs or woollens or tobacco or rice, or any of the other products of the vast Louisiana hinterland.

The moon had set before midnight and only the stars gave any indication of the shore just two miles under their lee. Any time now, Gresham reckoned, he'd start to see the first glow ahead as the sun nudged towards the horizon. Then they'd see what they would see.

He was on a reconnaissance mission, and there was no question of taking prizes. He had eight of a crew, far too many to handle the sails but barely enough if they had to use the oars, and they carried nothing more than two muskets and a pistol and cutlass for each man. Gresham had worried that so many men in a coasting lugger would look odd, but he really didn't want to be without the means to pull out of trouble if they should be becalmed, or if they had to escape to windward.

The French captain had spoken of line regiments gathering but he'd seen no transports while he'd been loading in the bay. No troop transports, no army supply ships and no navy escorts. The build-up of forces around New Orleans was just supposition, an extrapolation of a few rather shaky facts. What the Frenchman didn't know was that *Dartmouth* had chased an escorting frigate and what looked very much like four troop transports or storeships in the Old Bahama Straits. It was a good bet that they were bound for Mobile Bay or even New Orleans, but Carlisle wanted harder information to bring back to Jamaica.

Ah, there! The horizon was starting to glow – that was the only way to describe it – a point or so to starboard of the boat's bows. Gresham looked up and already the stars were growing dimmer, giving the three visible planets an unnatural and brief brilliance as they outshone those far-off points of light.

'The island's coming clearer now, sir.'

Gresham could see that for himself and he was trying to determine just where they were by comparing the shadowy outlines with his memory of the chart.

'Oh, sail ho!' said Souter in a conversational tone. 'There's another lugger astern of us, maybe two miles distant, following a couple of cables offshore of our track.'

Gresham nodded silently. He pulled his telescope out from under his coat where it had been protected from the falling dew. It wasn't as good as Carlisle's, or Beazley's but he'd bought it at Antigua on the promise that it was a night scope, and it did indeed enhance the images of ships and the land when the light was poor, at least to a certain extent. He stared astern at the following lugger. At this distance there was nothing to say that it wasn't another ship's longboat in disguise. It had the same long, low profile, the same light yard rigged diagonally across the mast and the same tanned-brown mainsail and jib. He could even see the mounds of cargo rising above the gunwales, just like their own. The only real difference at this distance was that the jib was smaller than the longboat's jib and it was set upon a shorter bowsprit with a distinct steeve to it, while the longboat's bowsprit thrust forward without any hint of an upward tilt. He was satisfied. Nobody would think twice about the longboat's assumed identity; it was a French lugger hauling bale goods from New Orleans to Mobile Bay for transhipment back to France, just like the fellow astern, nothing unusual at all.

Now the upper limb of the sun was just breaking the horizon and the whole of the coastline was coming clear. Out on the larboard quarter, far astern now, Gresham could see the passage between Dauphin Island and Massacre Island. There were two sails tacking out, a yawl and another lugger, and as he watched the yawl bore away and steered east for Mobile Bay. Well that verified at least part of the French captain's story. He'd insisted that the passage between Dauphin Island and Oyster Point on the mainland was too shallow for anything but canoes, that he wouldn't try it even in a ship's boat, not without the local knowledge that the Louisiana crabbers, shrimpers and oystermen had. Yes, there was a channel with perhaps half a fathom at low water, or so it was said, but if it existed at all it wasn't marked in a regular way. That yawl's actions tended to prove the point; it could have saved a few hours if the Oyster Point passage was available. Then it did appear that the shallow lagoon behind the islands offered no safe passage from New Orleans to Mobile Bay. Perhaps that was why Mobile was abandoned as the capital of Louisiana in favour of Biloxi; it was just too difficult to reach from the west. That was all well and good, but one look at Beazley's chart told Gresham that such a large, sheltered bay would never be completely discarded, not as long as it lay on the direct route from the old world in the east to this new world in the west.

'Nothing ahead of us, sir, and nothing to seaward. It looks like all the traffic is coming this way.'

'Yes, I expect so. It would be a hard beat out of the bay with this sou'-easterly. Probably they'll wait for the evening and take a night passage to the west, or choose a day when there's a good easterly.'

The longboat forged on and as the sun's rays warmed the land the sea breeze started to set in. Now they were making five or six knots on a broad reach and their larger jib and lighter load – the bales were filled with weightless junk – were allowing them to sail three miles for the two that the following lugger was able to make.

'There's the end of the island, sir, shall I steer for it?'

'No, there's a spit that runs south for three or four miles from the eastern end of Dauphin Island, it has no more than half a fathom over most of it. In fact you can harden up a point until the entrance is right on the beam, then we'll bear away. Now, let's see what that fellow does. Ah, he's coming up a touch also. I wonder whether he's following us, thinking that we know these waters?'

Souter laughed at that.

'I hope he doesn't have a nasty shock, sir. But it does look as though we'll be first into the bay today and with this sea breeze I can't see anybody trying to get out until the afternoon.'

***

The shallow water was obvious as they came closer. The waves weren't breaking on the spit but Gresham could see the darker water and the steeper waves as the swell was forced upwards. It was a natural place for a bar, with the flow from the Mobile River bringing down its silt and depositing it where the bay met the sea. The chart showed a deep channel between Dauphin Island and the long isthmus that stretched out from the east until they almost met. And there was an anchorage behind Dauphin Island, with some four fathoms of water, but then the whole of the rest of the bay was shallow with a few patches of three fathoms but mostly less than two. That made Gresham's task relatively simple. He could assume that any transports and stores ships would discharge at the mouth of the bay, and their escorts would likewise be unable to make the twenty-five mile passage up the bay to the fort.

'Is there no fort at the mouth of the bay, sir?'

Souter was systematically studying the passage into the bay. There were certainly some kind of buildings on the point of Dauphin Island, but they looked more like warehouses and wooden single-story homes than any kind of fortification.

'Not according to the French brig's master, Souter. The original settlers were more concerned with the Indians than they were with being attacked from the sea. The only fort is right at the head of the bay and I don't intend going that far. Those buildings that you can see are what passes for a port, just a lookout station and a customs post and a few houses and warehouses. Now, we should start to see something soon.'

***

The longboat ran fast with the following wind and the details on the shore rapidly became clearer. There were tall masts in the anchorage, although it was too far to see what they were. The lugger astern of them bore away into the longboat's wake; perhaps it was following them after all.

It seemed that any transhipment must be done at Dauphin Island rather than further up the bay. A quick look through the telescope confirmed what he had guessed: there was no sign of seagoing vessels beyond the anchorage. So far, the Frenchman's testimony was proving accurate. Perhaps this would be easier than he hoped. By the time he ran into the anchorage the sea breeze should be starting to fail and, if he was any judge, the wind would turn easterly, or even nor'easterly, mimicking the offshore trade winds that still had the power to penetrate this deeply into the Gulf. A quick count of the vessels with at least an estimate of what they were about, then they could reach out through the narrows and back to sea. *Dartmouth* should be waiting below the horizon and they'd be back on board before sunset.

The sun was well up in the sky as they passed through the narrows.

'Three miles wide, do you think, Souter?'

'Aye, three miles I reckon, sir. If they have batteries, it will be a long shot from either point.'

Gresham nodded. That was probably another reason why there were no forts here. A ship staying in the centre would be at the extreme range for guns sited on those low points of land, and the only men-of-war that were of shallow enough draught to use the bay were frigates. They made a poor target from a mile-and-a-half, particularly if they were sailing large. No, Gresham didn't fear any shore batteries.

***

Cousins At Arms

The vessels in the anchorage were becoming recognisable. A frigate and three merchant ships; transports perhaps, it was hard to tell at this range. Ah, and just behind them, well inshore, was a brig with a missing main topmast. It looked like a new one was being hoisted; at least there was some kind of activity around the main masthead.

'That'll be our convoy, for sure, sir.'

'Aye, that's for certain. Well, it looks like we'll get a closer look at them this time. Once you've cleared that point you can run down among them, just as though we were going to anchor and discharge our cargo.'

'It'll be a stiff beat out, sir.'

'That it will but there's nobody to hinder us as far as I can see.'

A flight of pelicans crossed their bows, heading to the east and flying low, their wing tips almost touching the water as they took occasional beats to keep them above the waves. But mostly they just glided, seemingly without any effort whatsoever. When they had passed ahead the lead bird suddenly gave a few energetic flaps and soared upward followed by all the rest, then one by one, as though there was some guiding intelligence co-ordinating their movements, they slipped sideways and plummeted head-first for the sea, folding their huge wings immediately before the impact. The fish that they sought must have been just below the surface for within moments each of the birds surfaced, flapping wildly, and bobbed around with their heads held up, apparently swallowing whatever they had caught. Gresham realised that the whole longboat's crew was transfixed by this spectacle, and to be sure it was a wonder to behold, a marvel of creation.

'Good eating, they say. I tried it once but it was a bit too fishy for me. Still, it's better than albatross. I can't abide them, nor petrels, nor stink-pots; they're well named if you ask me.'

'You've been in the Southern Ocean, Souter?'

'Aye sir, before the war I shipped as a deck hand with

the John Company. Two voyages to India and China, and you can't help coming across albatrosses once you're past Saint Helena. I won't eat them no more but my tobacco pouch is made from albatross skin and it keeps the wet out but holds the leaf's moisture. You can't get better than albatross for a tobacco pouch.'

Gresham smiled and remembered his own voyage to the east in the last war. It had all seemed so simple, a few years as a lieutenant, then he'd distinguish himself and be made master and commander into a sloop, and then to the barely-imaginable heights of being posted and his own real, rated ship. But somewhere along the line, and he could never identify where, he slipped from the path. Perhaps he enjoyed being a lieutenant too much and didn't push himself, and now his age told against him. Well, here he was, and barring a miracle he'd end his days as a half pay lieutenant. And at this moment, with the sun shining and his longboat standing into an enemy port, with pelicans performing to order, it didn't sound so bad.

***

'You can bear away now, Souter. Just pass to leeward of that ship-rigged merchantman on your bow then run down to the brig and then we'll beat our way out. Right, I want six of you to crouch down among those bales. Only Souter and two of you to show yourselves.'

It should do. The longboat had high gunwales and it would be difficult for anyone to see inside. He felt for his uniform coat which he was using as a cushion and looked keenly at Souter and the two seamen who were visible in the bows, past the bales. They'd pass for seamen of any nationality, he was confident. He pushed his telescope into the folds of his coat, so that it wouldn't be seen, and settled back to observe whatever he could.

'This first one's a transport, sir. Look, some of the soldiers are still on board, mustering ready to get into those boats, by the look of them. And there's a party shifting their dunnage. The second's the same, I think.'

Souter was speaking through the corners of his mouth as though that would look more innocent than speaking openly.

'That third one's a storeship, sir, and I'll bet the brig is too.'

Gresham just nodded. They weren't private merchantmen, that was for sure. Each of them had a white circle painted on the bow with a black number inside the circle. That was similar to the way that transports and storeships were identified in the British navy. In fact any vessels hired by the navy board were marked with a number so that they could be easily told one from another amongst dozens or even hundreds of their fellows. The only real question was how many of each type had come over in the convoy. Certainly there was one storeship; he could see them swaying casks and bales into a lighter alongside. It was clear that other two were fitted out for carrying soldiers, about a small company to each, he guessed. He wasn't sure about the brig, but he could now see that a main topmast was being prepared for hoisting. The brig seemed too small for soldiers on a winter Atlantic crossing, so it was another storeship then.

Gresham had resolved to keep his telescope hidden while they were in the anchorage, but he just had to see where the lighters were taking the soldiers. He scanned the shore to the north. Nothing, in fact it looked barely inhabited. Dauphin Island, then. Ah, now he could see a solid block of white-coated figures with the sun glinting off musket barrels and other accoutrements of war. They must have landed the troops there to organise themselves before they were taken on the twenty-five mile voyage up the bay to the fort, or the short sea passage to New Orleans. He'd seen formed bodies of soldiers before and knew what to expect. This looked like two under-strength companies ashore and a few more soldiers still to join them from the transports. He could guess what had happened; that blow when *Dartmouth* was in Havana must have disrupted the seaborne traffic all along the coast. It had delayed the lighters coming down from the head of the bay and the soldiers had decided to camp on the island rather than spend another day confined to the transports. Now, at last, their lighters and boats were gathering to take them to their destination.

'Beg your pardon, sir, but they're taking an interest in us on the frigate's quarterdeck.'

Gresham swivelled around so that he could see the frigate and he guiltily tucked the telescope back under his coat. It was a shock to see how far the longboat had come into the anchorage, and now the frigate was well to windward, blocking their escape to the open sea. It would be awkward beating out if they were discovered to be an enemy boat.

'He's calling to the other officers now, sir, and I think they're clearing away a gun on the fo'c'sle. Yes, I can see them taking off the sea lashings. There goes the tompion.'

Gresham could see that for himself. He could also see an officer running up the main shrouds with a telescope slung over his shoulder. He watched as he crawled hand-over-hand up the futtock shrouds then as soon as his feet were on the boards of the maintop he trained the telescope at the longboat. There was a shout, he couldn't hear just what was said, but it didn't matter, the meaning was clear from the bang and puff of grey smoke as the fo'c'sle six-pounder threw a ball across the longboat's bow.

'Here comes a boat, sir, one of those big yawls that they sometimes carry, and it's stuffed with men.'

***

CHAPTER EIGHTEEN

Trapped!

Saturday, Second of January 1762.
The Longboat, at Sea, Mobile Bay.

Gresham looked sharply around. It was clear that if he wanted to escape through the channel they'd used to come into the bay, they'd have to fight their way past that yawl. That would be difficult; the French boat was smaller than the longboat, but it carried more men and they were all armed, and the blue coats of a file of French marines showed among the oarsmen. The danger was that of all the pursued: while the pursuer could afford to have accidents and catch up later, for the fugitive, anything that stopped progress risked them being overhauled. And in this case there was another jeopardy: it could hardly be long before other French boats joined the hunt. No, an escape past the frigate just wasn't feasible. But there was another way and the officer in charge of that French yawl seemed to have discounted it by manning his oars rather than setting the sails.

'We've seen enough, Souter, we'll make our escape to the west over those shallows.'

'Aye-aye sir. There's a second boat pulling away from the frigate now. It's setting a sail.'

Boom!

The frigate had evidently managed to clear away one of the nine-pounders of her main armament. The shot fell wide, but it was a clear statement of intent. They must now be in no doubt of the nationality of the longboat, and they must be confident that they'd blocked its escape.

'You see where that smaller island lies off Dauphin? The channel – if it exists – will be close in to there, that's where the stream will scour the deepest after it swings around Oyster Point.'

'Five cables between the two, I reckon, sir.'

'That's right, and I won't be spilling any wind, so just you watch the water ahead and keep us off the mud. Now, let's get the men out from under and see to the trimming of these sails. Overboard with those bales, quick as you can, and the anchor. We'll keep the water cask.'

***

Souter stood to his task so that he could better see the water ahead. It wasn't encouraging. The little island to larboard lay barely above the sea with a tangle of old, rotten trees showing stark and white. He'd looked at Mister Beazley's chart too and he remembered that it was called Heron Island, and a more perfect place for a heronry he'd never seen. The water lapped at the very roots of the trees which suggested that there were extensive shallows on that side. He could imagine the ebb tide, strengthened by the flow of the Mobile River, encountering that obstacle and slowing, leaving a deposit of sand and mud that had built up over the years. Yes, shallows to larboard.

Over to starboard it looked a little more hopeful. The tip of Oyster Point was sand rather than mud. This, if anywhere, was where that ebb tide would have scoured a channel, and he could see a few withies sticking clear of the water. They could help, but he knew all about old, discarded withies. They may once have marked a channel, but channels shifted over time and some of those poles lasted for generations. At other times in other places he'd learned to look for painted withies, as a sign that someone used them, but if these had ever been painted, their colours had long ago faded.

Boom!

'Closer, but we'll be out of range soon. Do you see those withies, Souter?'

'Aye, sir, I see them. This must be the channel now. Last of the ebb, I reckon.'

Gresham looked over the side to see the water rushing past. The longboat must be making six knots on this dead run and it was difficult to see how deep the channel was. The water had been clear out at sea but here, with the constant churning of mud and sand as the tide flowed fast into the lagoon, he couldn't see deeper than a foot or two. But he could sense that he was in shallow water; he could feel the boat being retarded and it was settling down deeper in the water from the effect of their speed in such little depth.

'You see those birds, sir? I'll want to gybe in a moment.'

Gresham looked up to see that Souter was pointing at a small group of moderately sized brown birds in the water ahead. It took less than a heartbeat to realise that they were standing, not floating.

'I hope they've got long legs, sir.'

'You may gybe when you see fit, Souter.'

It was better to leave it to the coxswain. He could see that Souter had a better appreciation of this bar than he had. Last of the ebb. If they touched ground now the falling tide would leave them stuck fast and then there'd be nothing for it but to surrender.

'Gybe-oh!'

With this lug rig the mainsail was loose-footed – it had no boom – and as Souter pushed the helm over it quickly filled on the other tack.

'Dip the lug!'

Two of the hands grabbed the throat of the sail and bodily hauled the yard over to what was now the leeward side. Gresham had often seen luggers sail with the yard to windward, just for convenience. It was of no consequence usually, but today they needed every fraction of a knot, and to leeward it must be.

The brown birds on the starboard bow rose with one accord and took to the air shrieking their annoyance at being disturbed. Gresham had a moment to notice just how short their legs were.

Now the effect of the shallow water could be felt by everyone. The seamen cast knowing glances at each other.

'Off with your shoes, boys,' Souter shouted, 'we may have to push her home yet.'

***

Withies came and went in rapid sequence but it wasn't clear to either Gresham or Souter which side of the channel they marked. There seemed to be a definite flow behind the longboat, which suggested that the water was going somewhere.

Boom!

The ball fell short, closer to the pursuing boats than to the longboat, it must have been fired at the gun's extreme range. That was one danger past, the frigate could no longer influence this chase, but its boats could and Gresham watched as the first yawl set its sail and sped after its partner. The closest pursuer was perhaps two cables astern and making about the same speed as the longboat, and it was following exactly in the longboat's wake. Then these Frenchmen knew no more of this supposed channel than he did. But the fugitive's jeopardy still remained; any check in the longboat's progress, even if only for a couple of minutes, would surely see them taken. And those boats were smaller than the longboat and would draw a few inches less.

'How much further, sir? Did the Frenchman say?'

'No, he didn't and I don't expect he knew, but I expect the shallows run for about a mile, then we'll be in deeper water in the lagoon. Then ten miles perhaps until the first gap in the islands and we can make for the sea.'

Souter nodded, never taking his eyes off the water ahead. A darker patch to larboard made him bring up the helm. The longboat was close to another gybe and the mainsail leech lifted threateningly. They could all feel the boat slowing.

'Gybe-oh!' shouted Souter. 'I think we're touching, sir. I reckon the channel's to starboard of us.'

The longboat was slowing, there was no denying it. Their keel must be carving a path through the mud a couple of inches deep. Gresham looked astern; the French yawl was gaining on them while they were in the mud's clutches.

'Damn and blast it!'

The longboat was hardly moving and now that he looked over the side he could see the brown mud and the tendrils of green weed waving mockingly.

Then, with a gentle lurch they came to a complete stop.

'Over the side and push for all you're worth men. Souter, heave everything overboard that can be moved, just keep the oars and leave the sails sheeted. Then stay in the boat and steer.'

With that Gresham threw himself over the stern without shifting shoes, stockings or breaches. The water was warm and the mud was soft and cloying. It felt like his feet sank six inches into the ooze, and the water must have been nearly three feet deep. Two men joined him at the stern and the others heaved from the sides. Souter was madly jettisoning the boat's gear. Over went the boom and the gaff for their normal rig. Over went the water casks and the biscuit barrel and the packages of salt beef, and over went the gratings for the forefoot. The difference could be felt immediately as without the weight of the crew and emptied of everything movable, the longboat rose six inches in the water. Now the pushing was having an effect and the sails were still drawing. Slowly, slowly the longboat started to move forward. Gresham risked a look over his shoulder to see the yawl no more than a hundred yards astern. He could make out the individual faces, he could see the marines at the bow levelling their muskets. The French coxswain had chosen a path some twenty yards to starboard of the longboat's, perhaps he did know the channel after all.

Pop! Pop!

The marines had opened fire. Gresham felt horribly vulnerable with his broad back presented to the enemy. But the longboat was moving now. Was she free of the mud? Yes!

'She's underway, sir, and answering her helm.'

Souter moved the tiller to starboard and the longboat felt noticeably freer.

'Keep pushing, wait for my word… Now! Everybody in.'

The seamen scrambled over the gunwales while Gresham gave a few last mighty heaves on the stern, then he grasped the top of the transom and hauled himself up, with Souter grabbing the waistband of his breeches to drag him over and in.

Pop! Pop! Pop!

Another volley and Gresham felt a musket ball embed itself in the solid oak behind his back. There was a cry from forward and one of the seamen fell between the thwarts.

'Down. Everybody down below the thwarts. See to that man.'

He pointed at an older seaman who he knew had acted as a loblolly boy in some long-ago commission. He was no surgeon nor even a surgeon's mate but he should be able to apply a bandage or ease the man's last hours; one of the two was likely necessary.

The longboat was flying now and Gresham stood to look ahead, braving the French musketry. He hardly dared to hope but it looked as though they were through the worst. Ahead lay a long, long lagoon with gently rippling waves and not a wading bird nor a treacherous withy in sight. He was about to tell Souter when he heard the start of a cheer. He whipped around in time to see the lead pursuer's mast go by the board; it toppled forward as the yawl came to an abrupt stop. No gently shelving mud bank for the French, it looked like they had charged full tilt onto a hard oyster bed. That must have been the difference between the longboat's track and the twenty yards to starboard that the French coxswain thought was right.

That was one pursuer, the most deadly of the two dealt with. Now it was just the original yawl, the one that had thought to chase under oars. Gresham narrowed his eyes against the sun. The yawl was a good half mile astern and sailing no faster than the longboat. It was ten miles to the open ocean, so now it was a straight chase. But even if they were overhauled, he'd fight. Now that there was a clear path of escape he'd exchange musketry with any other boat. Aye, and he'd grapple with pistols and cutlasses or hand-to-hand if he had to.

'Bring her a point to larboard now, Souter. We still have the ebb with us so we should make the gap in an hour and a half and we'll see *Dartmouth* before the sun sets, but I fear we'll be thirsty by then. What, we have some water?'

One of the seamen in the bow was holding up a little breaker, the smallest example of the cooper's art, except for the staved flagons that he made in exchange for tobacco. The breaker held about three gallons of water; it was a permanent fixture in the boat, even when it was hoisted onto the spars in the ship's waist.

'Just that little cask, sir,' said Souter, 'It must have been under the thwarts and I overlooked it when I was jettisoning everything else.'

Gresham looked sharply at the coxswain. He didn't a believe a word of it.

***

By the time the longboat reached the gap between Dauphin and Massacre islands the pursuing yawl was more than a mile astern. Outside, in the open sea, the wind was blowing freshly from the nor'east and the yawl took one look at it and turned back for the lagoon. That French officer in charge could calculate that by the time they got back to the shallows the tide would have risen sufficiently to allow them easy passage and they could help the other boat as they passed. Anything was better than beating back to the east in this stiff wind with the near certainty of a night at sea and no provisions in the boats.

The bow lookout sighted *Dartmouth's* t'gallants with two hours of light left in the day, and the longboat nosed alongside as the great orange orb was just touching the western horizon. They handed the wounded man carefully up to the gangway with a bowline around his chest and his messmates placing his hands and feet so that he didn't slip. The heavy lead ball had passed right through his arm, breaking it just below the elbow. It was hardly a mortal wound, unless it became infected, and he was already looking forward to weeks or months of light duties.

'Well, Mister Gresham, you seem to have had an adventure.'

The first lieutenant gratefully accepted a glass of his captain's Madeira and settled down – with muddy shoes and stockings, breeches and shirt – to tell the story of the French reinforcement of Louisiana.

***

Enrico kept his watch on the quarterdeck as *Dartmouth* stood out to sea to reduce the risk of being seen by any of the coastal traffic that crossed and re-crossed between the French ports on the Gulf coast. It should have been the first lieutenant's watch as he was covering for Wishart who was away with the prize brig, but Gresham had spent the whole day in an open boat and Enrico had volunteered to stand the first watch.

Enrico loved this life with every fibre of his being. He loved the excitement, the danger, the friendships and the technical knowledge that was so necessary for a sea officer, and he found it all so much more satisfying than the life of a junior officer in the Sardinian cavalry. The regiment was all behind him now and in principal he was a lieutenant in the Sardinian navy, seconded to the British navy to learn the art of managing a square-rigged man-o'-war in anticipation of the day when Sardinia had its own fleet of frigates and fourth rates. Yet he knew that it was all a sham. The Angelini family's influence was spent and those plum appointments to the new frigates would go to men of the rising new families, those that leaned towards France rather than Tuscany. And it wouldn't have helped even if the Viscountess Angelini hadn't fallen out with King Charles Emmanuel, for the fact was that he had burned his bridges with his family after *Dartmouth's* last visit to Nice. He felt strongly that there was no way back. One day, when the minister of marine felt that he no longer needed the good will of the British navy, or when pressure from France became irresistible, his commission would be terminated and there'd be no reason left for him to tread the planks of a British quarterdeck, and what then?

He'd made enough friends in Antigua to find a place in one of the plantations, but that didn't appeal at all, he had no love for those islands. On the other hand he was well thought of in Williamsburg and felt that he could start a new life there, and that would be made all the easier if his cousin was back in residence in that house on the green, just down from the Governor's Palace. There were great opportunities in Virginia, and then there were the other twelve colonies, and now presumably Canada and the new territories that had opened up beyond the mountains to the west. Yes, his cousin would give him a roof over his head and he felt sure that he could talk his way into a respectable career in Williamsburg.

However, there was another option, one that he kept pushing to the back of his mind, barely letting it see the light of day. He could take a commission from King George. He was certain that he had a good enough reputation and the small matter of the lieutenant's examination would be no real obstacle; he'd surely learned enough in four years of war to satisfy any board of post-captains. He stopped dead in his walk, letting the dread possibility leave the deeper recesses of his mind – of his soul, it could be said – and find light and air. Every commissioned officer in the British navy had to swear an oath that *inter alia* – it was strange how he thought in Latin at times like this – renounced any faith in the Pope. In fact it went further and insulted the man and the office. He couldn't do that. He couldn't give the lie to the very principles upon which his early life was formed. With a stamp of his foot that startled the quartermaster he pushed the idea back to the darkness where it lurked, hiding from the bright daylight. He'd banished it, but he knew he hadn't heard its last; it was ready to ambush him whenever his mind was at ease.

Enrico hadn't realised how his heart had been racing as he thought through his future, and he counted the beats as it slowed down to a normal pace. He'd made himself anxious and for now there was no cause. For now he was master of all he surveyed on a glorious night, with a quarter moon hanging low in the sky, almost kissing the horizon, and the vast arc of the heavens ablaze with the fire of a million stars.

***

CHAPTER NINETEEN

Stay or Go?

Sunday, Third of January 1762.
Dartmouth, at Sea, off Mobile Bay.

'What are you going to do, Edward, now that you've determined that the French are reinforcing Louisiana? Will we fly back to Jamaica with the news?'

Breakfast in the great cabin was often a public affair, shared with the officer of the morning watch together with the master's mate and whichever midshipmen had been on deck for those four hours, but this morning Carlisle and Chiara breakfasted alone. Carlisle found the atmosphere all wrong. He was delighted with his wife's presence at supper, but he had discovered that her mind worked faster than his at breakfast, and he couldn't keep up with the constant stream of questions when he was still trying to make sense of the day to come. In this case, however, he thought he knew where the conversation was leading; Chiara was missing Joshua, their son. When they set out from Antigua a month ago the prospect of a spell without the cares of motherhood had appeared attractive and she passed Joshua into the hands of a nurse under the supervision of her manservant with hardly a thought. But the days and weeks were passing and a three-year-old boy changed and developed without any heed for an absent mother, and Chiara, although she wouldn't say it, was ready to go back to Antigua.

'Well, my dear, you're quite right, of course. This information needs to get back to Jamaica and to London, yet I believe it can wait a day or two. I have it in mind to annoy the French a little before I leave. They must know that there's a British man-o'-war in the offing, but I'll wager that they don't know whether they have to contend with a little sloop or a seventy-four. Although, on reflection, he's seen our longboat and will know that it's too big to belong to anything less than a fifth rate. He won't believe a sloop, then, but he could be deceived in believing we are about the same force as him, and in that case he will have to come out and look for us – the pressure from the merchants will force his hand – and I hope to bring him to action, or at least to scare him so that he'll hide away in Mobile Bay until the war is over.'

'And how long to make Jamaica, do you think?'

'Perhaps two weeks, if we're lucky. It's far to windward of us, you know.'

Chiara nodded, hiding her disappointment. She'd spent enough time at sea to know that the Caribbean was ruled by the trade winds, and they were almost dead foul for a passage from the Gulf of Mexico to Jamaica, and then right on the nose again from Jamaica to Antigua. That was why there were two distinctly different naval commands in the two areas, because communication between them was so difficult. She knew all that, but just at this moment what she needed from her husband was words of encouragement, not a stark statement of the facts.

'I need to talk to Beazley again but I have it in mind to take the Florida Straits past the Bahamas, make a long board out into the Atlantic and then the Windward Passage to Jamaica. I believe it will be faster at this time of year.'

'But still two weeks, you think?'

'I regret so, my dear, and then perhaps as long again to return to Antigua. However, as you know, there's no certainty that *Dartmouth* will be bound for Antigua. Whoever commands at Port Royal may have other plans. We could be doomed to the Jamaica squadron for months or years.'

Chiara knew all this of course, but she couldn't help a sigh passing her lips. Somehow she couldn't open up about her hopes and fears, not even to her husband. One part of her enjoyed the thrill and the mental stimulation of being involved in world affairs, and there was no denying that *Dartmouth* had been at the heart of things these past weeks.

She absolutely adored the times that she had to speak to important foreigners, and every conversation in a language that her husband couldn't easily follow cemented her position and her reputation. She knew that she had been helpful to him and to the ship's mission. No. She'd been more than just helpful. If she hadn't been involved this whole cruise would have turned out differently. And yet, and yet, she was being tugged mercilessly in the other direction. She missed her son and she missed her home. Every time she thought about what new faculties he had developed in her absence, it was all she could do to avoid bursting into tears. Deep inside she knew that this wonderful cruise must end soon and it was a hundred-to-one that she would never be able to repeat it. Her future lay in Williamsburg and her success would be measured by how well she managed a household and brought up a family.

She looked at her husband, seeing the man who had captivated her emotions so long ago in the Mediterranean. She knew that he wondered why she had left her life in Nice for him, but she could never tell him. She'd been running from a very similar dilemma to the one that she now faced. As a young woman in Sardinia and in Tuscany she'd been involved in matters of state, she'd been listened to and her advice sometimes heeded, but even then it couldn't last. Little by little she saw people's attitudes towards her change. Why was she concerning herself with these things? Why wasn't she married and manging her own household instead of trying to manage a nation? Yes, she'd run away from all that, but fate was pursuing her relentlessly, and here she was with just the same questions, but this time she knew the answers. She covered her rising distress by looking away as if fascinated by something beyond the windows, and changed the subject.

'This reinforcement of Louisiana, Edward. I'm surprised that the French think it's worth the ships and men when they are still fighting in Europe and when their navy has been so reduced. Surely they must know that America is lost to them.'

'Indeed, it's a mystery why they persevere. It would take a vast army to hold the American hinterland once my countrymen start moving west. The land up to the Ohio is only the start, you know, there's another two thousand miles to California and the north-western coast. And all that land is far to the north of Mobile and New Orleans, and of course the Mississippi flows south. It would be a huge undertaking to move an army up the river. And yet,' Carlisle paused in thought, 'you know, they held Canada with a pitifully small number of men against hugely superior British regular armies and colonial militia, and they did so through four years of war with barely any reinforcement from France. Perhaps they think they can do the same again.'

Chiara spread a thick layer of orange marmalade on her biscuit. It would have been better with toasted soft bread but the last of the Havana bread had been consumed days ago, so ship's biscuit it was. There wasn't much about British cuisine that Chiara liked and she often pined for the wonderful fresh foods of her native Mediterranean, but marmalade on toast was a delicacy and she had privately sworn never to be without a supply.

Should she interfere? Or now that her mind was made up to forego this dream-like existence, should she hold her tongue. Well, she had a lifetime of holding her tongue to come, and while she was free of domestic responsibilities, she'd make the most of it.

'However, there is perhaps another explanation, Edward.'

Carlisle looked up from his plate. He'd long ago learned not to dismiss his wife's insights on international affairs.

'If you were King Louis – no, don't laugh – and you believed that Spain would join the war this year, wouldn't you have some grand plans for co-operation? Something to mark this new family pact, something that would make an impact on the long series of French failures. Now, the invasion of England is an obvious one, and it would offer a rapid end to the war with the return of all their colonies in exchange for withdrawing their armies back across the Channel. But we know that it would be a risky venture and no army has succeeded for centuries. Even if an invasion could be attempted, it has little do with us in the New World, and surely they must attempt something here, even if it's only a contingency in case an invasion fails. Guadeloupe and Dominica would be vulnerable to a combined French and Spanish attack, and Jamaica of course, but the first two are far to windward of the squadrons in New Spain, and Jamaica is well garrisoned. What does seem credible is for the Spanish forces in Florida to join with the French in Louisiana and attack the southern British colonies. Georgia must be at risk, and if they succeed there, then South Carolina, North Carolina, Virginia even. Any one of those would make a powerful bargaining counter at the peace negotiations, and at this stage, that must be what Grenville and Choiseul and Wall are thinking of. Could we be witnessing the start of a grand design, a plan to be initiated when this secret treaty is enacted?'

Carlisle stared at the window, dumbfounded by his wife's analysis. It could certainly be true, and the idea of an attack on Jamaica might be a mere chimera. If the French and Spanish held Georgia and the Carolinas, Britain would have to offer anything – everything – to regain them, and Carlisle well knew how lightly they were defended. If Sir Henry Moore in Jamaica had this information about the troop concentration in Mobile it could change his plans.

Yet still, he could afford a day or two to test that French frigate's mettle, and test it he would.

***

CHAPTER TWENTY

Carpe Diem

Monday, Fourth of January 1762.
The Admiralty, London.

Lord Anson spread his coat tails to catch the heat from the fire. He was growing no younger and nowadays the cold seemed to seep into his very bones. Outside a brisk nor'easter brought occasional snow flurries and every kerbstone sported a miniature snowdrift that grew hour-by-hour. He could hear the sweepers outside, clearing a path for any visitors who looked as though they could spare sixpence, and even on this frigid January day there was a steady stream of hopeful half-pay captains and lieutenants looking for a ship. He spared them hardly a thought. After so long as first lord, his hide had become thickened and he no longer saw them as men like him, but as pawns in a chess game where the rules changed with each move and victory wasn't a defined state.

Today Anson wasn't concerned with pawns, but to draw out the analogy, his visitor today was at least a bishop or a rook, and by many measures he held the position of the queen on the chessboard of state. He was able to move freely through the body politic and leave a trail of broken opponents in his wake, but he was always vulnerable to counter-attack.

George Grenville was a younger man of about fifty and he looked entirely at ease with the weather; he hadn't as much as commented on it, which for an Englishman was unusual. Of course his short journey from Parliament to the Admiralty building would have been made in an enclosed chair with thick curtains and heated burlap-wrapped bricks at his feet to keep out the chill. A few infant snowdrifts wouldn't have affected him at all.

Cousins At Arms

Anson had been listening in silence for a good few minutes but now Grenville's monologue had ceased and there was an awkward pause while Anson considered the implications of what he had heard. He cleared his throat and blew his nose into a handkerchief.

'Then we're at war with Spain. Well, it had to come and it's better to seize the day rather than to allow the Spanish the luxury of choosing when to announce their intentions. As Machiavelli tells us, *There is no avoiding war; it can only be postponed to the advantage of others*. I offer that quotation freely, my dear Grenville, and you may use it in your next speech, if you wish.'

Grenville was a seasoned politician and he'd recently risen to the leadership of the House of Commons, following his brother-in-law William Pitt's resignation in October. He wasn't going to let an ill-considered quotation nor an inaccurate statement stand, even though he always felt ill-at-ease in Anson's company, intimidated even, and was usually reluctant to argue.

'Oh, that will never do my Lord. We're all Whigs, at least for the time being, and Machiavelli is still *persona non grata*, he's far too much of a Tory. I'd be hissed out of the place. Now, if you could find me an appropriate quotation of Plato's that justifies a pre-emptive war, then I'll be in your debt; he's the man of the day.'

Grenville fidgeted with his pocket watch; his time was precious and he had a lot on his mind.

'And I must insist that we are not yet at war. The Spanish ambassador has been sent for, my Lord, and there'll be statements in both houses this afternoon and *then* we'll be at war. It will be Britain against a Bourbon family pact all over again. Louis and Charles, cousins at arms. But you're right, and we do indeed need to seize the day.'

Grenville couldn't hide his anxiety. His brother-in-law William Pitt had resigned largely because he wanted to declare a pre-emptive war against Spain, and the King would have none of it. Now, here they were, about to do just that, and he knew better than anyone how vulnerable the government was after a *volte-face* of that magnitude, and how exposed he was in his own person.

'Well, Grenville, the navy's as ready as it'll every be. I can't believe we'll wring another penny out of Parliament and even if we could we'd be hard pressed to find enough men for any more ships. Tell me, if you can, what swayed the King and Parliament after so long with their heads in the sand? Spain has never had any love for us and any sensible man could see that we would have to fight them again. We could as well have called them out last year.'

'It's the treaty mainly, but also this embargo on our trade. Our merchants have been expelled from Spain and their goods in the warehouses have been seized, and that's not to be tolerated. Do you know, I'm constantly amazed at how these men of business fail to see the way of the wind. What sensible man would have kept full warehouses in Spain, after five years of war with the Spanish King's cousin, forsooth? However, as you well know, nothing moves the house like an immediate and tangible threat to our trade. The members can hold their noses at as many secret treaties as they like – and there will always be those who suspect that the government is inventing causes – but goods seized without any compensation will never fail to raise them from their seats.'

'Ah yes, the treaty. I suppose the French deliberately leaked it in order to force our hand, and to forestall any shyness on Spain's part, is that so? It's a pity because I've instructed Jamaica and the Leeward Islands to be as accommodating to the Spanish as possible. I heard from Sir James Douglas the other day that he sent a fourth rate to Havana to deliver the governor-general's furniture. Apparently the ship that was carrying it was wrecked and it fell into Sir James' hands. I do hope the Dons appreciate the gesture.'

'Yes, the French sent us a copy of this *secret* treaty by devious means, unattributable of course, otherwise we'd use it to drive a wedge between Louis and Charles. It's just such a damned inconvenient time.'

Anson turned to the fire to conceal a smile. It was well known that the King's advisor, the Earl of Bute, wanted an end to this war and would be prepared to give the French just about anything they wanted to bring about a peaceful resolution. That was why Pitt resigned, he couldn't stomach the thought of handing back all the British gains from the war. What in that case would it have achieved? Certainly the French should have their sugar islands, but they mustn't be allowed to harbour any designs on the American continent. And there was a clause in the secret treaty that committed France to giving Minorca back to Spain, that also couldn't be allowed. Minorca was the only sensible place for watching the French fleet at Toulon, and it would make any future war in the Mediterranean doubly difficult if it wasn't available to the British navy. The French fondly believed that bringing Spain in on their side would tip the balance at sea, and a Spanish invasion of Britain's ally Portugal would further stretch the navy and draw away British regiments that could otherwise have been fighting on the continent. And then there was that oldest of French strategies, the invasion of England. Anson knew very well that King Louis had no desire to rule in London, but a French army encamped in Kent or Sussex or Hampshire would force Britain to negotiate from a position of weakness.

'How will this affect your deployments, My Lord? You'll have to reinforce the Channel Fleet I imagine.'

Anson wasn't a man to be hurried and he left the secretary of state waiting for a good half minute, although there was no need to, it was just a ploy to keep him off-balance. He'd thought this through over the last year and his plans were made; they were just on hold until war with Spain was declared.

'This is too early for the Spanish navy; they need at least another six months to bring their fleet to full readiness. Well, I'd go further and say they need that time to achieve any sort of readiness, they really are dismally unprepared. Our informants have reported that most of their line-of-battle is in ordinary in Cadiz and Cartagena. They have a good squadron at Havana but they'll need that when the Jamaica squadron gets wind of this new war. No, I'll recall no ships, but all the first and second rates that are here will stay in home waters until we see how things lie. No doubt there'll be an army to be sent to Portugal and that will need a decent squadron, but all of that can be achieved without disturbing the foreign stations. In fact, I think we can consider going onto the offensive. I'll be interested to hear what our fourth rate found in Havana, if he was allowed in. We haven't had a man-o'-war in there for years, and I suspect the Dons may have let their guard down. We'll see. And then there's the annual *Flota*. I'll wager that King Charles would rather have seen *that* home before he was forced into a war. It's only the injection of New World silver that keeps Spain from penury.'

It was Grenville's turn to look thoughtful. He hadn't realised how eager the navy would be to take the offensive against Spain. For his part he could think of few worse situations than being at war with both France and Spain, and he knew how fragile the British economy was becoming with the constant demands for money from the navy and the army.

'You'll take your seat for the announcement, my Lord? The government will need support in both houses.'

'I hope so, my dear Grenville, I hope so.'

Anson wasn't unmoved by the need to support the government, but everyone knew that he was at best lukewarm in his backing for the Earl of Bute, the rising star who surely saw himself as the future king on the chessboard. One day, when Bute was feeling strong enough and the King was pleased to be compliant, Newcastle would be ousted and then Anson would lose his place as first lord of the Admiralty. But not now, not with the war entering a whole new phase. So for today he would support the government, but it did no harm to play fast-and-loose with Grenville, and it amused him to do so.

***

CHAPTER TWENTY-ONE

The Lure

Monday, Fourth of January 1762.
Dartmouth, at Sea, off Mobile Bay.

'High water at five o'clock tomorrow morning I reckon, sir.'

Beazley was studying the only chart that they had of Mobile Bay. They'd been off this coast for two days now and he had a good idea of the times of the tides and from that datum he'd be able to estimate the ebb and flow for as long as they stayed here. He'd listened to Gresham and Souter's account of the rise and fall and the flow in the mouth of the bay and in the lagoon to the west and had made his deductions. Add fifty minutes for each day that passed and it was as good as having a tide table of Portsmouth Harbour in his hand.

Carlisle nodded in agreement. Five o'clock was good enough for his purposes, nearly two hours before sunrise. But he knew all this already; he'd calculated it himself before he invited his officers into the cabin to plan this little expedition. They were all looking at him, waiting to hear what he had in mind for the annoyance of the enemy.

'Well Gentlemen, we have to lure this frigate out if we are to engage with him, and that won't be easy. He's seen our longboat and must be certain that it doesn't belong to a sloop or a sixth rate. Granted, it could just as well have belonged to a fifth, but I don't hold out much hope of persuading him of that. He'll remember us from the chase in the Old Bahama Straits and won't be persuaded that that there are two British men-o'-war lurking in the Gulf of Mexico. I think we have to assume that he knows who we are.'

Gresham glanced at Beazley. It was asking too much that a frigate, even a large one – a fifth rate – should voluntarily engage in a single-ship action with a fourth rate. It wasn't just the number of guns – and *Dartmouth* carried fifty to the frigates thirty-six – but a fourth rate also had much heavier guns, twenty-fours and twelves against the Frenchman's outfit of twelves. And *Dartmouth* was built with massive frames and planking to take punishing broadsides in the line of battle, while a frigate was built with speed in mind and her timbers were necessarily lighter.

'We have to put pressure on this French captain. Now, I've deliberately left two days since we last annoyed him, to let him consider his position. The coastwise traffic should be at a standstill by now and the merchants and the soldiers and the local governors will all be wanting to know what he's doing about it. Why has a single enemy ship managed to blockade a whole coast?'

He looked at Gresham and Torrance. They must know that a boat expedition was in prospect but Gresham was looking doubtful, wondering perhaps what could be achieved against an alert enemy, and Torrance looked blank. But they lacked imagination.

'Yes, I know that he won't be willing to come out and face us, whatever pressure is put upon him. At best he'll try to slip out without our knowing and summon help. That's what he'll be thinking. But he'll have to do something if we became enough of a nuisance and he might take the bait in a moment of passion, in the heat of a disturbance. Now, Mister Gresham, do you think you can cut out one of those transports or storeships with the longboat and pinnace?'

Gresham still looked dubious and he scratched his head as he remembered how the anchorage was set out.

'Well, sir, perhaps. It all depends on what measures they've taken since we were last there. If I were in that frigate I'd shift my berth so that I was to seaward of the anchorage and I'd have a boat rowing guard across the harbour entrance. I wouldn't trust a single vessel, not a coaster, nor a fishing boat, having seen how we passed off the longboat as a lugger. They looked handy enough and they cleared away that gun as fast as I've seen it done, aye and got a few shots at us before we ran out of range, and I expect they'll take all the precautions against surprise. So, as I said, sir, it may be possible but only if they don't know their business.'

'Good, that's exactly what I hoped you would say, Mister Gresham, and I'm sure you're right. It would be pleasant to make a prize of one of those ships but I doubt whether it can be done. However, by at least attempting to enter the bay we'll raise their level of discomfort. If we can persuade them that the longboat and the pinnace will spoil their sleep every morning from now 'til doomsday, perhaps we can encourage them to do something about it, to lay a trap for you, or to chase you again. That would take the pressure off that French captain, and he'd reason that if we lost our two biggest boats – he can't know that we already lost one in the Straits, which is a pity – then we'd be forced to withdraw.'

Gresham still looked doubtful while Torrance didn't dare give the impression of anything other than complete agreement with his captain. It was Carlisle's good word that would see him at the lieutenant's board when they were next in England, and he'd do anything to be assured of it.

'Don't you see? He must – he is absolutely bound – to do something to free up the coastal trade. Those companies of soldiers won't want to march to the Mississippi to start their journey up to the Ohio or wherever they're bound. They'll be expecting to go in small coastal craft that can sail along the coast to New Orleans. Every day that we keep them in Mobile Bay is a day lost on their expedition. I don't say that he'll willingly come out and fight but I do believe he'll do anything short of that, and we must be ready to take advantage. So, Mister Gresham, Mister Torrance, I want you to go into the bay tomorrow morning, or as far as you can without having to fight, and test their resolve. If you can do any damage, or take prizes, so much the better, but don't risk the boats or we really will have to withdraw.'

***

The moon had set in the middle watch and a light westerly wind brought a bank of cloud that blotted out the stars and planets. There was not a point of light on the whole wide surface of the sea and the watery world was as dark as the first moment of creation. *Dartmouth* was creeping towards the land under courses alone with two leadsmen singing out the soundings and the longboat and pinnace riding alongside on their painters.

'Two knots and a fathom, sir,' said Midshipman Young, touching his hat.

Beazley turned to the dark shape that he assumed to be his captain.

'Two knots and a fathom and we've ten fathoms beneath us, sir. I reckon we're two leagues off the mouth of the bay and a league clear of the spit. The tide will be on the ebb still.'

'Very well. Heave to here, Mister Beazley.'

'By the deep, eleven.'

There was a pause as the leadsman and the bosun studied the sample of the seabed brought up in the tallow-filled hollow at the bottom of the lead. Even in this moment that needed his greatest concentration, he noticed that it was Foster at the lead, the man who'd disgraced himself in the Old Bahama Straits. Evidently he'd redeemed himself sufficiently to regain the bosun's trust.

'Grey sand and mud, sir.'

The bosun's gruff voice confirmed that the ground was neither shoaling nor deepening, and *Dartmouth* was lying above the smooth, sandy plateau that stretched out from the shore before it descended into the depths of the central Gulf of Mexico.

'Mister Gresham, Mister Torrance, are you ready?'

They were all whispering. It was ridiculous; no voice could carry six miles to the land but even the bosun had moderated his accustomed deep roar to a soft rumble. There was something about boat operations at night on a hostile shore, something that brought the hackles up at the back of the neck and forced a hush upon the deck and solemn faces among the boat crews. Gresham answered for both of them.

'Ready, sir.'

'What's the course for the mouth of the bay, Mister Beazley?'

'Dead north, sir, at two leagues. That should clear the sou'eastern point of the spit but you gentlemen would be well advised to use the boat lead after you've gone a mile or so.'

Carlisle could see that Gresham and Torrance were taking careful note of the master's advice. He felt a touch on his elbow and saw that Chiara had come on deck to watch this expedition depart. She was wearing a dark cloak that swept the planking as she walked and spread out in the little breeze like a leeward studding sail. Yet even dressed thus and barely visible in the profound darkness, she contrived to look elegant. A good omen, perhaps? Carlisle thought so and probably so did his officers.

'Very well, remember that you are there to cause unease, not engage in any heroics. I can't afford to lose you or the men or the boats. If you can get into the anchorage without risk then do so, but if there's a guard boat or if the frigate has shifted its berth, then just let them know you're there and then come back on the tide before the sea breeze sets in.'

Gresham offered his hand as he always did at times like this. Torrance hung back but Carlisle grasped his hand also. There was no telling how boat expeditions would turn out and he had a deep affection for his officers. They turned away to the boats and with a few soft commands they were quickly lost in the blackness.

***

Torrance had a watch that he'd borrowed from Horace Young and a boat compass that Beazley had given him with dire threats if it was lost or damaged. He had a dark lantern that showed a tiny sliver of light when a little tin window was opened, and a good hand in the bow with the ten-fathom boat lead. That was all he had to navigate on this blackest of nights, except for a tiny pinprick of light from Gresham's boat where the longboat's dark lantern was shining from its transom to keep the pinnace in station astern.

He'd been on boat expeditions before, in fact he thought himself more experienced than most in this kind of work, but he'd never been on one quite like this. On every other occasion he'd had definite orders: to cut out a prize, to take soundings and bearings, to land marines. He'd been on all kinds of missions, but each one had been carefully planned. This time he had little more than his orders to follow the first lieutenant's boat and to use his best endeavours to annoy the enemy within the strict parameters that Carlisle had laid down. He really, truly, had no idea what would happen.

'Seven fathom.'

The leadsman was doing his duty well. He'd been told not to report unless the depth changed enough to be indicated by one of the markers on the line. There were to be no calls of *by the deep* – an approximation of a depth between two markers – until they were in less than two fathoms, and there was therefore no need to preface the calls with *by the mark*. Each additional word could be picked up by an alert enemy in a picket boat.

The oarsmen were keeping up a steady rhythm. It was easy work because the pinnace was far lighter than the longboat and needed much less effort to propel it through the water. The coxswain had the tiller and he could see the tiny light ahead as well as his officer could. All Torrance had to do was to ensure that the pinnace didn't creep up too close to the longboat, and to suppress the oarsmen's whispering. They were all excited at this novel expedition, and were inclined to chat to each other, and he knew how that could escalate. If he didn't check them, in no time someone would be laughing out loud. They each had a cutlass or boarding axe stowed under their seat and a primed pistol carefully wrapped against the dew lying on the thwart beside them. Torrance had told them what he knew but had realised how hollow it sounded, without a particular goal in mind. But it didn't seem to dampen their enthusiasm.

'Five fathom.'

On through the shrouded world with only that tiny glimmer of light to guide them. Torrance looked at the boat compass every minute, but there really wasn't any need. Gresham was steering a true course and even if he wasn't the pinnace must follow the longboat. If he saw the longboat steer wildly away from the course he'd catch up and have a whispered conversation, but the chances are that Gresham would have a good reason for anything he did.

'Three fathom.'

A pause as he heard the leadsman swing the line again. He must have detected that the boat was running into shallower water, otherwise he'd have kept to his normal rhythm of soundings.

'Two fathom.'

That must be the tail of the spit. With luck the water would get no shallower and they'd soon be over it and moving into the bay's mouth. If that was so they had just two miles to go, twenty minutes at this pace.

The coxswain, a man named Fulsome who had been in Torrance's watch on-and-off for two years, nudged him and pointed out to starboard, but Torrance had already seen it. The far horizon was lightening with the prospect of a new day. It did nothing for the inky blackness that surrounded them, but it gave notice that in half an hour they'd be naked to the gaze of anyone who cared to look to seaward. But wasn't that the point? To demonstrate to the French that they no longer held dominion over this part of the Gulf of Mexico? In fact, with *Dartmouth's* control over the waters between Mobile Bay and the mouths of the Mississippi, the French owned no part of the Gulf that could be remotely useful to them. The shoreline ahead was where their territorial authority started and ended; by their inaction they had ceded sovereignty of the navigable waters to a foreign intruder.

'Two fathom.'

Torrance suppressed an instinct to berate the leadsman for that unnecessary call; the water depth hadn't changed. But he remembered that he'd shown the leadsman the chart precisely so that he could make intelligent use of the lead line. He was pointing out that the depth had steadied, rather than leaving it to be inferred from his silence.

'And a half, two.'

Over the spit, apparently. Now, was that land he could see ahead, or just a thickening of the darkness? Yes, land for certain and it was becoming clearer every minute. Soon the sun would peep over the horizon and then the tropical twilight would end and a new day would begin.

He could see the longboat now, and over to starboard the eastern arm of the enclosing land thrust out into the channel. Ah, there was the western arm as well. He looked over his shoulder, out to sea. No hint of dawn there; in fact there was a sea mist that reduced the visibility to a bare mile. They'd have difficulty finding *Dartmouth* when this was all over, but probably it would burn off with the sun.

The longboat came to larboard, evidently making for the centre of the channel. A point would do it, and Gresham could steady up on about nor'-by-west. But Torrance was startled to see the longboat continue turning; two points, three, four. Then he saw it, low in the water and barely visible against the land, a boat, and not more than a cable distant.

'Pull away, men.'

There was a breathless twenty seconds as the pinnace picked up its pace and sped westward in the longboat's wake. Then a shout came over the water. A shout in French, an urgent question.

'Qui va la'

And again, louder and more insistent.

'Qui va la. Qui va la.'

A sliver of orange sun burst over the horizon and suddenly the whole scene was clear. There was a French boat rowing guard, something along the lines of *Dartmouth's* lost cutter, rowing eight oars with an officer at the tiller and a marine with a musket at the bow and stern.

A sudden puff of smoke showed where one of the muskets was fired, then the other. They'd have no time to reload. It was a warning to the frigate, he assumed, rather than an attempt to injure the longboat or pinnace.

'Oh pull, pull,' shouted Torrance, 'pull for all you're worth. Cut across the longboat's stern and get between the guard boat and the anchorage, Fulsome.'

The pinnace was catching up on the longboat, it was almost abeam. The guard boat knew its peril and was pulling fast for the safety of the bay. There was a flash of sunlight against steel as the marines worked their rammers to reload.

With an almost physical effort Torrance took a grip of his wild emotions. The French guard boat couldn't escape, not with Gresham going straight at him and the pinnace manoeuvering to block his retreat. He looked around, surely this wasn't all the French could do. He could see that a battery had been set up on the western arm of the bay's entrance, but both of the boats were well out of range. Beyond the twin arms of land he could see that the frigate had indeed shifted its berth and it was now in a good position to protect the transports and storeships. *Dartmouth's* boats were in no danger, not at nearly two miles distance, but what was that? Something was creeping along the shoreline taking advantage of the shadows and the glare of the rising sun on the eastern side, opposite the anchorage. Torrance stared for a moment, wiping the tears from his eyes as he looked straight into the sun. A boat, about the size of *Dartmouth's* longboat, and it was stuffed with men. He could see the twinkle of light reflected off muskets. It had that bulky look to its bows that generally meant that it had shipped a boat gun, a two-or-three pounder. They were rowing into a trap!

***

Gresham urged his men on, determined to capture the cutter before it could reach the protection of the frigate's guns, or slip close enough inshore to be covered by the battery on the point. It would be touch-and-go but Torrance seemed to have grasped the situation and had crossed the longboat's stern to intercept the retreating French boat.

'Pull… pull…'

Gresham beat the time, urging his oarsmen to a greater effort. He had to be careful, but the tide was still ebbing, he could see the evidence of it now, and if they grappled with the French boat, they'd all be set to seaward, away from that wicked-looking frigate. He heard a pistol shot from the pinnace. What was Torrance about? He was far out of range for taking shots at the guard boat.

'Mister Torrance has turned away, sir. Oh, there's another boat over the other side… there sir!'

Souter pointed urgently to the far side of the channel. Gresham took one look then turned back to the oarsmen. They could all have seen the new boat but were so intent on pulling a clean stroke that not one had noticed it. Now the stroke oar was looking nervously over Gresham's shoulder.

'One last effort, men, and she's ours. Don't worry about that other boat, Mister Torrance will hold it for us. Pull!'

***

CHAPTER TWENTY-TWO

A Lee Shore

Tuesday, Fifth of January 1762.
Longboat and Pinnace, at Sea, Mobile Bay.

Torrance turned the pinnace towards the fast approaching boat. He had no real idea what he would do when he came up with it, but he knew for certain that he must hold it off while Gresham dealt with the cutter. He remembered how difficult it was to point a boat gun even when the target was a substantial ship, and against a fast, agile boat like the pinnace, a hit would be achieved only by sheer chance. The same was true of musketry from an open boat: it was far better to get close and rely upon pistols and cutlasses. Knowing that gave him confidence that he could grapple the French boat, at least for a while, and then he'd just have to hope that Gresham would come to his rescue. One key factor was in his favour: the ebbing tide would take them offshore, away from the frigate and away from that new battery.

Crack!

The bows of the oncoming boat were hidden in the wreath of smoke as the bow gun opened its account. Torrance noticed that the shot pitched short and well to the left, but he really wasn't paying attention, he was more concerned with seeing that his men had their pistols, cutlasses and boarding axes ready.

'Let the men rest their oars, one pair at time, and prepare for grappling with that Frenchman.'

'Aye-aye sir.'

Fulsome touched the butt of his own pistol and ran his finger over the hammer to check that it was safe. There'd be time to cock the weapon when they were about to board. His cutlass was in its scabbard at his waist but he knew what he would use when they came to close quarters. The pinnace's tiller was four feet long and three inches thick and made of hard ash wood, and it was only secured in the rudder head by a loose pin.

Crack!

Another shot, closer this time but still hopelessly far from its target. Now he could hear muskets. There must be four or five men trying their luck, but the French boat was pulling as hard as the pinnace and it was the most unsteady of platforms for accurate shooting.

'Pull… pull… pull.'

Fulsome was calling the time, keeping the men in check so that they didn't arrive exhausted. The oarsmen all had their backs to the French boat now, and only he and Torrance could see their enemy. The pinnace rowed ten oars and Torrance and Fulsome made the total up to twelve. The French boat looked as though it had the same number of oarsmen but there were two men manning the gun and four blue-coated French marines firing over their heads.

'What'll you do, sir?'

What indeed? Torrance had been racking his brain for inspiration. He'd learned from his captain whose frequent cry was to avoid combat on equal terms, but if it became necessary, then do everything in your power to create chaos, to unsettle the enemy. It would do no good to just run the pinnace alongside the French boat and board it, they had more men and a bigger boat, and Torrance knew that he and his men would be dead or prisoners within a minute. So what advantage did he have? He looked again at the heavy lumbering boat on his bows. It must be slower, and less manoeuverable. It was probably twice the weight with all those men and the gun, and it pulled only the same number of oars as the pinnace. Now, whoever was commanding seemed pre-occupied with pointing that dammed boat gun, what if…

'Come three points to starboard, Fulsome. I want to force him to turn to keep that gun pointing, or to accept an attack on his beam.'

Fulsome grinned. That made sense; he could imagine how hard it would be to swing that boat's bows to keep pace with the fast-moving pinnace, and a crossing target was always harder to hit for a gun or for a musket. He pushed the tiller to larboard and the pinnace turned rapidly away from the enemy boat.

***

Souter steered straight at the French cutter. He looked over his crew. He could see that they were ready and now it was evident that they'd reach the enemy before they were in range of the frigate's guns. He glanced at the first lieutenant. Gresham was looking astern at the mist-shrouded sea then over to where the new battery was optimistically firing its first shots in the engagement.

'Straight at 'em, Souter.'

The French cutter was almost beam-on and the marines were still trying to reload. A musket ball hit one of the oars, momentarily throwing the oarsman off his stroke.

'Pull!'

'The frigate, sir, it's letting fall its tops'ls.'

Gresham glanced at the big French fifth rate. Souter was right and he could see the jib and fore stays'l being set. They must have slipped their anchor. Well, it was too late to worry about it now, he had a boatload of Frenchmen to deal with.

'Never mind the frigate. Ram that cutter, amidships if you can.'

The longboat was deep and wide and its planking was thick and heavy. The massive timbers of its bows hit the lightly-built cutter with a crash that knocked everyone off their feet, Frenchmen and English alike. Gresham had braced himself for the impact but still he had to haul himself out of the bottom boards. His shoulder felt like it had been kicked by a horse, and he could feel blood running from his nose.

'Board 'em lads! Over you go.'

It wasn't the solid wave of men that he would have wanted, half of his oarsmen were still trying to disentangle themselves from oars and stretchers, but it was still a respectable force and it overran the Frenchmen before they had a chance to react. A pistol banged beside Gresham's ear; English or French, he couldn't tell. In front of him the French officer was trying to gain his feet but Souter hit him a vicious blow with the butt of his pistol, laying him flat. Then it was all over. The French crew were all in the bottom of the boat with British seamen looming over them, daring them to arise. One of the French marines was bleeding from a gash to his head that had cut through his hat and almost severed his ear, but he didn't look in any imminent danger, and one of the longboat's crew was nursing a broken arm from the impact of the ramming. But that was all; it was a remarkably light casualty bill on both sides.

'Right, get all their weapons and oars into the longboat. The French officer is to come across also, the crew can stay in the cutter.'

There was a flurry of activity as the Frenchmen were pushed and pulled to reveal any pistols or swords. Everything that was found was passed from hand-to-hand back into the longboat. It was the work of just a few minutes and when the job was finished Gresham addressed the enemy officer in execrable French, mixed with whatever English words seemed to match the need. The Frenchman appeared to understand. The crew were being set adrift to make their own way back to Mobile Bay – the tide would turn soon and sweep them that way in any case – and the officer was a prisoner.

Gresham at last looked up again. The pinnace was almost grappling with the French longboat, a full mile away, so that was clearly where he must go. The frigate was underway – a seamanlike crew, certainly – and was standing out of the bay towards the longboat. He looked to seaward, praying for a miracle, hoping that he would see *Dartmouth* standing into the bay to save them, but there was nothing but that wall of mist that blocked out anything that was more than a mile distant. Gresham remembered what

Carlisle had said, that he would wait at the point where the boats had been cast off. He expected no relief from that direction.

***

Fulsome turned the pinnace back in towards the enemy longboat. It had come to a complete stop as it had backed one bank of oars to bring its gun to follow the speeding pinnace, and now it was wallowing in its own wake, pitching and rolling as the slopping waves caught up with it. The gunner's curses could be heard clearly across the water. It was a good plan of Mister Torrance's and it was ten to one against that boat gun scoring a hit, or even getting close.

'The frigate's getting underway, sir.'

He said it in a matter-of-fact tone. He knew that Torrance wouldn't disengage now. Not only would it leave the first lieutenant unsupported, but it would make them a much easier target for the gunner in the longboat. No, the frigate could do as it wished, the attack must go ahead.

'Right. Never mind that, be sure you strike the longboat amidships then push your tiller hard over. We'll board on our larboard side.'

Crack!

Torrance heard the longboat's gun fire at the same time as he felt the impact of the iron ball on the pinnace. It was the ten-to-one shot. It hit somewhere forward and threw up a spray of splinters. The larboard bow oarsman fell in a spray of blood, and his shattered oar fell over the side. The starboard bow oarsman reached across to help him, trying to keep his own oar clear of the water with his other hand.

'Stand by!'

The pinnace swept along the longboat's starboard side, throwing oarsmen to the deck and shattering their oars. A grapnel secured them alongside and Torrance, with a great shout, jumped across to the larger boat. There were bangs as pistols were fired and the sound of bodies colliding with bodies. The sheer ferocity of the attack swept the French from the stern sheets, but there were too many of them and

Torrance could see that they had twice his numbers still standing. He waved his sword and a half dozen men lurched forward, swinging cutlasses and boarding axes and the butts of their pistols. They levelled the front rank of the French, beat them down into the bottom of the boat and crushed them underfoot, but still they were outnumbered. Torrance saw one able seaman felled by a French musket butt and another slashed by a sword. Back they fell, back into the very stern of the French longboat.

Torrance looked over his shoulder at the pinnace. Could he retreat? Could he get his boat away despite this relentless barrage of blows? And where was Gresham? His field of vision had narrowed and now all he saw was the two boats, still locked together, and his own men falling as fast as barley before the farmer's scythe. Surely he'd done all he could. He looked around for a means of surrender. There was the French officer slashing about himself with his sword but he was so hemmed in that he couldn't make a blow land true. Torrance shouted at him, but there was no recognition. The Frenchman knew he was winning and had no time for anything else; he didn't understand that his enemy was trying to surrender.

Another crash and Torrance was thrown off his feet again. He lay for a second on the hard oak of the French thwart, hoping that it would all go away, that everyone would stop shouting, then his sense of duty drove him to his feet.

In that brief few seconds it had all changed. Somehow, miraculously, the French were turning about, facing a new threat from their bows. There was Gresham, thrusting with his sword as he led his crew from *Dartmouth's* longboat over the Frenchman's bows. Torrance shouted, rallying his men for a push that would squeeze the fight out of the enemy. Then it was all over, the French were dropping their weapons, raising their hands over their heads to ward of the blows from the victors.

***

Gresham looked around him as the last of the Frenchmen were forced down below their longboat's thwarts. The three boats were locked together with grapnels, their heads pointing in all different directions and under no kind of command as they drifted at the whim of the wind and tide. There were wounded and dying men on the longboat, both French and British, and a dead oarsman in the pinnace. Weapons were littered everywhere and the only man who looked unmoved was the French officer from the cutter who, with his hands bound behind him with a turn or two around a thwart was sitting helplessly, watching the dreadful scene unfold and hoping that the longboat didn't sink, taking him with it.

The tide was just on the turn and soon the whole assembly would be swept into Mobile Bay to be an easy prize for the French. And here, to seal their fate, was the French frigate under her tops'ls with both batteries of great guns thrusting through their ports. Gresham glared at it as though by his sheer ferocity he could turn it back. He wasn't a man to give up the fight, not while there was life in him, and he broke his stare to issue his orders.

'Throw all those French pistols and swords into the pinnace. Souter, take a man with you and tip that boat gun over the side, and all the oars. Where's that officer? Into the longboat with him, the rest can stay in their own boat and we'll tow them. Use the grapnel, it has two fathoms of chain. Take a couple of turns round the forward thwart. That's right, they won't cut through that in a hurry. Oarsmen back to your oars.'

There was a mad scramble to obey the first lieutenant's orders. The British wounded were dragged back to their boats and Gresham passed the line to tow the French longboat away.

'Mister Torrance, will the pinnace float?'

'Aye, sir, it will, unless there's a high sea.'

'Then stay in company and pull back to seaward. Let's see how far this frigate chooses to follow us. And let's see whether he's willing to fire at us with his own men so close.'

Gresham took the tiller; he was four men short on the oars and he needed Souter pulling. He had a brace of pistols beside him in case the French prisoners should try to cut their boat free or otherwise interfere with their escape. He would have liked to set them adrift as he had for the cutter, but he needed them as a shield against the French frigate's broadsides. Oh, he knew it would all be over soon, when the frigate got to windward and within musket range. Then they could fire into the British cutter without fear of hitting their own people. But where there was life there was hope, and he would play this out to the bitter end. He cast the lead, there was nobody else to do it. Two fathoms. Then they must be near the tail of the spit. He waved to Torrance and pushed the tiller hard to larboard and the longboat's bows turned west. That would delay the inevitable for half an hour at least as the frigate would have to skirt around the spit. Perhaps he could even pass into the lagoon between Massacre Island and Dauphin Island, and there start a whole new game of cat and mouse until the night came. Yes, there was still hope. He looked again out to sea but the mist hemmed them in as thoroughly as it had before. Surely the sun would burn it off soon. He held up his wetted finger. Yes, the wind was coming firmly from the south; the sea breeze had set in and the tide had turned, but still the mist persisted.

'The frigate's coming onto the port tack, sir.'

Souter had a better view of his pursuer. The frigate had been momentarily headed by the southerly breeze and had paid off with its head to the west. It was a brave move when he had still not passed to seaward of the spit. It was the tactic of a man who was determined that his prey wouldn't escape. Gresham watched in fascination, expecting at any moment to see the topsails bend and fall forward as the frigate slid up onto the sand. He watched almost breathlessly, but it wasn't to be and the two longboats, the pinnace and the following frigate crossed the spit and, in the faint breeze, stood on across the length of Dauphin Island. Gresham nodded his head in admiration at the French captain's persistence and at this display of seamanship. He looked ahead into the mist. It must be ten miles to the gap into the lagoon and his exhausted boat was making no more than two knots. Five hours then, at least, and the frigate would be up with them in no more than twenty minutes. Perhaps this really was the end. He looked back at the French longboat and waved a pistol to remind them not to attempt to interfere.

Boom!

A spout of water rose from the surface of the sea ahead of the boats. Souter looked questioningly at Gresham.

'Let 'em fire away. They won't fire right at us, not with those Frenchmen in tow. How are those officers doing?'

'Oh, they're well enough, sir.'

The two French officers were sitting in the bottom of the boat at Souter's feet. They could see nothing and they couldn't understand the rapid English being spoken around them. Everything else they heard only alarmed them and when the frigate started firing it must have seemed like the end of the world.

Gresham looked again at the frigate. It had shaken out its courses and now it had a good four knots speed advantage over the boats. He could see the marines lining its fo'c'sle and quarterdeck, some of them were already taking aim at the British boats. Once they were within fifty yards he'd have to surrender, but not before.

It had a dreadful inevitability about it. The nearest shoal water was two miles away to leeward and it might as well be on the moon for all the good it would do. The frigate was almost within musket range now and even the French officers could see what was happening. They were edging lower until they were actually under the stroke oar's thwart; nobody wanted to be a casualty of their own side's fire.

And at last the mist was lifting and the full glorious sun of a tropical day was pouring over the sweating oarsmen.

Boom!

A shot from a quarterdeck six pounder screamed low over the boats, a final warning. Gresham could see just what was happening. In a moment there would be a volley of fire from the marines' muskets. At that range there would be at least half a dozen hits on the boat, and he could expect two or three casualties. He gripped the tiller harder and raised his arm to wave to Torrance. Then he heard a broadside, at least twenty heavy guns firing in unison. He looked up at the frigate but could see nothing beyond. The volley of small arms never came and the frigate's bows came off the wind.

Gresham craned his neck to see what was happening. Somewhere behind the frigate another man-of-war had joined the fray, and he knew the sound of those twenty-four pounders well enough. It could only be *Dartmouth*.

Now the frigate was running before the wind. Gresham looked to the north where Dauphin Island had become visible. There was no safety for the Frenchman there. The frigate was trapped on a lee shore with an enemy of overwhelming force to seaward. He saw the courses furled hurriedly; he saw men running up to get the tops'ls in. The French captain was going to put his ship aground rather than have it taken by the British ship. He watched in fascination as the beautiful frigate ran under bare poles down towards Dauphin Island. When it came, the ship's end was almost graceful. It touched so gently that not a spar was lost, and within minutes the boats were in the water carrying out kedge anchors to prevent her being driven further ashore. He nodded in appreciation of the fine seamanship.

Slowly, wearily, the three boats turned their bows to seaward and started the long pull into the wind to where *Dartmouth* waited, hove to as close to this lee shore as the great ship dared come.

***

'What was the fellow thinking of, Mister Gresham? You were there, how did things seem to you?'

Carlisle looked amused at the turn of events, surprised

by the good fortune that had allowed him to force the French frigate aground on Dauphin Island. He could see that Gresham was tired, but he needed to know, to understand what had persuaded the French captain to leave the safety of Mobile Bay.

'It was the sea-mist, sir, I'm certain of it, that and the sight of his boats being taken before his very eyes. He hadn't intended to come out; he showed that when he slipped his anchor cable in such a hurry, and I'm sure it wasn't planned. I believe, sir, that the mist seeped into his head, so to say. He was overcome by the speed of events. I can't account for it otherwise.'

Gresham paused then spoke again.

'We lost three men, sir, and two more wounded, and the pinnace will need to be repaired. On the other hand the French lost more and I brought back two officers and a longboat, not unlike our own.'

Carlisle looked solemn. Three men were dead who yesterday lived and laughed with their shipmates. He never had learned the detachment that he'd seen in other captains, he still saw them as human beings, formed of the same clay as himself.

'Mister Angelini. My compliments to the doctor and I'd like to hear how the wounded men are doing.'

Carlisle and Gresham contemplated the stranded frigate. They were both thinking the same thing; How could they bring about its total destruction.

'We can't get close enough to bombard her, sir, it's too shallow, we'd be aground before we were in range. But I could take the boats in tonight and burn her, sir, just say the word.'

Carlisle gazed affectionately at his first lieutenant. His most endearing attribute was his constant readiness for any duty that could add to the enemy's woes. He shook his head sadly.

'I regret not, Mister Gresham. We know there are two companies of infantry and a few field guns camped on that island only two or three miles away. They'll be dispatched to protect the frigate, for sure, and I won't have you sent into that danger, not without a compelling reason. No, Mister Gresham, I fear there's nothing more we can do against him. Our work here is done and we'll sail for Jamaica by the Florida Straits as soon as this sea breeze dies.

***

CHAPTER TWENTY-THREE

Dispatches

Tuesday, Fifth of January 1762.
Pembroke, at Sea, off Cape Cross.

Captain John Wheelock drummed his fingers on his dining table and studied the young lieutenant in front of him. He'd spotted the brig at dawn and immediately saw it for what it should have been, a French merchantman working to windward having departed one of the ports on the southern side of Cuba, probably making for the Windward Passage. It was fortunate that he was a wealthy man and could shrug off the disappointment when he found that the brig was already a prize and belonged to *Dartmouth*. Well, Carlisle was welcome to it, but his officers didn't share that opinion; they were quietly seething at what they saw as the loss of *their* brig. *Pembroke* had been tied to the admiral's coat-tails in the line of battle for over year and hadn't taken a prize in all that time. This was their first real cruise since arriving at the Jamaica station, and now they found that their first prize was no prize at all. Yet that wasn't what concerned him at the moment, and he'd dismissed the oddly-rigged brig and its paltry cargo. The lieutenant's story was more interesting.

'Then Captain Carlisle told you that you may hand over these despatches to the first post-captain that you should find, or to the admiral's secretary at Port Royal, whichever came sooner, is that correct?'

'Yes, sir, just so.'

Wishart was wilting under the stern gaze. He hadn't had much to do with post-captains other than Carlisle, and he found this one intimidating. He felt as though he was being criticised, although for what he couldn't say.

'You know the contents of these letters, I assume?'

'In broad terms, yes, sir. Captain Carlisle explained the situation to me before we parted.'

Silence. Wishart could almost hear the post-captain's mind working.

Wheelock was evidently in a quandary. Despite what this lieutenant said, it was most unusual, unheard of in fact, for a captain to open dispatches that were clearly and indisputably marked for the commander-in-chief, and he knew that he would do so at his peril. It was entirely possible that Wishart had mistaken his verbal instructions and then, if Carlisle denied having given them, there could be trouble all round. Admiral Holmes' untimely death only made the matter more uncertain, for it was anyone's guess how his successor would view things. He'd heard that it might be Sir James Douglas from the Leeward Islands, or even Admiral Rodney, and it was to be expected that whoever it was would want to stamp his mark on this new station immediately. What better way than to haul a post-captain over the coals – or even order a court martial – for usurping the commander-in-chief's prerogative?

'Well, I'll decide whether I should open Captain Carlisle's letters after I've heard your story. Now, even your over-masted little brig should be able to round Negril Point on this tack, so there's no great hurry. Proceed, if you please, Mister Wishart.'

Wishart glanced at the clerk who was poised to record his words. It did nothing for the state of his nerves to know that whatever he said could come back to haunt him. He knew it would be difficult to get it all in the right order, but with a gulp that propelled his Adam's apple upwards beyond the top of his stock, he started.

Wheelock listened in complete silence as Wishart told his tale. The loggers of St. George's Island were interesting; indeed they were topical as he'd heard something of their situation before he sailed from Port Royal a week before. The lieutenant-governor had openly speculated on whether he should reinforce St. George's Island and the Yucatan shore if Spain joined the war. He'd spoken of recommending that it should be claimed for the King, if only as another bargaining chip in the peace negotiations. Carlisle wouldn't have known all that because it had happened after *Dartmouth* had sailed, but if he had known it would probably have changed his decision to head back to the Gulf of Mexico. Wheelock could pretend that he knew nothing of Sir Henry's musings; they hadn't made a single line in the orders that he'd been given for the cruise and there had been no talk of it in the commander-in-chief's office before he left Port Royal. But still, something should be done with this new information. He cast that aside for the moment; it was the secret treaty that really caught his interest. Of course, the two were inter-twined, and the loggers could expect to be attacked when a war started, as they had been in the past. It was a small matter in relation to Louisiana; the territory that the loggers called their own wasn't even claimed by Britain. However, Carlisle's opinion that the French were preparing an expedition up the Mississippi, perhaps with Spanish assistance, was of the utmost importance. It was becoming increasingly clear that the government viewed America as the lasting legacy from this war, and everything else could be sacrificed to keep it free of French influence.

A secret treaty, a Mississippi expedition, Yucatan loggers. Taken individually it was only the news of the treaty that warranted any action on his part, but taken as a whole, it painted a worrying picture of two nations plotting to pool their resources against Britain, and to do so at any moment. Of course, in Port Royal and in Kingston the talk was all about war with Spain and the threat to the island. Jamaica had been a thorn in the side of successive Spanish monarchs and their governors-general, and they had made plans in every war to invade the island and make an end to British interference west of the Antilles. This time, however, they would find the British navy with fewer ships in the Caribbean than had been the case in previous wars, and with no great, renowned Admiral to instil fear in the Spanish governors-general and captains-general. There was no

Vernon on the scene ready to make good his boast to capture Porto Bello with only six ships. If ever Jamaica was ripe for a change of ownership, it was now.

Captain Wheelock was so engrossed in his own thoughts that he didn't immediately notice that Wishart had finished and that he was sitting most uncomfortably waiting for some sort of reaction. Eventually Wheelock raised his head and fixed Wishart with a quizzical eye.

'This sergeant of artillery, he's on board the brig now, is he?'

'No, sir. He's in the boat alongside. I though it possible that you would want to question him yourself.'

'Good, that was sound thinking and it's saved some time, I expect. I may well want to transfer him to *Pembroke* but for now I'll take your word for his good faith.'

Wheelock stood and walked over to his writing desk. He took out a small clasp knife and cut the cords that enclosed the package, then he unwrapped the tarred canvas and removed the grape shot. Wheelock turned the unopened letter over and examined the seal. That must be Carlisle's family crest, but how a colonial had a family to speak of, more less a heraldic badge, was more than he could say. He tried it with his fingernail; yes it was firmly fixed to the paper, the letter hadn't been opened. Then he slid the knife underneath and twisted it upwards to break the seal.

Wishart thought that his torment would never end. Captain Wheelock read the letter once, then he read it again, and finally he stared abstractedly out of the stern windows, perhaps hoping that the Caribbean swell would give him inspiration.

He had to admit that Carlisle had handled this very well. The information about the treaty was persuasive, and even though it came from a mere sergeant of artillery, it was corroborated by the sighting of the troop convoy apparently heading for Louisiana. It was the physical presence of the sergeant that was so important in this case, and he must be available for his testimony to be examined back in Port

Royal. If it were true, then it would give the governor and the commander-in-chief – whoever that should be – a timescale for the start of Spanish aggression. It also gave them a timescale to consider their own offensive moves. He guessed that Anson would want to start the war against Spain by sending an expedition against an important Spanish port such as Havana, and that was another point of contact with Carlisle's cruise. He'd sailed through the Old Bahama Straits and added to the store of knowledge of the navigation of that difficult passage and he'd been to Havana and seen its defences. It suddenly occurred to Wheellock how little was known about the Spanish and French possessions to the west of Jamaica. It was the trade wind that was to blame, as always. Any ship passing beyond the Yucatan Channel was condemned to weeks of beating to and fro in an effort to return to Port Royal, and there had been few times during this war when valuable ships could be spared for so long.

As for French Louisiana and the Yucatan, that was additional useful information and it could well influence decisions in these last few months before the war at sea widened. He knew all about the euphoria in the British American colonies now that the French had been beaten in Canada. But he also knew how quickly that could turn in upon itself if the French strengthened the line of the Mississippi, confounding all the colonists' plans for expansion to the west. They'd held off vastly superior numbers of troops in Canada with a pitifully small army, could they do it again in the wide tracts of land that filled the belly of the continent? What part could Spanish Florida and Mexico play in that move, and could Louisiana become the foundation of a resurgent New France?

And Sir Henry, he knew, was bombarded with deputations of loggers every time one of their schooners came to Jamaica with logwood and mahogany and hides, and they all demanded the same thing: protection from Spanish raids. He guessed that the governor would do nothing, not until there was an outright war. And there was the rub. Britain and Spain could be at war already and in the faraway Caribbean, perhaps only the Spanish knew it.

He closed the dispatches gently, taking care not to further disturb Carlisle's seal, just in case it should become an issue. He knew now what he must do. Carlisle was busy on the coast of Louisiana and would bring back any further news but meanwhile these dispatches must be brought to Port Royal as soon as possible. One look at the brig beating painfully to windward under *Pembroke's* lee with its obviously jury-rigged topmasts told him that it could take a week if he handed the dispatches back to Wishart. Yes, the pieces had all fallen into place, as he knew they must if he considered long enough.

'Well, Mister Wishart, you've done well to bring these dispatches to my notice, and I'll be sure to mention you to the new commander-in-chief, when we see him. Meanwhile, I find that I must carry them to Port Royal myself, and I'll take the sergeant at the same time. Now, tell me, what would Captain Carlisle say if I were to send you elsewhere in the brig? How attached is he to his prize?'

Wishart almost smiled, then composed himself. It was a tricky question. The *Petite Marie* was the outright property of Captain Carlisle and the officers and men of *Dartmouth* and only a prize court could take it away from them. It wasn't unknown for prizes to be sent away on a cruise before they had been condemned, but it was unusual and he didn't know of a case of it being done without the capturing captain's express agreement. He could dig his heels in and state his captain's likely disagreement, but he knew it probably wouldn't be true. Also, he didn't know what Wheelock had in mind. It could be an opportunity for him to distinguish himself in some way. But still, it would be wise to throw the decision back onto broader shoulders.

'I believe Captain Carlisle would want whatever was for the good of the King's service, sir.'

Wheelock looked angry for the first time since Wishart had come into the cabin. He knew this lieutenant's game, he would probably have done the same in his shoes, but it didn't help in this case. If the brig should be lost after he had sent it away, he could be liable for its value. He knew Carlisle reasonably well – they'd been together at Quebec in 'fifty-nine when Carlisle had that frigate, *Medina* – but not well enough to be sure that he wouldn't be vindictive. And in any case, a captain was only acting on behalf of his officers and men when he negotiated on matters of prize money, and Carlisle could find himself compelled to take a hard line. The good of the King's service indeed! Bah, he'd had enough of this fencing.

'Then it's clear to me that you represent Captain Carlisle's interests here, Mister Wishart, so I ask you, do you give your permission for your prize to be sent away on the King's business? On the King's business, mark you, and I'll have a straight answer, if you please!'

Wishart gulped again and out of the corner of his eye he saw the captain's clerk smirking. He'd been outwitted – or outgunned – and he knew it, and his every word was being recorded. All that was left was to make the best of things.

'I do, sir. May I ask on what service the brig is bound?'

***

CHAPTER TWENTY-FOUR

St. George's Island

Saturday, Ninth of January 1762.
Brig Petite Marie, at Sea, off Turneef Cay, Gulf of Honduras.

The tropical sun burst from the sea astern, setting the sky and sea aglow, but Wishart had no eyes for the gaudy beauty of this new day. He was dog-tired, having navigated his brig across nearly two hundred leagues of featureless sea, steering only a point and a half to the south of west, cutting the lines of longitude almost perpendicularly and being offered no clues as to his westward progress. They'd passed well to the south of the Caymans, so they'd sighted no land and no sails on the whole four-day passage. He had his octant and his tables, so he had a good idea of the brig's latitude from his noon sights, but as for his longitude, that was in the lap of the gods. He'd heaved the brig to at sunset last night, for fear of running aground in the darkness, and now he was sailing with the utmost caution under a main tops'l with the monotonous sound of the leadsman reporting *no bottom, no bottom on this line*.

Somewhere ahead lay a jagged coral reef that guarded the eastern Yucatan coast, and by all accounts the seabed rose from an unimaginable depth to the wave-washed peaks of the coral in only a mile or so. To make matters worse, what dry land there was barely rose more than a few feet from the sea and even when he should see it, there was no real way of knowing what part of the coast he was looking at. He prayed for a chance meeting with one of the loggers' vessels, like the one that *Dartmouth* had encountered just under a fortnight ago. But meanwhile he was steering, as best as he could by dead reckoning, to pass close to the north of the archipelago that the locals called Turneef Cay. If he could find it, he would have a departure fix for the short crossing to the reef, behind which, if he could ever find the passage, lay the settlement of St. George's Island.

It had all seemed so wonderful four days ago when Wheelock had written out his orders, a great adventure far away from the critical eyes of authority. He would be his own master with his own brig and an important mission to fulfil. He was to sail with all speed – *all speed* for God's sake, in this jury-rigged tub – to St. Georges Island and there to make contact with the British settlers and warn them of the imminence of war with Spain. Under no circumstances was he to divulge the source of his information, nor was he to imply that his Majesty's government felt any responsibility for the fate of the settlers in this *terra nullius*, this no-man's land, unclaimed by any civilised king. He was to discover the situation of the settlers and their vulnerability to Spanish raids, by personally travelling the country if necessary, and he wasn't to hazard *Dartmouth's* prize, the *Petite Marie*, in any way. Then – the crowning glory of these wildly optimistic orders – when his mission was complete he was to lose no time in returning to Port Royal, some two-hundred-and-twenty leagues almost dead to windward. He'd be lucky if he saw Port Royal before the war was over.

***

'Beg pardon, sir, but I think I can see something, just about four points off the larboard bow. It could be land, sir, or it could be just a bit of a haze on the sea.'

Barker, the bosun's mate, stood in lieu of a first lieutenant, a sailing master and a bosun. He'd risen to the occasion and he could see that the lieutenant had a good opinion of him. He was almost convinced that it might carry him further in the service, perhaps even to the unimaginable heights of a bosun's warrant, and so he was being as obliging as he possibly could be. Wishart knew all this and he knew that Barker was susceptible to wishful thinking in his sightings of land and sails, so that he could claim the glory of being the first to report it, and it did seem strange that the masthead lookout had seen nothing from his lofty perch. Nevertheless, he took his telescope, the only one in the brig, and climbed up to the maintop.

'No bottom, no bottom on this line.'

He was tempted to order the leadsman to cease, but that would be dangerous on two counts. If the brig were to run aground, who would rescue them in this desolate place? And the first question that would be asked in an inquiry or court martial would be, *what were the sounding immediately before you struck the reef, Lieutenant Wishart?* If the leadsman had been dismissed, he'd have no answer.

He stared at the horizon on the larboard bow. Nothing, just the slightest hint of haze that a willing mind could imagine to be land. A pity because that was just where he expected to see Turneef Cay. It was another of the bosun's mate's will o' the wisps, but he didn't dare discourage the man; one day he would see the reef that lay in wait for them, and he didn't want there to be any hesitation in reporting it.

Another sweep of the horizon. His telescope passed the ship's head, then he came back. Now, was *that* something? The pole of a mast, perhaps, just showing as the brig rose on the swell, and perhaps a hint of the peak of a fore-and-aft mains'l. He looked up to where the masthead lookout was also studying the same bit of horizon, but with nothing more than the naked eye. Should he make the hail? It seemed somehow beneath a captain's dignity, and then the decision was taken from him.

'Sail ho! Sail right on the ship's head. It looks like a little sloop, sir, and it's coming our way.'

Wishart ordered the brig to heave to and await the unknown sail. If it was a friend then all well and good and he could expect to hear where in this wide, wide sea he was sailing. If it was an enemy, then he was in no state to escape. His jury-rigged merchant brig could neither fight nor flee; it was the natural prey of all the ocean's predators. He could only await his fate. Besides, he thought he recognised that tops'l.

***

'Captain Hookway, it's a pleasure to see you again.'

The logger timed the rise and fall of the two vessels and stepped briskly over the yard gap that separated them. He looked askance at this lieutenant in his blue coat apparently in command of a French merchant brig. Like Captain Wheelock before him, he was disappointed of a prize that he thought was his for the taking. Moreover, it was a prize that would never have to suffer the uncertainty of being condemned at the vice-admiralty court in Kingston, because Hookway had not a letter of marque to his name. The technical term, in civilised society, was *piracy*, and the British settlers on the Yucatan coast had practiced it through time immemorial. That was how they acquired all of their brigs and sloops and schooners, except for the few that made the voyage to Kingston or Port Royal, where the authorities cared about such things and could inquire into the provenance of a vessel.

'You were in that two-decker *Dartmouth* when last I saw you,' he said accusingly, dropping the *sir* as he mastered his disappointment. 'What brings you back here? Are you bound for St. George's or back to the Dons again?'

'St. George's this time, Mister Hookway, and I'd be grateful for a pilot if you have one.'

Hookway looked slowly around him. The brig appeared in good order, there was nothing amiss except for those odd, overweight topmasts, and even they looked good enough to a logger from the Yucatan Coast. He leaned over the gunwale and put his fingers to his lips, letting out a piercing whistle. The man at the helm of his sloop waved and Hookway pointed distinctly over to the sou'west where he'd come from.

'Then I'm your man, sir, and I won't cost King George a farthing in pilotage dues. You aren't far out in your direction and if you'd sailed on another couple of hours you'd have seen Turneef Cay on your larboard bow, a little further away than you'd perhaps have hoped. Now, if your steersman will just put up his helm we can bear away for St.

George's.'

Hookway glanced over to the east and the nor'east and nodded to himself.

'With this wind we'll be there before sunset.'

***

St. George's, as the settlers called it, was sweltering hot and plagued by biting flies. The insects didn't seem to bother the islanders, they must have become used to their constant attacks, but they saw Wishart as fresh meat and attacked in their droves. Wishart had worn his coat and waistcoat when he stepped ashore but he soon stripped off both and sat down with Hookway and two other men – *magistrates* they called themselves – in his shirt sleeves with the cuffs pulled well down over his hands. Now he was here he hardly knew how to start. His information seemed paltry and probably not as reliable as anything that these men collected by their own observation of the Spaniards.

'I've been sent to tell you the latest news about the war.'

If he'd expected wild rejoicing, he was disappointed. All he could read on the faces around the table was scepticism. Probably they'd been disappointed by King's messengers before. But still, they were listening.

'Spain will be an open enemy by May at the latest, possibly before, and it may even be that we declare war before they do…'

Still no reaction. Were these men made of stone? Wishart was searching for something more to say, something that would make his mission seem worthwhile.

'… and I regret that I can't tell you where this information came from.'

That broke the silence. One of the magistrates gave out an involuntary laugh and then the others followed. It took a few moments for them to regain their composure.

'You'll forgive our manners, sir…'

Wishart could see that Hookway was the leader of the group, or perhaps *first among equals* would be a better description. In any case, when he spoke they didn't interrupt.

'…that's no way to treat an officer of the King. It's just that we see the Spaniards every week and hear of them every day. War may come to England and Jamaica in May or it may come next week, but it's here today on the Yucatan. The Spanish are pushing their patrols closer and closer every time, and whenever they find our camps they destroy everything. Thank God we've been able to move our men out before they arrive, so far, otherwise we'd have deaths to tell you of, not just lost tents and equipment and men carried away to the Spanish hell-holes of prisons.'

'Yes, you must live a precarious life so close to the Spanish.'

Wishart had the impression that once these men started talking about the woes of life on the Yucatan peninsula and the injustices that they suffered at the hands of their neighbours, they would never stop.

'Yet open war is a different matter altogether. I expect you all remember the last war with Spain.'

Wishart looked from face to face. They were all men in their forties and fifties, the elders of the island community, and each one was old enough to have been here when the Spanish swept through the Yucatan with fire and sword. It had barely made a few words in the London broadsheets and it was largely forgotten outside the island, but these people would remember. They had been forced to flee from their homes and had spent a few years struggling to make a living on Jamaica. He could see that he'd touched a sore point.

'Aye, we remember.'

The man who spoke now looked like the oldest of the group, and he had a sad look in his eyes as though he was recalling painful memories.

'I lost a boy when they surprised our logging camp; he'd be just about your age now, if they hadn't killed him. I told him that it was no use fighting those odds, but he picked up his axe anyway and they shot him before he could come close to them.'

Hookway reached across and laid an arm on the older man's shoulder, but he kept his eyes on Wishart.

'You see, sir, this is our land, and we hold it in our own right. Oh, we've petitioned for the King to claim it and we'd be right happy to be subject to King George's law and to Parliament, but I suppose it's not profitable enough.'

Wishart nodded in sympathy. The land barely supported a few hundred logging families, but that wasn't the chief impediment to its being claimed by the Crown. It was a foothold on the Spanish Main, and even though Spain didn't effectively govern this part of the peninsula, it would be a running sore in the relations between the two countries. It was barely important enough to be a bargaining counter in peace negotiations, yet its geography made it a point of contention.

'I really don't know anything about your business here,' Wishart said, to steer the conversation away from the subject of sovereignty. 'How far afield does your logging take you and how close have the Spanish come to the island?'

'Well, we don't have what you would call a territory, sir, but we don't go west of the New River or south of the Sibun River. For the most part we've been left alone within those limits when there's no war, but in the past year the Spanish have come over the Sibun and raided our logging camps. They don't stay, they're not looking to claim the land, not yet, but they destroy our camps and recently they've been carrying away – stealing, it should rightly be called – any felled timber that they find.'

'Is there no logwood to be found beyond those rivers?'

'Oh, my word! There's logwood aplenty and mahogany too, deeper into the country, and in the past few years we've made more for each load of mahogany than we do for logwood. It's a right good business and they say, with the demand for brown furniture in London and Paris, it can only grow. No, it's not the timber that keeps us within our territory; we don't go beyond the rivers for two reasons. The first is that there's plenty of timber this side of the rivers, enough to keep us and our grandchildren busy, at any rate of felling, I reckon. But the second reason is that it avoids clashes with the Spaniards or with the Indians. You see, we call this our territory, and we have done for generations, but there are no papers that give us title and no army or navy to keep our borders safe. If war comes we will have to abandon the camps and bring everyone back to St. George's. When it seems right we can send out scouting parties, and if it's clear we'll send out logging expeditions. We can hold the island against anything other than a determined attack, and even then, well, you've seen the reefs, no ship can approach without a pilot. It'll be hard, but we won't give up the island without a fight. As long as we have our homes here, we can always return to the forests when the war's over.'

Wishart nodded in understanding. Well, he'd carried out the first part of his orders but he hadn't seen the dangers that the loggers faced at first hand. And he was intrigued to see how they carved a living from these daunting forests.

'Well, gentlemen, I feel it would be helpful if I can return to Jamaica with a first-hand account of what's happening in your logging camps. Is there anyone who can guide me?'

***

Wishart walked the length of the island with Hookway before the light faded. It was a strange place to be the *de facto* capital of a territory. The island was shaped like a shepherd's crook, just a mile long and varying between one and two hundred yards wide. He saw about sixty houses; all of them were single storey with palm-leaf roofs except for the building where he had met the magistrates, where a red tiled roof covered what looked like the largest structure on the island. There were a few tiny gardens, but the soil was too sandy for any serious agriculture. Where the houses and gardens ended it was just scrub and the inevitable palm trees, all bent to the west in obedience to the wind.

'It looks a mighty precarious place in a hurricane, Mister Hookway. How do you get along in the season?'

'Oh, we just stay here, the island's protected by the reef. We lose a few roofs every year and we lost nearly all of them three years ago, but as you can see, they're easy to replace.'

He swept his hand around to show the palm trees whose branches provided the raw material for the roofs.

'The southern end of the island flooded in that big one of 'fifty-nine, but we don't build down there in any case. You know, the most important thing is that the island can be defended. We'd be more comfortable on the mainland, and when things are quiet most of the families spend their time in logging camps all over the territory. But now the Dons are on the move again, it's only the men who go into the forest.'

It only took an hour to view the island, but by the end of their walk Wishart thought he understood how these hardy folk could make a living here, and more importantly, he'd be able to describe it when he returned to Jamaica.

He spent the night in Hookway's house on the island with his large family, his dogs and his chickens running about the place in what looked like a hopeless chaos. He'd seen to the security of the brig; it was anchored snugly to the west of the island in a two-fathom patch of sand beside two sloops and a handy-looking schooner. It was safe from the trade wind, if it should blow up, and they were well past the hurricane season. That schooner had raised envious thoughts. It would make the passage to Port Royal in half the time that the brig would take, and it was built to carry the baulks of logwood and mahogany in its hold, so it would swallow the brig's cargo of furs and timber with ease. Oh, how he longed for a fast, weatherly schooner.

The islanders were right. No man-of-war of any force could get close enough to bombard the island, and none could pass through the enclosing reef without a pilot. The only way to attack the island was in boats that could sail inside the reef from Punta Cacolla, and that was forty leagues away. It was as safe as any settlement could be so close to Spanish forces.

Wishart spent an uncomfortable night and not just because of the biting insects. Despite his clear and written orders from Captain Wheelock, he wasn't at all certain that he was acting correctly in plunging into the Yucatan forest in the company of a group of loggers. If he was taken by the Spanish, it could spark a diplomatic incident. Such an incident could even be used as a *casus belli* by a Spanish governor-general keen to shift the blame for war onto the British. It was that consideration that had made him determined to go without any of the brig's crew. He'd carry his sword and a pistol, but no other weapons, and his fate would be in Hookway's hands.

***

CHAPTER TWENTY-FIVE

Evidence

Monday, Eleventh of January 1762.
The Yucatan Forest.

'Now, sir. If you want to see what the Spaniards do to our camps the best that I can do is take you to where they made their latest raid, just two days ago. It's five or six miles up the Belize River and we can do that by canoe in half a day. Of course, all our camps are on rivers, it would be too difficult to shift the timber otherwise. We make rafts of the lighter stuff and load it with the logwood and mahogany, then float it all down the river to the coast. We pick it up in our boats and tow it to the island, then to Jamaica in our sloops and schooners. I can't offer you a massacre; the men at the camp had word of the Spanish raid from the Indians, so they took what they could and came back down the river. However, you'll see where they burned the huts and tents and made an attempt to burn the timber. It was too wet to burn through, of course, but it's spoiled now and of no value.'

***

They set out at dawn, Wishart and Hookway and two burly loggers in a small canoe. Hookway had a huge brass blunderbuss of the sort that was carried in stage coaches in England and the loggers had their axes; they were equally useful for hewing wood or for defence and were always near at hand. Wishart had a sword and pistol, and that was the sum total of their armament. It didn't seem adequate for a trip into an untamed forest, let alone a forest that the Spanish army had so recently raided.

St. George's Island lay seven miles off a broad peninsula where a low bluff forced the mouth of the Belize River south into the coral lagoon. The canoe threaded its way through the shallows, past reefs and sandbanks and small islands. The water was crystal-clear and no more than a fathom deep, sometimes less. Shoals of fish, some of them two-or-three feet long, scattered when the canoe's shadow passed over them. Sea birds were everywhere, diving for fish, wading for the worms and crabs that teemed in the mangroves and squabbling among themselves for the right to the booty. To add to the delights, as soon as they left the island the sand flies left them alone. It was something of a paradise: the world as Adam may have known it, before his fall from grace.

On the right bank of the estuary, the mangroves had been cleared and there was a raised path, a sort of causeway that led to firm ground where the roofs of a few huts could be seen. The canoe didn't stop and the men paddled noiselessly into the river. The sounds of the sea faded and within two hundred yards any hint that they were near the coast was gone. Here it was all virgin forest except for the weathered stumps where long ago the first loggers had taken the most convenient trees. After a mile the river narrowed and started to meander first this way and then that in an utterly bewildering manner, and the trees grew closer overhead. There was no sign of movement except for the occasional swirl in the water where some creature of the river dived at their approach. Wishart was feeling the heat now, and the insects. These were a different sort to the sand flies on St. George's Island; here in the forest the flying insects were larger and more colourful. There weren't so many and they weren't so bloodthirsty, but when they did bite on the exposed hands and neck, they caused a burning sensation that seemed to follow the course of his blood vessels. None of this worried Hookway and the two loggers. They appeared oblivious to the discomfort and the canoe continued its slow ascent of the river.

The results of the loggers' industry was easy to see. The thick forest that came down to the river bank was interrupted every few hundred yards by a clearing where logs had been dragged down to the water. Presumably, the lesser trees that had been felled to make the clearing were used for the rafts that Hookway had described. Between the clearings the forest was thick and apparently impenetrable, and there was no sign of life except for the occasional gaudy bird and great flights of outrageously coloured butterflies. Wishart had the unsettling feeling that they were being watched from the shadows of the trees, that their journey was being observed and noted by unfriendly eyes. A glance a Hookway showed him that he at least wasn't concerned.

After two hours of paddling the canoe rounded a bend and Hookway pointed ahead at the left bank.

'There, that's the encampment. There was a jetty but the Dons destroyed it; we'll have to clamber through the mangroves.'

Wishart started to take off his shoes, but Hookway stopped him with a laugh.

'You don't want to cripple yourself, sir. Those mangroves are thick with little clams that'll cut your feet to shreds. Even the Indians wrap their feet in tree-bark before they go into the swamp, and *they* spend their whole life without shoes.'

Wishart thought ruefully of his good leather shoes. He'd only brought one pair when he'd been sent into the prize, that had seemed enough for a quiet passage to Jamaica. However, as soon as he left the canoe he saw that Hookway was right. If he had tried this barefoot he'd have been crippled for days, even though it was only half a dozen yards through the swamp.

They reached the cleared path that led to dry land, and a hundred yards more brought them to the camp, or what was left of it.

'We'd been here for a couple of years. There were fourteen men here or out in the forest felling trees when an Indian told them that a Spanish raiding party was only two miles away. That's at least an hour's march for soldiers even when there's a cleared path, so our people had time to load up their tools and some of the food and a few tents. They had to leave the rest, and you can see what happened.'

Wishart surveyed the desolate scene. There had been huts here, four by the look of it, and what looked like hearths and some tilled ground, but it had all been burned and the enclosing trees had been scorched by the flames. He could see the remains of the stacks of massive timber. He knew little of logwood and mahogany, but he assumed that the greatest logs were the prized mahogany. They weren't utterly destroyed, but they were blackened and he could imagine that it wouldn't be worth trying to trim them down to make them fit to be sold. It had been a neat operation by the Spanish, and a harsh lesson to the loggers about the risks that they would have to take if they wanted to earn their living in the Yucatan forest. It was easy to see where the Spaniards had come from and which way they had departed, for there was a wide beaten path heading away to the sou'west with the undergrowth all flattened by the captured tents and spare canvas that the raiders had dragged away. If that was all that they took, then it wasn't for booty that the raiders came.

Hookway pointed down the path. Wishart could only see about fifty yards of it before it turned and was lost to his sight.

'That's the way back to the border of Guatemala and then on to Punta Cacolla. Of course there's no border to be seen and no agreement as to where exactly it runs, but that raiding party will be half way home by now and in territory that the Spanish really do control. A few miles upstream the river bends around to the southwest and there's a sort of ridge, a watershed you could call it, between the right bank of the river and the smaller streams that run east into the sea. There's a track along the ridge, used mostly by the Indians. The raiding party won't have wanted to be crossing those streams, some of them are deep and wide, so I expect they made for the ridge. They typically don't stay in this area, just burn and destroy – kill if they can – then run for home. They live in fear of the Indians around here, who have no love for them and will attack the raiding parties if they think they can get away without casualties.'

***

Hookway and the two loggers searched the clearing for anything useful that could be taken back to the island. They found a cooking pot, an axe with a broken shaft and a pair of iron hinges that had burned away from the door of one of the huts. Wishart had seen all that he had come for and he took a folded sheet of paper from his pocket and sat down to sketch the scene. He knew that a picture would be worth more than all his words when he was called to describe the burned camp. A smell of wet woodsmoke clung in the air and for the first time since they had started up the river, there were no birds or butterflies in sight. He'd always imagined that these tropical forests teemed with life, that there was a jaguar or a great ape behind every tree, but so far he'd seen no four-legged animals at all.

There was a sudden sound of movement from the path that the Spaniards had taken. Hookway hefted his blunderbuss and Wishart dropped his sketch and cocked his pistol while the two loggers reached for their axes.

A figure walked carefully into the clearing, holding his hands wide and staying close to the cover of the trees. He was a well-made man of moderate height with a barrel chest, clearly an Indian. His hair was tied above his head and his face was painted with smears of some ochre substance. He carried a bow in his hand and a few arrows tucked into a loin cloth. Hookway lowered his blunderbuss and called a greeting in the Indian's tongue. As he did so, two others emerged from the path dragging a makeshift sled with a human figure strapped tightly to it.

'He's a friend of ours,' Hookway explained, 'and he appears to have brought us a wounded Spaniard.'

Wishart studied the figure on the sled, touched the cold face and felt the flaccid hand.

'A dead Spaniard, I believe.'

Hookway poked at the dead body and nodded in agreement.

'So they didn't get away unscathed.'

He asked the Indian a few questions then turned back to Wishart.

'The Indians saw the burning and followed the Spaniards as they withdrew. They were heading for the ridge, as I thought. This man wandered a little too far from their camp during the night and our friend here shot him with an arrow and dragged him away before his friends could intervene. He must have died before the morning. I wonder why they brought the body all this way.'

Hookway asked a few more questions and the Indian held out what appeared to be a folded sheet of paper. There was a brief argument, Hookway was demanding and the Indian refusing. Wishart only saw the paper for a moment before the Indian hid it behind his back, he'd seen that there was no seal and no address on the outside but there was writing on the inside.

'He found a letter on the dead Spaniard. He can't read, of course, but he knows that letters can be valuable. He wants a gold piece for it. I told him that he has the Spaniards clothes and his dagger, and that the letter is of no use to him, but he's insistent. He'll burn the letter if he doesn't get his gold.'

Hookway waited for Wishart to say something. Pieces of gold were a King's officer's business, not a logger's.

'Will he let me see the letter before I decide?'

Hookway spoke to the Indian again, but he just shook his head and coyly showed a corner of the letter from behind his back.

'He's a crafty one. I've dealt with him before and he'll give away nothing if he can't see an advantage for himself. Now don't consider taking the letter from him, sir. We have a good understanding with these people and I don't want to see it spoiled.'

'What will he do with a piece of gold?'

'Oh, bore a hole in it and hang it around his neck, I expect. He has no other way of profiting from it, and he can hardly walk into Punta Cacolla and buy wine at the tavern. It makes no sense, I know, but they value gold as a mere ornament. In any case, you won't get the letter unless he gets the coin.'

Wishart shrugged. Probably the letter was of no value, but he'd come this far and may as well see it. He reached into the purse that he kept tucked inside his breeches and felt for the smallest coin he could find without showing the rest of the contents. Luckily it was gold, a Portuguese half-joe, but that was far too much to offer. He considered asking to borrow an axe to cut it into quarters but one look at the Indians face told him that he wouldn't get the letter for a mutilated coin. It was wanted entire, as an ornament as Hookway had said. With a wry last look at the coin, he offered it in the palm of his hand. The Indian bit the coin, smiled broadly and without further ceremony handed over the letter.

Wishart sat on a burned stump at the edge of the clearing. Hookway, the loggers and the Indians untied the dead Spaniard and started stripping his clothes. In this forest everything was valuable and a Spanish soldier's uniform and accoutrements were particularly prized. He could see the loggers bargaining with the Indian for a few items and they handed over copper coins in exchange for shoes and what looked like a silk neckerchief and some smaller things. They refused the bloodied shirt and waistcoat and breeches and the Indian grinned at their foolish niceties and rolled them into a ball and handed them to his followers.

He opened the letter. It was in Spanish, of course, and Wishart spoke almost nothing of that language. It had been written in a clear, precise clerkly hand, as though it was some sort of official document rather than a personal letter. He scanned it quickly, but it wasn't until he reached the end that he found a clue to its meaning. There, below a neat, tight signature in a different hand, was the name of the person under whose signature it had been written. He could read that, at least: *Don Alonso Fernández de Heredia: Governor and Captain-General of Guatemala.*

***

Wishart's head swam. After all this effort, the flies and the heat and the discomfort, this letter may at last have made his expedition worthwhile. He studied it again, digging back into his knowledge of Latin and French to try to tease out the meaning. It was an instruction, that much was clear. Now here was an interesting phrase: *Colonos ingleses.* Could that mean English colonists, or English settlers? And here was another word he recognised, *Yucatan*, it must be the same in Spanish as in English.

'Mister Hookway, do you have a moment? What rank would you say our Spanish friend was?'

Hookway glanced again at the now-naked corps which the Indians were dragging into the undergrowth.

'Not an officer, sir, not like yourself, nor even a sergeant, but he's not a common soldier. I'd say he was some kind of clerk. Here's an ink horn that I gave the Indian a ha'penny for, I doubt whether a soldier would carry that.'

Wishart turned the ink horn over in his hand. It was literally a horn, from some kind of small animal like a goat, and it had a brass cap that was held in place by a leather tie. He looked inside to see a half inch of dark ink in the bottom. A clerk, then, and it must have been a significant size of patrol to include such a person.

'Would you ask him how many Spaniards there were?'

'Oh, I already did. It was the greatest number they've seen since the last war, fifty or so. That's why the Indians didn't dare to do anything more than pick off this one wandering soul.'

Wishart thought for a moment.

'Can you read Spanish, Mister Hookway?'

Hookway laughed, it seemed that everything Wishart said amused him, perhaps it was because their lives were so different and the common points of reference so few.

'Read Spanish, sir? I can't even read English. There's not much call for it on the Island, although a few of the younger men can read, aye, and write a bit. Just enough to be certain that we're not being cheated by the Jamaica timber merchants. I speak a fair amount of Spanish, although that'll do us no good with him over there dead as a doornail.'

Wishart grimaced. It was galling to realise that he wouldn't know what the letter said until he reached civilisation. But then a thought occurred to him.

'If I read this letter to you, making the best that I can of the Spanish words, could you tell me what they mean in English?'

'Well, that's a thought, sir. We have a reader and a translator; shall we give it a go?'

***

It wasn't a long letter and a few of the words meant nothing to Hookway, but in twenty minutes Wishart had discovered who this letter from Don Alonso was addressed to, and had teased out a broad understanding of its meaning. It must have been written very soon after the governor-general landed in Punta Cacolla, before he set out for his capital at La Antigua. It was an authority – no, an instruction – to the local captain to harass the British loggers on the Yucatan peninsula. It pointed out that Spain and Britain were at peace but there was a phrase that Hookway couldn't translate; it might have said that they were at peace for the present time. It asserted the illegality of the loggers' presence on the mainland and described them as pirates.

Hookway snorted his disgust at that.

'That's the usual way that the Don's justify attacking us. They've been calling every Englishman that they find beyond the line a pirate, ever since Drake's day. It's them who're the pirates.'

Wishart read on. The captain was to destroy any camps that he found on the mainland but was not to interfere with St. George's Island, although there appeared to be a caveat to that restriction and the words were similar to the previous untranslated phrase. Possibly the captain was being told to leave the island alone while the two nations were not at war. Loggers were to be unharmed but again there was a difficult phrase: *unless they resist?*

Wishart sat and stared at the letter. It was important, he knew that. He remembered what the sergeant of artillery had said about the secret treaty, that there was a timeline in Spain's march to war. Don Alonso must have thought that there was no chance of this letter falling into English hands in the four months left. Then the leader of this expedition was presumably the captain to whom the instruction was addressed, and the dead Spaniard his clerk. This was no casual incursion into the loggers' historic territory, but a planned and important first step on the road to war in this part of the Caribbean.

'Well, now we know where we stand, sir.'

Wishart had forgotten about Hookway and the loggers for a moment. The letter was of some importance to the lieutenant-governor of Jamaica and the commander-in-chief, but it was critical to the settlers on St. George's Island. It meant that they'd have to take precautions whenever they set foot on the mainland. They'd need pickets down towards Punta Cacolla to give them warning of Spanish raids and they'd have to arm the logging parties. Well, Hookway knew the facts, but Jamaica didn't and Wishart's duty was clear; he must make all speed to Port Royal. He grimaced when he thought of the long beat to windward in that jury-rigged tub of a brig. Perhaps…

'Mister Hookway, you have a schooner just returned from Jamaica, I believe.'

'Aye, sir, she should be loading these logs in the next week,' he pointed at the blackened piles of useless logwood and mahogany, 'but there's no cargo for her now.'

Hookway looked thoughtfully at Wishart, why did he want to know? He thought he could guess.

'Then I have a proposal to make. I'll charter the schooner from you, I can give you a note in hand against the navy board, and you can redeem it in Port Royal. I'll shift the cargo into the schooner and leave the brig at St. George's Island. When you have a cargo of timber, you can use the brig to carry it to Jamaica, and exchange it for the schooner in Kingston.'

Hookway thought for a moment. It was certainly in his interest that the news of the Spanish raids should reach Jamaica as soon as possible – perhaps a miracle would happen and they'd get some help against the inevitable raids – and he could turn a profit on the charter. The brig could be useful too, that fat belly suggested a cavernous hold within. The logging parties would bring a lot of cargo down to the coast when they withdrew from the forest, more than the schooners alone could carry. Yes, it was a good proposal. He spat on his hand and held it out to Wishart.

***

CHAPTER TWENTY-SIX

A God's Eye View

Tuesday, Twelfth of January 1762.
Dartmouth, at Sea, Crooked Island Passage.

Chiara had grown quite accustomed to the life of a mariner and since leaving the Gulf of Mexico she'd developed the habit of rising before the dawn. She slept undisturbed through the bells tolling the half hours until some inner receptor heard four bells in the morning watch. Then she was up and out, hurrying so as to catch the first loom of the sun while it was still below the horizon. With a cloak against the early chill, she walked the poop deck for an hour while she watched the daily miracle of the light's rebirth, for all the world like an admiral on his flagship. It wasn't such a poor analogy either, because the officer of the watch, the mate and the midshipmen greeted her with the kind of reverence normally reserved for those who had hoisted their flag. Coffee? A biscuit? May I send for a chair? Nothing was too much trouble for Lady Chiara. Carlisle watched all this with his usual amused smile. When he came on deck – the lord of all he surveyed –he received nothing more than a doffing of hats and a report on the weather, the course, the speed and what sails were set; none of his officers thought to offer him a biscuit, or a chair.

A fixed habit, yes, but today was different. If all went well and the trade wind held, tomorrow morning they'd be nearly through the Windward passage and back in the Caribbean Sea, and the next morning they'd be threading between the cays into Port Royal. The cruise was nearly over and it was time to think about what she should do next. It had been wonderful in so many ways; to be so close to her husband for more than the week or so that was her normal lot, to have her voice heard in the ship's councils and to be free from the cloying embrace of motherhood. And yet, she was starting to miss her son, and the loss had grown day by day until it outweighed all other considerations. She'd left him back in Antigua in the charge of her manservant and a nurse, and she'd heard not a word since she'd so light-heartedly waved goodbye two months ago. Yes, it was time to go back to Antigua and then… and then to Williamsburg. If she had been saying that out loud there would have been a definite emphasis on the last word, but as it was said in private, the only outward evidence was a softening of her features. For she felt she had crossed her own Rubicon and at last shaken off a lingering desire for the Ligurian Coast.

She hardly dared hope that *Dartmouth* would be sent back to the Leeward Islands, even though that was Carlisle's proper station. If there was no immediate prospect then she'd take the next decent-sized merchantman that was heading that way. A week or so at the rented house in St. John's, just to say farewell to friends, then she'd look for a passage to Hampton Roads from where it was just a carriage ride to her beautiful home at Williamsburg. She'd miss the worst of the Virginia winter too, and the crocuses would be out on the palace green in front of her house, and the old shepherd who was so attentive to Joshua would be fixing his hurdles in anticipation of the lambing season.

'Good morning again, Chiara.'

She realised with a start that she'd been so engrossed in her thoughts that she hadn't heard her husband's first greeting. How long had he been watching her? She knew that her face would have betrayed her mood, and she would so much regret it if she had hurt her husband's feelings. She knew how hard he had tried to make the cruise comfortable and stimulating for her, and she harboured a suspicion that he'd left that grounded French frigate to its own devices for fear of putting her in danger by running his ship alongside and pounding her broadside-to-broadside. How much of his career had he sacrificed for her? She would never know for sure but she did know that there was an undefinable store of goodwill that each sea officer owned, and it had to be jealously guarded and used sparingly. Carlisle had expended much of it in taking her on this cruise and he would have to work hard to replenish it. The bell struck five; half past six on this new day.

'Good morning, Edward. Sunrise in fifteen minutes, I believe.'

Chara always recovered quickly from a bout of morbid introspection. Carlisle had become used to it, but it still gave him joy every time.

'You're quite the creature of the sea, my dear. Sunrise, according to Mister Beazley, is at forty-seven minutes past six. You'll have noticed that it's a few minutes earlier each day due to our eastward passage.'

'Yes, and with the lengthening of the days since the solstice. I do pay attention you know Edward, and some of your mystic arts do stick.'

They stood together on the larboard side of the poop deck, watching for the very moment when the first sliver of burning orange orb appeared over the horizon. The ship lifted to the swell and they held their breath. Almost. Half a minute passed and the stern rose again and this time they caught a momentary sight of a glowing golden grain, it was nothing more than that, but it was that special moment. Carlisle felt his hand taken by Chiara's and they watched in rapture until the full expanse of the sun had cleared the horizon.

'How wonderful. It will never cease to delight me, and the sunrise is never the same on land. I'm truly grateful for having been on this cruise, Edward, but I feel it's time to go home.'

'Home to St. John's?'

Carlisle asked the question with hidden trepidation. He had a secret fear that when Chiara said *home*, that she really meant Nice, the Mediterranean city on the Ligurian coast where she had spent most of her years. He dreaded that one day he would wake up and that she'd be gone.

'No dear, home to Williamsburg. I fear missing the spring and I want Joshua to see it now that he's older, and I want your father to see little Joshua again. He's not growing any younger, you know.'

They stood in companiable silence until Carlisle was called away by the cares of his command, but it was a special period to him, one that he would remember until he died.

***

Chiara stayed on the poop deck through the change of the watch, absorbing as much of the beauty of the new day as she could. Eventually satisfied, she looked around the deck then craned her neck to see the main topmast crosstree where a lonely figure sat, apparently at ease, with its legs around the mast.

'Mister Gresham, what is Mister Young doing so far up the mainmast? Is something in sight, something that hasn't yet been reported?'

Gresham glanced forward to where Carlisle and Enrico and the carpenter were considering the repair to the pinnace. He would have preferred not to discuss the discipline of the ship with Lady Chiara but he could see there was no help to be found from the captain.

'Sky parlour, Ma'am,' he answered with a deadpan expression.

'Sky parlour? I don't believe I've heard that expression before, Mister Gresham.'

'Ah, perhaps not Ma'am. Mister Young is supposed to keep a station bill for his watch and when I called for it this morning I found it to be deficient. He's been contemplating the error of his way since he left the deck half an hour ago at the end of the morning watch and he will do so until eight bells. We call it *sky parlour* to ease the shame of it.'

'Then he missed his breakfast?'

'Yes, Ma'am. We find that it concentrates a young man's mind wonderfully, and he'll enjoy his dinner all the more.'

'And what class of person is subject to this particular punishment, Mister Gresham? Now that I think of it I've seen a few of the junior officers in that position, although I had taken them for lookouts.'

'Oh, just the young gentlemen, Ma'am. It's not a punishment for the seamen.'

Chiara thought for a moment and her eyes rested on her cousin.

'Could Mister Angelini be sent for sky parlour?'

Gresham smiled at that.

'On, no, your Ladyship. A commissioned officer couldn't possibly be sent to the masthead, nor a warrant officer. It's just for the midshipmen and the volunteers.'

He caught the quickly concealed look of regret in Chiara's face. Just for a moment she'd reverted to her childhood state of mind and the attractive thought of her cousin being punished while she escaped censure.

'Well, I hope that Mister Young's station bill is improved by the loss of his breakfast and now mine is calling. Thank you for explaining this new phrase to me and good day to you Mister Gresham.'

***

Carlisle and Chiara had just finished their own belated breakfast when a knock on the door brought a midshipman, not Horace Young who was still lounging in his sky parlour.

'Beg your pardon, Lady Chiara.'

He bowed low, and his acknowledgement of his captain looked like a mere nod in comparison.

'Mister Gresham sends his regards, sir, and he wishes you to know that we've raised Cape Mays two points on the starboard bow.'

'Very well, I'll come on deck.'

The sun was well above the horizon and *Dartmouth* was bowling along with the wind just forward of the larboard beam.

'Seven knots, sir,' Gresham said as Carlisle came out onto the quarterdeck, 'and we'll be able to set the stuns'ls when the cape is on the beam.'

Cousins At Arms

A most glorious day, the sort of day that he'd remember long after his seafaring years were over. And there was nothing for him to do. By the end of the afternoon watch they'd be in the Windward Passage and then Jamaica was less than two days away. His mission was complete and the daily work of the ship could be safely left to his officers; it was only Wishart that troubled his mind. That old brig with her makeshift topmasts could still be struggling along past Cuba for all he knew. In fact, given the general lawlessness of the Caribbean, Wishart and his men could have fallen prey to any number of privateering and semi-piratical factions. He had sent Wishart off with the dispatches and the sergeant with so little thought, but he was starting to realise that the young lieutenant's mission was the most important of all. By comparison, his return to the Gulf of Mexico looked frivolous. He just hoped that he'd arrive in Port Royal to find the brig swinging at anchor with the prize agent's men crawling all over it. But there was nothing he could do to help Wishart and for now, he could cast his cares aside and enjoy the day.

'Captain, sir, Mister Young reports a sail two points forward of the larboard beam. He's at the main masthead, sir.'

Gresham had removed his hat and he was looking rather sheepish, as though caught in a transgression.

'Indeed? I didn't hear the hail from the lookout.'

'He meant to report when he was relieved, sir. My fault, I think. I told him to expect to see one of the squadron ships blockading Cape François, and he felt it could wait for the minute until he came down. Mister Young beat him to it, although he called very softly, as he's not a rightful lookout.'

Carlisle gave his first lieutenant a hard quarterdeck stare then looked aloft. It was Able Seaman Whittle at the masthead now. He was sharing the crosstree with Young and squinting under his hand towards the sail that had been reported.

'I do hope things are not becoming slack at the end of the cruise, Mister Gresham.'

'No, sir…'

'Deck there. Sail forrard of the larboard beam, it has the look of a Frenchman, a frigate maybe.'

Carlisle picked up the speaking trumpet and pointed it up at the main masthead.

'You're sure, Whittle?'

'Aye, sir. Her t'gallants have that high-cut foot. Could be a frigate or a ship-o'-the-line, sir, but she's French, for sure, or a prize that hasn't been into the yard yet.'

'Beat to quarters, Mister Gresham, and clear for action. And tell Mister Young he may come down on deck and take his proper station. Ah there you are Mister Beazley, take the deck, if you please, and come up as hard as you can.'

The marine drummer beat the stirring tattoo and the deck became a hive of activity as men poured up from below, some hastening to the guns and some running to the tacks and sheets to bring *Dartmouth* as close to the wind as she would come. The sound of the carpenter's mallets knocking out the cabin partitions reminded Carlisle that his wife was still below and knew nothing of the hostile sail.

'Mister Young, it's good to see you on deck for once. My compliments to Lady Chiara, and she will soon find herself without a cabin. Would she care to join me on the quarterdeck?'

'Right in the eye of the wind, sir.'

Beazley had taken a bearing of the stranger and was waiting until a few minutes had passed on this new course before he took another. Then he would know whether they were the hunter or the prey.

'Deck there. It's a frigate, sir, a French one, and he's under all sail with stuns'ls aloft and alow.'

Carlisle stopped dead at that last report. A frigate coming boldly down against a fourth rate? That captain was playing a dangerous game, unless there were greater issues at hazard today.

'How far to Cape François, Mister Beazley?'

'Thirty leagues, sir, east-sou'east. If he's come from the Cape then he must be steering for the Old Bahama Straits. There's nothing for him if he takes the Crooked Island Passage.'

The Straits again! Beazley was right, any French man-of-war leaving Cape François for home would naturally take the Caicos Islands Passage, but this frigate was already too far to leeward. The Crooked Island Passage held no advantages. So it must be the Straits, in which case it was either business with the Spanish at Havana or with French Louisiana. But this frigate must have deliberately altered course to run down to *Dartmouth*. Its captain must by now have recognised that he had a ship-of-the-line to deal with, so why was he so frivolously squandering his windward position? Unless…

'Deck there. I see another sail to the right of the frigate and further off. I can't make it out yet.'

Carlisle resisted to temptation to demand an identification. Whittle was a reliable man. In fact Carlisle had known him almost all his life, since he'd been raised on the Carlisle family plantation, the son of an indentured servant. If Whittle had anything useful to add, he would have said it already.

'The ship's at quarters and cleared for action, sir. What do you think of our friend over there?'

One of Gresham's characteristics was that he recovered from a rebuke faster than any man Carlisle had ever known, and he never bore a grudge. Nobody would have imagine that only fifteen minutes before he'd been rated by his captain.

'Whittle knows a French frigate when he sees one, Mister Gresham, and that one looks like it was steering for the Straits until it saw us. The other sail will be French, I'm sure, otherwise why would the frigate bear away to look at us? I can't imagine what happened to the blockading squadron.'

'Well he can't think we're French, so there must be more than two frigates over there.'

Carlisle opened his mouth to agree, but his words were cut off by another hail from Whittle.

'Captain, sir. The second one's a ship-o'-the-line and French, for certain. Steering the same course as the frigate, maybe three miles astern. I can't see any other sails.'

Carlisle picked up the trumpet again.

'Good work, Whittle.'

There was no need to remind Whittle to report anything new, nor to keep a sharp lookout, he'd do both of those things without unnecessary orders, particularly after a very public congratulation from his captain.

'Well, so that's it. The blockading ships are off station and a frigate and a ship-o'-the-line have taken the opportunity to escape from the Cape. They're not heading for France, so it must be Havana or Louisiana, and they're not in a hurry, they seem perfectly happy to pick a fight.'

'There's something odd about that, sir. They never cruise against the enemy like we do. They always have specified orders, so they're reluctant to fight. And there must be a risk that another British ship will appear.'

Carlisle nodded distractedly. He was thinking along the same lines. There was something distinctly unusual about the behaviour of these two ships.

The second set of sails was visible from the deck now. They could see the girth of the ship's topmasts and the breadth of the tops'ls.

Gresham looked quickly through his telescope.

'Third rate, I reckon, sir. Not a seventy-four, more like a seventy.'

'You know, Mister Gresham, I don't believe they have a set mission. They've seen the opportunity to escape, couldn't believe their luck, and they're out looking for something they can take on. They may have heard about a British two-decker in the Old Bahama Straits, and thought they'd investigate. Just look where we were when the frigate sighted us, we could have been coming out of the straits, after a hard beat to windward. I wouldn't be surprised if they really are on their way back to France, and have decided to take the long way around through the Florida Channel. Well, I wish them *Bon Voyage*; a third rate and a frigate are no business of ours. Mister Beazley, square away and shave Cape Mays as close as you can. We're bound for Port Royal. Mister Gresham, keep the ship cleared for action but you may dismiss the watch below for the time being.'

'Sail ho! Sail on the starboard beam. Three ships beating up through the passage, sir. Could be a frigate and two of the line. British by the look of them.'

'Belay squaring away, Mister Beazley. Belay dismissing the watch on deck, Mister Gresham.'

There was an edge to Carlisle's voice, his mind was working fast to understand what this new information meant to *Dartmouth*. A frigate and two ships-of-the-line, that would be the blockading squadron for sure. The Lord only knew why they weren't on station, but it was clear that they were beating back to Cape François through the Windward Passage. There hadn't been a better chance to catch a major French unit in these waters for years. But it was certain that as soon as the French frigate got sight of the British squadron, both he and the third rate would abandon all their glorious designs and flee north through the Crooked Island Passage, or west through the Straits.

'Hold your course, Mister Beazley. Make the signal for enemy in sight to windward. No, wait. Bend it on but don't hoist it.'

***

Things were moving fast now as the three groups of ships sped towards a meeting.
'I'll be in the maintop.'

Carlisle slung his telescope lanyard over his shoulder and ran up the ratlines, perhaps not as fast as a young topman, but fast enough to do credit to a man of his age.

From here it was all clear, he didn't need to ascend any further. Those were certainly French ships to windward – a frigate and a third rate, probably a seventy as Gresham had suggested – and they surely had designs upon this lone fourth rate that was standing towards them without a care in the world. The ships to leeward were British, without a doubt; a seventy-four, a sixty and what could be one of those nine-pounder, twenty-eight gun sixth rates, like his friend George Holbrooke's *Argonaut*. Neither the windward nor the leeward groups were aware of each other's presence and if *Dartmouth* hadn't been there, they would have passed on their peaceful occasions without ever knowing they had come so close. But Carlisle could see everything, and he knew that with a bit of good fortune he could bring about an action that could hardly fail to favour the British squadron. But how long before the French suspected something?

He was lucky; if he'd started to bear away then come back on the wind it would have looked suspicious, as though he'd suddenly seen something to change his mind. And if he'd hoisted that signal – even if the French didn't know its meaning – they'd know that he was signalling to someone, to a ship or squadron that was to leeward. In either case a prudent French captain would haul his wind and stand away to the nor'west, or beat back to Cape François. Then how long? how long before they saw the ominous t'gallants breaking the sou'western horizon? He needed to draw them south to give the advancing British ships a chance of bringing them to an engagement.

Carlisle stayed in the maintop watching the closing forces. It was fascinating being in this position, having a god's-eye view as it were. Ten minutes passed with no change. Carlisle set to studying the British squadron, trying to decide which ships they were, who commanded them, and were they senior or junior to himself?

'Whittle! How long before the French sight that frigate in the lead there?'

Whittle was far above Carlisle's comfortable position in the maintop. He had climbed above even the main topmast crosstree and onto the t'gallant yard to get the best view possible. Nevertheless, they were alone on the mast and it lent an intimacy to their conversation.

'Ten minutes, I reckon,' he replied, 'if their lookout's doing his job and he's not skulking in the maintop.'

Carlisle let Whittle's humour pass. He was indeed skulking in the maintop and he had no plans to go higher. Ten minutes. Then it was time to spring the trap.

'Mister Beazley! Mister Beazley. Put the ship about onto the starboard tack, full and by. Mister Gresham, beat to quarters again, just to remind everyone, and hoist the signal: enemy in sight to windward.'

***

CHAPTER TWENTY-SEVEN

A Promising Action

Tuesday, Twelfth of January 1762.
Dartmouth, at Sea, off Cape Mays.

There was something about a hard beat into the trade wind; the steady fresh breeze heightened the pulse and had all hands straining to make the ship go faster. It wasn't like this in most other parts of the world where the winds were more fickle and a beat to windward meant frozen hands and sleet-battered faces. *Dartmouth* plunged northwards tossing the warm spray aside, with her own miniature rainbows keeping station on the bows.

'*Centaur*, seventy-four, I believe, sir, and the sixty's *Pembroke*. I'm not sure about the frigate, it wasn't in the Jamaica Squadron when we left, but it's one of those new twenty-eights.'

Gresham was studying the British ships through his telescope. They were right astern now and they'd crowded on sail when they saw *Dartmouth* tack, although the probably couldn't read the signal yet. They knew that there must be a good reason for a British fifty-gun ship to apparently flee from them. She could have been taken by the French of course, but it was more likely that she'd seen the enemy and was leading the way. In either case, they would follow at best speed, like hounds on a scent.

Simmonds was jostling for Carlisle's attention.

'Captain Forrest has *Centaur*, sir. He was posted in 'forty-five, and Captain Wheelock has *Pembroke*. He's below you on the list, sir, June 'fifty-nine.

'Thank you, Mister Simmonds. Let me know who's the captain of that frigate as soon as it's been identified.'

Carlisle knew Arthur Forrest. He'd been on the station for as long as anyone could remember and was making a fortune from prize money and his interests in plantations.

Nothing would shift him from Jamaica, and their Lordships knew better than to interfere when a man was so obviously suited to a task. He'd taken a French sixty-four last year, along with *Hampshire*, and of course he'd commanded at Cape François in 'fifty-seven when they'd sent the French back into their harbour in ruins. His own frigate had been there, but he'd been back in Jamaica recovering from a wound, and his first lieutenant had commanded *Medina* at the battle. He knew John Wheelock too, they'd both been at Quebec when it fell in 'fifty-nine. Well, it was quite clear that Forrest commanded here, unless that frigate had a strangely senior captain.

'The French have hauled their wind a point, sir.'

Whittle was having to bellow against the stiff breeze whipping past his face.

'Ha! They've taken the bait. They're chasing us.' Gresham pounded his fist into his palm in sheer delight at the prospect of a battle. 'Now, what will they do when they see our friends to leeward?'

Beazley glanced at the chart. He knew it by heart, of course, but the dynamics were changing fast.

'They can't make the Crooked Island passage without getting past us, nor can they make the Old Bahama Straits. They'll have to beat back to windward and make for the Caicos passage or to Cape François if they don't want to fight against three of the line. It's a bad situation for them either way, and any moment now they'll realise it.'

Carlisle could hear his officers discussing the coming battle, for they all thought it was inevitable. He wasn't so sure. It all depended upon that French captain's orders. If he was on his way home then surely, as soon as he saw those t'gallants on the horizon, he'd haul his wind and make for the Caicos Passage. He'd be through before Forrest could come up with him and then he'd have the whole, wide Atlantic and the blessed cloak of night to aid his escape. If, however, he was bound to the west, to Havana or Louisiana, then he'd make for the Straits and hope to brush *Dartmouth* aside. Would Forrest chase him into that tangle of reefs and sandbanks? Probably not, his station was off Cape François, and he could argue that a French ship-of-the-line and a frigate fleeing to the west were none of his business. Nevertheless, he'd fight if he could, and if *Dartmouth* could just hold the French for an hour, then he'd have his engagement. And Carlisle had a feeling about these Frenchmen. War with Spain was coming, and he'd seen the preparations on the coast of the Gulf of Mexico. It made every sense for these ships to be making for Havana and then on to Mobile. He'd have to throw his little fifty-gun ship into the path of a third rate and a frigate. Well, so be it. He'd pin them fast until Forrest should be able to come up and settle the matter. But there was one thing that he had to do before that.

Chiara had watched all these warlike preparations from the poop deck rail. She was out of the way there, and she could see everything and hear most of the conversations on the quarterdeck. She'd absorbed the ways of these sea officers like a sponge, and she knew that a hard battle was in prospect. The next thing that would happen was that her husband would ask her to go below to the relative safety of the cable tier in the orlop. There, protected by the thick oak sides and the huge coils of the anchor cables, she would be immune to the enemy's guns. She'd done it before and meekly obeyed, and she'd suffered the agonies of apprehension as she heard the awful din and felt the mighty crashes of a battle at sea. Well, she was damned if she'd endure that again. He was coming now, striding up the poop deck ladder with that pleading look on his face. Well, he always told his officers to put the enemy off his stride.

'Don't worry, Edward, I'll go below to the cockpit before the first shots are fired.'

She noticed how her husband nearly tripped over the coaming at the top of the ladder. Really, it was too easy to destroy his self-confidence. She almost smiled, but she knew that wouldn't help her cause.

'The… the cockpit? Oh no my dear, the cable tier. It's much the safest place and Walker will see to your comfort. You should go now, before we are engaged.'

'No, Edward. I can be of use in the cockpit if there are any casualties. It's quite safe down there and I'll have something to do rather than sit in the dark and worry about you.'

'But… but...'

Edward was stammering and she knew she had won. Just a last push. She spoke softly in the hope that nobody else would hear this defeat of their captain's will.

'No, Edward, I won't be moved on this. If you want me to go to the cable tier you'll have to send Sergeant Wilson with a file of marines to take me there. Now, I'll stand here out of the way. I know how far these cannon can fire and I'll go below in plenty of time. I won't be incarcerated among the cables. Did you know there are rats down there?'

Carlisle knew when he was defeated; it just took him a little longer to realise it than his wife. A file of marines indeed! Well, he'd at least put a brave face on it.

'The cockpit it is, then. But allow me to tell you when the enemy is almost in range.'

Chiara held her husband's hand, feeling the life pulsing through his veins.

'Are you sure there will be an action, Edward?'

'Oh yes, there's little doubt of it. Look at those fellows over there, they can see Forrest's squadron, they know what they're up against. If they were going to make for the Caicos Passage or Cape François, they'd have done so by now.'

Chiara nodded. She knew what that meant, she could guess at the punishment that *Dartmouth* would have to take in barring a seventy gun ship's passage, and she knew how vulnerable a captain was in such an engagement. She reached up and kissed her husband on the cheek.

***

'Three miles, I reckon, sir.'

Beazley looked pointedly up at the poop deck, and Carlisle followed his gaze. But Chiara had been as good as her word and had gone. She must have slipped quietly down the ladder to the quarterdeck then down again to the upper deck and through the main hatch. In any case, she was gone and as far out of harm's way as she would consent to be.

'Very well, Mister Beazley, lay me alongside her as close as you can. Half pistol shot will do nicely.'

'Aye-aye sir. Half pistol shot it is.'

There was no good in manoeuvering. The Frenchman wanted only to get past *Dartmouth* and run to the west. No doubt her captain would willingly take a raking broadside from the bow because then he'd be past and gone while this awkward fourth rate lost speed as it bore away to follow him. No, the only way to stop him was broadsides, and if *Dartmouth* started to take so much damage that she couldn't hold position, then he'd run her alongside and board the Frenchman if he could. That would ensure that Forrest could come into action.

He looked astern again, astonished to see that the British frigate was now only three miles or so behind while *Centaur* and *Pembroke* were a good four miles further off. The frigate seemed amazingly fast and with this breeze she could join the battle in under an hour. Even those nine pounders would be useful; she could lie off the Frenchman's bows or stern and batter her with impunity while *Dartmouth* took the heavy blows from her broadsides. Ah, the French frigate was bearing away. She was going to cross the third rate's stern and prevent the British frigate from joining the battle. Very well, that was the correct response. Then *Dartmouth* could expect no help until the two ships-of-the-line came up.

'Mister Gresham, Mister Angelini, stand by the starboard battery. Mister Pontneuf, if I call for boarders you'll lead with the marines.'

It was all happening fast now. The seventy-gun ship was less than two miles away and the frigate was slipping out of sight on *Dartmouth's* starboard quarter. Forget the frigate, focus on the third rate.

Carlisle cast an eye along the upper deck. The crews were crouching over their guns but they weren't adjusting their aim yet. Gresham had told them that *Dartmouth* would bear away soon, and they were to hold their fire until he gave the word. It would be a point-blank engagement; no need to adjust the quoins for elevation when the target was but yards away.

The third rate disappeared in a pall of smoke. Carlisle heard a roar like thunder and the sound of chain shot screaming overhead. The Frenchman was squandering that first, carefully loaded and aimed broadside in exchange for the chance of shooting away an important spar. Carlisle nodded his approval. It was the right tactic and had it succeeded the Frenchman would have escaped. There was a hail of odd blocks and lengths of cordage that bounced harmlessly off the splinter net. He looked up to see torn sails and loose sheets, but nothing vital had been hit. Well, the Frenchman could only do that once.

Carlisle heard Beazley's orders. He saw the few men that were needed running to the sheets and braces, and he felt *Dartmouth* turn fast off the wind. Now the two ships were on a converging course and only a hundred yards apart. He could see the French officers on the quarterdeck. He didn't look but he knew that there'd be marksman in the tops, and swivel guns too. It was a strange feeling to know that he and he alone was the prime target of so many lethal weapons.

'Stand by Mister Gresham.'

The muskets and swivels were already firing and he could see that the French crews had almost reloaded the great guns, the first dark muzzles were pushing out thorough the gunports, and this time it would be round shot, the true ship-breakers. He wanted to catch them while they were still running out; just a few more seconds.

Gresham was watching him, waiting for the order.

A quarter of the French guns were run out. Now!

Carlisle blew his whistle.

'Fire!'

Gresham's voice cut through the sound of musketry and a second later *Dartmouth's* starboard battery erupted in flame and smoke.

Twenty-four pound shot at that short range made dreadful holes even in the thick planking and frames of a seventy-gun ship, and with their opponent so close, every shot hit. There was an interval – a brief pause – in which Carlisle heard the screams of wounded Frenchman, then the response came and *Dartmouth* reeled to the impact of heavy round shot. The Frenchman had more guns and on his lower deck he carried thirty-two pounders. They smashed into *Dartmouth's* lower deck destroying gun ports and sending showers of splinters scything through the gun crews. It wasn't much better on the upper deck, where the Frenchman carried twenty-fours to oppose *Dartmouth's* twelves. A gun was upturned and its crew lay in deathly attitudes around it. Now he could hear English screams. Gresham was everywhere, encouraging, helping, threatening, anything to get the battery reloaded. He was a lieutenant short as well. The upper gundeck was usually Enrico's responsibility but with Wishart gone, Enrico had taken charge of the lower deck, leaving Gresham to manage the upper.

'Fire!'

The starboard battery spoke again. Carlisle noticed that two guns didn't join in, the attrition had already started. How long before his battery fell silent? He heard Gresham shouting that they should fire as soon as each gun was loaded, rather than wait for the whole battery.

Dartmouth staggered again as the French guns bellowed. They were fewer in number too, but then they had ten guns more on each broadside, they could afford to lose a few and still outgun *Dartmouth*.

The din was continuous now and men were falling all over *Dartmouth's* deck. How long had they been engaged? Twenty minutes? It seemed like a lifetime. *Dartmouth* was being hit hard and couldn't take much more of it. Now or never.

'Mister Beazley, lay me alongside. Mister Pontneuf, Mister Gresham, boarding parties ready. Marines aft, seaman forrard. Bosun! Grapnels, and be ready to cut their boarding nets.'

Another French broadside and he felt *Dartmouth* shudder as though the ship had been swatted by a giant hand.

He looked over to larboard. The two frigates were alongside each other; they were grappling, but who was boarding who? He couldn't tell. Beyond the frigates the two ships-of-the-line looked glorious under a full spread of canvas. Forrest probably didn't care to reduce to fighting sail and risk missing the battle entirely. If *Dartmouth* still had hold of the Frenchman when they came up, it would be all over without *Centaur* having to fire a shot, and the enemy would surely bow to the inevitable and strike her colours. But there was the rub. *Dartmouth* had to set its teeth into the larger ship like a terrier at a bull, and at any risk to herself prevent the enemy running to the west.

'Boarders ready, sir!'

Dartmouth was closing in, the gap between the two ships was reducing yard by yard. Beazley couldn't just throw the helm over and put his bows to the enemy, if he did that they would inevitably pass under the seventy's stern. Carlisle wanted no mistakes; they must be beam-to-beam to give his boarders the widest front for the attack. Beazley had to slant in gradually, watching the relative bearings all the time, and it took nerves of steel as the French guns kept firing while half of *Dartmouth's* crews were away grabbing their weapons and crouching under the gunwales ready to leap up and board.

Thirty yards, twenty yards…

Carlisle heard a crash over his shoulder but ignored it.

Ten yards…

Beazley's voice sliced through the noise.

'Mizzen topmast's going sir. Hard a starboard quartermaster.'

Carlisle looked back to see the massive topmast lurching to larboard. It was the leverage of the after sails that was keeping *Dartmouth's* bows to the wind. Without it she'd start to slew to larboard. Would that helm order be enough?

Carlisle held his breath. For a few seconds he thought they'd do it, that the ship's momentum would allow the rudder to bite sufficiently to overcome the loss of sails aft.

'Drop the jib, drop the fore stays'ls.'

Carlisle realised he was screaming his orders, but he didn't care. If he could reduce the pressure forward, perhaps the bows would swing back to starboard. He only needed a few more yards. He could see the marines formed up in ranks with the indomitable Sergeant Wilson keeping them in check with his halberd. The seamen were less organised but still eager to be upon the enemy's deck. He knew in that moment that if he could board he'd win the day, nothing could stand against these men.

The jib and stays'ls came down in an untidy heap, smothering the swivel guns on the bows. It was going to work. He saw his ship's bows edge to starboard as the swell swept under her keel.

'Stand by to board!'

He felt the stern drop gently into the trough and watched appalled as the swell travelled forward and his bows paid off. The gap was increasing now and the Frenchman was running away from him.

'Belay the boarding. Stand by the starboard battery.'

It was a forlorn hope but all that he had left. The ship was swinging to larboard seemingly whatever Beazley tried to do. In a moment, his whole starboard battery would be pointing at the enemy.

Gresham saw the opportunity at the same time. He drove the confused boarders back to the guns. All along the line the gun captains were raising their hands. Guns Ready!

Gresham waited for no order from his captain, he knew what to do.

'Fire!'

Carlisle had a moment to notice that it was a good broadside, probably the best and most timely that his ship had ever fired. He saw the Frenchman's stern windows disintegrate and the taffrail dissolve into a shower of splinters. Roundshot must have travelled the length of the gundecks; there would be casualties aplenty and smashed gun carriages. A magnificent broadside, but nothing important was hit. The enemy's rudder was still functioning, he had lost no masts nor even yards and he sped on westward in disdain of his puny opponent.

Carlisle could have wept with frustration.

***

CHAPTER TWENTY-EIGHT

Reunion

Tuesday, Twelfth of January 1762.
Dartmouth, at Sea, off Cape Mays.

Carlisle watched impotently as the French third rate ran fast to the west, straight as an arrow for the Old Bahama Straits, to carry out its unknown mission. His enemy was ragged around the edges and they'd be burying dozens of men before they reached the open ocean, but in her essentials the ship was unimpaired. She'd call at Havana, no doubt, and Carlisle had seen the excellent dockyard facilities at the head of the bay. The Spanish shipwrights would repair the damage in a week, although her captain's cabin would take longer to be restored to its former glory. Now he must try to drag his mind in another direction. There was still a French frigate somewhere to the south and he should at least try to block her escape.

'The French frigate has struck, sir. Our frigate is fast alongside her. They've stopped firing.'

Midshipman Young was almost hopping with excitement, and it took a growl from Beazley to restore what dignity he ever had.

Then that was that. It was over and he could let his racing mind slow down. There'd be no catching that French third rate, and Forrest would know it. Nevertheless they'd gained a handsome frigate and all four British ships were in sight when the colours came down, so the day could be counted a success, but at what cost? Carlisle had seen with his own eyes a dozen men carried below, and a half dozen apparently lifeless bodies had been pushed into the scuppers, to await the end of the battle. He looked up at the mizzen topmast that lay drunkenly across the poop deck hammock nettings. Port Royal was to leeward and the wind looked set fair; they could make it without a jury rigged mast.

'Mister Gresham, what's the state of the guns and the crews?'

Gresham's face was stained dark grey by the powder smoke except where he had run a hand across his eyes and mouth leaving long streaks for the natural flesh colours to show through. There was blood below his ear and his coat was torn, probably by a splinter. But Gresham was unconquerable, and although his voice was louder than normal through his being deafened by the guns, he sounded as though he'd just finished a pleasant breakfast, rather than fought a desperate action against a superior foe. The first lieutenant had cheated death for so long that he and his shipmates no longer found anything remarkable in it.

'There's one gun carriage destroyed on the lower deck, sir, but the gun's unharmed and it's being secured now. There's at least two dead down there, and some wounded, I don't know how many. One of the twelve-pounders was struck on the muzzle, that'll have to be returned to the ordnance wharf, and two carriages are slightly damaged, the carpenter will be able to deal with them. There are three more dead on the upper deck and I saw a dozen carried below. I'll have the surgeon report as soon as he knows the numbers, sir.'

'Very well. The men did well, Mister Gresham.'

'That they did, sir, that they did.'

They both surveyed the devastated deck. There was much to be done, but first they had to see that all was well with the frigate.

'The surgeon asked me to pass a message to you, Edward.'

Carlisle turned around, astonished to see his wife. He couldn't have been less surprised to see an archbishop in full purple standing there. He suddenly felt guilty that he hadn't inquired after her.

'He has fifteen wounded men below. Now, I know he will have to take off two arms, and there's a leg that looked like it might have to go too. One bad head injury but the rest should do well. And you are unharmed, I see, and Mister Gresham, Mister Beazley? She suddenly stopped and looked swiftly around.

'Where's Enrico…'

Gresham smiled broadly and the flash of his teeth and pink lips broke through the grime.

'Mister Angelini is very well, your Ladyship. He's on the lower deck supervising a gun that needs to be secured. He may not look his usual self, not quite up to his normal standards of elegance, you understand, but he's fit as a fiddle, Ma'am.'

'Thank you, Mister Gresham, you've put my mind at rest. Now tell me, what are those ships doing there? They appear to be in an embrace.'

***

Chiara had to wait for an answer for *Centaur* was bearing down upon them and altered course to pass within *Dartmouth's* hailing range. Carlisle recognised Forrest's stocky figure standing on the hammock nets holding onto a shroud.

'Good morning, Carlisle, are you badly damaged?'

'No, sir, just the mizzen topmast and some gun carriages. Six dead and fifteen wounded. We can make Jamaica well enough.'

'Well, I'm sorry for your men. Now, just run down there would you and see that all's well.'

He pointed to the two frigates. They were firmly locked together and with their sails still set were running willy-nilly to the west-sou'west, towards Cape Mays. It appeared that they were all too busy to reduce sail or heave to.

'I'm going to see that fellow off the premises. Wait for me here or to windward, I'll be back tomorrow, I expect. If he loses a spar before the dog watches I'll have him, but I won't chase him into those straits, not at night. That's no place for a sane man.'

Carlisle forbore to point out that he'd chased into just those same straits only a few weeks before, and at night. That experience had convinced him that Forrest was right.

Pembroke came next, tight in *Centaur's* wake. Carlisle knew John Wheelock a little, but it appeared that he wanted to speak and he briefly backed his tops'l to take the way of his ship.

'I fell in with your prize brig a week ago, Captain Carlisle, off Cape Cross. I took your dispatches to Port Royal and gave them to the admiral's secretary.'

'Thank you for that. How was my lieutenant, Mister Wishart?'

'In fine form. He's taken the brig back to St. George's Island to warn them of the Spanish moves. I gave him written orders to cover him and told him to return to Port Royal soonest.'

Carlisle kept his surprise to himself. Written orders? It sounded like that was Wheelock's idea, and if so it was a damned liberty to send his prize off on an errand. It would be a hell of a legal situation if the brig was lost on that coral reef before it had been condemned by the vice admiralty court. Well, this wasn't the time to discuss it.

'What frigate is that. Who's commanding her?'

Wheelock's answer was lost as at that moment a gust caught his ship and drove it forward. He saw Wheelock look ahead to the growing gap between him and *Centaur*, and in a moment his main tops'l was drawing and he surged ahead of *Dartmouth* and hurried away before Forrest could send a rebuke for his station keeping. The two ships sped westwards in their pursuit of the fleeing enemy with *Pembroke* in his leader's wake but three cables astern of his rightful distance.

Carlisle shrugged; it was ten-to-one that the frigate's captain was below him on the captain's list, and if not, he'd soon be told.

'Mister Beazley, run down to those frigates if you please.'

***

Dartmouth rounded to under the British frigate's stern and moved slowly up on her larboard side. They were busy as bees on the deck. A few hands were furling the courses but the main part of the British crew was on the Frenchman's deck, securing the prisoners.

Beazley stared then reached for the telescope and studied the frigate's hull as it rolled to the waves.

'Good Lord, look at that! Her bottom's been coppered! That's why she was so fast.'

Each time her boot-topping came clear he saw the smooth, green underside with hardly a weed or any other kind of fouling showing.

'I'd heard that *Alarm* had been coppered, sir, but I didn't know about any others.'

There was no sign of the British captain on the deck, but a man who looked as though he could be the sailing master waved to them.

Ha! I know him, that's Josiah Fairview,' said Beazley with a knowing look. 'I heard that he had a ship, although I could hardly credited it. A frigate, that sounds about his mark.'

Carlisle ignored him and shouted across the gap.

'What ship?'

But before the sailing master could answer, a tall man, dressed in the uniform of a post-captain, jumped across the gap between the two quarterdecks and swung himself down from the hammock nets. The sailing master – Fairview as Beazley had named him – quite rightly waited for his captain to answer, but before the tall man had drawn a breath, Chiara cried out in delight.

'Isn't that George Holbrooke, Edward? Oh, I'm sure it is.'

'*Argonaut*. Captain Holbrooke at your service, sir, and well met on this fortunate day.'

'Ha, ha. It's Holbrooke all right.'

Carlisle called across to the frigate with a new vigour.

'Well met indeed, George. Did you suffer much? What assistance can I offer?'

'Your marines, if you please sir,' Holbrooke answered without hesitation, 'and your Marine lieutenant, if he's at leisure. I have a couple of hundred prisoners to deal with. I've lost one man dead and a few wounded, but there's no real damage to the ship. He considered his position as soon as that third rate showed us its heels. With Captain Forrest coming up fast and you blocking the way to leeward, he threw his sword and his hat onto the deck and struck his colours without further ado, and I can't say that I blame him. He was in such a rage that I thought he might stamp on his hat, but no such luck. That's him at the taffrail, *sans chapeau bras*, and much cooler. Is that Lady Chiara? My compliments your Ladyship.'

***

By the evening *Dartmouth*, *Argonaut* and *La Méduse* were on the larboard tack working their way in a leisurely fashion across the windward passage to get clear of Cape Mays. Enrico had been appointed prize master, with a prize crew drawn from both ships. He had no Frenchmen to worry about as the prisoners had been distributed between the two British ships, all securely battened below decks. The burials would wait until the next day, that was only decent, and the wounded were all quiet if not comfortable. Holbrooke had left his first lieutenant in charge of *Argonaut* and had been rowed across to *Dartmouth* for supper.

'Well, I must say that you are the last person I expected to see here in the windward passage, George. The last I heard of *Argonaut* was that you were at Belle Isle, then I heard that you were sick at your home. I've had no letters from you, but with us shifting from the Leeward Islands to Jamaica then being sent away to the ends of the earth, it's hardly surprising. Come to that, I've had no letters from anyone for months. What strange winds blew you here?'

Holbrooke was nursing a glass of Carlisle's Madeira. It brought back good memories of their time together in *Fury* and then in *Medina*, although it all seemed like lifetimes ago.

'Well, I wasn't really injured, I just rather overstretched myself and my officers had to bring *Argonaut* home, with me adrift in my wits in the great cabin. It's embarrassing to admit, so I won't dwell on it if you don't mind.'

Chiara pressed her hand on her husband's knee to prevent him probing further.

'However, I was up and about in a few weeks and fully recovered by the time *Argonaut's* repairs and coppering were complete, so there was no question of being superseded. We were sent out to Antigua by way of Barbados, and then after a few weeks there, like you I was packed off to Jamaica. You sailed just a few days before I arrived.'

'We must talk about the coppering when we have more leisure, but how do you find it so far?'

Holbrooke thought for a moment.

'I can't answer for its long-term effectiveness, but in the few months I've had it there have been no problems, and I'd swear that I have an extra knot of speed, perhaps more. The weed won't cling to it, you understand, and I'm told that the worm can't reach the hull through the copper plates. However, we'll have a better understanding at our next docking or careening. For all I know the hull could be rotting away underneath it. In principle it should reduce the need for careening, or perhaps eliminate it all together, but I understand that it's ruinously expensive. The coppering was the main reason for me being sent to the Caribbean, to test it against the worm.'

Carlisle nodded. It was an intriguing new development that could mean ships spent more time at sea and less time in the yards. It could also increase their service life.

'I did manage to call at St. Johns while I was in Antigua,' Holbrooke added, 'three or four times in fact, and renewed my acquaintance with Joshua. He's a fine little chap and doing very well under his nurse. Black Rod keeps an orderly house, as you can imagine. I suppose I should call him Mister Black now, although it doesn't sound quite right.'

Cousins At Arms

Chiara's made an involuntary gasp and nearly cried out.

'You saw Joshua? Oh. How I wish I was with him now.'

'Yes, and with a little prompting he sent his love to his mother and his duty to his father. Here, I have some drawings that he made for you. They've chased you across a thousand miles of ocean, but better late than never.'

Holbrooke brought out four sheets of paper, somewhat crumpled, with charmingly crude stick figures of his father and mother and his grandfather in Williamsburg and Uncle George who he hoped would pass on the artwork.

Chiara held the drawings for a moment, searching them for anything that could be identified as coming from the son that she had so easily left behind in Antigua. Holbrooke looked away to spare her embarrassment as she shed her tears.

'Well, and Ann is thriving?'

'Yes, sir, she's doing very well, and young Edward is a year old now. Ann is making quite something of the house, and she hopes you will be able to visit some time. Her father is ailing, however, and her stepmother doesn't know what to do with herself. Do you remember me writing about the Austrian Major of artillery who has dogged my steps since we first met at Emden?'

'I do, you told me he was in service with the Breton militia. Have you heard from him?'

'He's living at Mulberry House! He had a disagreement with his French hosts and had to leave the country, and there seems little prospect of his returning to Austria, not while the war continues, at least. When I left he was a sort of manager in my father-in-law's corn business. Whether that will come to anything I can't say, but it's convenient for both parties.'

They were interrupted by Walker serving supper and when he left the subject had subtly changed.

'I gather, George, that you'll be with Mister Forrest carving a furrow off Cape François for a few months. My commiserations.'

In all the wide spread of the seas that came within the Jamaica Squadron's responsibility, the Cape François blockade was the least desirable. It meant a life of constant beating to and fro in an attempt to stay to windward of the French naval base, with every yard of leeway to be recovered by hours and days of sailing hard on a bowline. There was little chance of another squadron action to relieve the monotony, not with the French so depleted in the Caribbean.

'Oh, it's only for few days, I'm just a substitute. Robert Carkett was supposed to be with Captain Forrest but *Hussar* sprung a butt end two days before the sailing date. The master attendant believes it can be made good at the careening wharf and she can be breamed while she's there, it should only take a week. I have to be back in Port Royal on the twentieth whether I'm relieved or no, there to await my fate which I believe to be a convoy. You'll hardly be there before I join you.'

***

Dartmouth, *Argonaut* and the French prize made their way slowly to windward, tack upon tack, but not too far to the east, because Carlisle was eager to be away for Port Royal as soon as Forrest should return. In any case, with her wounded mizzen it was difficult for the two-decker to keep her head to the wind, and by the Wednesday evening the three ships were still somewhat west of the longitude of Cape St. Nicholas.

Centaur and *Pembroke* found them before the light faded. They'd chased the French third rate as far as prudence would allow and they'd caught a providential backing of the trade wind to make a single board back to the east. Forrest wasn't inclined to socialise. He had to work his squadron to its proper station off Cape Monte Christi, to windward of Cape François, and with the trade wind blowing hard and regular, that would take a couple of days at least.

'Carlisle!' he shouted across the tossing waves between the two ships, 'take the prize back to Port Royal and let whoever pretends to be in charge know about that third rate that's gone west. Stir up the master attendant and Carkett, if you can. I want *Hussar* here without delay so that I can send young Holbrooke back and still have a frigate. Carkett may suggest that he needs a week to set up his rigging or some such nonsense, but you may tell him from me that I expect him to clear Port Royal no more than two days after he's afloat. There are too many Sirens on shore for my liking and for his health.'

Carlisle smiled broadly as Forrest gave him a knowing look and what could have been a wink, although he was too far away to be sure. He didn't know Carkett well enough to guess whether he had succumbed, but more than one captain on the Jamaica Station had not been so well prepared as Odysseus to encounter the Sirens. Port Royal, with its warm tropical nights and its huge distance from home, made it prime Siren territory.

'You'll look after that prize now, and make it quite clear to Holbrooke's agent – you have the same man, I believe – that we were all in sight when he struck. It's as clear a decision as can be but I don't want any misapprehensions at the prize court. You know how those things can drag on if the facts aren't reported correctly at the first telling.'

'Do you have any letters, sir?'

'No. You saw how it went and you can report on the action as well as any letter of mine. We chased that fellow as far as fifteen leagues past Cape Mays but we never came closer than three miles. He showed every inclination to press on under all canvas, so we may yet hear that he's grounded on one of those reefs. But I wouldn't be thanked for being stranded a hundred miles to leeward of my proper station.'

Carlisle raised his hat in farewell. Enrico knew very well that he'd be following *Dartmouth* back to Port Royal in the prize, so there was no need for signals or orders.

'I wish you well, Captain Carlisle. I wouldn't be surprised to see you on this station in a month or so. My respects to

Lady Chiara.'

Ships didn't dawdle in the Windward Passage, not if they had to make way to the east to watch the French at Cape François, and in a moment the two ships-of-the line and Holbrooke's frigate were hard on the wind making their offing to be clear of Hispaniola during the night. *Dartmouth* and *La Méduse* squared away for the two-day run down to Port Royal.

***

CHAPTER TWENTY-NINE

Family Decisions

Friday, Fifteenth of January 1762.
Dartmouth, at Anchor, Port Royal, Jamaica.

There was no commander-in-chief at Port Royal. Charles Holmes had been buried and all the indications were that Sir James Douglas would move across from the Leeward Islands station. However, the Leeward Islands were busy. Admiral Rodney had arrived with a fleet and an army under Brigadier Monckton. Their objective was Martinique, that fabulously rich sugar island, and the operation to capture it had already started.

There was no commander-in-chief but a series of commodores and post-captains manoeuvering for position with the lieutenant-governor pulling strings from the side-lines. Carlisle was hoping to hand his report to the commander-in-chief's secretary – who appeared to sail serenely above the turmoil – and to retire to the familiar and comforting task of hounding the master attendant to repair his damage and prepare his ship, and to securing a passage for Chiara to Antigua.

'I wish I could give you some better direction, Captain Carlisle, but as you see, with Captain Forrest off Cape François, there's no clear candidate for the *interregnum*. What I can say is that you're needed here in Jamaica, and I hope you weren't set on returning to Antigua. They have all the ships-of-the-line that they need, what with Admiral Rodney arriving with so many for the attack on Martinique.'

Carlisle nodded and smiled wryly. He knew that the secretary was too polite, and too good a secretary, to point out that Rodney had no use for fifty-gun fourth rates.

'Well, I'll just have to find a passage in a comfortable merchantman for Lady Chiara, because she must return to St. John's for the sake of our son. In the meantime, I won't be causing you disturbance, I hope. *Dartmouth* will need a month of repairs before she's seaworthy again and I'm no contender for the crown.'

The secretary bowed. It was clear that the thought of Carlisle contending for the position hadn't entered his mind.

'The lieutenant-governor will wish to see you, of course.'

Carlisle's heart sank, but he knew he should have anticipated it. With no settled commander-in-chief the usual channels through which the lieutenant-governor heard news that the navy brought in had collapsed. It was only natural that Sir Henry would want to meet a captain who had been to Havana, Louisiana and the Gulf of Honduras. After all, Jamaica must be assumed to be a first objective for combined French and Spanish arms in the event of Spain joining the war, and Carlisle had the latest word from the west.

'However, if I may advise you, I would wait for a summons. It will do no good to appear too eager and I'll brief him on the contents of your report this afternoon.'

Carlisle changed the subject.

'I didn't see *Hussar* in the anchorage or at the careening wharf. Has Captain Carkett sailed already?'

'Oh, yes, sir. He had Mister Forrest's words ringing in his ears and he sailed the day after he floated off. I expect Captain Holbrooke to return soon to claim his prize.'

'Yes, those envious stares that I received rightly belonged to him. *Dartmouth* and the other two weren't engaged at all with the frigate; that was all Mister Holbrooke's doing.'

'*Memento mori*, Captain Carlisle, *memento mori*. It's not good for these young fellows to receive too much adulation. We who have seen the world turn a few times are largely immune, but like the Roman emperors in their triumph, our brilliant young captains must be reminded that they are mortals, not gods, don't you think?'

Cousins At Arms

Carlisle wasn't so sure, and he didn't much like being cast as one of the older men, but the secretary was a powerful person who moved the levers of influence without ever letting anything more than his shadow be seen. It would be foolish to disagree over a trivial matter. He nodded in cautious agreement.

Carlisle walked back to the wharf where his boat waited, lost in thought. How could they ever have come to this state of affairs with one of the most important overseas stations apparently leaderless? In principle, post-captains held their seniority relative to their fellows according to their date of posting; there should be no discussion on the matter. However, their Lordships, in their desire to promote the best officers to senior commands, raised post-captains to the temporary rank of commodore whenever they saw fit. While it was well understood that a commodore ranked above a post-captain, by reason of his appointment, it wasn't at all clear who was the senior when it came to stepping into the shoes of a deceased commander-in chief. Well, he hadn't progressed far enough up the post-captain's list for it to concern him, but he could see that others, nearer hoisting their flags, would be very keen for the opportunity to show their worth.

***

The pinnace shot across the bay to where *Dartmouth* lay at anchor. The lieutenant-governor would call for him, or he wouldn't, there was nothing he could do about that and he had his own concerns. *Dartmouth's* repairs would hardly take any of his time. Gresham, the carpenter and the bosun were more than capable of dealing with the master attendant and his minions; he had other more personal concerns.

The passage back to Port Royal had a *fin de siècle* feeling to it. He'd delighted in having his wife follow him to the Caribbean and he'd even enjoyed the cruise with her as a cabin companion, once he'd become used to it. He was sure that Chiara had also appreciated it, but now she wanted to see their son and to return to their home in Williamsburg. It should have been easy. There were merchantmen and packets dashing here and there from Jamaica and some of them had accommodation suitable for a lady. However, it was an astonishingly small number that made the passage from Jamaica to Antigua. It was the trade winds of course, those arbiters of all journeys in these latitudes. The secretary's damned Roman slave could as easily have whispered to a Caribbean admiral that he must remember that everything he did was with the consent of the trade wind, as he could remind an emperor that he was only mortal. His mind wandered for a moment as he tried to render it in Latin. *Memento artis ventis*. But he didn't quite like the *artis*, it suggested an artisan, a mere tradesman, rather than the majesty of the global trade that underpinned the wealth of nations. *Memento ventis*, that was better, *remember the wind*; he must ask the carpenter to paint it on the ship's binnacle. Or on reflection perhaps not. It would be a permanent hostage to a nautical sense of humour and when word of it got out, he'd be a laughing stock throughout the squadron. No, better not. Nevertheless, he was secretly pleased to find that he hadn't forgotten everything from his abbreviated time at the grammar school in the college of William and Mary.

Carlisle was jolted back to the here-and-now as the pinnace nudged heavily against the ship's side. Souter stared in silent wrath at the bowman who should have sacrificed his very hands if necessary to avoid his captain being inconvenienced.

'Beg pardon, sir,' he said, privately promising that the bowman would live to regret his transgression.

Carlisle remembered his own dignity and climbed steadily up the side, supported by side boys and greeted by the shrill pipes of the bosun's mates. He was greeted by the stamp-and-slap of the marines' salute and the massed ranks of his officers. Gresham removed his hat and bent low.

'The post has arrived, sir. Simmonds is sorting it in your cabin, and the master attendant has sent word that he will wait on us this afternoon, if we can send a boat. His own has been hauled out for repair.'

'Very well, I'll be in my cabin. I expect to step ashore later with Lady Chiara to find some suitable lodgings.'

***

The post. A veritable mountain of letters that Simmonds had already sorted into four piles. The first consisted of the official letters that the captain would need to see, and these he had opened. The second was the captain's personal correspondence, the third was for the officers and the fourth, the smallest pile, was for the people of the ship.

'Good morning, sir. Much of the usual but there's one letter from the Admiralty Secretary that you may wish to read first.'

It was hot in the cabin and Carlisle stood while Walker helped him out of his coat, then, in his shirt and waistcoat, he sat to read the letter that Simmonds thought so important. Perhaps he was right in thinking so. It was unusual for a captain to receive a letter directly from their Lordships, they normally channelled all orders, admonitions and advice through the appropriate commander-in-chief. It was in fact two letters, one enclosed within the other, and he opened the outer one first, and read with a growing sense of sadness.

It was from the Sardinian Minister of Marine and addressed to Lord Anson, who had passed it on to Carlisle. He remembered the minister as a closed, devious man who could be trusted only as far as the extent of his master's interests. He passed over the laborious salutations and found the few paragraphs that mattered.

Mister Enrico Angelini's commission as a lieutenant in his Sardinian Majesty's Navy is revoked with immediate effect. Mister Angelini has been informed of this decision and it is expected that he will take the first opportunity to rejoin the Royal Piedmont Cavalry in Milan where he will take up his duties in his former rank.

There was more but it was of no consequence, just the minister assuring his Lordship of his continuing regard etcetera, etcetera. There was a note on the turn-back from the Admiralty secretary stating that their Lordships consented for Mister Angelini – it saddened him to hear Enrico's naval rank so suddenly and completely erased – remaining in *Dartmouth* as a supernumerary, borne for rations but not pay, until a passage should be found for him.

'The enclosed letter is for Lieutenant Angelini, sir. I expect that is what the minister meant when he said he has been informed.'

Carlisle sat back, stunned by this sudden blow. He could see that it had affected his clerk too; he and Enrico were good friends. Of course, he knew that Enrico would be recalled one day, but he had assumed that it would be to use the skills that he had learned in *Dartmouth* to the benefit of the resurgent Sardinian navy, to command a sloop or even a frigate. He had never imagined that his wife's cousin would have to suffer the indignity of reverting to the rank of lieutenant in the army, a rank that was immeasurably lower than a lieutenant in the navy. It was brutal and spoke volumes about the Angelini family's standing in the country.

It would have to be done immediately; he could see that. From this moment Enrico could no longer be paid, he could not benefit from any captures taken after today, and he was not sheltered by a commission; he had no authority on board *Dartmouth*, or anywhere else, come to that.

'Well, a sad day, Mister Simmonds. Would you pass the word for Lieutenant, Angelini? And mark you, he is a lieutenant until the moment he reads this letter, and he is to be treated with all respect as long as…'

Carlisle paused in mid-sentence. He had been about to instruct Simmonds to inform all the other officers how they should treat Enrico, but it occurred to him that there was someone else who should be consulted before he spoke to Enrico.

'Belay that, Mister Simmonds, would you knock on the door,' he nodded towards the dining cabin where he knew his wife was reading, 'and ask Lady Chiara to join me? And not a word of this to anyone until I have spoken to Mister Angelini.'

***

Carlisle was certain that the letter would cause Chiara distress, and he knew no better way to introduce it than to pass it directly to her. She studied it in silence but he could see that she grew more furious with each line. She read it twice then laid it on the table, took off her spectacles and slapped her hand onto the letter, as though to punish the very paper on which it was written.

'The man is an ill-bred lickspittle, Edward. I knew his family well and they were all the same, climbers of any greasy pole that came to hand as long as there was a pot of gold at the top. This is an outrage and an insult to the Angelini family name. I cannot imagine how the viscountess has taken it.'

Carlisle let her rage boil over. She loved her cousin and was infuriated at this treatment, but as for her aunt the viscountess being similarly outraged, well, when she paused for thought she'd remember how Enrico had been as good as chased from the country by his family. It was more likely that the viscountess was an instigator of this than that she was a victim.

'My poor, dear Enrico, what is to become of him? He won't go back to Sardinia you know.'

Chiara stood and gazed out of the windows at the busy harbour with Kingston over the bay and the mountains beyond. She turned, and Carlisle was struck by how old she looked, old and sad. And he knew that it wasn't just this letter that was affecting her. She needed to see to the stability of her family, she needed her son and her home.

'However,' she said with a deep intake of breath, 'I shouldn't be surprised. If Spain enters this war then Sardinia's position becomes precarious, with all of the

Mediterranean at odds with Britain. The King must be considering taking sides. And, you know, the Viscountess Angelini is no friend of King George, and has no love for Enrico. I often wonder what she thinks of me. I fear for Enrico if he should go back to Milan. If one commission can be revoked, why not another? And you know, assassination is still a common way of dealing with family disagreements in Sardinia. No, he cannot go back, and I imagine he can't stay here with you.'

Carlisle slowly shook his head.

'You are correct, my dear. That note on the turn of the page comes with Lord Anson's approval but it's conditional. I can only allow a berth for Enrico until he can find a passage to wherever he chooses to go.'

'Do you think he would choose Williamsburg? There's plenty of room for him at our home, and we could take passage together. He would be the best safeguard that I can imagine.'

Chiara looked at her husband carefully. She was aware of man's jealous nature where a wife was concerned, and she had often wondered how he perceived the obvious friendship that she had for her cousin. She knew that it was perfectly innocent and always would be, and on board her husband's ship it couldn't be anything else. However, for Enrico to escort her all the long sea-leagues to Antigua and to Williamsburg, and then to live under her roof while Carlisle was away at sea? Perhaps that was too much to ask of any man. She hoped that her husband would detect her concern, that he would say the right things to ease her distress. But Carlisle still could not really read his wife's mind, even after four years of marriage.

'Well, let's see what Enrico wants,' he said, and opened the cabin door to tell the marine sentry to pass the word for Lieutenant Angelini.

***

Enrico read the letter in silence and with an impassive face.

'I've been expecting something like this, although I still hoped that it may just have been a recall to a post in the Sardinian navy. I made up my mind months ago, sir. I won't go back to Milan. I have it in mind to settle in Virginia, in Williamsburg, perhaps, and to see if I can make something out of a map-making business. I've spoken of it to your cousin Mister Dexter in a roundabout way as it has some similarities to his bookselling business. Or perhaps I'll study for the law, I have enough in prize money to last until I'm established one way or another…'

'Oh, oh!'

Chiara couldn't hold back the tears.

'Well,' Carlisle said as he placed his hand on his wife's arm, 'you're welcome at our home for as long as you like.'

'And you can escort me, dear Enrico, me and Joshua, for we are bound for Williamsburg too, as soon as we can find a passage to Antigua.'

There was a knock at the door and Midshipman Young stepped in. He looked uncertain as he saw the emotional scene in the cabin, but he delivered his message manfully, if in a rather abrupt voice, as he sought to pretend that he had seen nothing untoward.

'Mister Beazley's respects, sir, and there's a little schooner passing close alongside us with Mister Wishart calling out to ask if he may come aboard when he's anchored.'

'Mister Wishart, on a schooner? Are you sure, Mister Young?'

'Mister Wishart it is, sir, large as life, and the prize crew from the brig.'

'Then where's the brig? Oh, off you go Mister Young.'

He stared in bemusement at Chiara and Enrico.

'Are there any more surprises?' he demanded, 'because I'd appreciate having them declared now, so that I can enjoy the rest of the day without going completely mad.'

***

By the time Wishart came aboard from the tiny gig that was the only boat that the schooner possessed, half of the ship's company was in the waist and on the fo'c'sle openly speculating on the fate of their prize and commenting unfavourably upon poor Wishart. He hurried below to Carlisle's cabin.

'Well, Mister Wishart? Perhaps you can explain how you lost a French brig and gained a scruffy little schooner?'

Wishart didn't know whether his captain was genuinely angry, whether he should smile or look solemn. Like Midshipman Young, he chose to deny the existence of any emotion whatever and make his report as though he were bellowing it to the masthead in a three-reef gale.

'I met *Pembroke* off Cape Cross, Captain Wheelock, sir. As you ordered I gave your dispatches to him and stayed as he opened them. He decided to deliver them himself, the brig being rather unweatherly…'

'Yes, yes, I met *Pembroke* in the Windward Passage and had a quarterdeck to quarterdeck conversation with Captain Wheelock. He told me you turned around to run back to St. George's Island. That was rather irregular with the prize not being condemned, but we'll pass over that for the moment. Now, how did you come to take possession of a schooner, and where's the brig and its cargo?'

Wishart took a deep breath and told the whole story. Carlisle's face alternated between flashes of anger and grudging approval as each phase of the story was told.

'You are sure that the letter was from Don Alonso?'

'Yes, sir, I have it here.'

Wishart brought the letter from his pocket. It was somewhat crumpled after its long and arduous journey, but still perfectly readable. Carlisle started to read it and then realised there was someone much better versed in the language than he, and he knew that she was in the adjoining cabin, talking to Enrico.

'Chiara,' he said, poking his head into the dining room, 'may I use your linguistic skills again?'

Chiara read the letter through with an impassive expression, then she read it back to Carlisle in English and the full extent of Don Alonso's duplicity became clear.

Carlisle scanned the letter again, looking intently at Don Alonso's signature as though he could understand the man better from his handwriting.

'Well, it seems that this is a day for betrayals. We clasped a viper to our bosoms. He must have decided on this course of action before he even left Havana. I wonder that a man in his position could so take advantage of our hospitality.'

Chiara took the letter and read it through once more.

'Betrayal? I don't believe I would put it quite like that, Edward, and I wonder whether it's quite wise to judge kings and princes and colonial governors-general by the same standards that we might judge a friend or colleague. The stakes are high for those men and finer sentiments must surely come second place to hard decisions concerning their realms. Did your last King George withhold his clemency from Admiral Byng out of sheer spite? Did the last Henry sever the necks of two of his wives to satisfy a bloodlust? I think not. If Byng had not been punished, where would our navy be now? and Henry was advised from all sides that only a male heir would keep the kingdom from descending into anarchy. Perhaps they deserve our pity for having to make such judgements.'

Carlisle heard his wife in a thoughtful silence, forgetting the presence of Wishart for a moment.

'Thank you, my dear, you are very perceptive, and I had never thought of it quite like that. Now, I'll call for Simmonds and perhaps you would read it to him in English so that he can make a fair copy. Meanwhile, Mister Wishart, you must shift into something respectable for we are bound for the lieutenant-governor. Oh, and if you think you've come back to your comfortable three-watch system, you will be disappointed. Mister Angelini will enlighten you, no doubt.'

**

CHAPTER THIRTY

A Solution

Wednesday, Twentieth of January 1762.
Dartmouth, at Anchor, Port Royal, Jamaica.

Argonaut sailed into the navy anchorage under her tops'ls on the stroke of eight bells in the afternoon watch, with all of Port Royal watching to see how the latest captain to win a single-ship action handled his frigate. The ship backed its tops'ls and swung its bows into the gentle breeze from the land. In a flash the tops'ls were taken in and furled, the mizzen brailed up to its yard and the jib and stays'l came down with a rush to be smothered by the fo'c'sle hands. The anchor cable smoked as it ran through the hawse and with the last of its sternway, *Argonaut* laid out its cable in the Port Royal mud, and every watcher would swear that it lay straight as a ruler, with never a bend in its entire length.

They watched in deep appreciation from *Dartmouth's* quarterdeck, some covertly timing the manoeuvres on their pocket watches. Wishart was there, but he was a shadow of his usual exuberant self. His story about the brig had been frankly disbelieved by many of the crew, and they, after all, had a monetary interest in that hull. Nothing that could be said about the cargo being safe and sound in the schooner, nor any assurance that the schooner was worth as much as the brig, could satisfy them. They were all hungry for prize money and they could see the prize court spinning this one out until they were all cold in their graves. So David Wishart kept to the far side of the quarterdeck, shunning the company of the other officers, and affecting a disinterest in his old friend Holbrooke's frigate. He was on the far side of the quarterdeck but as the land breeze was still blowing, that was the side that faced Fort Charles and the twisting route through the cays beyond, and that was why Wishart saw the brig before anyone else, and he would swear that he recognised the logger Hookway standing by the taffrail conning her boldly into the navy anchorage.

***

Holbrooke took supper with Carlisle and Chiara in the same lodgings that he remembered from the first time that he came to Jamaica.

'It was a strange affair, almost like a committee, or a junta or a triumvirate perhaps. In any case, three very senior post-captains, all evidently warming the bell on their flags, gave me their orders, each eyeing the others to ensure that they spoke as one. I'd imagined that I might have a cruise up towards the Yucatan, or perhaps I'd be bound for Cape François, or a convoy through the Windward Passage to England, but nothing of the sort. It appears that every ship that can mount a gun in the Leeward Islands is with Admiral Rodney at Martinique, and they have a convoy that must be cleared for New York. They haven't so much as a brig-sloop to escort them. At the same time there's a convoy gathering here, also for the American colonies. The solution appears to be to send *Argonaut* to Antigua with the Jamaica convoy, then I'll pick up the rest at St. John's and reach right across for Savannah, Hampton Roads, New York, Boston and Halifax. Hey ho, for the life of a frigate captain! I beg your pardon, sir, have I said something amiss?'

He looked from Carlisle to Chiara, who in her turn was looking at her husband in amazement. There was an unspoken question in that gaze, and Holbrooke caught the tiny nod of assent from Carlisle.

'My dear George,' Chiara said as she leaned over and grasped his hand. 'You have no idea, no idea at all how timely is this meeting. May I, oh may I take passage with you to Antigua? I can find a berth in an Indiaman from there, for me and Joshua and Mister Black, but I so much yearn to go home! Oh, and Enrico will be joining us, he's no longer a sea officer you know, and he's going to be a Virginian!'

***

HISTORICAL EPILOGUE

At Sea

In early 1762 British forces commanded by Admiral Rodney and Brigadier General Monckton captured Martinique, leaving the French Antilles possessions reduced to only those in the southern part of the island chain. With their navy yet to recover from its defeats at Lagos Bay and Quiberon Bay and its futile attempts to reinforce Quebec, there was every prospect that St. Lucia, St. Vincent and Grenada would soon also fall into British hands. To make matters worse, the loss of Belle-Isle in 1761 had provided an excellent base of operations for the British blockading squadron; France's Atlantic seaboard was locked down tight. The French shipyards were busy building replacements for the fleet and French agents were scouring the shipyards of Europe for spare capacity to build men-of-war. Meanwhile, and until the new ships should be available, all that the French navy could do was to try to keep a fleet in being, protected in its main bases at Brest and Rochefort, and hope that Spain would soon join the war and add its large, undamaged fleet to the Bourbon cause.

Western Europe

Prince Ferdinand continued to frustrate the French armies that poured into Westphalia and the other German states with each new campaigning season. It was this failure to capture Hanover that was King Louis' greatest concern because he and his ministers were convinced that Britain would exchange anything to retrieve the King's personal German fiefdom. However, if they noticed that George III didn't have the same attachment to Hanover as his grandfather had, they failed to take it properly into consideration, and it is questionable whether it would have been the bargaining chip for which they had hoped.

Central Europe

In Central Europe, Frederick of Prussia continued to raise new armies to hold his territorial gains against the combined armies of Austria and Russia. Nevertheless, a tactical mistake in the autumn of 1761 left the Prussian state on the verge of collapse and it was only saved by the death of Empress Elizabeth of Russia in January 1762. Her successor Peter initiated peace negotiations with Frederick, taking the pressure off his army and saving Prussia from defeat and destruction.

North America

French territory in North America was reduced to a few settlements in Louisiana and in the centre of the continent to the west of the Ohio and south of the Great Lakes. The English-speaking people of the thirteen colonies were starting to come to terms with the idea that they were no longer threatened with enclosure by French soldiers and settlers moving down from Canada. Louisiana was so far away that it was of little concern except to the people of Georgia, who also worried about Spanish Florida on their southern border. The mood in America was one of expansion to the west, and they were impatient with the continuing war which they largely saw as none of their business. They felt increasingly constrained by the demands of their colonial masters in Whitehall and although it's difficult to find evidence of anyone openly considering independence, many were thinking of ways in which the leash could be loosened.

The Long War

France had lost territory in North America, the Caribbean, West Africa, the East Indies and, most humiliatingly of all, their own home island of Belle Isle. There was no consolation in Germany where they were no more than holding ground. Their only conquest that had any bargaining power in peace negotiations was Minorca, and they had already promised that island to Spain as part of the secret treaty. King Louis saw Spain's entry into the war as critical, and if they could take back some of the sugar islands and if Spain could successfully invade Britain's ally Portugal, all may not yet be lost. Thus, Britain's declaration of war with Spain in January 1762 was greeted with joy in Versailles. However, the Spanish navy had not been given enough time to mobilise and the army wasn't ready for the stern test of invading its neighbour across a difficult border. For France and its allies, the prospects of a favourable outcome from the war still looked bleak.

***

FACT MEETS FICTION

The Third *Pacte de Famille*, 1761

There were three Bourbon family pacts during the eighteenth century. The first was in 1733 during the War of Spanish Succession and was agreed between Philip V of Spain and his nephew Louis XV of France. The second was made in 1743 during the War of Austrian Succession and was also between King Philip V and King Louis XV. The third Bourbon family pact and the one that we are concerned with was agreed between King Carlos (Charles) III and King Louis XV. Charles and Louis shared a common grandfather in another Louis, known as The Grand Dauphin, and were therefore first cousins. Charles had only been on the throne two years when he was persuaded into this disastrous treaty and it seems likely that he was heavily influenced by his older cousin who had, by that time, ruled France for forty-six years. The treaty committed Spain to join the war in May 1762 if France had not achieved a peace settlement by then. Britain, being aware of this secret treaty, decided that it was better to fight Spain before her ponderous bureaucracy had managed to bring its fleet and army to full readiness. King George duly declared war in January 1762.

***

Don Alonso Fernández de Heredia

Don Alonzo was a successful soldier and administrator. After some years in the Spanish army he became at various times the governor or captain-general of Honduras, Florida, Yucatan, Guatemala and Nicaragua. There is little on record about his personality but there is a wonderful portrait on his Wikipedia page that shows a strong, stern military man dressed for a campaign. It's very unlike the portraits of Englishmen or Frenchmen of that station in that period, who are usually shown in their finest uniforms or court dress. I've used that portrait as the basis for his character in this book, as I did previously in the third book in the series, *The Jamaica Station*. Don Alonso married the Countess San Clemente. They had one daughter, Maria, who in *The Jamaica Station* pursued Carlisle relentlessly on their way to St. Augustine. You may gather from my sympathetic treatment of Don Alonso that, as I wove him into these adventures, I grew to like him.

***

The Old Bahama Straits

The straits have been tamed today, and a combination of satellite navigation, excellent charts and extensive buoyage and lighting have rendered them safe for prudent navigators. It was not always thus, and in the first three hundred years that they were known to Europeans they claimed ships and lives aplenty. The problem was threefold: first, although a chart will show a channel some sixty miles wide between the islands, in reality at some points there are only twenty miles between submerged obstructions; secondly, the rocks and shoals are so far from the land that there is nothing to take a fix upon and the seabed rises so rapidly that a mariner could be aground between casts of the lead; then there is a constant current that sweeps westward coupled with the trade wind that blows almost constantly from the nor'east. A difficult navigational problem indeed.

***

The Yucatan Loggers

British buccaneers had been using the Yucatan coast of the Gulf of Honduras since the seventeenth century and gradually they found that harvesting logwood was more lucrative than stealing it from Spanish ships. Logwood is a tropical hardwood that can be used to make dyes, and in the eighteenth century it was a valuable commodity. The first permanent British settlements appeared in the early eighteenth century, and by the middle of the century St. George's Island – near present-day Belize City – was a thriving if unofficial centre for the export of logwood and later mahogany. Britain didn't claim ownership of the territory and the loggers lived a precarious existence when each new outbreak of war would see Spanish raids destroy their good camps and settlements. The British government and the colonial governors were reluctant to interfere in the peninsula and the settlers, on their own initiative, elected magistrates and established English common law.

***

Louisiana

One has to be careful when defining the historical area of *Louisiana*. The land mass that was called by that name in 1761 is different to that of the famous *Louisiana Purchase* of 1803, which is different again from the modern state of Louisiana. At the start of the Seven Years War, France claimed the whole of the American hinterland, leaving just the east and west coasts to Britain and Spain respectively. They called the territory that was based upon the Mississippi basin, south of the Great Lakes, Louisiana. Its boundaries weren't defined and most of it hadn't been explored by Europeans although the native Americans knew it well.

The problem with claiming Louisiana was one of access. The French could only reach it through the St. Lawrence or by navigating the Mississippi from the Gulf of Mexico. Once Quebec fell, the northern route was lost, lending new importance to the Gulf ports of Mobile, Biloxi, Pascagoula and New Orleans. The geographical value of Louisiana provides the background to Carlisle's operations in the Gulf of Mexico.

***

Chris Durbin

THE CARLISLE & HOLBROOKE SERIES

There are now thirteen Carlisle and Holbrooke Naval Adventures. The series starts in the Mediterranean at the end of 1755 when Captain Edward Carlisle's small frigate *Fury* is part of the peacetime squadron based at Port Mahon to watch the French fleet at Toulon. Carlisle is a native of Virginia but in those days before American independence it was quite normal for well-connected men from the colonies to take the King's commission. In fact, there is an information board at Mount Vernon that records George Washington's wish to join the navy and his mother's refusal to allow it. Imagine how things might have been different if he had found himself on the quarterdeck of a man-of-war instead of leading the allied armies to ultimate victory against the British during the war of independence.

Carlisle has a master's mate, George Holbrooke, who is the son of an old friend now retired in England. Holbrooke's heart isn't in the navy; he wanted to become a lawyer but the family finances wouldn't stretch that far. His performance is disappointing as a sea officer, to the extent that Carlisle is considering dismissing him. However, when war breaks out the following year Holbrooke rises to the challenge and as the navy struggles to mobilise for war he achieves rapid promotion and is soon in command of his own ship.

Each book in the series is centred on one of the two principal characters, either Carlisle or Holbrooke, and they take centre stage in alternate episodes. There are broadly two books for each year of the war and I hope to carry the series through the period of strained relations between Britain and its American colonies, into the war for American independence.

The series is available in Kindle, Kindle Unlimited and in paperback formats, and I plan to publish two new books each year. The easiest way to obtain a copy is through Amazon.

I am also releasing audio editions of the books and I hope they will be published at the rate of four a year. The audio books are available through Amazon, Audible and iTunes.

***

BIBLIOGRAPHY

The following is a selection of the many books that I consulted in researching the Carlisle & Holbrooke series:

Definitive Text

Sir Julian Corbett wrote the original, definitive text on the Seven Years War. Most later writers use his work as a steppingstone to launch their own.

Corbett, LLM., Sir Julian Stafford. *England in the Seven Years War – Vol. I: A Study in Combined Strategy*. Normandy Press. Kindle Edition.

Strategy and Naval Operations

Three very accessible modern books cover the strategic context and naval operations of the Seven Years War. Daniel Baugh addresses the whole war on land and sea, while Martin Robson concentrates on maritime activities. Jonathan Dull has produced a very readable account from the French perspective.

Baugh, Daniel. *The Global Seven Years War 1754-1763*. Pearson Education, 2011. Print.

Robson, Martin. *A History of the Royal Navy, The Seven Years War*. I.B. Taurus, 2016. Print.

Dull, Jonathan, R. *The French Navy and the Seven Years' War*. University of Nebraska Press, 2005. Print.

Sea Officers

For an interesting perspective on the life of sea officers of the mid-eighteenth century, I'd read Augustus Hervey's Journal, with the cautionary note that while Hervey was by no means typical of the breed, he's very entertaining and devastatingly honest. For a more balanced view, I'd read British Naval Captains of the Seven Years War.

Erskine, David (editor). Augustus Hervey's Journal, The Adventures Afloat and Ashore of a Naval Casanova. Chatham Publishing, 2002. Print.

McLeod, A.B. British Naval Captains of the Seven Years War, The View from the Quarterdeck. The Boydell Press, 2012. Print.

Life at Sea

There are two excellent overviews of shipboard life and administration during the Seven Years War.

Rodger, N.A.M. *The Wooden World, An Anatomy of the Georgian Navy*. Fontana Press, 1986. Print.

Lavery, Brian. *Anson's Navy, Building a Fleet for Empire, 1744 to 1793*. Seaforth Publishing, 2021. Print.

***

Chris Durbin

THE AUTHOR

Chris Durbin grew up in the seaside town of Porthcawl in South Wales. His first experience of sailing was as a sea cadet in the treacherous tideway of the Bristol Channel, and at the age of sixteen, he spent a week in a tops'l schooner in the Southwest Approaches. He was a crew member on the Porthcawl lifeboat before joining the navy.

Chris spent twenty-four years as a warfare officer in the Royal Navy, serving in all classes of ships from aircraft carriers through destroyers and frigates to the smallest minesweepers. He took part in operational campaigns in the Falkland Islands, the Middle East and the Adriatic and he spent two years teaching tactics at a US Navy training centre in San Diego.

On his retirement from the Royal Navy, Chris joined a large American company and spent eighteen years in the aerospace, defence and security industry, including two years on the design team for the Queen Elizabeth class aircraft carriers.

Chris is a graduate of the Britannia Royal Naval College at *Dartmouth*, the British Army Command and Staff College, the United States Navy War College, where he gained a postgraduate diploma in national security decision-making, and Cambridge University, where he was awarded an MPhil in International Relations.

With a lifelong interest in naval history and a long-standing ambition to write historical fiction, Chris has completed the first thirteen novels in the Carlisle & Holbrooke series, which follow the fortunes of a colonial Virginian and a Hampshire man who both command ships of King George's navy during the middle years of the eighteenth century.

The series will follow its principal characters through the Seven Years War and into the period of turbulent relations between Britain and her American colonies in the 1760s and 70s. They'll negotiate some thought-provoking loyalty issues when British policy and colonial restlessness lead inexorably to the American Revolution.

Chris lives on the south coast of England, surrounded by hundreds of years of naval history. His three children are all busy growing their own families and careers while Chris and his wife (US Navy, retired) of forty-one years enjoy sailing their Cornish Crabber on the south coast.

Fun Fact:

Chris shares his garden with a tortoise named Aubrey. If you've read Patrick O'Brian's *HMS Surprise* or have seen the 2003 film *Master and Commander: The Far Side of the World*, you'll recognise the modest act of homage that Chris has paid to that great writer. Rest assured that Aubrey has not yet grown to the gigantic proportions of *Testudo Aubreii*, though at his last weigh in, he topped one kilogram!

***

FEEDBACK

If you've enjoyed *Cousins At Arms* please consider leaving a review on Amazon.

Look out for the fourteenth in the Carlisle & Holbrooke series, coming soon.

You can follow my blog at www.chris-durbin.com.

***

Printed in Great Britain
by Amazon